# LEAVING NORMAL

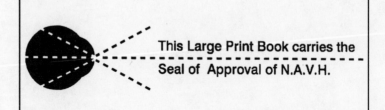

This Large Print Book carries the
Seal of Approval of N.A.V.H.

# LEAVING NORMAL

## STEF ANN HOLM

**THORNDIKE PRESS**
*An imprint of Thomson Gale, a part of The Thomson Corporation*

**THOMSON**
TM
**GALE**

Detroit • New York • San Francisco • New Haven, Conn. • Waterville, Maine • London

**THOMSON**
**GALE**
™

**LIBRARY OF CONGRESS CATALOGING-IN-PUBLICATION DATA**

Holm, Stef Ann.
    Leaving normal / by Stef Ann Holm.
      p. cm.
    ISBN-13: 978-0-7862-9226-4 (alk. paper)
    ISBN-10: 0-7862-9226-1 (alk. paper)
    I. Title.
    PS3558.O35584L43 2007
    813'.54—dc22                                    2006031726

Published in 2007 by arrangement with Harlequin Books S.A.

Printed in the United States of America on permanent paper
10 9 8 7 6 5 4 3 2 1

This one is for Millie Criswell.
As things happen in life, there are the ups and downs, joys and pains. You were there for me in those times, and I will never forget how kind, generous, wise and steadfast your friendship was and continues to be. I believe Arnette is smiling at us from Heaven.

# ACKNOWLEDGMENTS
## AND THANKS

Thank you to all the Boise firemen who kindly answered my questions and let me ride along with them. I'm especially grateful to Station 3 under the command of Captain Bill Sipple, Station 8 under the command of Captain Don Fry, Station 6 under the command of Captain John Peugh and Station 9 under the command of Captain Dave Muir.

The hero in this book was one day away from being recast as a police officer if it hadn't been for the two firefighters who work out at my Gold's Gym. I'm sure when I first approached them to help me they didn't know what they were getting themselves into. They allowed me to ask detailed questions and both were forthcoming with their answers.

Many thanks to Hoseman Rob Townsend, who has the body to be shirtless on the cover of a romance novel (and who is the hot guy for the month of May in the Boise Firefighter Calendar) — you rock, dude.

A very heartfelt thank-you to Hoseman Matt Owen, who let me shadow him on the job. The fictional depiction of the hero in this book was influenced by your generosity, thoughtful insight, masculinity and sense of humor.

Lastly, thanks to Hoseman Shawn Res, who tolerated me writing down a lot of what he said. You know it — "I hear ya."

To all who wear the Maltese cross, stay well and be safe.

Stef Ann Holm

# ONE:
# HAIL, SAINT
# THÉRÈSE!

Natalie Goodwin's dream of owning her own flower shop would be a reality in less than one month. Joyous excitement fluttered in her heart, especially now that her business loan had been approved.

Hat and Garden would open just in time for Christmas.

The old 1904 house that she was converting into a flower and gift shop was located in Boise's North End. The oak floors were original, as were the heavy banisters and narrow stairs that led to the second floor. Each room upstairs was going to be decorated with a distinct theme: the teddy-bear room with cute little bears in all shapes and sizes, the nature room with gifts that celebrate the great outdoors and the Victorian room with its china tea sets for sale.

Natalie's vision of her shop was a place brimming with one-of-a-kind items from local suppliers.

To inspire her family members who were helping with the setup of the store, the holiday smells of burning cranberry and pine candles perfumed Hat and Garden while Christmas carols played through hidden speakers in every room.

"How high do you want this shelf, Natalie?" her father, Fred, asked. He held on to a shelf, raising and lowering it for her approval.

Stepping back to assess, she imagined the inspirational display of Saint Thérèse figurines and wanted them at eye level. "About right there," she said.

"Okay, I got it."

The fact that her dad didn't object, offer a critique or alternate suggestion relieved Natalie. As far as he was concerned, Target was the best — the *only* — store in town.

Fred Miller had retired from civil service a few years back having been a U.S. mail carrier for thirty-one years. Now his days were spent feeding the squirrels and birds, keeping his lawn green and his many trees and shrubs trimmed to perfection. Widowed twelve years ago, he had never remarried. Sometimes Natalie grew sad when she thought about him living alone.

He had been somewhat of a hardhead when Natalie and her sister, Sarah Brockner, were growing up, but he'd mellowed since Mom died of breast cancer. Still, there was a part of him that couldn't resist offering a strong opinion without being asked.

So when he took her direction about the shelf, Natalie smiled and thought he was turning into an old softy.

Colorful Christmas decorations still in their boxes filled the main level. The place overflowed with everything from fireplace garlands to ornaments from Germany, to strings of multicolored lights.

Sarah approached, holding a snowman. "Where does this go?"

"Right over there with the snowmen display."

The two sisters looked as different on the outside as they were on the inside. Natalie was the fairer of the two, taller and more curvaceous. She wore a size larger in clothing than Sarah, and dressed far more conservatively than her younger sister.

Sarah had curly dark hair, was petite in every way — and the spitting image of their mother. She was friendly, more outgoing than Natalie, and verbally expressive when it came to topics of sex, romance, men, dating and anything else found in the pages of *Cosmo*.

"Where's the hunky-man display?" Sarah

questioned with a lift of her eyebrows. "I saw the new firefighter calendar at my gym. I keep telling you, if you filled a rack of them, they'd be sold out in one day."

"I'm not putting any hunky men in my shop," Natalie declared.

"But I'll bet plenty of hunky men will come and buy flowers and things from you. Maybe you'll date one of them."

"I'm not dating anyone. I don't have any time, nor do I have the interest."

Sarah frowned. "You've been divorced for almost two years and the only relationship you've had since being single went bust, but that's in the past. It's time for you to get back out there."

"Hmm." Natalie hoped her noncommittal response would end the discussion. She didn't like talking about Michael Williams, didn't like being reminded about the short-term relationship that ended disastrously just under a year ago. She'd felt more pain going through that breakup than she had ending a twenty-one-year marriage.

"Michael Williams was your transitional guy," Sarah went on, ignoring Natalie's warning glare. "So you dated some duds after him, so what if none of them panned out? You can't expect to meet Mr. Right when you *do* five men in five minutes."

"It was called speed dating," Natalie clarified, trying to tamp down her agitation. "And it was eight men in eight-minute increments. And, at the time, I wasn't looking for Mr. Right. I would have settled for Mr. Right Now to share the basics with — dinner and a movie."

"You were on the rebound without a clear perspective."

"I hate all this divorced-people language — rebound, transitional and newbie. It's all so horribly depressing. Sarah, I'm done with dating. I just don't want to go there anymore. I need to focus on the shop."

Hat and Garden had come to fruition at a time when she was looking for an outlet to channel her creativity and to make positive changes in her life. She'd always been a gardener, loved sunshine and flowers, making things grow, so this new shop offered a perfect blend of all her interests.

When her daughter, Cassandra, had entered high school, Natalie finally took a part-time job. As a floral assistant she learned a great deal, and found a deep sense of satisfaction in the work. She knew then what she wanted to do with herself.

Greg, her husband at the time, never thought she was up to the task of opening her own shop. Which is one of the reasons he was now her ex-husband.

There had been a time in her marriage when she'd been blissful and alive: her courtship, her wedding day, those years before she got pregnant. Even after Cassandra had been born, Natalie knew a limitless peace and satisfaction. But then things had changed when Natalie went back to work.

It wasn't so much being out of the house as it was discovering who she was without Greg. She'd married in her early twenties and had never completed college. She had been content to stay at home with her baby, loved every minute of it and didn't want to change a thing. She would forever be grateful to Greg's income for allowing her the opportunity of being a stay-at-home mom.

But when she was arranging flowers, blending colors and creating bouquets, she found a piece of herself she hadn't known had existed. She felt a self-worth that had purpose beyond that of being a wife and mother.

Natalie began to realize that she needed more from her marriage than what she was getting from Greg. Her husband had been content to maintain the status quo; doing no more and no less each day. Get up, go to work, come home, watch the evening news, eat dinner and go to bed. He liked the routine, the safety of it all. Natalie had become, in her older years, more of a risk taker. Life was short — she wanted to embrace it.

And yet, she hadn't had the courage to do so at the time because she worried about the effects of divorce on Cassie. She stayed with Greg who, in all fairness, hadn't changed from the man she'd married.

But she wanted more for herself: emotional balance and the desire to be loved and nurtured. They'd gone to marriage counseling, but the sessions only frustrated her and added conflict to the relationship. She hated the tension, the feeling of things unraveling with no way to knit them back together.

When Cassie entered her junior year at high school, Natalie could no longer live in the strained marriage, so she finally filed for divorce.

There was no one to blame. Not herself. Not Greg. It was just one of those things. You either grew together in a marriage or you grew apart.

They'd grown apart.

The twenty-one year union that had been dying a slow death for years had been dissolved. At forty-three, for the first time in her life, Natalie had confronted facing things on her own, making her own decisions — both good and bad. And, in the past two years, she'd lived with the consequences.

It had taken a year to regroup financially, going from part-time work to full-time to support herself. Then she'd temporarily been distracted by her brief romance with Michael. A mistake she was not going to repeat.

In a moment of retrospect, Natalie conceded, "Sarah, I don't want to be alone all my life, but I'm not going to worry about it. I'm going to enjoy what I have around me." Sitting on the cash-register counter was a box of miniature Saint Thérèse statues. They could be arranged in houseplants or in window gardens.

"She's pretty," Sarah said. "Who is she?"

"Thérèse of Lisieux. The saint of flowers." Natalie sighed, a feeling of contentment settling through her. "To me, she also represents patience and simplicity. I love appreciating the curling detail of rose petals as they form a flower, the textures and smells around me. I have to live for the moment, Sarah, and not focus on the big picture or I'll go crazy. In my marriage, I focused on my husband and what was going wrong and how I could fix it. Even when I was with

16

Michael, I repeated history. I can't fix the whole world, but I can fix what's going on in front of me. From now on, I'm going to enjoy taking pleasure in the small things."

Sarah's expression grew introspective, still not surrendering to the battle. "But you have so much going for you. With the perfect man —"

"You've already taken the perfect man. Steve is the best." Natalie laughed, trying to make light of everything. Then in all seriousness, she added, "I'm happy, Sarah. Truly. I've worked hard to get where I am. This is the best time of my life and I don't want to miss any of it because I'm blinded by love — or blind by what I *think* is love."

"I understand that, Natalie, and I agree. Hat and Garden is going to be fabulous. I'm proud of you." Gazing at the snowman in her arms, she added with a sparkle in her eyes, "He's cute, but he'd be even cuter with a Mrs. Snowman."

Natalie shook her head. "She's too busy making snowballs to throw at a certain sister. Besides, she got tired of him leaving the toilet seat up."

"I did not. I made sure I put the dang thing down," their dad grumbled, coming toward them carrying a string of holly berries.

Smiling, Natalie assured, "Not you, Dad."

"Oh." His expression relaxed. "Where did you say you wanted these hung?"

"Over the front door. Weave them through the pine boughs."

"They'd look better on the counter."

"I have more for that."

"Where'd you get these? I hope like hell not at that big 'W' store. Target has the best selection and quality. I could run up and buy some extras."

"I don't need any more."

Fred Miller grew silent, a sullen look spreading across his face. He was a handsome man for his age with silver-gray hair, and a full head of it. He kept it cut in a half pompadour, half crew, combed back from his high forehead. Thin age lines bracketed the corners of his eyes, his nose straight and slightly wide, his mouth generous. The upper lip was thinner than the lower, his teeth a nice neat row, thanks to dentures — something he was not happy about — but they had never looked artificial to Natalie. Of course, she was biased, but she thought her dad quite distinguished.

"Well," he said at length, "if you do, they've got plenty."

Sarah went back to work and her dad headed for the front door. As Natalie walked through the shop, she knew in the back of her mind that she had to do something, but with so much going on, she couldn't think what it was.

Hands on hips, she stopped to ponder, then walked into the living room.

BreeAnn and Sydney, Sarah's daughters, who were ages eleven and thirteen, assembled the train set that ran on a track between the two fir trees displayed in the front window.

"How's it coming?" she asked.

Sydney looked up. "Good, Aunt Natalie."

Since she was unable to remember what she'd intended to do next from her list of a hundred different things, Natalie gravitated toward her office.

In what used to be a parlor in the old house, Natalie entered the room and slipped behind her desk. Stacks of papers, invoices and envelopes spread out before her. Paperwork wasn't her strong suit, but she did have a method to keeping track of everything.

She sat down, gazed at her surroundings and allowed herself to reminisce — a moment when she dared to dredge up memories — if only to analyze the whys and the hows. To tell herself that she really meant what she had said to Sarah about being single.

In thinking back on her marriage to Greg and to her brief encounter with Michael, Natalie told herself that she would much rather be alone than with either man.

In the beginning, Michael had been wonderful. They were so alike. Both had had marriages that had failed for similar reasons, and both had daughters the same ages. It was the girls' junior years in high school and Michael had suggested they take them to Hawaii for spring break. Natalie thought the trip would be great, ran the idea past Cassie who had no objections. In fact, she was looking forward to surfing and shopping on Waikiki with Brook, Michael's daughter.

But on the vacation, something went wrong. Natalie felt it in Hawaii, and sensed it when they returned home. In the following weeks, Michael distanced himself emotionally. In hindsight, she realized he'd never really made himself available. She was too open, too trusting, and she'd allowed herself to be vulnerable.

She wore her heart on her shirtsleeve and it had cost her.

Michael would have continued the relationship if she hadn't started a discussion about it one evening, at his place, just before he was about to go out of town on business. She asked him point-blank if he wanted to be in the relationship or not. He got this stupid smirk on his face that spoke volumes: "Ah, you caught me." Then he said he never had any time to himself. She thought this strange since he was always inviting her to be with him — a family reunion, outdoor activities, dinners in his home and weekends spent together. He said he felt pressured to be "a couple." Then he'd rambled on about the women in his life — the way they'd mistreated him. She had listened, then quietly commented that he was penalizing her because she was a woman — and once a woman had done him wrong, none were to be trusted.

He reassured her that that wasn't the case and said he'd call her when he came back to town, and they'd talk about things further. He told her not to worry.

Numb, she went home that night, lay in bed reliving all the things she had done or said, wondering what had happened and how they could work to resolve the issues between them.

But she never heard from him again.

It was a rude awakening into the dating world, one that rocked her off her axis and left her in a funk for months afterward. She knew now that it was the lack of closure, the feelings of frustration . . . of not being able to put him in his place . . . of being able to tell him that he had led her on.

His disappearance had not only affected her, but Cassie and Brook had been comfortable thinking of the adults as a couple, and now they were dazed and confused.

As painful as it was, Natalie had taken both girls out to dinner to tell them the breakup was no one's fault. All Natalie had gathered from Brook was that her father had explained to her that Natalie was a "nice lady," but there was no chemistry between them anymore. Within a week he had a new girlfriend and Brook was trying to deal with that.

Even now, months later, Natalie hated to think about Michael's easy-come/easy-go behavior. The reality was that she'd been tossed aside and so easily and quickly replaced — it still hurt her sometimes if she allowed it to.

Her first summer as a divorced woman had been a disaster.

It had taken autumn and into the winter months for her to recharge her emotional battery. She'd had some dates since, but nothing to write home about. She was at a place in her life where she really had come full circle.

She actually enjoyed spending time alone, being her own best friend. Family surrounded her, Sunday dinners were evenings to look forward to. At Sarah's, her dad's and they all took turns hosting the weekly meal. It was always fun to see the family gathered together. Natalie was doing okay.

In fact, she was better than okay.

Turning her attention to the computer, Natalie logged on to the Internet and downloaded her mail, hoping to find a note from Cassie. Her daughter was in Chicago, attending her first year of college.

An e-mail from Cassie registered in the in-box.

Natalie opened it.

Mom . . . I'm low on cell-phone minutes. Call me on the dorm phone when you get a chance. Hugs and kisses, Cassie

Natalie was already dialing the phone, any number of Cassie's crises flashing through her mind.

Cassie was paged, then came on the phone. "Hello?"

"Cassie, it's Mom. Is everything all right?"

"Hey, Mom. Yeah. I'm fine."

"I got your e-mail and I was worried."

"I'm sorry. I just used a lot of cell minutes and I didn't want to go over. I need to buy a calling card for the dorm phone."

"I can send you one."

"Okay. How's the shop coming along?"

"Wonderful. Aunt Sarah and the girls are helping today. So's your grandpa."

"I wish I was there."

"I wish you were, too, but you'll be here in a few weeks."

"That's what I'm calling about."

Natalie, who'd been absently shuffling paperwork on her desk, froze. "You're still coming, aren't you?"

"Yes. Of course. I have my ticket. Dad sent the money like he said he would."

"Good. Then what's the matter?" Natalie knew when something was on her daughter's mind.

"I wanted to ask you something."

"Ask me what?"

"Austin can't go home for Christmas. His mom is taking a cruise and I hate the idea of him staying in Chicago all alone over the holidays."

Natalie's muscles tensed. Over the course of the semester, she'd heard all about Austin Mably, Cassie's new boyfriend. Natalie had never seen him, but, from Cassie's descrip-

24

tion, he sounded like a metal rocker or something along those lines.

"Well, Cassie," Natalie said, putting a lightness into her tone, "I'm sure there are plenty of things for him to do. Colleges know that not all students can make it home for the holidays, so I'm sure he'll be fine."

"But I want him to be with me."

"Cassie . . ."

"I told him he could come home with me."

Disappointment registered heavily in Natalie's mind and she was at a loss for words. It took her a few seconds to find her voice. "I really don't think it's a good idea, Cassie. We're already missing you for Thanksgiving, and it'll be your first Christmas at home since being at college. I've been so looking forward to seeing *you*."

"But you'll be busy with Hat and Garden's grand opening."

"Never too busy for you."

"You won't even know Austin's around. I promise."

Hearing the strain in her own voice, Natalie tried reverse reasoning. "But, Cassie, I've never met him — and I don't even know what he looks like — and besides, where would he stay?"

"With Dad. I'll e-mail you pictures of us together."

"With Greg?"

"Yeah. I already talked to him about it and he said it was fine."

Natalie gritted her teeth. "Well . . . I just wish . . ."

"Mom, Austin already bought his ticket."

"Oh."

There was a heavy silence on the phone. Natalie hated being so upset over this, especially since she knew Cassie had her own life now. Her daughter was an eighteen-year-old living independently away from home — albeit not completely financially independent. It was inevitable something like this would happen. She'd only hoped it would be later rather than sooner.

"I guess it'll be okay, Cassie."

"Thanks, Mom. I knew you'd be cool with it. I told Dad you would."

Hanging up, Natalie rose to her feet, the thought of Greg and Cassie discussing her reaction not sitting well with her. It irked her and put a frown on her face. She hated to think that Greg would offer his home just to rattle her cage. He'd never been the malicious type — it took too much effort. But their divorce *had* been rather strained.

With a sigh, Natalie acknowledged there would be a slight damper on Christmas, but nothing she was going to dwell on. Cassie would be coming home and that's what mattered most.

Returning to the area by the cash register, Natalie finally remembered what it was she had to do.

As she focused on a row of toy soldiers painted with bright enamel colors, Natalie smiled, recalling the hours she'd put into her store these last few weeks. She forgot about Austin Mably. Even Greg and his doubts about her abilities to pull off a business venture were no longer a sticking point.

She was proving to herself — and to no one else — that she could do this. And, from all indications, everything she'd hoped Hat and Garden could be was coming to reality.

# TWO:
## ROMANCING HOME DEPOT

Sarah examined the blue, cordless Makita screw gun. Gripping the trigger, she squeezed, and the gun turned over in a fast whir of air power that startled her. "This thing has some kick to it."

Natalie and Sarah sat on the instruction risers at Home Depot for the Do-It-Herself Clinic. The topic was "You Can Organize Your Closet."

As the instructor talked, Natalie spoke beneath her breath. "I want to turn the closet underneath the stairs of Hat and Garden into a storage area."

"Sounds ambitious."

"Can you believe it?" Even Natalie was surprised at her willingness to tackle such a large project. "Two years ago I didn't know a lug nut from a bolt. Last week I had to figure out what kind of washer I needed for my sink faucet." She paused thoughtfully and spoke before she could stop herself. "It would almost be worth having a boyfriend to do all these things for me."

"Now you're talking."

"Talking crap," Natalie whispered. "I like my independence. Want to know what I did the other morning?"

"What?"

"I made myself a piece of toast in the nude."

Sarah slanted her a glance. "Why?"

"Because I could. When Cassie was living at home, God knows how many times she had girls sleep over and I had to look halfway presentable in the morning — no walking around in short-shorts with a wedgie. I rarely had the house to myself. The phone would ring and it was never for me."

"I could help you with that. Steve was telling me about this guy he works with who's single and —"

"I don't need my phone to ring that bad." Natalie mused aloud. "I wasn't sure I would, but I'm enjoying having an empty nest. I miss Cassie, but I don't miss all that went with a teenage girl. It's rather nice not to run out of hot water when I want to fill up the bathtub."

"Gee, what's that like? By the time the girls are out of the bathroom and Steve's finished a few loads of laundry, I'm lucky to have even a tepid shower."

"A hot bath is great. Especially with a glass of wine."

Natalie had enjoyed her bath last night, indulging herself with some Chardonnay. She'd lit all the candles surrounding her big tub, leaned her head back, closed her eyes and mulled over everything she still had to do for the grand opening. There'd been no giggling girls, no ringing phones, no stereo and TV blazing simultaneously. She'd had the entire peaceful moment all to herself.

Glorious. Bliss. Heaven.

It was fun being in her mid-forties without those daily parental responsibilities. She was settling in quite nicely, enjoying every second of her transformation.

Sarah set the screw gun on her lap and gazed directly into Natalie's eyes. "You really *are* happy, aren't you, Natalie?"

Natalie thought for a moment before answering.

These days she was content with her life, but there was no question she'd weathered a lot of changes. Small as they might be, she had some habits she wished she could break.

Sometimes she woke up in the middle of the night and couldn't go back to sleep. And every time she woke, she was always back on her side of the bed. Each night, she was determined to sleep in the middle of the queen-size mattress — claim her middle ground, so to speak — but each morning she was right back on the right side, as if Greg were still sleeping on the left. It annoyed her that she was finding it hard to break this habit.

She wanted to break rules, try new things, start over. Have fun.

And that's what she planned on doing. Hat and Garden would be her outlet, her place to begin again.

"Yes," she responded with a smile. "I really am happy."

She'd learned a lot about herself these past two years — but mostly that she was way more adaptable than she'd thought. Early on, refinancing the house and car in her name had been the least of her hurdles. Financial restructure had been easy compared to the mental restructure. Going from being married to single had been an adjustment. It was almost as if the carpet had been pulled out from under her. Even though the divorce had been her choice, she'd gotten used to the routines in her marriage.

Greg had done certain things — picked

up the dry cleaning, carved a Thanksgiving turkey, handled the yard work and a variety of other labors of love. She hadn't realized how integral he'd been in her life until after he'd left it.

Now everything fell on her shoulders. And while she was up to the task, she'd let a few things slip.

Up until recently, she usually grabbed whatever was in the fridge and ate it in front of the television. Now she made a point of cooking a real dinner and eating at the kitchen table with a linen place setting — making her evening meal something special, even if it was just for one person. She'd always made a habit of setting a nice table for the three of them, so why would she do any less for herself? She thought about it and didn't like the answer: She didn't think herself worth the trouble. How wrong she was. Now, more than ever, was a time to pamper herself, to take all the little pleasures life had to offer.

Taking her turn squeezing the screw gun's powerful trigger, Natalie then passed it to the woman beside her. "I'm going to have to buy one of these so I can get to work on that closet. Less than two weeks to go and I open Hat and Garden. I'm so excited. Now if only I'd stop having these damn night sweats. Do you remember how old Mom was when she went through the change?"

"I think I was out of high school," Sarah said.

"They say that however old your mother was, that's probably when you'll go through it. My periods have been whacked out lately — more so than usual."

"You've always had irregular periods."

"Don't I know it? I'll be so glad to give them up." An unpredictable monthly was the reason she'd had only one child. Looking back, getting pregnant almost seemed like a fluke.

She and Greg had tried for many years after Cassie to have a second baby, but Natalie had never been able to conceive. She hadn't wanted to endure the uncertain trials of fertility treatments, so they told themselves if it happened on its own, it happened. But it never did.

"I do remember Mom saying once she was finished with the change, she didn't have to shave her legs as often. Now, *that's* something to look forward to."

Natalie choked down a laugh.

Her younger sister was the queen of optimism, and the cheerleader for true love and romance. Sarah had been married for sixteen years to a wonderful man, and working as a Pampered Chef consultant made use of her bubbly personality.

Sarah's gaze left the instruction area and went to the aisles where the home-improvement store teemed with holiday customers. "Have you noticed how many men are in here?" Her careful perusal came to a grinding halt. "Oh. My. God . . . It's the May Hunk-of-the-Month."

"What are you talking about?" Natalie asked, her eyebrows lifting in confusion.

"The firefighter calendar! It's the guy for the month of May. Look at *him*."

Natalie followed her sister's gaze to the entrance of the electrical aisle and watched a man come forward.

There was only one way to describe him: larger than life.

His masculine presence domineered the shoppers walking past him. Well above average in height, broader in the shoulders than other men, he had clipped short black hair that framed a strong face. Standing somewhere around six foot four or five, he probably weighed in the two-hundred-and-forty-pound range — but every ounce was lean muscle; a solid chest, pumped biceps, a flat belly. Taper-leg jeans encased his thighs.

He wore a hooded, Kelly green sweatshirt with a front pouch pocket. Natalie recognized the IAFF logo — International Association of Firefighters — and the Maltese cross on the left corner of his chest. The words *Engine 13* were above it with *Lucky 13* below.

"He's gorgeous," her sister sighed.

"He's my neighbor."

Eyes wide open in disbelief, Sarah gazed sideways at her. "Mr. May is your neighbor? Since when?"

"Since about four months ago."

"How come I've never seen him?"

"How often do you come over, aside from Sunday-night dinners?"

"Obviously not often enough. We should move Thanksgiving from my house to yours."

"We should not," Natalie countered swiftly. "I'm doing Christmas."

The sisters stared as her neighbor smiled to one of the female clerks who had apparently asked him if he needed help. He had one of those boyish smiles, Natalie thought. Okay, so she had admired him . . . from afar. He was definitely good-looking. The best-looking man she'd ever seen. She'd only spoken to him a few times since he'd moved in with his wife and little girl.

"He's very married," Natalie caught herself talking aloud.

"Too bad for you."

"No, not too bad. He's clearly younger than me."

"Younger is better."

"Not when younger is in the thirties. I'm forty-three."

"You don't look forty-three."

"I do when I'm naked."

The corners of his mouth softened as he laughed at something the clerk said, then she pointed and he continued on. The clerk, like Natalie and her sister, watched him retreat.

Natalie conceded that he walked away as good as he approached, his behind just as great a view as his face. No question about it — her neighbor was the type of man who could make a woman lose her mind and every bit of common sense she possessed.

"I'm happily married, but a man like that . . ." Sarah said, blinking out of her stupor. "He's incredible."

Natalie couldn't deny that. She also couldn't deny he was very much a married man and, as tempting as he was, he was off-limits.

However, he did attract her attention whenever she caught a glimpse of his silver Dodge Ram pulling into the driveway across the street. She had a vague notion about his schedule; he seemed to work one day on and then was off for two.

She'd never conversed with his wife — very attractive, of course — and wasn't sure what the woman did for a living, but assumed it was something out of her house. She was usually at home during the day.

"He's just a guy who lives across the street from me," Natalie finally replied.

"He's not just any guy." With a slow, secret smile, Sarah added in a soft tone, "He's the real thing. The romance hero in the books I read."

Natalie tucked her hair behind her ear, recalling the dozens of books Sarah had loaned her after the divorce. They were meant to give her hope that she'd have a second chance in love. Instead, they'd depressed her. "Those books you read are made-up fluff. The men in them don't really exist. When I'm ready, I just want a normal guy."

"I don't think there *are* any normal guys. Steve bought bikini briefs the other day and I had a fit."

"Why would he buy those?"

"He said it was a mistake, but I think he wanted to see my reaction. And I gave him one — I told him if he ever wore them I'd have to revert to the granny panties I wore when I was pregnant."

The sisters traded glances, then laughed at the absurdity of their banter. The instructor gave them a frown and they didn't say anything further for the rest of the class.

When it was over, Natalie felt inspired. "I'm going to buy a screw gun so I can get to work on that closet remodel. You know, I think we had one of these cordless jobs but Greg took it with him."

"I saw Greg the other day," Sarah said, walking next to Natalie toward the check stands.

"Is he still dating that woman — Renee?"

"Yes."

"I figured he'd get remarried sooner rather than later. He's had two years on his own, and statistics say he should have been on his second wife by now. I hate to admit it, but I didn't think he could take care of himself for this long."

"Leave it to Greg to go against statistics." Sarah gave her a hug. "I've got to run. The girls are home alone and, at their ages, anything could be going on when they're not fighting over the phone."

Waving, Sarah said, "I'll talk to you before Thanksgiving."

"What do you want me to bring?"

"Your smile," Sarah called over her shoulder. "And that good-looking fireman if he becomes single between now and next Thursday."

Good-naturedly Natalie shook her head and smiled.

She walked the giant warehouse and went down the power-tool aisle filled with numerous boxes of testosterone-enticing equipment. The very idea that she was going to buy something in this store was amazing.

As she read about the features on different types of screw guns, she became aware of someone behind her. Normally she wouldn't have paid much attention, but whoever it was pulled at her subconscious like a blip on a radar screen.

Turning slightly, Natalie casually glanced over her shoulder to see who'd come down the aisle.

*Her neighbor.*

All she saw was his sweatshirt-clad back and the bold letters Boise Fire Dept. That, for some inexplicable reason, snagged her heartbeat and kicked it up a notch.

Standing in close proximity to him, she realized just how tall a man he truly was. Glancing at him from across the street was far different from being next to him.

Facing forward, she forced her breathing to remain calm. Should she say hello? She did, after all, know him — even though she'd never spoken to him and didn't know his name. Maybe he wouldn't recognize her. Then the moment would be awkward.

Natalie burst into a smile about her ridiculous thinking. My God, he was simply her neighbor. Her *married* neighbor.

This was so incredibly stupid!

Somewhere between the smile and the thought "stupid," she must have laughed out loud because a masculine voice spoke to her.

"Hey, how are you?"

Turning around, she thought she was prepared to make small talk, thankful he knew who she was. But the moment she looked into his face, she grew distracted by his powerful masculinity.

Natalie practically melted.

His mouth was incredible, his teeth were slightly crooked but very white against his lips. He had the nicest dark brown eyes and his face was more handsome than any one man should be entitled to.

"Hi," she returned. "How are you?"

"Pretty good. Haven't seen you outside lately."

Socializing in Boise came to a semi-standstill in the winter. Days were short, the air was a frigid thirty-some degrees and snow lingered on the ground. Mail was quickly collected from the boxes, half the time from the car before pulling into the garage; garbage cans made it to the curb in record time if one was dressed in office wear. Aside from that, nobody was in their front yard for conversations unless they had to shovel snow.

"Bad weather." Natalie couldn't stop staring at his mouth. "I don't do well in the winter."

"You're not a native?"

"Born and raised. I just never get used to the cold."

"Neither do I."

A momentary silence fell and Natalie became a little nervous. He unnerved her in a way she hadn't anticipated, and she thought it silly that she, a woman of her intelligence and age, was breathlessly affected by him.

"My name is Natalie," she said several seconds later, opting to take charge.

"Tony," he replied. "Tony Cruz."

"Natalie Goodwin."

He extended his hand and she hesitated briefly, then accepted. His fingers were strong, almost viselike, but without crushing her small hand in the slightest. He knew just the right amount of pressure to apply.

His skin was warm and felt firm, his grip solid; maybe there were calluses on his palm. She couldn't be sure.

"Nice to meet you," he responded. His deep voice resonated through her every nerve ending.

She combated an annoying blush. "Thanks. Now I have a name to go with your face. I've only thought of you as 'the fireman.' "

"And I've only thought of you as 'the neighbor,' " he countered with an easy smile, making her feel comfortable because he played along with her comment and turned it back on her. Folding his arms over his chest, his eyes fell on the Makita. "Good choice."

"I can't believe I'm buying it, but I'm doing a little renovation work. I'm in the process of opening my own flower shop in the North End — Hat and Garden."

"I know where that is. I saw the sign go up." His voice had a deep timbre. "My wife would probably say I should visit a florist more than I do."

"My grand opening is on the first. I'd love to have you stop by, and bring your wife, too."

"Maybe I will."

Natalie struggled to say something without

thinking about his wife and how Mrs. Cruz must look forward to this man coming home to her each day — with or without flowers.

"Well, in case I don't see you again," she said lightly, "have a happy Thanksgiving."

"You do the same. Hopefully we'll have a white Christmas this year."

"That would be great. My daughter's coming home from college for Christmas." As soon as she'd said it, Natalie instantly cringed. Saying she was old enough to have a daughter in college — she might as well have waved her driver's license in front of him and declared she'd probably been in middle school while he was entering kindergarten!

"That'll be nice to visit with her. I don't think I've seen her around."

"No, she's been away since the summer." Changing her stance, she commented, "I noticed you have a little girl. She's very cute."

"She's my stepdaughter." His brown eyes softened, a smile hooking itself on the corners of his mouth. "But I love her like my own."

*Endearing.* The man was utterly endearing and heroic . . . Natalie shrugged off further wayward thoughts. "Well, I have to get going."

"Me, too. See you later."

After he'd gone, Natalie's heart ached for reasons she couldn't begin to explain. She was unable to move, her feet planted to the concrete floor while she tried to make sense of what had happened. She had *never* been attracted to a married man — wouldn't even consider it. But Sarah was right — there was something about Tony Cruz. His male confidence exuded without effort.

Unwillingly, she found herself responding to him, knowing full well he was married.

Then it hit her.

He was safe. Unlike a single man who she'd have to put herself out there for. With Tony Cruz there wasn't any emotional investment. It was just plain lust.

Of course. That was it.

She wanted him because she couldn't have him.


"Someone in the city just shot himself with a .45," Tony said as he unloaded Station 13's dishwasher.

The bells had just gone off through the station, a female dispatcher's voice relaying the information on the radio speaker. Every

Boise Fire Department was hooked into the same system so they could hear where the other engines were being sent.

Station 5, the busiest in Boise, was being called to the scene. It was a morbid thought, but Tony thought it just the same: Now, *that* would be a good call.

One thing about the holidays, shit happened 24/7. The fact that it was seven o'clock in the a.m. didn't mean anything. If someone was going to harm themselves, they didn't necessarily do it when the bars closed. The guy had probably been up all night contemplating shooting himself; he just now got the courage — or someone found him and tried talking him out of it, and that alone was all the catalyst he needed.

"Number five," Captain Rob Palladino commented over the open newspaper on the table. "Those guys never sleep."

The blades of a blender spun, churning through the words of Jim "Wally" Walcroft as he said, "Toss me that aspirin from my food locker, Captain."

The captain tilted back on his chair legs, reached for a small plastic bottle and threw it across the kitchen. Wally swallowed two tablets, then kicked up the speed several levels and blended his protein shake.

Hoseman Tony Cruz, Captain Rob Palladino and driver Jim Walcroft were coming off A Shift as sunshine tried to break through the gray winter sky. Their three reliefs from B Shift gathered with them in the kitchen. The six heavily built men wore blue pants and blue button-down shirts with the IAFF logo.

With the dishwasher unloaded and having already taken out the trash, Tony leaned his backside into the countertop, his big arms folded across his chest. He lowered his right hand, laid it flat on his belly and thought about eating a slice of the half-eaten pumpkin pie on the table — food had been coming in steadily since Thanksgiving. Citizens had this need to feed firemen and the doorbell to the station house was always ringing with someone bearing food — especially during and after the holidays. The guys were committed to doing Atkins after the first of the year.

While coffee brewed, Tony talked with his relief, Doug Frye, and filled him in on the calls they'd taken during the last twenty-four hours. All of them had been medic calls. People didn't understand that firefighters didn't fight many fires. Whenever the bells sounded for that, they were in their turnouts faster than they could think, but, usually, they were sent out to be EMTs.

Rob Palladino glanced at Tony. "How many carbs do you think are in beer? I've got a wedding to go to on January fifth."

A rough calculation was made by one of the reliefs and Rob's expression became contemplative as if he were figuring out how many he could drink without blowing his diet five days into it.

The conversation moved away from Atkins as pie was dished up by two of the firemen.

Wally drank his shake in several long gulps, taking a breather to say, "Yesterday we got a call when Tony was making an omelet. Had it pretty nice — cheese, mushrooms, salsa. We get back and half of it's eaten."

Tony frowned, still pissed as he recalled the care he'd taken cooking that damn omelet, only to get a nursing-home call and having to leave his masterpiece on the plate — uneaten. His voice tight, he clipped his words while explaining, "Station 3 thought they'd come over for a visit while we were out."

Rob continued the story with a grin. "We get a call to Spring Brook and when we get back — Tony's omelet is half gone."

One of the reliefs laughed. "Gable. You

know it's gotta be him."

"I know it was Gable," Tony said, crossing his booted feet over one another in a casual stance. "He's that kind of guy."

The phone rang. The incoming captain snagged the receiver. His eyebrows lifted. "Gable. We were just talking about you."

Tony's mood darkened. So it was only an omelet, but he wasn't much of a cook and he'd really taken his time on it. Perfection didn't come easily and that damn omelet had been perfect. Pranks were always happening between the firehouses, and Tony had participated in many. But this time he wasn't laughing.

With the receiver next to his ear, the captain gazed at Tony. "You really want me to ask him that?"

Lifting his chin a notch, Tony asked, "What?"

"He wants to know what kind of cheese you used."

"Give me the phone." Tony took two long strides to reach the captain who was holding out the receiver and laughing. "Gable, you shit. I'm going to get you back."

Several choice f-bombs were traded, the call ending with Tony good-natured and planning his revenge. He was thinking an open can of tuna taped somewhere discreetly beneath one of Station 3's kitchen cupboards. In a couple of days, they'd be wondering what had died.

Fifteen minutes later Tony was in the fire-station garage helping Doug wash the engine. If he had time he usually pitched in with the daily duty. It was sort of therapeutic. A wind-down from the adrenaline surges that were always ready to go full throttle while he was on a twenty-four-hour shift.

The radio was playing and, as Tony hosed water off the red paint, he sang along to an old Bread song. " 'I want to make it with you,' Doug."

Frye's face soured. "You're making me nervous, Tony."

Tony simply grinned.

Tony Cruz had a masculine confidence that rarely, if ever, buckled. He was secure in himself, knew what he was good at, what his strengths and weaknesses were. He didn't have an ego, wouldn't know what to do with one if he did. Acknowledging he was well liked was something he prided himself on. If he gave his word, he meant it. If he said he'd take someone's shift, he was there.

He stepped around the shoreline — the electrical cord that kept the engine charged to a battery. When the truck was washed and dried he stepped out of his work pants and boots, put on a pair of jeans and Nikes and he swapped the button-down for a long-sleeved, navy tee with Boise Fire Dept. written across the back.

As he drove down the residential street where the fire station was located, he noticed all the people out shoveling snow. The skies had dumped six new inches on top of an already heavy snow cover.

Tony dialed his cell phone with one hand, waited for the rings and then a voice picked up.

"Rocky's Tavern."

Tony cracked a smile. "You wish."

"When I retire, Cruz. Just wait and see."

Hoseman Rocky Massaro worked the A Shift at Station 6 on Franklin Road. Assigned to the ladder truck, he sometimes forgot to be humble on the job, but it was that trace of arrogance and pride that Tony respected in his friend. He and Rocky had graduated from the same fire-academy class and had formed a pretty tight friendship during the last eight years of service in Boise.

After their shifts they often met at the local gym to work out together; mostly they talked bullshit about the job while lifting weights. Sometimes their talks got serious if one of them was having personal problems. Rocky was single, no steady girlfriend; he just dated a bunch of women and kept things easygoing. Tony felt comfortable telling Rocky about Kim and the pressure he struggled with in not wanting to start a family right now. Nobody knew about that, not even his mom. It just wasn't something he discussed with everyone, but Rocky didn't criticize him. He pretty much just listened, and offered a little advice when he was asked.

"I heard Gable raided 13 last night," Rocky chuckled.

"You don't even know how pissed I was."

"I know you well enough that I can figure it out. What's the payback?"

"Still working on ideas. Maybe Nair in his shampoo bottle — the guy's already blowing a gasket about going bald — or a lady's thong in his duffel. Frye told me Gable just started seeing a woman he likes."

"I say go with the thong." The radio in Rocky's car was blaring to a rock-and-roll song. "So are you thinking what I'm thinking?"

"Probably. The roads suck. Let's forget the gym this morning. I just want to go home and crawl in bed with my wife."

"Reading my mind. I want to go home

and crawl in bed with your wife, too."

"Shut up." Tony shook his head while laughing. "I gotta go. Talk to you later."

"Yeah, later."

Tony drove down the sanded roads, traffic moving at a slow pace.

He hated the winter. It was long and cold. Thinking about how many Kelly days he had banked, he could take a two-week vacation this summer. He wanted to go someplace tropical. Hawaii. Cabo. The Virgin Islands. Kim had mentioned the latter.

His wife would be waiting for him at home, just getting Parker up for school. He'd been married for just over two years and had bonded with his six-year-old stepdaughter. She had irresistible dimples, and a head of white-blond hair. She'd been after him to get her a kitten for Christmas and he'd been thinking about it. In fact, he'd gone to the pet store yesterday just to see what they had. He'd opted out of buying one, deciding to go to the animal shelter instead.

Pushing through the morning commute while the radio played in his truck, he thought about all he had going for him in his life. At thirty-four, he had a great job — an eight-year veteran with the Boise F.D. — he owned his own house and had a fairly solid marriage. The sex was good . . . but it was the lack of emotional intimacy that sometimes kept things more unsettled than they should be.

He loved his wife, was faithful to her, but there was something in his heart that kept him from committing to having a child with her. It was an indefinable thing, but the uncertain emotions were there.

Kim had wanted a baby with him for the past year and he just hadn't been able to give himself over completely to the idea. At first, he thought his reservations stemmed from the fact that he wanted Parker to feel important to him, safe and secure, before he brought another child into the house. But that wasn't it.

The intangible reasons troubled him because, more than anything, he wanted a child of his own. Kim had been waiting for him to come around, but Tony had sensed a distance in her lately. He worked one twenty-four-hour shift, then was off for forty-eight. Recently, during the time when he was away overnight, he'd begun to get an unsettled feeling.

Tony pulled into his driveway and caught sight of Natalie Goodwin across the street. She was tackling the snowpack blocking in her car.

Killing the ignition, he climbed out of the Ram and paused. He was dead-ass tired, really wanted to go inside, take a hot shower and go to bed with his wife after Parker left for school.

But something stopped him. A recollection of something Natalie had said.

He pocketed his keys and walked across the street.

"Mornin'," he greeted, catching Natalie unaware. She looked up, a line of worry on her forehead. The tip of her nose was red from the cold air, her cheeks flushed against her pale complexion. Green eyes lifted to study him with a sense of hope.

Folding his arms over his chest, he said, "Having your car stuck in the garage is a bad way to start off the grand opening."

The firm set of her shoulders softened and she sighed.

Then she did something he hadn't anticipated. She threw her arms around him and gave him a hug.

# THREE:
# HAPPY HOLLY-DAZE

Tony was no stranger to being shown appreciation — a touch on his arm, an embrace, smiles and thank-yous. But he'd never had a physical reaction like this. Natalie's soft body pressed against his felt incredibly good. Her cheek slightly touched his as she stood on tiptoe, arms wrapped around his neck.

His breathing shortened, caught in his throat. A fist of arousal hit him low in the gut. The rapid, and almost reckless, way he responded threw him for a curve.

"You remembered," she said, her breath warm against his face.

Without his being aware, his hand had come around her back and he held her in return.

She backed away, her expression guarded, if not embarrassed, as if she just realized what she'd done. "I'm sorry. I didn't mean to . . . I'm a little stressed out." She gave a nervous laugh. "Okay, a lot stressed out. Do you think you could . . . I hate to ask, but —"

"Don't worry about it. I was going to offer." He grabbed the shovel. "You're wearing the wrong shoes for this kind of job."

She gazed at the pointed-toe black shoes with heels that she had on. "You're probably right."

"No probably about it."

"I was in too much of a hurry to change into my snow boots."

She wore a long coat and slacks, and nice shoes that were meant for an office and not clearing a driveway. A forest-green scarf wrapped around her neck, an almost perfect match to her eye color. Her makeup wasn't overdone, and she'd applied a shade of pink lipstick he thought attractive.

Her lips parted, and he couldn't help but smile when she confessed, "I set my alarm two hours earlier than necessary, but I hit the snooze and that was a big mistake. I barely got ready on time."

"Really?" he responded in jest. "I thought you wore mismatched gloves on purpose."

She stared at her hands, noting one brown and one black leather glove. "Oops."

He chuckled as she dashed into the house and came back wearing a matching pair of black gloves. "Thanks. My mind is just crazy today. It did have to snow buckets last night." Her breath misted as she spoke. "I can't believe this . . . I'm going to be late for the biggest day of my life."

"I always thought a woman called her wedding day the biggest day of her life."

"Actually, I think that's what I called my divorce."

A half smile gathered on his face.

"Oh, that was horrible of me. My ex-husband isn't that bad."

Tony ran the shovel across the width of the driveway in one long run, lifting a weighted scoop without effort. As he moved to the opposite side of the walkway, she followed him.

She put a hand over her heart, sincerity in her gaze. "This is really nice of you and I appreciate it."

"Not a problem."

"I'm sure I could have done it, but it would have taken me twice the time and . . . really, this is just so incredibly nice of you."

She gave him a warm smile.

He couldn't really guess her age — whenever he dealt with patients, he never made assumptions. Perhaps Natalie was a little older than him. If she was, it couldn't be by much. The fact that she owned her own business and seemed to be financially stable was an attribute he commended. Not every woman could be single and self-sufficient to live this comfortably.

She lived alone, her daughter was in college. He wondered if she ever got lonely. God knew he did, even sometimes when Kim was home. They'd sit on the sofa together, each at their own end, and watch a TV program without really talking to one another. During those times, he wished he was at work.

But there were nights at the station when he'd come in from a call at one, two or three in the morning, and he just couldn't fall back asleep. It was the adrenaline, the fact that he'd been woken up in a foggy sleep that kept him from crashing hard again. Once awake, he had to struggle to capture that completely relaxed state once again. The room where he stayed was small with just a bed and a locker and sometimes he'd lay in his twin bed and read. Other times he'd go into the television room, pick one of the many recliners to lie in and watch the tube. If he was lucky, he'd doze off with the clicker in his hand.

"I want to thank you in some way. Please come by the shop," she insisted. "Pick out whatever flowers you like and I'll make them into something nice for your wife."

"I might just do that."

"I wish you would. I'm sure you had a rough night and this is the last thing you need to be doing."

"It's actually a good stress reliever." He'd never minded shoveling snow; in fact, he liked the tediousness of it after a night of unpredictable events.

In a thoughtful tone, she asked, "Did you have some difficult calls?"

He shrugged. "No more than usual."

"I guess I'm curious. Anything in particular you've found hard to deal with?"

Thinking to himself, he was reminded about that DOA — a code blue called in by two people who worked with the victim. A sixty-two-year-old woman who'd been dead in her home for a couple of days, as far as the coroner could tell after a cursory exam. Idaho Power had killed her electricity — a notice was tacked to the door. No heat in the house. While it was obvious to assume that she died of exposure, that wasn't the case. She had failing health; a half-dozen medication bottles were on the kitchen table.

Tony recalled the fecund odor of cats in the dingy house, only able to see as far as the beam of his flashlight stretched. Mixed-breed cats. Two of them meowed at the blue-black corpse sitting upright on the sofa. One more day and the cats probably would have got to her.

"No," he said at length. "Nothing hard to deal with."

"You hear about terrible accidents at this time of year." Natalie stuffed her hands into her coat pockets. As she breathed, tiny clouds of misty air left her pale lips.

He completed the task, then rested the shovel against the wall of her garage. He ran cold fingers through his short, damp hair. He'd worked up a light sweat. As he'd been standing in only a long-sleeved T-shirt, his skin was hot.

"Thank you so much for the help." She seemed calmer, a little less keyed up. "And please, come by Hat and Garden anytime."

"Tony!" A little girl's voice called from across the street.

Parker stood in the front of their house wearing a coat and snow boots, her backpack on her shoulders.

"Hey, Parker."

She had her hair in pigtails, the blond strands appearing silky and curled. "Look at my snowman."

He hadn't noticed it when he'd pulled into

the driveway. His gaze was redirected to the lopsided snowman in the yard. It wasn't very tall. Patches of dormant grass were visible where she'd rolled the large ball of snow to make the body. She'd decorated it with a scarf, a carrot and what looked to be some charcoal briquettes for the eyes.

"Come see it, Tony."

"Okay. I'll be right there."

"You better go," Natalie hastened to say. "I shouldn't have taken up your time."

"Hey, don't apologize. I was happy to help." He gave her a smile, one that he knew would be contagious. She returned the smile just as he knew she would.

Tony crossed the street, heading toward Parker, who was fixing the scarf on the snowman. Kim stood in the doorway wearing a pair of sweats and an oversize shirt — one of his. He loved the look of her hair, tousled and sleep-messed. The corner of her mouth turned up, a half effort that said she was only half-awake.

In that moment, he realized with a certain clarity that he'd missed his wife last night. Missed sleeping with her.

As soon as they got Parker off to school, he was going to show her just how much she meant to him.

■ ■ ■ ■

"Who is that man?" Sarah questioned from behind the sales counter. "This is the third time he's been in the shop in the last three weeks and each time, he stares at you."

Natalie gave the man a cursory look. About fifteen feet away, he stood by a rack of greeting cards; their eyes met, and he quickly looked down with a shy smile.

She was assailed by a strange sense of familiarity and got the vague impression she knew him but couldn't remember from where.

He was tall, broad in the shoulders in his suit, and his brown hair was cut short and neat. His facial features were masculine; he had a mustache and his lips were full.

"I haven't noticed him in here before," Natalie replied. Which was the truth. She'd been running on overload for the past three weeks since Hat and Garden had opened. Sales were doing well. She had a steady stream of customers and Christmas was mere days away.

Sarah put her hands on her hips. "I think you should say hello to him. Ask him if he needs any help."

Natalie frowned. While she normally had

no problems with that, it was Sarah who was outgoing enough for the both of them and she always made it a point to greet everyone with a smile and offer of assistance. It was Natalie who preferred to be in the flower shed out back, making the arrangements.

The shed was an old garage they'd converted into a workstation. All the fresh flowers were stored in a large refrigerated unit, plus there was a long bench that had every color of ribbon imaginable on various spools; on a shelf below were vases of all sizes. Baskets, too. Floral tape, putty and foam to create stellar arrangements. Natalie loved the creative end of owning her own business. The paperwork end left her less than enchanted, but it was all part of proprietorship.

She'd hired a young clerk, Meagan, to help Sarah inside the shop. A male student, Carl Brewster, who went to Boise State University part-time, made deliveries in the mornings, and on Friday and Saturday afternoons, her dad came in and drove the delivery van. Sarah worked several days a week at the counter, and a few times Steve brought BreeAnn and Sydney after school to help with inventory. It was a good blend of people who were all helping to make the flower shop a success.

"I have to look at some receipts in my office," Natalie countered, not in the mood to spar with Sarah. Sometimes her sister's romantic energy and enthusiasm for finding Natalie a boyfriend got on her nerves.

"You do not. You just don't want to talk to him."

"I have nothing to say to him. He clearly knows what he wants. A greeting card. Let him pick it out himself — sentiments are very personal and I'm sure he has something in mind for whatever the occasion is."

"He doesn't want a greeting card," Sarah insisted. "He's looking at you."

Natalie glanced toward the man once again and caught him staring. She straightened, smoothed her hands down the front of her green apron and said, "Fine. I'll go talk to him."

Her acquiescence was more out of curiosity than to quiet her sister.

Weaving her way around the coffee-cup display, Natalie approached him.

"Hi. Is there something I can help you find?"

"You don't remember me, do you?" His voice was deep, resonant.

Just then she knew she knew him but couldn't quite place how.

She caught a hint of nice cologne surrounding him. Dark in color, his eyes connected with hers. "You used to work at Blooming Floral."

"Yes . . . I did."

And in that instant, she knew. She'd done the floral arrangements for his wife's funeral about three years ago.

His name was on the edge of her mind. She struggled a moment, then uttered, "Jonathon Falco."

He nodded, a slow and sad acknowledgment. Sympathy came to her, full-blown, as if he had just buried his wife yesterday.

"I hope you've been doing all right," she said, the sentiment seeming so mechanical.

"We're getting along pretty well these days. My sons are playing in home games tonight at two different schools and I'm spread thin. These are the times I wish I had a clone." The pleasant, albeit stressed, laugh was added to the latter.

Natalie smiled. "Well, is there anything I can do to help you on your way?"

He grew quiet, thoughtful. "Actually, I was wondering if you were still married. I noticed you aren't wearing a ring anymore."

"Oh . . ." Automatically, she gazed at her left hand. "I'm divorced."

"I'm sorry."

"Don't be. It's fine. For the best," she hastened to add.

"Well, good. Then I was hoping you'd join me for dinner one evening."

Taking a moment to let him continue, she regarded him.

"I know you probably get asked out a lot, and you don't know me," he went on. "But the first time I came in, I recognized you and I've come back a few times now just to buy some things I don't really need."

His confession warmed her heart, made her smile widen.

"I realize it's the holidays and everyone's busy," he added. "But I'd really like to take you out to dinner."

Natalie suddenly felt nervous, noticing he looked at her with more than casual interest. How long had it been since a man had caught her attention? Jonathon was nice-looking, pleasant to talk with, and he was a widower. They were a different breed. No baggage, no ex-wife. He'd had a good marriage and that was a plus.

Why, then, didn't she just accept?

"I think your offer is very generous, Jonathon, but you're right about the holidays. I just opened the store and my daughter's coming home in a few days and she'll be with me through the holidays."

He nodded, shrugged. "I understand about family." In a voice that was both soft, yet firm, he added, "Maybe you can find the time after the first of the year. I'd really like to take you out — if you're not seeing anyone."

For the briefest of instants, Tony Cruz's face flashed before her. It was utterly ludicrous that she'd even think about him right now.

"No, I'm not seeing anyone. I've just been too busy."

"Then it'll do you good to have a relaxing dinner. After the first, can I call you?"

She licked her dry lips and, unbidden, glanced over her shoulder at Sarah, who was fixated on them. "All right." She slipped a hand into her apron pocket, and pulled out a Hat and Garden business card. "You can get hold of me here."

"Thanks, Natalie. I'll look forward to it." He pocketed the card. "I hope you have a merry Christmas."

"Thank you. Same to you."

He left and Natalie returned to the cash-register counter, raising her hand to silence Sarah before she could open her mouth. "I really am busy and I really might go out to dinner with him and I don't need any input. I have to check on Dad. I sent him out on deliveries over an hour ago and I see he hasn't returned, so honestly, Sarah, I don't need to hear whatever it is you want to say."

Sarah's mouth dropped open, then snapped closed. A few seconds later, she gave Natalie a scowl. "I was only going to say that we're all out of gingerbread-man cookies for the tea cart and I'll go get some more."

"Hmm," Natalie responded, more of a hum than a reply. A quick glance to the tea cart with its carafe of spiced apple cider and its silver tray empty of shaped-iced cookies, Natalie bit back anything further she would have said.

Indeed, they were out of gingerbread men.

But she was quite certain Sarah would have been mentioning a different sort of "man" had she been given the chance.

Fred Miller drove the 1997 Ford Econoline van with *Hat and Garden* scripted in pink across the side. The big gas guzzler was filled with flower arrangements, and the interior air was perfumed like a hothouse.

Absently, he sniffed his shirtsleeve and wondered if he smelled like flowers. Hard to say. He detected a hint of starch from the dry cleaners where he had his shirt laundered.

A Big Gulp sat in the drinks console, and as Fred turned the steering wheel, crushed ice inside the cup sloshed up against the lid. Dr Pepper was a second choice over what he really would have liked to be drinking. He wished he had been sent in the direction of Target; he would've made a quick pit stop for a white-cherry slushy, but Natalie had him delivering to southeast Boise.

Glancing at the road map he'd printed from Natalie's computer, he checked the cross streets, signaled and proceeded. The subdivision was fairly new, kept up nicely but didn't have mature trees. A yard needed a bunch of mature trees in order to attract squirrels.

Squirrels were God's gift to the retired.

At sixty-one years old, he was amazed by how much he depended on those squirrels to entertain him. He had a big yard up on the Boise bench and he could sit out there for hours and watch them. His favorite thing to view was when they'd lift the lid off the peanut box and take a nut out. He had often wondered how they'd figured that out. How did they know that the lid could lift up? There were bite marks on it, little tooth scratches so, at one time, they had thought to gnaw their way through the wood. Then one of them must have been smart enough to figure out that the lid came up. It was something that would remain a mystery to him.

Hell, he had time to figure it out. He was in no hurry.

He'd rushed all his life delivering mail. It was always hurry up and go. Now that he'd been retired, he did everything slow. He got up in the morning slow, he read the paper slow, he dressed slow, he drank his coffee slow, he ate his lunch slow . . . Everything he could do, he savored and he enjoyed.

Making flower deliveries for Natalie wasn't a full-time job and, after Christmas, he probably wouldn't be doing it as much. He was bothered by the fact that his daughter insisted on paying him. He would have helped her out for nothing.

While working for her got him out of the house, he liked his off-days, when he could take his time with all that he had to do.

Scanning the mailboxes for the correct address number, he pulled over to the curb. Shifting the gear column into Park, he pressed down on the brake. This van was a fuel monster compared to his Hyundai Elantra with its sporty sunroof.

He loved his car.

AARP said that when a man retired he needed to trade up to one of those big luxury cars. To hell with that. He wasn't a Cadillac kind of guy. Not even a Buick Century kind of guy. An economy car did him just fine, although there were those rare occasions when he caught himself getting in on the wrong side to operate it. Old habits died hard, and the older he got the more he regressed to the old days. He'd used the passenger side for so many years to operate a government Jeep, he sometimes forgot the right way to start up the Elantra. And damn if it didn't get his Dutch up when he did that.

Stepping out of the van, he ambled to the back, opened the door and got the iris arrangement. The thick cluster of flowers were a deep purple-blue with yellow eyes. The card read:

*Luis C—*

Sarah's handwriting couldn't find its way out of a paper bag it was so sloppy. All he could make out was the "C" of the last name. The rest was one big squiggly line.

As Fred took the walkway up to the front door, he thought whoever sent Iris some irises was pretty clever.

He punched the doorbell and waited for an answer.

The door opened and a woman stood in the opening. At first glance he assumed she was younger than she was by the nice shape of her figure. On closer inspection, she was actually a more mature lady. Not mature in a way that was aged and unbecoming, unflattering or unappealing. But mature in a very lovely way.

She was tall, too. Probably a couple inches taller than him.

He gazed at her feet to see if she was wearing heeled shoes. No.

He hadn't dated much since he'd been a widower. The first several years had been hard ones, then he'd gotten into the swing of things being on his own. He'd had a few dates his girls didn't know about. Decided real quick that women his age were no fun. Amazing how many didn't want to go to the lake because they didn't swim, or the sun was too hot or they didn't water-ski because of their hip. Or didn't want to in-line skate or bike. Didn't want him to open the sunroof on his car because the wind gave them an earache. Or didn't want to go to Las Vegas because plane travel upset their stomachs. Those who took a shine to him had only been interested in being taken care of by his retirement checks. He was no woman's keeper. He'd only done that for the single love of his life because she had been the mother to his children, and nobody else could ever replace that special spot in his heart.

"Flowers for Iris," Fred found himself saying, staring into a pair of nice brown eyes.

"I'm Iris."

He should have known.

She was very attractive. He liked her hair. The light shone on it in a soft, kind of warm way that looked nice. Her eyes were brown and she actually wore makeup. Many of the ladies his age had forgone makeup and styling their hair. They'd gone over to the dark side — bouffants and Marlene Dietrich eyebrows.

"Then these are for you."

"How sweet." She took them, paused and said, "Oh, let me thank you for your time."

He knew what she was getting at — a tip. "No thanks necessary. I was happy to do it."

And he was. Happier than he realized when she smiled at him. But that only made him think of something else —

Who in the hell had sent her the flowers? A boyfriend? A husband? One of her kids, if she had any?

Why did he even care?

"Have a merry Christmas," he muttered as he stepped off the porch, only to catch himself glancing over his shoulder at her as she pressed her nose into the flowers with the sweetest smile he'd ever seen.

Fred climbed into the van, cranked on the heater and braced himself by gripping the steering wheel. What had come over him?

The cell phone he'd set on the dash chirped and startled him.

He answered and Natalie asked him where he was.

"I'm just now done with Iris, um — whatever her last name was," he replied, wishing he'd had the foresight to read what had been written on the card before he'd made the delivery.

"I know you like to take your time, Dad, but we have a bunch more deliveries."

"I'm heading out to the next stop now." He turned over the ignition, took a sip of his Dr Pepper, the ice having melted enough to knock some of the carbonation from the syrup. He made a sour face. "Hey, none of my afternoon deliveries happen to be in the direction of the Milwaukee Street Target, are they?"

"No."

"Well, hell."

He clipped the phone line dead, punched his foot on the accelerator, and snuffed out thoughts of how tasty a white-cherry slushy would be.

"I hope Austin doesn't look as rough around the edges in person as he did in the photos Cassie e-mailed me," Natalie stated above the noise of the airport's PA system.

Sarah's expression went from enthusiastic over Cassie's imminent arrival to guarded. "Don't get your hopes up. He did look a little . . . uh, not really right for Cassie."

"I know."

Natalie mulled over the very real possibility that this new boyfriend of Cassandra's was not good enough for her daughter. Of course, very few boyfriends of eighteen-year-old daughters were worthy of baby girls. It was just that Cassie seemed to act a little differently when she was with Austin.

There were those times when Natalie had called Cassie, and Austin was in her dorm room with her — something that rather distressed Natalie. She mentally went over all the "girl talks" she'd had with Cassie

75

about birth control and safe sex. Yet it seemed that whenever he was with Cassie she got silly and giggly. Goofy. Cassie wasn't a goofy girl. She'd always been fairly solid, a grounded young lady with a good head on her shoulders.

Austin Mably made Cassandra Goodwin breathless.

No doubt about it, her daughter got that lightness in her voice when she talked about the boy. Natalie could only hope the relationship wasn't too serious, or that it wouldn't last for long.

Cassie needed to focus on her education.

That was a big bone of contention for Natalie. She'd dropped out of college and hadn't pursued her degree. She'd married and taken on a set of family responsibilities. Not that she regretted any of it. She just wanted a better life for her own daughter. Cassie had so much potential. She was an excellent artist — a great visual person who'd always won awards in high school.

A new batch of holiday travelers came through the glass security doors of the Boise airport. Family and friends waited in a designated area. Forgoing the vinyl chairs Natalie and Sarah stood at the top of the escalator. Passengers rolled carry-on luggage through the concourse.

Natalie was anxious to see her only daughter, to reconnect and visit. Give her a big hug and a kiss. To reaffirm the familiar bond. She wanted to hear all about her college life this past month, how she was doing in her classes. Her daughter had always excelled academically and she carried high hopes for becoming an advertising designer. Natalie wanted to know more about who her friends were, although Natalie suspected Cassie had chosen Austin above making new girlfriends.

Cassie hadn't come home for Thanksgiving due to class scheduling and a project she had to complete. Natalie had missed her greatly and was glad she'd be here for a week this time. Part of the time would be spent with her and the other time with Greg.

Sarah scanned the crowd while saying, "What are you going to do if you don't like Austin?"

"What can I do about it? Cassie likes him." Natalie held a white-frost bouquet for her daughter, a welcome-home gift. The sweet smell of white carnations, lilies and roses overpowered the fast-food odors of the airport.

Sarah thoughtfully asked, "Remember Kyle Provant?"

"How could I forget? You dated him in

the tenth grade. Dad hated him."

"That's sort of why I dated Kyle — I mean, I thought he was cute. But Dad wouldn't let me get my learner's permit until my grades were better, so this was my one way of getting back at him."

"All I remember about Kyle is that he had to go to juvenile court for car theft."

"Yeah. His house was on Dad's mail route and Dad delivered the court notice. When he came home from work that day he gave me holy hell about it, asked me if I knew I was dating a delinquent. I told him it was no big deal. He had a fit. Said I couldn't date Kyle anymore."

"That's right."

"So my point is — I only picked Kyle because there was something I wanted more than him. And that was to get my learner's permit."

"And this has to do with what?"

"Leverage. I told Dad I'd stop seeing Kyle and get my grades up if he'd let me get my learner's permit."

"Dad never said you could do that."

"I know. But Mom did. She was always on my side." Sarah smiled, a pair of dimples coming out on her cheeks. "Mom never liked to argue."

Natalie smiled in fondness, an image of

their mother coming to her mind. Mom had always been the peacemaker in the house.

"So I'm thinking — why do you think Cassie wants to date a boy you probably won't like? What does she want?" Sarah asked.

Baffled, Natalie shrugged. "She hasn't asked me for a thing."

"Well, there has to be something exciting about this boy."

Tamping down the anxiousness that struck a chord, Natalie uttered with dismay, "She wanted me to up the limit on her Visa and I said no. Oh, God — do you think this is about me not letting her go shopping?"

Sarah folded her arms beneath her breasts. "When I was her age, I might have thought about it." Sarah's stream of thought was cut short, her gaze narrowing. "Is that her? I think it is. She's wearing a red beret."

Natalie stretched on tiptoe to see. She caught sight of her daughter coming toward her on the ramp, a smile on her travel-weary face. A red felt beret was angled on her blond-highlighted hair, her cheeks wintry pale and appearing fuller. She looked exhausted, as if she hadn't slept much last night. The zipper of her coat was undone, the edges hanging open. She wore bleached jeans and a gray sweatshirt, very nondescript. Cassie had always had a snap more fashion flare.

Maybe she really did need to go shopping. . . .

"Doesn't look as if Chicago has turned her into a big-city girl," Sarah commented, waving to her niece.

"She looks great," Natalie replied, her heart warming and a smile spreading across her mouth. "Tired, but great."

Natalie hadn't realized how much she'd missed her daughter until this moment. So much had happened since she'd sent her only child off to college. It was good to have her home so they could catch up, and Natalie could show her Hat and Garden.

Cassie approached with a lightness to her steps, carrying an overstuffed travel bag.

In that moment, the tagalong boyfriend was forgotten.

"Mom!" Cassie said, dropping the bag and putting both arms around Natalie.

Natalie held on tight, breathing in the scent of her daughter, reveling in the feel of their embrace. "Cassie, honey, I missed you."

"Me, too, Mom."

Pulling back, Natalie brushed the long hair from Cassie's left cheek. She'd lost that innocent high-school demeanor, the look of a flighty senior ready to move away. In its place was a college student, more mature and self-sufficient. "You've changed."

"No way."

"Yes, you have. You look . . . different."

"I'm tired. I didn't sleep well last night, too excited to come home, I guess."

Sarah hugged her niece. "The girls have been asking about you."

"I brought them something. It's in my suitcase — if it made it here. O'Hare was crazy. We almost missed our flight."

Natalie presented her daughter with the white flowers, giving her a buss on the cheek. Her skin felt smooth and warm beneath her lips.

"They're beautiful." Cassie breathed in the fragrance.

"Are you going to introduce your friend?" Sarah questioned.

"Austin, come here. I want you to meet my mom and my aunt."

It was then that Natalie homed in on the boy standing three feet away from them. He wasn't exactly a *boy*. He was a young man, twenty years old. Call it a mother's instinct, but Natalie didn't get a good feeling about him from the outset.

The photos had been correct; now seeing

him in real life, Natalie's premonition was correct.

He had too much product in his hair which was a dull brown color. The style seemed greasy. His eyes were gray like fog, the eyebrows above flat and thick. A smile curved on his mouth, his teeth marginally crooked, but not overly so. His face was pleasant enough if she were being generous. But the fact remained Natalie didn't think he was good enough for her daughter. That conclusion was hammered home when she noted the sleeves on his plaid flannel shirt had been rolled up, revealing forearms colored with tattoos.

"Mom, this is my boyfriend — Austin Mably."

*Boyfriend?* Did Cassie have to call him that?

Cassie had never had a serious steady in high school, and that pleased Natalie. Her daughter was involved in school activities, big groups and sports. Barely four months had passed since she'd started at Columbia College Chicago. That seemed so soon to land a boyfriend, much less bring him home for Christmas.

Natalie stiffly extended her arm to Austin's outstretched hand. "Hi, Austin."

"It's nice to meet you, Mrs. Goodwin."

"Natalie," she clarified before she thought better of it. She had to give him credit for addressing her respectfully, but she hadn't thought of herself as a missus in quite some time.

"This is my aunt, Sarah," Cassie said.

Sarah said, "So, your mom told me you two met at orientation."

"We didn't like each other at first." Austin scratched the light bristles of beard. Certainly not a day's growth — more like a few days'. "I thought she was too country for me."

Natalie stood taller. "Idaho isn't the country."

"He thought Idaho was where Iowa is." Cassie's laughter was soft.

If it hadn't been a common mistake, Natalie might not have nodded. "Where are you from?" she questioned Austin.

"Minneapolis."

"Not exactly New York City." There was a slight bite to her remark. Sarah caught it and nudged her with her shoulder. Natalie was wishing that she could rewind the moment and watch Cassie come toward her again, only this time, without Austin in the background.

"I'm not much for New York." Austin

settled his hand on Cassie's shoulder. "I like Chicago."

Her daughter's face lit up as if it had been illuminated by a host of holiday lights. A stab of jealousy worked through Natalie, leaving a bitter taste in her mouth. She didn't want to share her daughter, not now. Not this Christmas. It was going to be difficult enough with Greg taking their daughter for half her stay.

"Well . . . I guess we should get your luggage," was all Natalie could think to say.

As they walked to baggage claim, Cassie snuggled next to Natalie, hooking her arm through hers. In a low voice she said, "I want you to like him. Give him a chance, Mom. Please."

Natalie kept her gaze straight, her throat tight while her pulse beat at the base of her throat. "Honey, I've reconsidered the issue of your Visa card. I'll extend your limit."

"You will? Thanks, Mom."

"I just thought maybe it would be something to make you feel happier."

"But I *am* happy."

"I mean like . . . happier about your life in school. Maybe refocus on the schoolwork."

"My grades are doing okay."

Panic momentarily held Natalie. "Just 'okay'? Cassie, I really don't think —"

"Mom, not now." Cassie squeezed her arm, smiling up into Natalie's face. "We just got here. I have to call Dad."

"Dad?"

"Austin's staying with Dad, remember? Unless you say it's okay to stay with you?" Hope raised her voice an octave. "I never asked because I thought for sure you'd say no. But, Mom . . . would you?"

"Let him stay in the same house as us, you . . . and me? Cassie, now, I don't think that's a good idea."

"I didn't think you would, which is why I didn't ask. But modern moms are cool with it, you know. My friend in art history — her mom is letting her boyfriend stay in her bedroom with her."

"Not a chance. At the very most, he could sleep on the foldout bed in the den."

"Oh, thanks, Mom!" Cassie stopped, kissed Natalie's cheek and then turned to Austin. "Change of plans. My mom said you can stay at her house with me — but in the den."

Stunned, Natalie's jaw dropped. In a half daze perpetuated by the events of the past few minutes, she replied, "I . . . I hope you'll be comfortable."

"Thank you, Mom." Cassie kissed her cheek. "Love you."

"Love you, too." Natalie gave her only child a sideways glance.

Then she let her gaze stray to Austin whose gait was slightly shuffled, his hands shoved into the pockets of his overly baggy jeans. He grinned at her, startling Natalie. She was helpless to do anything but smile in return, all the while thinking she should have upped that Visa limit when Cassie first asked.

# FOUR:
## 50%-OFF
## CLEARANCE DAYS

Kim and Parker didn't show up for the Christmas Eve party at the fire station.

While the other wives, girlfriends and kids were having a good time, Tony kept his feelings to himself. Call it a hunch, but he didn't feel any immediate worry for his family's safety. He suspected this was just another piece to his marriage puzzle that was becoming increasingly more difficult to understand.

Things between them had grown progressively strained in recent weeks. He'd attributed some of the tension to the holidays. But in many ways, he knew that wasn't necessarily the truth. The rift in their differences had been widening, slowly and steadily. Now there were obviously signs of strain.

Two days ago, he'd been helping Rocky tune up his snowmobile and he'd had to drive back home for a minute to get a tool they needed for the gears. He went into the house to say hi to Kim, and his unexpected return had sent her into the laundry room where the hum of the dryer muted the last remnants of her phone conversation. When Tony had asked her who she was talking to, she'd flushed quickly and said Laurie.

Laurie was Kim's best friend, someone she'd been spending a great deal more time with — both in her company and talking on the cell phone.

In the pit of his gut Tony knew something was off, but it was just too much to deal with at Christmas. The thought of spending it alone, in discord with his wife, wasn't an option he wanted to get into. Besides, he'd rather keep things neutral because Parker was really looking forward to Christmas and this was no time to rock the boat.

But he had been expecting Kim and Parker to show tonight.

Tony went into the captain's office for some quiet to call the house, but there was no answer.

Sitting in the desk chair, he stared out the window, seeing first only darkness, then his reflection. His eyebrows were knit together, his mouth a taut line. He laid his palms on his thighs, ran them over his pants to his knees and leaned forward.

"Hey, Cruz, where's the wife?" Captain Palladino walked past the open doorway, pausing briefly, his arms filled with toys.

"She must have got hung up doing something. I'm sure she'll be here soon."

"My wife wants to talk to her about a Web site design. Is Kim still doing that?"

"Yeah, she is."

After Captain Palladino was nudged down the hallway by Walcroft's twin boys, Tony called Kim's cell phone. It took numerous tries and forty minutes later for her to pick up.

"Hullo?"

"Kim, where are you?" Swallowing tightly, Tony tried to curb the resentment in his tone.

"I'm so sorry, baby." Her voice was level, even. "Parker and I went to Laurie's house and I had too much wine. I fell asleep. I'm on my way home now. Parker's sleeping in the car. We're just too tired to come to the station."

Deep down, Tony knew that Kim was just as unhappy with their relationship as he was. He'd barely known her four months when they got married. Several months later, he acknowledged to himself that they'd probably made a mistake. But for Parker and the stability the little girl finally had, Tony stayed and hoped he was wrong about everything.

Tonight's phone call with Kim only added to his suspicions that she was lying to him about where she'd been. More important, with whom. He didn't have any proof she was being unfaithful, just a feeling that held him in its grip long after he disconnected the call.

The next morning, Kim wasn't home when he got off shift. He went into the house, the thermostat tripping on the furnace as he closed the door, leaving the cold air in the garage. The tree lights were still on; he felt the bulbs and they were warm to the touch. They'd been on all night. He'd told Kim to unplug them before going to bed. Even the new safety ones could be a fire hazard on a fresh cut tree. Dirty dishes and cups were stacked in the sink. A pile of mail lay unopened by the phone, including a number of holiday cards with red and green envelopes.

Merry Fucking Christmas.

Scratching the back of his neck, Tony stood in the kitchen and tried to figure out what he was going to do.

He'd just started cleaning up the dishes when Kim pulled into the driveway.

Parker burst into the house, ran to him

and squeezed his legs. "Hi, Tony! Can I open my presents now? I've been waiting and waiting."

He didn't ask her where she'd been waiting; he laid his hand on top of her head, smoothing her hair.

Kim came trailing in, a poinsettia in her grasp. "I think we got the last one in town." She set the red-leafed plant in its shiny gold foil wrap on the countertop. Then she came to him and put her arms around his waist and held on.

She smelled differently. He couldn't bring himself to embrace her in return. "I didn't think any of the stores were open today," he said.

"Oh . . . um, no." She inched away, not meeting his gaze, then went to the sink and finished loading the dishwasher. "I got it yesterday."

"Where's it been?"

"At Laurie's. We ran over there this morning to pick it up. I forgot it last night."

Tony showed no emotion. His muscles were tight, like iron bands in his body that held him rooted to the spot.

"Can I, Tony? Mommy said when we got home, I could open them."

"Sure, Parker."

Keeping a smile on her lips, Kim dried

her hands and took Tony's to lead him into the living room. The skin on her palm was cold, her fingers loose around his. He let her take him to the sofa and sit down, cozy next to him.

"That one's for Tony, Parker." Kim's face was flushed, her blue eyes startling next to her pale complexion and pink-blushed cheeks. She was a beautiful woman on the outside with classic good looks, and she had a very confident personality. Her liveliness and vitality for living life on the edge were infectious. That was what had attracted him to her in the first place.

Tony took the gift, and the others to follow. The three of them spent the morning opening presents and he pretended to enjoy himself as if nothing were wrong — as if his life was not somehow off-kilter.

Later on while Parker played with her new toys, Tony cornered Kim in the kitchen as she put on a fresh pot of coffee.

"Where were you this morning, Kim?"

Looking insulted for the first time since coming through the door, she said, "At Laurie's."

"Why don't I believe you?"

"I don't know."

They merely stared at one another, allowing a ridiculous span of silence to be broken only by the playful hums of a six-year-old who was completely oblivious to the two adults at odds with each other.

"I'm going to Rocky's house to get the kitten for Parker," Tony finally said in a soft voice, picking up his keys.

"She's going to love it, Tony."

"Yep," he replied in a clipped voice.

After punching the garage-door opener, he realized Kim's car was in the driveway blocking him in. Rather than move it, he opened the door to the Mazda coupé and got inside. The small vehicle swallowed his large body, making him feel closed in. Almost suffocated.

Feeling for the lever under the seat, his hand touched a cold object.

Kim's cell phone.

It must have fallen on the floor mat. He tossed the cellular onto the shifter console, made an adjustment to the seat and slid it back as far as it would go to accommodate his long legs.

He put the car into gear, rested his wrist on the steering wheel and turned down the radio that heralded holiday tunes. He punched another station, not in the mood for fa-la-las.

Driving down Fairview Avenue, he headed to Rocky's house to pick up the kitten.

Rocky had two playful rottweilers who Tony hoped like hell had left the kitten alone. Rocky had agreed to keep the kitten overnight so he could surprise Parker with the Christmas present today.

The anxiousness he'd been feeling about watching her face when he gave it to her was now diminished. While he didn't want to believe Kim could do such a thing, he wondered if she had told Parker not to tell him where they'd been last night and this morning. If Kim had devised a "game" to play with her little girl . . . If that was the case . . .

Tension built in the back of Tony's eyes, around the sockets where moderate pain grew into a vague headache.

Stopped at a red light, he was jolted out of his thoughts by the chirp of an incoming call on Kim's phone. Startled into action, he reached over and punched the answer button.

"Hello?"

Nothing.

"Hello?"

The line went dead.

Tony glanced at the ID, but the LCD reading blinked to gray.

"Shit," he muttered, fumbling with some of the task buttons, trying to figure out where the Received Calls feature was. While doing so, the phone rang once more.

"Hello?" he answered gruffly.

Again, no response.

"Who is this?"

Once more, the line disconnected.

A car horn blared behind Tony as the light changed and he didn't accelerate. He quickly went through the car's gears, grinding them from first to third as he pulled into the nearest business driveway.

Sitting in the empty Kmart parking lot, he figured out Kim's call log. The incoming was from a Boise number, the prefix 938. That was north of Boise around Eagle. Searching deeper in the phone menu, he found the outgoing-call list.

He licked his lips, scanned the dates and times and found that that particular number had been called sixteen times last night and once this morning.

Not moving for long moments, Tony stared at the phone. Then he hit *67 so Kim's ID wouldn't appear on the incoming call and dialed the number and waited.

"Hello?" a man's voice answered.

"Who's this?" Tony demanded, his voice a low curl that rumbled in his chest.

No answer.

He went on. "Listen, I know you're involved with my wife. Who are you?"

Silence, then finally a response. "I think you'd better talk to Kim."

Then the line disconnected.

The light traffic on Fairview Avenue became a blur as Tony clenched his jaw, his hands gripping the steering wheel.

He barely remembered getting to Rocky's, pulling into the driveway and ringing the doorbell. The sound of barking dogs echoed through the large house.

Rocky stood in the opening wearing a pair of sweats and a T-shirt. His resemblance to Nicholas Cage was a little uncanny as he held on to a glass of orange juice.

"Dude, I hate to tell you this, but the rotties made cat chow out of your kitten." He chuckled, then seeing Tony's troubled expression he said, "Not really. I'm just bullshitting you. Don't look so worried."

Tony let himself inside, speaking while walking, uttering aloud what had been at the back of his mind, but too potent for him to say it until this moment. "Kim's having an affair."

Rocky followed him into the kitchen. "You're sure?"

Upon seeing Tony, the two big black-and-brown dogs in the backyard wiggled their butts, wet noses smearing up the glass on the slider.

"I told you I suspected it. The guy just called her on her cell phone. I drove her car over here and she'd left her cell phone under the seat. *Fuck*."

Tony ran his hand through his hair, thought he'd prepared himself for this, but he hadn't. Not really. How could any man be prepared for something like this?

Because his suspicions were finally confirmed, all at once Tony was relieved, yet upset at the same time. The impact hadn't fully hit him. Not yet. He did feel betrayal. Betrayal was frickin' huge and it left a nauseating taste in his mouth.

In all the years he'd been with the fire department, all the overnights he'd had, he had never once strayed. He'd had the opportunity. He knew plenty of women who were willing and made their intentions obvious, but being unfaithful to his wife was crossing the line.

"Jesus," Rocky muttered. "Want a beer?"

"No. I need to keep a clear head."

He was left with a bunch of unanswered questions, and a shock wave of overwhelming uncertainty.

"Do you know who the guy is?" Rocky asked.

"Not a clue."

A host of questions came at Tony.

Why had she cheated on him? Who was the guy? How long had it been going on? Had they ever had sex in his home, his bed?

One moment his life had been complete, and now it felt discounted. Less than what it was. A clearance. A markdown.

"What are you going to do?" Rocky set his glass down and leaned next to the countertop.

"Don't know." Tony exhaled slowly, trying to focus. "Talk to her."

There were a million things going on in his head, but only one thing surfaced with clarity:

He still had to get the kitten for Parker. No matter what happened with him and Kim, he loved that little girl.

"Mom, these are fifty-percent off." Cassie searched through spools of clearance ribbon at the craft store.

"Pick out all the red velvet ones." Natalie usually bought notions from her suppliers, but the after-holiday sales were really great. At a fifty-percent discount, it meant she could save a lot of money.

Rummaging through the craft ribbons, Natalie wasn't really focused on the palate of colors. This was one of the rare opportunities she'd had this holiday to be alone with her daughter.

Every day had been spent with Austin in tow, her daughter's arm slung around him or Austin's hand grabbing for Cassie's. Resentment had surfaced, a niggling little claw that pulled at the hairs on the back of her neck. Natalie had so looked forward to spending some time alone with her daughter, yet they had barely had a moment together.

She and Cassie had gone shopping together while, thankfully, Austin stayed at Greg's to watch football. Natalie had made a discreet phone call this morning to her ex-husband, planting the idea that he invite Austin over for some "guy-time" since Austin had ended up at Natalie's house for four days. They'd dropped Austin off on the way to the shopping complex.

"So how are things going at school?" Natalie asked, her tone upbeat. She wanted to enjoy every second of this moment. "Tell me how your life is going."

"It's going great, Mom."

"Are you enjoying your classes?"

"Sure." Cassie had thrown her hair into a ponytail, her eye makeup a little darker than she normally wore it. She'd applied a frosted lip gloss that smelled like angel food cake.

"Which one is your favorite?"

"Art design. Austin's in that class with me."

Natalie kept a lightness to her tone. "What does he want to be?"

"He's not sure yet. He's still trying to decide." Cassie had seemed a bit disinterested with their conversation, but then her face lit up. "Did I tell you he's in a band?"

"I believe you mentioned that over Christmas dinner."

"Grandpa thought it was cool that Austin plays the drums."

Fred Miller did have a way with making lemonade out of lemons.

"What about his family?"

"I've never met them. I talked to his mom once on the phone when she called and Austin was in the shower."

The spool of plaid ribbon in Natalie's hand dropped to the floor. She didn't readily move to pick it up. "What were you doing in his room when he was in the shower?"

Cassie's laugh wasn't reassuring. "Mom, I was in his room while he was in the *dorm* shower. Chill out. Jeez."

Natalie's heart slowed, resuming a normal

rhythm. "Well . . . oh." A thought flashed through her mind. She wondered if she should even bring it up, then opted to just go ahead and say it. "Remember how you and I had all those talks about sex, Cassie?"

"How could I forget? You bought me a *Playgirl* when I was in high school and you told me you'd rather me see what a penis looks like in the magazine versus me doing anything stupid out of curiosity."

Natalie did recall doing that. At the time, it seemed a very sensible and liberal thing to do. But to hear Cassie retell it now . . . it sounded a bit over the top.

"My intentions were good," Natalie said. "I was trying to expose you to human sexuality without you having to see anything, um . . . exposed to you."

"And your point is?"

"My point is —" Natalie had sort of wished she'd forgotten the point, but she hadn't "— I'd like to think you're being cautious and adult in your decision making now that you don't live with me. I hope that you learned something about abstinence and, at the very least, about safe sex . . . if you and Austin are . . . well, you know what I mean — I'm just saying, you need to be careful."

*"Mom,"* she groaned. "I haven't *done* anything, so quit freaking out."

Relief rushed through Natalie like a breath of fresh air. The feeling of falling over a cliff while trying to reach out and grab something thankfully left with her daughter's reassurance.

"Good for you, honey. I'm proud of you. I know it's hard to hold out, but . . . good for you." She reached out and gave Cassie a hug. Cassie rolled her eyes, but gave her mom a hug in return.

The very fact that they were having this conversation in a craft store seemed disconcerting, but there had been no other alternative given that they hadn't had time in the past several days to talk privately.

Before she could stop herself, Natalie blurted, "Cassie, I can't see you with a boy like him. You're so opposite."

"I know." Cassie's smile was beautiful. "That's what I like about him. It's the fact that we are so different. We bring out the best in one another, Mom."

An unforeseen feeling of emptiness settled in Natalie's stomach. She remembered what it was like to have that feeling in her life, first with Greg, and then even with Michael Williams. The fact that Cassie was on her own and experiencing a connection with a boy made Natalie both happy . . . and sad.

She missed her little girl, but the woman she'd turned into seemed to have a level head on her shoulders.

"If he's what makes you happy, then I'm glad you met someone at school who you can share your time with." But she added with motherly caution, "Just make sure this romance doesn't interfere with your grades."

"It won't." Cassie's automatic assurance didn't do a whole lot to alleviate Natalie's concern. "I'm getting hungry for dinner. Are we almost done?"

Tonight Natalie was facing Greg over a Chinese dinner. It was the "transfer" night from one house to the other, and Cassie wanted the two of them to meet at the restaurant. Natalie knew that Cassie would always try to get her and Greg back together, however misguided her heart. It wasn't as if Cassie disagreed with the divorce — Natalie had talked to her about it. Cassie just wanted her parents to live in the same house again, and she would probably have those feelings for a lifetime.

"I'm almost done," Natalie said.

Moving through the craft store, a basket looped over her arm, Natalie buttoned her coat. There had to be something wrong with the heating system because it was just as chilly inside the store as it was outside.

The cold atmosphere didn't help gather the warm front she needed to put on tonight. She'd put this dinner out of her mind, but now she'd have to go through the motions. It wasn't as if she carried any animosity toward Greg. It was just that whenever she was in his company, she was reminded about why she'd divorced him. He always did this stupid thing with the check: he was so anal about a tip he always took out a pocket calculator to make sure he tipped exactly fifteen percent.

As she headed for the cash register, Natalie saw three Boise firemen coming toward her from the back of the store. They were in their turnouts and helmets, all carrying axes.

Slightly alarmed, Natalie wondered if there was a fire in the store.

Cassie paused, her voice raising an octave. "Mom, there's a fire."

"I don't smell anything burning, and no announcements have been made."

"Then how come the fire department is here?"

"I don't know."

She recognized Tony Cruz almost immediately. He stood out among the others, his shoulders broad and his face so good-looking that every female shopper within shouting distance stared with obvious appreciation. He made eye contact, giving her an easy smile and a lift of his chin to acknowledge that he knew her.

Unexpectedly, his friendly gesture went straight to her beating heart and gave it a jolt. Why did she have a physical reaction to him whenever she saw him? She knew he was off-limits.

"Mom, do you know that guy?" Cassie asked. "He's hot."

"Oh . . . he's . . ." Natalie felt a sudden loss for words, thinking that, yes, Tony Cruz was hot. Blankly, she formed words to counter what she was really thinking. "He lives in the house across the street."

Tony approached them.

"Is there a fire?" she asked him, keeping her tone even.

His voice was calming, reassuring. "The heater tripped an alarm. It turned off the switch. The heating and air-conditioning company's coming out to fix it."

No wonder it was so cold in the store.

The other two firemen continued to walk ahead, but Tony held back.

"Hi," he said to Cassie, and Natalie remembered she wasn't alone.

"This is my daughter, Cassie. Cassie, this is Tony Cruz."

"Hi," Cassie replied. "You guys rock."

Tony grinned. "Thanks."

"A girl in my college dorm set off the sprinkler system when she had a fire in her room."

Natalie gazed at Cassie. "You didn't tell me that."

"Yeah, I did." To Tony, she went on. "She was burning candle wax on a hot plate, forgot about it, and the heat blew up a can of air freshener on the counter. A shelving unit caught fire."

"I would have remembered this," Natalie said.

Cassie shrugged. "Then maybe I told Austin's mom when I was on the phone with her."

Natalie bit back a sharp pang, not taking any time to examine it.

"It was nice to meet you, Tony," Cassie remarked; then to Natalie, "I'm going to see if they have confetti and those blowers for New Year's. Me and Austin are going to have a party."

Cassie excused herself, leaving Natalie with her thoughts spinning. A New Year's party? Would that be a private party? Or a big beer party? Or . . .

"Pretty girl." Tony's comment intruded on Natalie's musings.

"Thank you." She stole a look at his face without being obvious.

While he gave the appearance of being relaxed and in control, she sensed an undercurrent of something different charging through him. A tension that was unwelcome, and an anxiousness that told her something had changed inside him. She saw thin lines at the corners of his eyes that hadn't been there before. An old scar at his right temple, just at the tip of his eyebrow, was now clearly defined.

He looked tired.

Happening to glance out her front window, she'd seen him twice this week — coming and going in his Dodge Ram. She hadn't spoken to him since that day he'd shoveled snow for her. He'd been a godsend.

"How was your Christmas?" she asked politely.

"Fine." He nodded, an almost perfunctory gesture, as if he'd done it a thousand times on various calls, then he shifted his stance in a way that made him stand taller. Natalie took in the scope of his presence, almost a little intimidated by his formidable size.

He wore large black boots with zippers running up the tops. His feet were big. His body was big in the reflective-striped turnout. Everything on him looked immense — from his helmet to the oxygen tank strapped on his back — but the whole image of him in uniform was presented in a way that wasn't threatening. To the contrary, his ready-for-action appearance was quite reassuring.

If she hadn't seen the restless mix of uncertainty and dull pain in his eyes, she would have sworn he had no worries in his life. But she had seen that spark of emotion, however fleeting, and it compelled her to ask about his welfare.

"Have you been busy with calls?" she questioned, but really meaning — *"Is everything okay at home?"*

She wasn't sure how she was able to sense that something was wrong, but she was. Maybe it was because she had seen those same lines on her face while coming to the realization that her marriage was in trouble.

"No more than average." His eyes were a deep brown, not really an intense color, but very dark. "I've got to go. See you around."

Tony moved through the double-glass doors, feeling Natalie's gaze on his retreating back. He grew annoyed with himself by the transparency of his feelings — something she clearly saw, judging from the way she'd spoken to him. He never let his private emotions show on the job, yet here he was looking pathetic enough that his neighbor noticed.

The last few days had been hell, a chain reaction of events that left him numb. Kim hadn't denied her affair when he'd confronted her, and her subsequent admission of how long it had been going on was, in the end, inconsequential to him.

His marriage was over. The end had been a long time coming and now he was faced with a new set of uncertainties. Where was he going to live? What was going to happen to Parker?

For the past week, he and Kim set aside the chaos in their dissolved marriage for Parker's sake while Kim made arrangements to move out and in with her "boyfriend," a man Tony didn't know by name — didn't care to know by name. Kim would be taking Parker and the kitten with her. Tony had a hard time reconciling that. He had no legal claims on the little girl, but he loved her as if she were his own. He'd formed a bond with her, and yet the law said he had no rights. It was a hard truth to swallow.

He and Kim hadn't discussed divorce details. It was the unknown that unsettled Tony to a point of near distraction.

The down payment on their house had

been made with his money, even though the title was in both their names. He regretted doing that; a stupid move of trust on his part. He was living in the home alone now, worried she would want her share of the equity, if not the entire house for herself. Tony knew he had to hire a lawyer, he just hadn't gotten around to it yet.

He filled the hours with overtime, taking shifts other than his own so the guys could spend the holiday week with their families. He hadn't told anyone at the station that his family had fallen apart.

Maybe in the deepest recesses of his mind he was in denial. At this point, even if Kim asked to take him back, he probably wouldn't. His reservations were too great. He could take the affair out of the equation and he'd still feel the same way. They'd just never been the right couple. He'd sort of known that from the start, but he'd turned a blind eye to his better judgment because he'd wanted to be married, to have a family. To be fair to Kim, he probably hadn't been there for her in the ways she needed.

Now he couldn't go back.

Tony climbed into the fire truck, flipped down the SCBA seat in the back and buckled himself in. Then he fit the heavy weight of the oxygen tank into his seat.

It was the dead of winter, the skies were a vibrant blue, not a cloud in them. The temperature was in the mid-forties and the parking lot was full of cars at the after-Christmas sales.

Tony slipped his headset on and listened to the captain talk into the microphone. Comments between the firemen were exchanged about the call, nothing significant for Tony to add to. He remained quiet, a rarity for him as he usually had a joke to tell.

As the driver turned over the engine, Tony rolled down the window. His skin felt hot in the turnout and he shrugged out of the coat and pulled off his fireproof hood.

The engine rolled forward, moving through the parking lot. The other two firefighters in front participated in a conversation while Tony gazed out the open window.

Little kids were getting out of a minivan, the mom smiling as the truck slowly drove past. A boy about ten years old waved with excitement; so did his siblings who were bundled up in winter coats. The mom joined in. They all waved and Tony waved back.

A part of him had always liked the attention, but public admiration wasn't what had made him want to be a fireman.

But right now, when he was filled with

self-doubt, a part of him needed that assurance, needed to know he was a good guy.

# FIVE:
## WHOOPS-A-DAISY

"Now, don't come unglued — but Dad had a minor accident with the van," Sarah said, walking into the floral shed where Natalie was arranging roses for a twenty-fifth wedding anniversary.

She dropped her work shears. "He *what?*"

"It's nothing and he's okay."

"Nothing!"

"He ran into the curb and all he did was puncture the tire."

Her breathing shallow, Natalie gasped, "What happened?"

"He swerved to avoid hitting a squirrel."

"Great! Better to hit the squirrel than to kill himself in an accident."

"But Natalie, he's all right. I'm heading out there and Steve's going to leave the office for a minute to go and change the tire."

"I should go."

"No, you stay here."

Sarah was walking back to the shop, Natalie following. The outside air was brisk with a bite to it. Once inside the cozy store, Natalie was picking up the phone.

"Don't you call him," Sarah cautioned, her eyes sending a warning glare. "I promised him you wouldn't."

"Well, I like that." Natalie set the receiver down. "He's driving my company van, and he's in an accident, and I'm concerned."

"He said you'd mother him and he wasn't in the mood."

Natalie was vaguely affronted and would have debated the issue if there hadn't been a modicum of truth to it. As the eldest daughter, and after Mom died, Natalie had taken on the role of making sure her father was nurtured and looked after — not that he needed her to do it.

She'd barely digested the bad news when a customer entered the shop, pulling Natalie's attention away from the accident.

And he wasn't just any customer.

In the midst of a crisis, Tony Cruz had appeared. She painted an instant smile on her mouth, all the while wishing he'd come at a different time — a time when she was mentally prepared and not under duress. She wanted to make a good impression.

Hat and Garden, with its charming atmosphere, had become the beat in her heart, the stride in her step, the first thought on her mind when she woke up each morning.

Letting Tony see that about her, knowing that this was a special place to her . . . well, she couldn't explain why, but it was important.

Instead of being calm, she felt the chaos building in her pulse as she greeted him. "Hi, Tony. I'm so glad you stopped by."

"Yeah, I should have done it sooner. But I've been working a lot."

Sarah was grabbing her purse and car keys from under the counter, giving Natalie a silent wave, when Meagan appeared from around a corner where the ladies' room and utility area were located. Meagan grabbed Sarah and mumbled something to her.

Natalie wondered what it could possibly be, but she had to tune out the two women. "I'm sure the fire stations are busier during the holidays."

"We had a pretty busy New Year's Eve a couple nights ago."

"Oh." Distracted, Natalie didn't like the look coming over Sarah's face as she and Meagan disappeared down the hallway.

Addressing Tony, Natalie remained pleasant, masking her distress. "Well, I'm glad you finally made it here." *Had she already said that?* "What can I help you with?"

"I need a bouquet."

"What's the occasion?"

"Birthday."

Natalie smiled. He was a sweet man. "Well, there are all kinds of flowers you can choose from in the cooler here. We have an assortment from mums to daisies, roses to asters. I'm sure your wife will like whatever we come up with."

When Tony didn't readily respond, Natalie looked up at him, realizing he'd been quiet longer than a moment.

His expression darkened. "They aren't for my wife. They're for my mom."

The way he said it put a hitch in her heart. She couldn't find words fast enough.

He ended up continuing, "My wife moved out. We've split up."

"Oh," Natalie mouthed, adding nothing further for a few drawn-out seconds. "I'm sorry to hear that."

No wonder he'd seemed preoccupied when she and Cassie had run into him at the craft store. How could it have escaped her that his wife was no longer living across the street?

But with Cassie's visit, then departure, the shop, the craziness of the new year . . .

Her heart went out to Tony; she knew all too well what he felt like.

116

Sarah returned with Meagan in tow just as the shop phone rang. It was answered by Meagan, while Sarah said a brief hello to Tony. "Hi, I'm the sister — Sarah. I hate to interrupt, but I need Natalie for a second."

Natalie was steered away toward the exit porch, and the two of them stood just inside the doorway.

"What's the matter?" Natalie hissed in a lowered tone.

"The bathroom toilet flooded and the floor's all wet. We shut off the water, but I think it's a main water pipe or something. It's still trickling. I threw down a roll of paper towels to sort of keep it under control."

The pulsing knot in Natalie's head was tightened to a degree that she knew she'd need some aspirin to see her through. "Wonderful. Just what we don't need."

Still processing that piece of news, Meagan called softly to them, and when Natalie didn't respond, she said louder, "Natalie, phone call for you. It's Jonathon Falco."

Natalie smothered a groan.

Could things get any more complicated?

Natalie rang the doorbell, drawing in a deep breath of chilly air while she waited; her cheeks and nose were already cold. She hadn't thought to put her coat on — in fact, she really hadn't thought anything through.

She heard footfalls, then the door opened, and Tony Cruz's wide shoulders filled the opening.

"I brought you a bottle of wine," she uttered without preamble.

She recalled how yesterday, at the shop, he had seemed very restrained. She'd greeted him with her mind elsewhere and had been unable to offer her undivided condolences over his news. She thought this goodwill gesture might somehow make him feel better.

He put his forearm over the doorframe and leaned his body forward without speaking. Black lashes spiked his eyes. His eyes were darker than she recalled, a brown that was remote and distant.

"I'm sorry probably doesn't help . . . but I'm sorry." She tried to make her voice sound casual, nondescript. Understanding, yet not as if she'd come to be his confidante or therapist.

His gaze pierced the short distance between them, his mouth grim. Tired lines bracketed the corners of his eyes. He appeared as if he hadn't slept much lately. His clipped black hair was ruffled, and she fought a strange urge to smooth it.

The rich timbre of his voice enveloped her when he asked, "You want to come inside and help me drink it?"

She licked her dry lips, looked past him into the large, empty living room. Indecision caused her to hesitate. She hadn't really thought about drinking the wine with him. Or maybe she hadn't wanted to acknowledge the thought had crossed her mind.

"I can't stay long. I have to . . ."

She didn't have to do anything.

Today was Sunday. Her store was closed. All that was waiting for her at home was a house to clean and laundry to wash.

Tony took the bottle of sauvignon blanc from her, then stepped aside. She urged her feet forward. She held back a little, letting him take the lead and bring her into the house.

Instantly grateful for the warm interior, she shivered off the outdoor cold that lingered behind her. She wore soft-washed jeans and a pale-pink knit sweater, the weave clingy over her arms and breasts.

The front entry and subsequent living room created a spacious area, made more so by the lack of furnishings. All that was left was a wide-screen television and a sound system that looked as if it cost a small fortune. The walls were bare except for one lone picture of a landscape. Where the sofa had been, there were four imprints of furniture legs in the carpet pile . . . some candy wrappers and coins scattered about on the floor.

The symbolism of an empty space was more than just what met the eyes. She felt the disconnection . . . she relived her own moment in time when this had happened to her.

"I'm sorry," she repeated as he went into the kitchen.

The sentiment seemed too trite for the occasion, but she uttered it a third time just the same.

His back was to her as he set the bottle of wine on the countertop. "What are you going to do?"

She took a second to process his comment and not take it literally. "I suppose you'll get on with your life."

"Yep."

Natalie watched as he rummaged through the cupboards.

Tony looked at her across his shoulder. "She took the wineglasses. All I have are these."

He poured the wine into two drinking

glasses and offered one to Natalie, then took a sip of his before setting it down. She noted that he already had an open beer. Moisture rolled down the amber bottle, his hand holding on to the neck as he brought it to his mouth for a drink.

As he swallowed the beer, his throat tightened. His neck muscles were taut, rigid. He was so tense, he could snap that bottle in two with little effort.

A gray T-shirt stretched across his muscular chest; his lean legs were encased by dark denim. He wore white socks that, for some reason, made her smile.

Captured by his compelling presence, she couldn't help staring, watching as he moved.

"I'd offer you a seat but I don't have any," he said, leaning his backside against the counter.

"That's okay. I can't stay long."

"She took the things we bought when we got married — couch, lamps, table and chairs. It's just stuff, I really don't give a shit. At least I have my TV." The latter was spoken with a quirk to the corner of his mouth, the first hint of amusement she'd seen on his face since he'd opened the door.

"It's a big television." She left the kitchen, glanced at the large, dark screen in the living room.

"I don't watch much television in the summer, but the wintertime is different."

"Football," she surmised.

His smile broadened a little. "That and HBO. *The Sopranos.*"

"Hmm." She had cable, but never really watched much of anything. Working six days a week she was always too tired at the end of the day to do anything more than have some dinner and go to bed.

Tony took a seat on the floor, leaned his back against the wall and brought one knee up. The black remote control for the TV unit was at his hip. "Sit down?"

Reclined against the wall, the window above him, she studied him in the winter's light. Awash in muted grays and vague shadows, he still had a monopoly on virility.

He hadn't shaved today. A dark bristle dusted his jaw and chin, his upper lip. Once more, she noticed a thin scar line on his temple, and wondered about it. His brown eyes were now leveled on her. He was look-ing, and not casually, either . . . but sort of intently regarding Natalie as if he were wondering or thinking . . .

Natalie squirmed inside.

She managed to sit next to him, an arm's length away. She left her legs out in front of her, one hand in her lap and the other holding on to the glass, the wine warming beneath her fingers.

They sat in solitude — quiet for a long moment. The scent of his warm skin came to her, a muskiness that filled her head and mind with his presence. Even three feet away from him, she felt too close. Too intimate. She shouldn't have come, but now she was powerless to leave. Not yet.

When he finally spoke, she almost started. "She was having an affair."

At the same time, shock, surprise and sympathy were all etched on her face. "How awful for you."

"I suspected it for a while."

"That still wouldn't take away the disappointment."

She gazed at his profile, the strength of his jaw and cut of his nose.

Tony sighed. "I'm not all that disappointed. I'm relieved."

"I think I know what you mean. I felt the same thing."

He drank a slow swallow of beer, then licked his upper lip. "How long have you been divorced?"

"About two years." She organized her thoughts quickly, then spoke them before she had time to think otherwise. "I filed. It wasn't anything my ex-husband did. We just grew apart over the years. Sometimes that happens in a marriage. It's nobody's fault. I don't mean to sound callous, but there were moments when I wish he had had an affair, then there could have been blame, a definitive reason."

"I can see your thinking, but a reason still doesn't make it easier."

"Oh, I'm not saying it would. What you are going through must be horrible. I can't imagine. And the little girl . . . that has to be difficult."

"I have no rights to her. Just what I feel in my heart." On that, his voice weakened, barely discernible but she heard the change in his tone. It was enough for her to react without thinking — she reached out and touched his hand.

She settled her fingertips over his, a light pressure. A small measure of comfort. He was warm, his knuckles rough. She noticed he'd removed his gold wedding band.

Smiling reassuringly, she removed her hand, feeling self-conscious about the familiar gesture.

She drank her wine, welcoming the heat that fanned through her stomach and slowed the surge in her heartbeat.

Tony hunched his shoulders slightly as he reached for the TV remote and absently flipped it around through his fingertips. "She served me at the fire station yesterday."

"That was harsh," Natalie criticized, eyebrows raised in disapproval over a matter she wasn't personally involved with. Even so, she thought about the way she'd handled her divorce. She'd handed Greg the complaint at a local notary's office, not wanting to publically humiliate him at work. They'd been married for twenty-one years. A margin of respect for the vows that had lasted that long was the least she owed him, that and a semblance of civility.

"I'm going to need a lawyer," Tony thought aloud.

"I know of a good one." She thought about Chuck Hays, the man who had been her rock while representing her. "He isn't a lawyer who goes for the jugular, but he's fair. That's all I wanted out of mine. A fifty-fifty split, everything as amicable as possible."

"Kim's said she doesn't want to get into it with me. I don't know if I believe her. I made the down payment on this house. I'm thinking I should keep it."

"You'll have to ask Chuck about that. I'm sure he'll steer you in the direction that's best for you. I'll get you his number."

"That would be great. Thanks."

Tony rubbed his jaw, the rasp of a beard beneath his fingernails. "I have to buy a new bed."

The offhand comment was jarring, and the implication sent a clear image to her mind: His wife and her boyfriend must have been together in their bed.

She wished he didn't have to go through this.

He was big and strong, and yet she detected an emotional fragility to him right now. She'd seen it in the craft store, in Hat and Garden. The brief window of hurt that barely surfaced before he closed it off, removing all traces. She had so much empathy for him.

"Kim said I could visit Parker whenever I wanted, but that would mean going to her new boyfriend's house, and I can't trust myself not to kick his ass." Tony mistakenly punched a button on the remote. The TV came alive and he muted the sound. A picture spread over the screen. ESPN. "I know my wife isn't innocent, but I can't help wanting to get in his face. He knew she was married. Why did he pursue her? Or maybe he didn't. Hell, maybe she pursued him. She never gave me a real answer."

Natalie let him talk, sensing he needed to unload, get things off his chest. It was good to vocalize the feelings of resentment, of failure. She had done the same thing with Sarah.

"I mean, shit . . . something like this makes a man question what he was lacking. What was it that I couldn't give her?"

He grew quiet. She still didn't speak.

"A baby," he said beneath his breath. "I just couldn't do that."

His explanation was surprising. Infertility was the reason many marriages broke down. Her heart went out to him.

"I don't know anything about that, but there are doctors —"

"It wasn't a matter of getting her pregnant. I just didn't want to make a baby with her."

"Oh . . ." she murmured, enlightened. Now the topic was definitely quite intimate. No doubt he had his reasons. But she wouldn't ask.

He didn't elaborate and she was actually relieved not to hear the details of something between this man and his wife.

Tony clicked through the channels, as if needing something to do. He paused on an episode of *Gilligan's Island.* When Mary Ann and Ginger screamed and ran away from headhunters, Tony cracked an amused smile. His interest in a show like this was surprising — until he elaborated.

"I once had a call where a cross-dresser was made up like Ginger. He'd fallen off his platform heels and cracked his forehead open on the curb. When we got there, he was lying against the gutter crying because there was a hole in his gown."

"So *Gilligan's Island* inspires Boise's cross-dressers? I didn't know we even had any," she commented, trying to make light of the show, make light of the dark mood that had surrounded them prior to the television being turned on.

"I've come across a few. Seen other things I'd rather not have, as well. A lot of overweight people stuck on toilets."

In spite of herself, Natalie laughed. "Really?"

Tony gazed at her. "And they're always naked."

"Oh, my."

"That's not what I'm thinking." A half smile touched his mouth. "I have seen some things you wouldn't want to know about."

"I can only imagine."

Somberly, he replied, "You don't want to."

"Do you ever get depressed?"

"Absolutely."

"I admire you," she said, not withholding

her true feelings. "It takes a special person to do what you do."

"Not really. You just have to pass some tests."

"Don't discredit yourself. You deserve the praise." She took a sip of wine, relaxing more. "Did you always know you wanted to be a fireman?"

"Nope. My parents got a divorce when I was in junior high. My dad moved to Portland afterward and he wasn't a big part of my life. I wanted to play on the summer baseball team, but I didn't have a dad to watch me or coach me. So I asked my neighbor if he'd want to sponsor me, help me out. He said he would." A fond expression overtook Tony's features. "He was a firefighter and he took me to the station and I got to hang out there. After that, I knew that's what I wanted to be. A firefighter like him."

"That's a fabulous story."

"I met my best friend in the academy. Rockland Massaro. He's a good guy."

"Is it hard to become a firefighter?"

"Not really." Tony shrugged. "I passed the written, scored in the top one hundred. You're tested on English, math, reading comprehension. Some mechanical-aptitude stuff. Then you take a CPAT."

"What's that?"

"Candidate Physical Aptitude Test. It's a series of physical tests."

He tipped his face to the window, and she followed his gaze. A light snow had begun to fall, the sunshine fading to a murky blue-gray.

The beer bottle in his hand lowered to rest on his knee. "You have to walk on a treadmill with seventy-five pounds on your back, then you drag some hoses. You can go down there and practice ahead of time. You drag a dummy. Hit some pegs with a sledge-hammer, pull apart some ceiling tiles and crawl through an area that simulates a small space. Just basic stuff."

He made it sound so effortless, but she was impressed. She was sure not just anyone passed these tests.

His profile was sharp and confident. She wavered, trying to collect herself. Why was it whenever she was around him she felt out of sorts? She had to conquer these involuntary reactions to him. He might be separated, but he was still married and in for a long road ahead if he was really going through with a divorce.

Natalie tried to refocus her thoughts. "How long have you been a fireman?"

"Eight years."

"Can you see yourself doing the job until retirement?"

"Oh, yeah. Very few people quit."

They directed their attention back to the *Gilligan's Island* episode, and Natalie rolled her eyes at the outlandish comedic antics of Gilligan and the Skipper that, back when she was younger, she thought funny. Now the acting just seemed silly. "I remember this show from my day." Cutting off a gasp, she immediately cringed and ran the topic in a different direction. "Do you have cable or a dish?"

"Cable," he said shortly. His eyebrows lifted. "What do you mean — 'my day'?"

She groaned and figured she'd just make a joke about her age. "Back when there were black-and-white televisions."

"Give me a break. How old are you?"

Natalie drew in a breath, expelled it, then closed her eyes a second. She wished she'd never brought up the subject. Bucking her composure, she stated in a bland voice, "Forty-three." Then slanting a glance at him, she dared herself to ask, "How old are you?"

No hesitation marked his reply. "Thirty-four."

She gave a choked laugh, confused by her

unexpected response. His age should have been of no consequence to her, and yet, her stomach flip-flopped. An unexpected heaviness settled in her heart and she faltered in the dry silence that engulfed them.

A nine-year difference was a large enough gap to give her pause. It might as well have been ninety years.

"You're only as old as you feel," he said simply, intuitively knowing that's all he needed to say. Then he clicked through the channels once more, stopping on a movie with Matthew Broderick.

*Ferris Bueller's Day Off.* A classic. She hadn't watched it in ages.

Ferris and his friend were calling the school principal to get Ferris's girlfriend out of class for the rest of the day. The scene was priceless, and Natalie's misplaced sense of their ages being an issue faded. It wasn't as if she were looking for anything but friendship.

As Matthew Broderick grabbed the telephone from his friend, Natalie laughed; an undiluted sound that came out soft and buoyant, very natural.

In that moment, she forgot she'd made a date with Jonathon Falco and had been indecisive about it ever since. Sarah had coaxed her — more like backed her into a corner — into returning Jonathon's call. Natalie had told herself it was a mature thing to go out with an adult of the opposite sex, and that it would do her some good to get out there again, to circulate and just . . . well . . . she didn't want to think about that date right now.

She allowed herself to simply enjoy right now, to not analyze the whys or hows. To just . . . feel alive.

Feel good. No worries. No cares.

"You have a really great TV," she commented, enjoying the movie even more because the screen was so large and the sound was crisp and theater quality.

"It's a guy thing," Tony replied, standing up. "We have to have the biggest TVs and the biggest garages for the biggest trucks." He went into the kitchen. "Can I pour you some more wine?"

Gazing into her glass, she realized she'd finished what she had. She probably should be going home, start a load of towels.

Disregarding the idea of being sensible, she said, "Please."

He came to her, poured, and then grabbed himself another beer.

Resettling next to her, they sat with their backs against the wall and their legs stretched in front of them.

Outside, the snow came down in fluffy, featherlight wisps. Tranquility and peace seemed to surround them as they were amused by a movie with teenage humor.

Inwardly, Natalie smiled.

The shadows that had touched her heart over the holidays lifted. It felt good just to sit. Just to breathe. Just to laugh.

To be reminded that life moved on in its strange ways, and today was a day she wouldn't soon forget.

Tony sat at his mom's kitchen table, the morning paper open to the obits where she'd been looking at the columns. She had this interest in reading about people after they'd died. It wasn't a morbid thing, she just said it was interesting to see how men and women had lived their lives, what they had done and accomplished.

The aroma of coffee grounds filled the air, the sound of it perking broke into the silence as his mom leaned against the counter to wait for the coffee to finish.

She looked great at fifty-four, better than she had in her forties. She was five foot eleven and stood out among other women. She wore her hair shoulder length and layered. She kept the color dyed a dark brown with some brassy red in it. He'd inherited her deep brown eyes, the shape of her jaw and her smile.

"How did your last meeting with the attorney go?" she asked.

"Okay. He had everything written up like we'd discussed. I only made a few changes."

"Are you sure he's good?"

"I liked him. I interviewed a couple and I thought he was fair."

"How'd you find him?"

"My neighbor recommended him." Tony gave pause. Every now and then, especially late at night at the fire station if they came in from a call and he had to try and fall back asleep, he caught himself thinking about Natalie Goodwin, and it sort of took him by surprise. He found her attractive, smart and resourceful, but maybe there was more to it. He definitely felt a pull toward her, although examining why hadn't been a priority for him, not with everything else going on.

She'd come to his house on a day when he'd felt as if his life was turned inside out, wondering what he was going to do, and she'd listened to him when he'd needed to talk. He hadn't realized how well timed her visit was until she'd rung the doorbell.

Guys kept their emotions bottled up. It was a macho thing, although Rocky and him had had a few beers and conversed briefly about the way things had ended for him and Kim. But it wasn't anything constructive, just guys being guys and letting off steam by drinking alcohol and playing pool.

Natalie lent a softer side. Basically — true compassion was what she brought to the table, something he appreciated without even being aware of how much he needed it until it was offered.

His mom poured two cups of coffee, set one in front of him. "So did the lawyer say how long the divorce would take?"

"Kim signed the complaint and Idaho processes a divorce in about twenty-one days."

"That's amazing. You spend all that time married and it's over in twenty-one days?" She sobered, looked at him. "I didn't mean that in a bad way against you, Tony. I was speaking figuratively about how sad it is that people can be divorced so quickly. I know that what happened with you and Kim was irreconcilable. I don't think Kim was ever really happy. Although I am so heartbroken for Parker."

"Me, too. But there's nothing I can do. I have no legal rights." Tony was going to take her out to lunch today and he looked forward to it.

He no longer missed Kim, strange as that was. He had missed her the first week she moved out but that was it. Then it finally hit him, it wasn't really her — it was his family he missed. He missed the familiar, the routine.

Now he came home to a quiet house, to nothing, really.

He tried to fill the void by working extra shifts, by lifting at the gym, going over to Rocky's and watching ESPN. Still, it was no substitute for the one thing he'd really wanted.

A wife, a kid . . . family life.

But it wasn't meant to be with Kim and he'd known that for a long time, he just hadn't been willing to accept it. Tony couldn't let what had happened bother him. But life had to move on.

After having coffee with his mom, Tony left and drove to Kim's new house. He got out of the truck but wouldn't go inside. He waited at the frosty curb, not even stepping onto the walkway.

Kim held back in the open doorway and he didn't really look at her. Didn't think about the way her hair used to fall over her shoulders in the morning. He willed himself to forget he'd ever held her, touched her . . . loved her.

Parker appeared, bundled in a pink coat and snow boots. She ran to him.

"Careful, Parker. It's icy," he cautioned.

As only a child can do, Parker managed to slip and run her way to him without falling. She reached him and stretched out her arms. He picked her up, pressed his cool check next to her smooth warm skin.

"Hi, Tony."

"Hey, Parker."

"I miss you." Her mouth puckered into a frown. "How come you can't live with us, too?"

His chest tightened as he carried her to the passenger side of the truck. He opened the door and set her on the leather seat. No matter how many times he'd told her, she always asked. Elaborating, he said, "Because your mom and I are living in different houses now."

"How come?"

"Because your mom and I aren't going to be married anymore."

"How come?"

"She loves somebody else now."

"How come she doesn't love you?"

"She loves me, but —" the lie tasted ugly on his lips, but he spoke it just the same "— she loves Brian the most right now and they're going to live together and they both love you."

*Brian McKinney.*

Hotshot piece of shit who Tony still had never seen up close — had no desire to. Fucking prick business consultant needing a Web site to launch his project-management company, and had to jump in bed with his soon-to-be-ex-wife while he was at it.

The anger that simmered beneath Tony's surface was welcome. It was a lot better than the shock and numbing pain. Or even the quiet grief of acceptance that he was getting a divorce.

Yeah, anger was good. Anger carried a potent strength and a mind-sharpening sense of purpose — within reason. He knew he'd have to let it go soon — get back to normal. Whatever the hell normal was.

Tony climbed into the high truck, then made sure Parker's seat belt was fastened. It seemed just like yesterday that he was getting used to having a small child, learning how she behaved, how he should react when he was with her.

When he met Kim, Parker's dad was out of the picture more than he was in it. As far as Tony knew, the guy was still an absentee father. Tony had given the little girl the first sense of stability she'd had and it cut him to the core for her to think he was bailing on her.

"Do you still love me, Tony?"

Just before turning over the ignition, her words gave him pause.

Turning toward her, he stared into her small face, the white-blond hair that framed her red cheeks, the rosebud shape of her mouth.

He fought off an emptiness that left him hollow. His voice cracked slightly. "Always, Parker."

"Me, too, Tony."

He started the truck and pulled away from the house. "So do you want Burger King or McDonald's for lunch?"

"McDonald's."

"Okay."

He'd taken Parker out to lunch on his weekend days off ever since the first of the new year. Either on a Saturday or a Sunday. He'd come at noon, but didn't go into Kim's house. She didn't come out to talk to him. They were both talking through lawyers now, not particularly arguing, but it was obscene that they were paying strangers to represent them.

He wondered when this would get easier on him, on Parker. He had no way of anticipating when Parker would one day say she would rather be with Kim and Brian, wouldn't want to come anymore.

He wondered when she would gradually phase him out of her life to begin her new one. He'd see less and less of her — until he stopped seeing her at all.

It was a truth he had a difficult time reconciling.

So for now, he promised himself to make the most out of the time he had with Parker.

"Toe-Knee," she said in her silly voice. "Do you know what the toy is in the Happy Meal today?"

"Nope. But we'll find out."

"Are you going to get a Happy Meal, too?"

He glanced at her and smiled. "Yeah. I think I will."

# Six:
# Renegades and
# Outlaws

The window of Hat and Garden was filled
with Valentine hearts and cowboy-clad
teddy bears. A saddle was used as a prop
for a plant sitting in a cowboy boot, a big
red satin bow spilling over the side of tooled
leather. Varieties of silk flowers in shades of
pink and a sprinkling of red glitter hearts
finished off the display.

Tony cupped his hand, peeked into the
window before going inside. The last time
he'd been here his mind had been elsewhere
and he hadn't paid much attention to the
flower store.

He did now.

The inside of the shop smelled good.
Candles burned on the counter and in
several other strategic locations. Sweet roses
and other fragrant scents collected in the
air. A large cooler with an assortment of
flowers in tall buckets took up one wall, the
other areas were small coves with theme-

filled items.

Valentine's Day was about two weeks away and Natalie had her store ready for the increase in business.

A female clerk greeted him, and asked if he needed help. He recognized her from his last visit. She was young and fresh, and had a friendly smile. She gazed at him with an eagerness he had seen in women's faces many times before. He knew he stood out — was bigger than most men. Most of the time he forgot about being so tall, so filled out. Other times, when women were all smiles and acting as if he were a pair of shoes to try on, he grew more aware.

Suddenly, after reminding myself why he'd come, he felt self-conscious. "Is Natalie working today?"

"Yes, she's outside in the flower shed making arrangements. Is there anything I can help you with?"

He gazed around, but didn't really look at his surroundings. "Do you think she'll be coming back in soon?"

The young woman smiled. "I can get her if you want."

"Yeah," Tony caught himself saying. "That would be good."

"Can I tell her who's here?"

"Tony."

"I'll be right back." The clerk headed out back but not before gazing over her shoulder at him once, giving him another smile.

He smiled automatically; hers broadened with a show of teeth, and then she disappeared.

Tony was left to wander around, to study the rest of the shop. Natalie was original and organized, and pretty clever because of the Idaho cowboy and Western theme she presented for Valentine's Day instead of the standard cupids and arrows.

More than once during the past month, he'd thought about the day she'd come over with a bottle of wine. While he hadn't been in the best frame of mind, he appreciated the fact that she'd stayed and watched television with him. For a short while, he had forgotten to be pissed at the world and he'd actually laughed.

Remembering their discussion, he wouldn't have guessed her age right if she'd asked him to. She looked younger than forty-three. She was uptight about the number, no doubt. Why women got that way he couldn't understand. He could give a damn he was thirty-four. Age was a state of mind. It was all about how he felt, how he thought, how he kept busy.

He'd been spending too much time at the

fire station, losing himself in long twenty-four-hour shifts that ran one right into another. He'd finally told the guys on the A and B Shifts that he was getting a divorce.

The news surprised Captain Palladino because Tony hadn't spoken much about his crumbling marriage at work. He kept most of those things to himself. It wasn't as if he didn't want to talk about it with the men he worked with. He respected them and they were like family, but there were just some emotions a man kept to himself — like how he'd felt discovering Kim's infidelity. He hadn't spoken about what had been the actual cause of their breakup, but the implication was pretty much there.

A pink cow-poodle figurine caught Tony's eye. His mom had enough style and an open-minded quirkiness to like this. He picked it up, checked underneath for the price. Just as he was doing so, Natalie came up behind him.

"Hello."

He set the figurine down, turned and was immediately aware of how good she smelled. Her scent caught him off guard; he wasn't prepared to breathe her in, but he recognized a primal need to pull that smell into his lungs and savor it.

She didn't smell like any perfume he'd

ever smelled in a department store. It was more pure, more natural. A fragrance of flower petals, a mix of sweetness and muskiness.

At the base of her throat, a pulse beat, and from that warmth came the smell of her skin, all fresh and flowery.

His palms suddenly felt fiery hot, his body overtly warm in the heavy Boise F.D. sweatshirt he wore.

"Hi," he returned, clearing his throat.

Studying her, Natalie seemed a little out of sorts, pressing her hands down the front of her work apron. "Meagan said you were here."

Meagan? Then he recalled the young female clerk. She'd returned to the cash register counter and, hearing her name, she gave him another smile. He shot one back to her, then focused on Natalie.

"I came by for some advice."

Her eyebrows rose. "Advice?"

"On some flowers."

"Oh," she replied in an exhale of breath, as if she were expecting him to ask him something else. "Of course, I can help you with that."

She moved to the cooler, waited for him to follow.

"Who are they for?" she asked, sliding the

door open. Cold air spilled out of the refrigerated space.

He thought about who he had in mind — the sole reason for his visit to Hat and Garden. "A woman."

For a second he thought he saw a brief flash of envy flicker into her eyes. "The occasion?"

"There is none. I just think she's a special woman." Tony looked at the different sizes, shapes and colors of flowers. "Why don't you pick out the flowers that you like."

"All right." She slid the cooler door open. "Do you have any color in mind?"

"What's your favorite color?"

"Pink."

"Do that."

"We can do lots of things in pink." She began pulling stems and making a collection. "There's roses, tulips, carnations, gerbera daisies, freesia and lilies."

"Those work."

"All of them?" she questioned, her hand filled with textures and the smell of flowers.

He nodded.

"Did you want them delivered?"

"No, I'm delivering them myself."

Once more, he recognized a hint of longing in her expression and he tried to make sense about why that pleased him.

"All right . . . it'll take me a moment to make this bouquet up. Can you wait or do you want to come back?"

"I can wait."

She went out the back door. Out to a shed, he assumed. The flower shop was a converted historic home, so he figured the shed was a garage. While he waited, he went through the rooms, then climbed the stairs to discover other rooms done in hues of purple, sage and white. Music played in the white room, a soft melody that he didn't recognize. He grew increasingly more appreciative of the effort she put into her business.

Most of the things Natalie sold were items he wouldn't normally buy. A lot of collectible knickknacks. His mom had some dust-collector stuff in her living room, but she was more practical about her decorating and put energy into kitchen gadgets rather than hand-crocheted doilies and teddy bears.

Tony was on his way downstairs as Natalie came through the back door holding on to a big bouquet in a tall vase. He was immediately impressed by how the flowers were put together with greens and other delicate accents.

"Is this all right?" she asked, setting the vase on the counter. Her cheeks were flushed from being outside, or maybe not just from the cold. He could see that she hoped for his approval by the way light played into her green eyes when she looked at him.

"It's great. Thanks. I appreciate it."

"You're welcome." She rang up his order.

He put his wallet in his back pocket. "And my mom really liked what you made for her birthday."

"I'm happy to hear that." Her face looked radiant, pleased. "Do your parents live in Boise?"

"My parents are divorced. It's just my mom. She lives in Meridian. My dad's in Portland." Conversely, he asked, "And your parents?"

"My mother passed away. My dad lives in Boise. He's retired."

"My mom still works, but she enjoys it."

"Dad helps me with the flower deliveries, and while he grumbles about the van he has to drive, I think he likes coming in."

He noticed then that they spoke in polite undertones. Gone was the level of comfort and margin of familiarity they'd shared in his living room. He realized they were at her place of work, but he missed hearing the humor in her voice. He couldn't nail down why, exactly. Only that he'd liked it when she was laughing at *Ferris Bueller.*

He moved to take the flowers and she stopped him.

"Wait — you'll need a box." She went into a closet underneath the stairs and came out with a box which she turned upside down. Using a box cutter she sliced slits in the bottom as if she were cutting up a pie. "Set this on the floor of your truck and stick the vase inside. It'll stay upright and the water won't spill."

"Good idea."

She simply smiled, and the curve to her mouth made her appear more youthful and very pretty. Through soft laughter, she said, "After so many years at this, I do come up with some good ideas every now and then."

He grinned at her frankness and gave her his best smile. The one that made women blush. He wasn't sure if the smile would get to her or not; it seemed she had a lot of reserve when she put her mind to it.

She blushed and turned away.

Inwardly, he was satisfied. Not in a way that was overconfident. He just took pleasure seeing that he could affect her — even in a small way.

Maybe it was a macho thing with him. Maybe he liked knowing that he could make her breathing jagged with little effort.

"You're all set," she said, her voice slightly edgy, as if she were trying to take command of it. "I hope your friend likes the flowers."

"I have no doubt she will."

" 'I hope your friend likes the flowers.' That's what I said to him. It just came out and I hated how I felt when he replied he had no doubt she would. I don't want him buying flowers for another woman, not now. Not so soon. I mean, he's still married and going through a divorce. Oh, why do I even care?" Natalie groaned.

"Because you like him," Sarah said, dipping a corn chip into salsa. "And now that he's going to be available you need to act fast, because a man like him will be taken out of circulation quickly."

"I don't want to take him out of circulation."

"Of course you do. I can see it on your face — he probably did, too."

Natalie raised her hands to her cheeks, feeling the burn of a blush.

Sarah said blandly, "Let's face it, if he's buying an expensive bouquet for a female friend already, he's moving on and you need to move in."

"I can't." Natalie pinched the bridge of

her nose, then took a drink of her water and ate a chip.

The Mexican-inspired decor at Café Fiesta created a fun ambience. Green-and-white painted walls, red vinyl booths, velvet paintings hung on the walls. And a neon Corona Beer sign hung in the window. When it was a patron's birthday, an oversize gold-and-black sombrero was put on their head and the servers sang "Feliz Cumpleaños" to them. Natalie knew this firsthand, as she'd had it sung to her on her last birthday when Sarah and her dad had taken her here.

She and Sarah had snuck out for a quick lunch at the restaurant, taking a break from Hat and Garden and leaving Meagan and her dad minding the shop.

"Why not?" Sarah brushed salt off the tiled table surface. "You told me you think he's good-looking, intelligent, nice, considerate, and now he's going through a divorce, so he'll be single."

"That's even worse. I refuse to be his rebound woman."

"Maybe you wouldn't be. Maybe you two would be perfect for one another."

"I hardly think that. He's got to deal with being divorced first, then there's the age thing."

Sarah lowered her voice but remained distinctly optimistic. "I know you hyperventilated when you told me before — how old is he again?"

In a smothered groan, Natalie responded, "Thirty-four."

"Nine years isn't so big a gap."

"Maybe not if he was nine years older than me."

Leaning into the booth, Sarah crossed her arms beneath her breasts, her expression sour, as if she'd sucked on a lime before a shot of tequila. "How long are you going to do this?"

"What?"

"How long are you going to resist falling in love again?"

Swallowing the heaviness in her throat, Natalie said, "Every mistake I could have made as a newly dating divorcée, I made with Michael. I lost my identity. I forgot what I liked, what I wanted to do because I wanted to be in love so badly." With a shake of her head, she sighed. "Stupid. I was too nice, I was too available. He chased me, he won me over — heart, mind and soul — then he threw me away for someone new. It *hurt*."

"I know. I was there with you every day," Sarah sympathized. "But that's in the past.

You're over him — aren't you?"

"Yes . . . yes." Natalie said it almost in disgust. "I hate the man for what he did to me, to Cassie and to his daughter, Brook. He came across as so wonderful, said all the right things."

"He's a jerk. A serial monogamist. You and I have covered this ground before. He never sleeps with two women at the same time, but he never stays with the same woman for more than a few months. He has classic commitment phobia, and the man couldn't communicate his feelings until you wanted answers from him about why he backed away from you after your trip to Hawaii. You don't need his baggage and lame excuses. He needs a good therapist and a reality check. He's got low self-esteem and moves from pretty woman to pretty woman — all to feed his ego."

Sarah gave a wan smile, one that spoke volumes: compassion, love, empathy, faith and hope. "Natalie, it's understandable why you fell for the guy. You didn't have love in your marriage for a long time. We all want to have those feelings."

"I know." Natalie fought the sting of tears that gathered in her eyes, mad that she even allowed herself to feel such vulnerability. "I want them again. But I am afraid to get hurt. It was horrible with Michael. The worst thing I ever went through." She pulled in a shaky breath.

"Maybe now's not the time to be asking, but what's going on with you and Jonathon Falco?"

"We're on for tonight — no matter what." Natalie gave a half laugh. "He's had to reschedule three times. His two sons are the center of his world, something I find very admirable, but fitting me in between their sporting events at school has been a challenge for him."

"I am so glad I had girls. I was watching BreeAnn dance at halftime during a boys' basketball game, and those boys are sweaty and aggressive. I can't even think about one of them with one of my girls."

"I understand. I don't like the idea of Austin and Cassie together."

"What's new on that front?"

"They had a fight a few days ago. I can only hope they'll break up."

"A fight about what?"

"She wouldn't tell me, but I have the worst feeling it has to do with sex and, if it does, a part of me doesn't want to know."

"It's the nature of men. They all want sex. I remember I had this blind date once. I made arrangements in advance with the bartender so that if things weren't going the way I wanted, he would call me a cab." Sarah smiled in remembrance. "I had a code for 'help.' "

"A code?"

"Yes. If I suddenly ordered a screwdriver, that meant I needed a cab sent around to the back of the bar so I could be picked up. I barely lasted fifteen minutes before I was ordering that drink. The man was vulgar."

"I would have never thought to do that."

"Because you were married younger than I was. I was a seasoned dater before I met Steve."

"I wish I could find someone without all the dating. You know, like maybe meeting my best friend."

"The fireman is already your neighbor, and neighborly friendship is a very good place to start." Before Natalie could deny that probability, Sarah asked, "Where are you and Jonathon going?"

"We're meeting at the Stonehouse. It's walking distance from Hat and Garden and, since I sometimes run late closing, I didn't want him to be inconvenienced and have to pick me up."

"Men need to be inconvenienced, Natalie. It makes them appreciate us more. Take my word on this one. Promise me."

Natalie put her hand on her heart, and said in fun, "Of course. Yes. You are the expert."

Sarah laughed, then raised her eyebrows as if she'd just remembered something important. "Your hand over your boob reminds me — I made our mammogram appointments for the first week in March."

"Let me know the exact day and I'll mark it on my calendar."

Ever since they'd lost their mother to breast cancer, the sisters religiously went for their yearly mammograms together.

"I will. I think it was the seventh."

Their food arrived and they ate while continuing to discuss family matters, then returned to the flower shop to discover the plumber had to be called once more to take another look at the leaky pipe in the restroom. This was the third time he'd come out to work on the pipes.

And Jonathon had rescheduled three times.

For some reason, Natalie felt as if it was a bad omen.

Later that night, after closing Hat and Garden, Natalie walked to the Stonehouse to meet Jonathon. She wore boots and, by the end of the sixth block, she wished she'd driven over. But the winter sunset was pretty and the outside temperature hadn't felt that cold when she'd started out. Now her cheeks were numb.

So much for her worries about keeping Jonathon waiting — he'd called to say he was running late. His eldest son had to be fitted with a new mouth guard and there was a holdup at the dentist's office.

Jonathon had two sons — a sixteen-year-old who attended Centennial High and a fourteen-year-old who went to Lowell Scott Middle School. The two boys played any game imaginable depending on the season. They'd been on the football team, the soccer team, baseball and hockey. Right now they were thick into basketball and wrestling. Jonathon's schedule revolved around his sons' games.

Natalie had never been really big into sports, perhaps going to a Boise State football game or two in the fall to get into the college-town spirit. Aside from that, she bypassed ESPN.

She questioned whether or not she and Jonathon had some common ground, then quickly discounted that thought. She was here just to have fun, to enjoy a man's company, to not put undue pressure on herself to make anything more out of it.

Natalie had freshened her makeup at the flower shop before leaving and now wondered if she should have changed into something less businesslike for an evening date.

*Date.*

The word had become almost foreign to her. It had been months and months since she'd been out. After those last few encounters, and doing the speed-dating session, she'd sworn off of dating.

What in the world was she doing here now? She'd barely talked to Jonathon on the telephone for more than five minutes at a time; she didn't know him. So she'd done the floral arrangements for his wife's funeral; that was years ago. He could have hang-ups, but she had no way of knowing about them until it was too late.

The back of her throat tightened, her palms grew damp.

*This is insane.*

She proceeded to the bar, trying to keep a modicum of composure. Glancing at the time on her watch, she took a seat at the end of the bar, hating every second of sitting alone, looking as if she were trying to be picked up.

"What can I get you?" the twentysomething bartender asked her.

"I'm waiting for someone. I'll order when he gets here."

He moved down to the end of the bar, took another order, then came back by her to fill a glass with beer on tap.

Licking her lips, Natalie contemplated asking him something. Then she just went ahead. "Have you ever been asked to order a cab for a woman if she needed one?"

"Sure."

"How do you know she needs one?"

"She just tells me," he replied, shrugging.

"But what if she couldn't tell you — what if the guy she didn't want to be spending the evening with was right next to her?"

"Never happened before."

Making a quick decision in what was perhaps a moment of lunacy, she replied, "If I ask you to make me a screwdriver, that means call me a cab."

"Excuse me?"

"I'm meeting a man and I didn't drive over here and I'm thinking I might need a backup plan." Although why she might need such a plan, she had no clue. But Sarah had put the germ of the idea in her head. "Where is your ladies' room?"

"In the back."

"Is there a back door?"

"Yes." His blond hair, shaved in a precise

160

crewcut, picked up the backlights from the mirrored bar.

"Good. So if I ask you to make me a screwdriver, call me a cab and have the driver pick me up in back."

"Uh, okay."

She reached into her purse, collected a bill and slid it toward him.

He raised his hands. "That's okay. I've done worse for nothing."

Almost twenty minutes later when Jonathon hadn't shown up, Natalie's nerves were stretched taut. Her bad feeling returned tenfold and she was borderline calling for a cab herself and going home.

But then a tall man approached the bar.

Jonathon.

Although looking stressed and tired, he was very handsome. He had on a dress shirt, suit coat and slacks.

"So sorry I'm late," he apologized. His eyes appeared as kind as she'd remembered. He didn't look awful, didn't come across as self-absorbed or as if he had planned on letting her wait so long.

"My days are crazy." He laughed, a show of white teeth beneath his mustache. "Sometimes I wonder if I can keep this up."

His cell phone rang and he cut himself short, glancing at the caller ID. "Excuse me.

It's my son's coach." He answered the phone, and the earlier optimism Natalie had felt just faded.

She waited, gazing pointedly at the bartender and smiling, trying not to convey the tangle of indecision flitting through her. She thought about the mound of laundry she'd yet to complete, and the data she could be inputting into Quicken tonight for Hat and Garden's books.

It was a sad commentary that she considered such mundane events more important than a drink and dinner with a nice-looking man.

Jonathon disconnected the call. "Sorry. My boy's been benched for the last several games because he has a hairline fracture on his big toe. I told the coach he's not shooting a ball with his damn toe but with his arms and hands. He's in great shape and I think he should be used in the game. He is one of the best players they've got." He stopped himself. "Anyway, let's not talk about basketball."

She hadn't been.

They sat at the bar together, settled in while drinking glasses of wine, and Natalie forced herself to relax. They talked about the basics, how long he'd been married, how he was coping with being a single parent and she having an empty nest.

They talked about his job and — actually, mostly about his life and job and how stressful it was. He didn't ask her too much about herself or her work and, call it instinct, she got a weird feeling about him at this point. Natalie didn't offer any answers to questions that weren't asked.

They conversed long enough to drink two glasses of merlot before it was close to their dinner-reservation time.

She set her glass on the cocktail napkin, wondering why this man was on a date when, in such a short amount of time, he'd made it evident he was only interested in hearing himself talk.

She tried to attribute it to nerves — he did confess he was still rusty in the dating department.

But as she was making excuses for him, his question broke through her musings. "So what do women your age do?"

"About what?"

"Sex. A lot of the ladies I've met who are your age — they don't have much of a sex drive left, or so they tell me when I ask them. I'm forty-six and I wake up every morning with an erection — and it takes care of itself. If you get my meaning. I don't even have to touch it."

Natalie sat there, stunned. Was this the same man who'd come into Hat and Garden, smiled softly at her, and almost shyly asked her out on a date?

Knocked out of her stupor, she blinked back the disillusionment that swept through her. So much for getting back into dating. If this man was a sampling of her options, she'd rather go it alone.

"Bartender, I'd like to order a screwdriver." Then to Jonathon, "Excuse me, I need to visit the ladies' room."

The bathrooms were in the back, so was the door. She opted to wait inside rather than stand in the cold back alley.

For a moment, she thought about going back there and telling him to his face that he'd been out of line. Then she opted out of confronting him. Then again, he knew where she worked.

Feeling the pulse of a headache building, Natalie wondered what in the world she was going to do if he called her again. Her disappearing act should have been signal enough that she was not interested.

She leaned her butt against the restroom sink and folded her arms with a shake of her head. She was holed up in a toilet, walking distance from her car, but not wanting to brave the frigid February air, much less the dark streets alone, with Mr. Take Care of Itself perhaps following her.

Long ago, she might have put up with the man just for the sake of finishing a date that she knew would be a first and last. But no more.

Natalie Goodwin had turned into a dating renegade.

Pulling into her garage not forty minutes later, Natalie got out of her car and went down the driveway to collect the mail out of her mailbox.

She was glad to be home, relieved to have made an escape from the date from hell. Shock still encompassed her, reeling her senses. How could he have said such a thing to her?

As Natalie returned up the walkway, she paused. A splash of color out of place on the front porch caught her attention.

She slowed. Rather than retracing her steps and going into the garage, she went to the porch.

Flowers.

There was a bouquet of flowers on her porch. And not just any bouquet — but the very one she'd made for Tony Cruz.

A moment's panic flashed through her. As she thought of all the reasons he might have returned them — dissatisfaction, change of heart . . . whatever the case, none prepared her to kneel down and see her name written on the card.

She opened it.

Natalie. These are for you. Thanks for being there when I needed a friend. Tony

She swept her hand over the petals. They were cool, not cold. They hadn't been sitting here very long.

Straightening, she felt her heartbeat skip.

Unbidden, she glanced across the street to his house, only to find it dark. Was he home? Asleep? Or watching to see if she came home and got the flowers?

She caught herself pressing the card to her lips, thinking this was an infinitely better end to her evening — above and beyond anything she could have imagined from the way it had begun.

Knowing that Tony Cruz thought of her as a friend was almost too much for her to grasp. The man could have any woman he looked at, and yet, he'd gone out of his way to show her his appreciation.

Why this pleased her immeasurably was something she hesitated to grasp for fear she wouldn't be willing to accept the answer.

But the thought came to her just the same. . . .

He might want to be more than friends.

# SEVEN:
## IT'S RAINING MEN

"What are all these good-looking men doing in my room?"

Ninety-one-year-old Elsie Fisher lay in a twin bed, her nightgown twisted about her spindly legs. The assisted-care facility's white sheets bunched at her knees and a pillow was laid flat beneath her head.

There was a translucence about her skin, as if it were tissue paper covering her veins and weak muscles. Lamplight gave her skin a yellow tone. From the large medical bag at his feet, Tony got the blood-pressure cuff and pulse ox.

Captain Palladino, James "Wally" Wallcroft and Tony Cruz attended Elsie, three big firemen standing over a slight and elderly human being. Their presence in the tight quarters, wearing long-sleeved blue shirts and boots, had the potential to overwhelm even the fittest patient.

Tony knelt at Elsie's bed, the bottoms of

his boots hitting the wall in the small space. Half-aware of a plant bowl and glass table behind him, he focused on his job. Elsie gave him a little resistance as he held her fragile wrist and slipped the oximeter on her finger to measure the beats of her heart.

"What are you putting on my finger?" Her voice was uneven, a mix of bossiness and fright.

"A pulse oximeter," Tony explained in a reassuring tone while wrapping the cuff around her upper arm. "It reads your oxygen saturation to see if you're getting enough oxygen."

"What did I do to get all these good-looking men?" she asked once more.

"You threw up, Elsie." Captain Palladino stood next to the charge nurse of the Swallow Hill Assisted-Care Living Center. To her, he asked, "What did she eat for dinner?"

"Seafood Newburg."

"I ate that yesterday," she insisted, feebly touching her gray hair in confusion.

There was a pink stain on the beige carpet where the attendants had cleaned the vomit.

"How much did she throw up?"

"I don't know. It was cleaned up before I was called into her room."

Captain Palladino inquired, "What's her

medical history?"

The nurse referred to Elsie Fisher's chart. "She has mild dementia impairment, cardio-vascular disease and here's a list of her meds. At nine o'clock she had her last pills."

"I don't have dentures," Elsie complained.

Tony read the oximeter and determined she needed oxygen. He got out the narrow canister and airline, explaining what he was going to do. "You need to have this by your nose, Elsie."

"Have what?"

"It's oxygen. It'll help you breathe better."

"I'm breathing just fine. I'm not dead." Looking beyond the bed to the sitting area of her residence, she asked, "Who are you?"

"Wally, ma'am."

"What do you want?"

"We're here to help you."

Walcroft stood back in the small bedroom area as three paramedics from Medic 51 arrived and were briefed by Captain Palladino.

There was an unspoken reluctance to give up medical territory from the firemen, who were usually first on the scene, to the paramedics. While the medics worked for Ada County, they were an independent source of transport for patients. Tony didn't always agree with their tactics to get a patient to one of the local hospitals. When a patient gave consent to be taken by the paramedics, a trip on the gurney set someone back about a thousand bucks. Most, if not everyone, thought the ride was a courtesy of the city. Not true.

As the paramedics worked on Elsie, Tony rose to his feet and backed away. His leg knocked the glass table and the plant tipped over. *Shit.*

Reaching down, he gathered the cluster of bulb stalks and placed them back into the polished rocks where they'd been rooted. He did his best to straighten the plant and make it look as good as it had before, but his efforts weren't entirely successful.

Sometimes he felt like a bull in a china shop in these tiny rooms.

The medics talked to Elsie, tried to convince her that she should go to the hospital. Tony gritted his teeth, saying nothing. The fact was, he couldn't be one-hundred-percent sure if she would be okay here, or if she should be admitted.

"All these good-looking men are for me?" Her voice was feeble, her breathing slightly labored.

Tony wouldn't say that all six of them were that good-looking. Two of the medics were slouches, but that was just his opinion.

"Elsie," one of the medics said in a calming voice, "we're going to have to start an IV on you."

"Oh, not that!" she cried. "No needles."

"I promise I will do my best not to hurt you."

"No needles!" She waved him off with her hand, tears gathering in her watery blue eyes.

A measure of compassion worked through Tony, an amount that he acknowledged wasn't nearly as strong as it had been when he first started the job. He felt badly for patients, but if he took in everything he saw and internalized it, he'd take things too personally — unless they were kids. He had a fourteen-year-old boy die last summer. It was a bad scene. Family was over at the house for a reunion and the boy died unexpectedly. No medical problems, no drugs. The medics thought an embolism broke loose in his lungs. Tony had thought about that boy for days after, still did.

Easing out of the room, Tony talked to Walcroft, then glanced at the kitchen and sitting area while Elsie was being worked on. It was human nature to be curious about cleanliness, pictures, hobbies.

Elsie Fisher was more than just a patient he was attending, she had a life and family.

He couldn't help but think about that.

A bouquet of old flowers were centered on the kitchen table. Petals fell on a doily, sprinkled across the table's surface. He was reminded of a different bouquet, the one Natalie had unknowingly made for herself.

He wondered what she thought about him giving her the flowers last night. He'd waited until early evening to put them on her porch. Knowing that she usually didn't get home until after six, he'd taken a chance she'd arrive at her normal time and the flowers wouldn't be ruined in the cold. When she didn't arrive, he'd had to shove aside disappointment. He waited for a while, glancing out the window, then went to bed.

Natalie had crossed his mind several times today. He had a vague dream about her, one that caused him to wake at three in the morning to an empty bed. He couldn't remember much about it, just that he smelled her in his sleep. That feminine scent of roses and carnations.

Continuing his cursory glance, Tony noted there were a lot of china figurines on the shelves, the coffee table and the side table. Thank God he hadn't broken one of them. Elsie collected angels, lots of them. There was a wall with photos and he leaned closer to make out a framed letter. She'd been a nurse in WWII. Black-and-white photographs when she'd been younger were sitting on a shelf. He didn't touch them, didn't pick them up, but allowed his eyes to skim over her life's history in still photos.

He could figure out which man was her husband, and there was one group photo of the two of them surrounded by children. Then there were the senior portraits of the four boys. Wedding photos. Grandchildren.

Tony's lips felt dry; he licked them.

A feeling came to him, one he didn't immediately recognize. Then he defined it.

Envy.

He envied Elsie Fisher her full life, her marriage. Her children and her grandchildren.

Tony wanted kids. He hadn't wanted them with Kim. But just because they were getting a divorce didn't mean he was giving up on the idea of being a father. He wanted a child of his own, one that was his. As much as he loved Parker, he wanted to be more than a weekend dad.

He wanted a son. Or a daughter. He didn't care.

The problem was, he didn't have a woman in his life. He'd have to be in love, committed to a forever future to create a baby.

He'd also have to be remarried.

Right now, he couldn't think about that.

After five minutes of conversation, the paramedics coaxed Elsie to agree to the hospital and readied her for transport.

A gurney was brought in, following behind was one of the staff nurses. Tony knew her, the whole station did.

Alisa had a thing for firefighters — especially Tony.

He couldn't remember her last name even though she'd brought him cookies on several occasions. Once she even came by the firehouse with a deli platter.

She was okay-looking, no great beauty. But it wasn't her appearance that had made him keep his distance in the past — and would continue to do so now that he was going to be single. The way in which she'd thrown herself in his path, knowing that he wore a wedding ring — or used to, anyway — turned him off.

"Hi, Tony," she said, her voice slightly out of breath as if she'd been on the other side of the facility when she'd heard Station 13 had come on a call to a patient's room.

"Hey, Alisa."

"Oh, Mrs. Fisher." Wrinkles of concern formed on her forehead as she lifted her eyebrows. Her brunette hair was swept into a soft ponytail that contrasted with her starched nurse's smock. She was probably in her mid-twenties. "I had a feeling it was her."

Tony stepped out of the way as the gurney rolled past him. Elsie lay strapped in with her purse propped on top of her stomach, both her hands over the closure.

"Are all these good-looking men coming to the hospital, too?" she asked as they pushed her through the door.

Alisa held back, watching as Tony put away the pulse ox and cuff in his medical bag. He hitched the strap on his shoulder and took precautions not to bump into anything on his way out of the room.

"I saw you at Albertson's the other day, but you were leaving as I was driving into the parking lot." Alisa followed him out the resident door. "I waved but you didn't see me. Have you been busy tonight?"

"A little."

She trailed after him down the carpeted hallway. The gear in his bag rubbed together, made his footfalls sound heavier than they were.

Alisa had to be barely five foot one. He towered over her as she kept up with his long stride.

"Have you been called to Spring Brook tonight?"

"Not yet. I hope we aren't."

He caught her eyeing his wedding-ring finger and the lack of a ring on it.

"How's your wife?"

"Fine."

They passed the nurses' station and Alisa paused. "I guess I'll see you around, Tony."

"Yep." He exited the double glass doors as they whooshed open for him automatically.

Cold air hit his face as he stepped into the dark night that cloaked the trees and bushes in shadows.

The engine was parked out front at the main doors next to the paramedics' van. The guys were in the process of situating Elsie.

Tony put the medic bag away in the engine's lift compartment, then climbed into the cab. It felt strange, but exciting to be in command.

He was swinging up to become a driver, driving a set number of shifts to add to his checkoff sheet. He fit the headset over his ears and fired up the engine with a push of a button. A deep rumbling sound came to life, followed by an idle that was smooth and steady.

Tony liked being in control of the 450-horsepower diesel engine. His foot stayed on the brake as the captain and Wally pulled their seat belts on and secured their headsets.

Captain Palladino's voice came through the earpieces. "Did you switch the wigwags on coming down here?"

"Yeah."

Tony checked the buttons, glanced in his mirrors. There was always that slight bit of edgy nervousness that flickered in him for a second before he let the engine go.

Pulling out of the parking lot, he steered the big engine onto the road and cruised through the intersection.

Typing notes into the computer under the mellowness of a red light that didn't blind the driver, Captain Palladino commented, "Did you see that rookie medic they had with them tonight? I'll bet he's in for shit."

"IV drip?" Walcroft questioned.

"Probably."

Standard operating procedures to initiate rookies was stringing an IV line through the ceiling tiles of his room, leaking a small drip on him while he was trying to sleep.

Tony worked the steering wheel, turning the engine at a corner and applying pressure on the gas.

Less than a mile from the station, Captain Palladino said, "Dispatch, available in quarters."

Wally mentioned, "*Pulp Fiction*'s on HBO tonight."

"I didn't see it in the lineup," Tony said through his microphone.

"The Latino HBO channel."

Tony snorted, "Jesus, Walcroft, you've watched it ten times."

"Only in English."

Captain Palladino inched his chin up as Tony approached the fire station. "If you scuff the tires on the curb when you pull in, you've got to clean all the toilets."

Walcroft cut in, "I say clean out the reefer with soap and water. C Shift forgot about some leftovers in there weeks ago — I can smell it even when the door's closed."

"No toilets and no refrigerators." Tony accelerated, his hands firm on the driver's wheel. "I'm not hitting anything but smooth pavement all the way into the garage."

And true to his word, that's exactly how Tony brought E–13 — Lucky Engine 13 — into quarters.

The veterans' home was decorated for Valentine's Day. Red heart garlands hung from the hallway handrails, and shiny foil cupids were tacked to the wall with push-pins. Big-band music played through the sound system, a tune that Fred Miller hummed as he walked alongside Natalie, pushing a cart filled with buckets of mixed flowers.

The staff at the nursing station at the front entrance greeted them.

"We're ready for you. The men are so excited," a nurse wearing a daisy-print smock said. "Do you need any help getting the flowers to the recreation room?"

"No," Natalie replied. "I brought my dad to help me."

They rolled the cart down the hallway, following the nurse as she led the way.

Natalie had volunteered to show the residents how to put together a simple floral arrangement for their lady friends, wives or any female family members and acquaintances.

The activity was a good way for Natalie to get out of the shop — and a very well-timed outing that she'd looked forward to. She needed some space today. She'd gone into her office this morning and punched the answering machine's blinking light with a feeling of dread. Sure enough, Jonathon Falco had had the audacity to leave her a message, stating his confusion over her disappearance — as if he couldn't have a clue as to why she'd fled! He called once more later in the morning and she'd spoken curtly to him, asking him not to call her again. Then she hung up.

The stress of those calls had kept Natalie distracted and took away from her earlier preoccupation with Tony Cruz.

She hadn't been able to thank him for the arrangement he'd left for her. She'd knocked on his door early this morning, her heartbeat racing a mile a minute. When he didn't answer, she figured he was working today and had already left. She didn't have his phone number to call and thank him because he wasn't listed in the phone book. She'd have to try and catch him tomorrow.

"Where do you want these, Natalie?" her dad asked.

"Right there along that wall would be great."

The large room was filled with chairs and about ten patients. They wore varying degrees of clothing. Some in gowns and others fully dressed. One man wore a suit and tie. He wasn't in a wheelchair like some of his counterparts; rather, a normal chair. Wrinkled and weathered, he looked very old, but he wasn't shaky or sickly-like in appearance.

"Most of these guys have short attention spans," he commented as they passed him. "You better talk fast and repeat yourself."

She grinned. "I'll do my best."

He smiled in return, a great smile that was infectious. His eyes were pale blue, the irises little dots of black.

"I don't suppose you know Dr. Cooper?" he asked.

"Um, no."

"He performed surgery on me. My ticker is still going strong. I used to be in the lumberjack business up in Idaho City."

"That's nice."

He gazed at the bald man who'd rolled up beside him. "Hi, Ralph." Then to the male nurse, "Did you get his Lap Buddy on securely? Last time he got up he fell on me."

"It's snug, Maynard. Double-checked."

"Good. I'll hold you to that."

Ralph began to sing with the Muzak playing throughout the room and Maynard made a face. "I wouldn't mind him if he sang on key," he said to Natalie, then to the man beside him, "Ralph, you couldn't carry a tune if it came in your coat pocket."

Grumbling, Ralph sang louder.

Fred nudged Natalie and whispered, "Why'd you have to volunteer to come here? These men are old. They're making me feel every year of my retirement."

"Because they need people to come in and make them feel better."

"At the expense of making me feel worse?" Fred quibbled. "It smells like old man in here and it's making me nervous."

"It does not. That's room freshener."

"To disguise the real smell."

Natalie rolled her eyes. Her dad could be cantankerous sometimes. He really needed to find other interests, pursue something that was out of his comfort zone. Namely, she'd like him to consider finding a woman friend. He had a lot to offer and she had always thought it a shame that he hadn't expressed any interest in female company.

Ralph stopped his singing, gazed pointedly at Natalie and in a very calm tone asked, "Do you think you can get me some Viagra?"

Before she could respond, Maynard was butting in. "Ralph, quit asking every visitor that question. They aren't getting you any sex pills."

Fred frowned, his face clearly indicating that he wished he could leave right now.

All these old men in here were making him aware he was no longer in his prime.

Natalie went with the head nurse to get something and Fred was left alone by the flower cart.

Ralph asked, "Have you had any operations?"

"Nothing to write home about," Fred supplied tightly, recalling the vasectomy he'd had in his thirties.

Not letting up on his interrogation, Ralph's next question threw Fred for a wallop. "Any penile implants?"

"Hell, no."

Ralph laughed. "Your secret is safe with me because I won't remember it tomorrow, anyway."

Maynard cut in, his disgust evident in the abrupt way he rose to his spindly legs. His suit appeared to be a size too large; it hung on him. "Ralph, you're embarrassing yourself and you're too lame-headed to even know it."

Getting behind the wheelchair, Maynard rolled Ralph to the back of the room, then came back and took his seat. "That's what happens when you let them put you on that dang cholesterol reduction pill. I take an aspirin a day and they want me on some other things, but I told the doctor here to go screw himself."

Fred started, unprepared for the crass comment from a spry geezer who had presented himself as fairly polished.

Intrigued by the change in his demeanor, Fred asked, "How old are you?"

"Ninety-eight. You know how you can tell when you're getting old?" Maynard's blue eyes narrowed. "Everything dries up or leaks!"

Just what Fred Miller didn't want to know.

His life sort of flashed by him in that moment, and he was struck by an image of himself dying alone. He hadn't really thought much about it up to this point. He'd been content to cope with life on his own. But now he had this horrible thought about never finding love again.

"Have you ever been married?" he asked Maynard.

"For fifty-nine years."

"When did she die?"

"She didn't," Maynard supplied, his eyes tearing up. Fred hoped the man wouldn't start crying. "She lives at Oak Valley . . . dementia. My son takes me to visit her. She doesn't know who I am."

Deeply saddened, Fred said with all sincerity, "I'm sorry."

"Me, too. But we had a good life together. I just . . . miss her. You ever been married?"

"Once. My wife died some time ago."

"Ever have a girlfriend?"

"No."

"Why not?"

"Not interested."

"Why not? Are you queer?"

"God no." The corners of Fred's mouth turned down. "I'm not . . . No."

"Then get yourself a woman. Treat her right. Light the fires in your heart before it's too late."

Natalie returned, ready for the class to begin. The men were lined up at a long table and given flowers and baskets, along with green florist foam she used to stabilize the stems.

Fred didn't pay the activity much mind.

He thought about what Maynard had said. Fred looked at the man as he made an arrangement for a wife who wouldn't know it was from the husband she loved, had married.

A piece of Fred suddenly felt sad . . . bereft.

Life had been sailing by and he hadn't realized he'd been missing a ride on the boat.

# EIGHT:
## BIDALICIOUS

"Do you think anyone would care if we left?" Tony asked, taking a drink of beer then scanning the crowded banquet room.

Rocky grinned. "I'm not leaving. How often do I get the chance to be auctioned off to a woman? I want to see who's going to buy me."

"I really wish we hadn't done this."

"It's for charity. I can suffer for a few hours."

Reconciling himself to having to go through with the event, Tony rested his arms on the bar and contemplated how he'd ended up here.

Tony wasn't feeling real enthusiastic about being auctioned off to the highest bidder for a date. The fire department had roped him and Rocky into participating in the hospital's annual air-flight support auction and black-tie dance.

While Tony thought it a worthy cause, the

idea of being bid on made him uncomfortable as all hell.

Rocky and him wore the required monkey suits, but Tony was thinking about his worn jeans and a pullover shirt. Dressing up wasn't his style. He liked comfort.

The event was sponsored by the local morning-radio show, members of the Boise Kixx women's soccer team and Bistro Owyhee — a trendy café on Eighth Street. Chef and owner Salvatore Pietro had catered the evening.

The auction was being held at the Boise Centre on the Grove.

Red tablecloths covered round tables and, in the centers were candles with floral arrangements. The soft flicker of candlelight illuminated the name cards on the tables.

Tony glanced at a program left on the bar. A name stood out and he picked up the folded paper. Hat and Garden had done the centerpieces.

Straightening, his gaze traveled the roomful of dark-suited men and women in evening dresses, looking for one woman in particular.

He couldn't see Natalie Goodwin, and wondered if she'd even come. Just because her shop had done the arrangements didn't mean she'd be here. Actually, he hoped she wouldn't show. He would feel even more idiotic with her watching the live auction.

They'd talked a couple of weeks ago, when she'd come over in the morning and thanked him for the flowers. He'd told her it was nothing, something he'd wanted to do. A blush had worked across her cheeks. He'd liked that. He liked her. Maybe too much.

He hadn't spoken to her since.

"What a way to celebrate being newly single," Rocky chuckled. He wore his sandy-blond hair spiked up for tonight. "How many days has it been now?"

"Five."

Tony's divorce had been recorded with the Ada County courthouse this week. Idaho was the only state he knew of that could grant a divorce in such a short time. He was officially a single man now.

But all the decree meant was a legal term on paper. The day he found out Kim had been unfaithful to him, in many ways, had been the day he'd felt the marriage was over.

Barely a bachelor for a week and look at how quickly he'd landed into trouble. He pulled his mouth into a frown. "I never should have said I'd do this."

"It's for a good cause," Rocky countered.

Tony gazed at the stage, the podium that

was decorated with hearts and cupids. In less than fifteen minutes, the night was going to start and he'd find out what opening bid would be placed on him. Right now, there were silent bids on the items, and every time a woman walked past and smiled at him, he had the urge to leave.

"I know it's for a good cause," Tony replied. "I'd rather just write a personal check and make a donation that way."

Rocky left to use the men's room, then came back with a crooked smile on his face. "A woman pinched my ass — a hit-and-run. When I turned around, she'd already left." A gleam lit his eyes as to who the offender could have been.

"How do you know it wasn't a guy?" Tony asked with a grin, taking another drink of beer.

"You had to say that." Rocky's gaze skimmed the crowd. "I was hoping it was her."

Tony followed Rocky's gaze.

A woman stood by the stage, her back to them — a back that was fully exposed in a plunging cocktail dress. Black fabric draped her hips and hugged a slender waist. The hem was sexy-short, several inches above the knees. She had on heels, really high ones. Her blond hair was swept up in sparkling hairpins, and loose curls fell against the slim column of her neck. She turned slightly and spoke to a man at her side.

Familiarity punched Tony in the gut.

Natalie Goodwin.

An arc of heat pulsed through the blood in his veins. He'd thought she was an attractive woman in many ways. Now he saw she was unbelievably sexy, as well.

"Do you know her?" Rocky questioned, dragging him out of his thoughts.

"She's my neighbor. She lives across the street."

"Ding-dong," Rocky said, his voice filled with admiration . . . and sexual appreciation. That bothered Tony. Something squeezed his chest and made him fight off the feeling of misplaced jealousy.

Rocky drank a swallow of beer, his eyes leveled on Natalie as she smiled at the man beside her, then laughed. "If I lived across the street from her, I'd be knocking on her door to ask for some sugar."

Natalie turned toward them and walked across the ballroom.

She looked up, saw Tony, and her eyes met his. Her lips looked fuller, pinker.

"Hello," she greeted. "I saw you were on the program. You're brave." She spoke with an easy lightness, a tone he'd never heard her use before.

"Not brave," Rocky interjected. "Good sports." Then he extended his hand. "Rockland Massaro, but you can call me Rocky."

She shook his hand. "Nice to meet you."

"I can be bought for cheap, honey," Rocky said, encouraging Natalie to bid on him.

Tony slanted his friend a look, wishing he wouldn't have said that, but didn't utter anything to the contrary.

Tony and Natalie exchanged a brief glance. There was something more to the visual exchange than he could identify. Maybe, for a moment, she was thinking about bidding on him.

Diamond earrings dangled from Natalie's ears. She wore a delicate necklace that hung low on a chain. The jewelry rested next to her skin where her breasts created a shadowed valley in the black fabric that was cut low. She showed a lot of skin — skin that looked soft and golden and very feminine. She wore a distinct perfume — not flowers exactly but maybe a trace. She almost smelled like limes. Limes and something really sweet. Whatever it was, he was very aware of how it clung to her warmth.

Natalie said, "Well, I should go —"

"How's your daughter?" Tony asked, dragging a subject from his mind that he knew would engage her in conversation. He didn't want her to leave, not yet.

"Cassie's doing well, thanks." Her green eyes were large, the lashes long and her makeup applied heavier than usual. Instead of looking overdone, it looked good. Exotic almost. "I talked to her yesterday. School is good, she's having fun."

An announcer began speaking through the microphone and asked everyone to take their seats.

"I'm going to sit down." She smiled, a smile that hit Tony hard. "Good luck to you. Thanks for doing this."

"Remember — I can be had for cheap," Rocky said, "but if you have deep pockets, I'm worth it."

Being a good sport, she laughed. Tony wondered if she'd take his friend up on his suggestion and bid on him.

Natalie sat at a table near the front. Tony sat woodenly in his chair at a table he and Rocky had been assigned to, drank half his beer in long swallows, then loosened his tie some more. He couldn't recall the last time he'd worn the double-breasted dark suit, and couldn't recall when he'd last felt like ditching an obligation.

It was all he could do not to drum his

fingers on the tabletop in edgy-nervous anticipation. After introductory speeches, the auction started and went on far too long before it got to the bachelors.

He had to stand up, walk onto the stage and smile as if he meant it. The strong floodlights rendered him almost blind to the sea of faces gazing at him. He was very conscious of where Natalie sat, and didn't want to look in her direction. To everyone in the room, he gave the illusion of confidence and easygoing masculinity, but in reality he was willing himself not to sweat.

In what felt like long and agonizing minutes to get through, Tony Cruz "sold" to the highest bidder, a woman he couldn't see because she sat at the back of the crowded room and the lights drowned any image of her.

Now he had to go on a date of her choosing and they would have to dance the first dance of the evening after all the auctions were completed. He had never been a great ballroom dancer. His mom had made him take private lessons before going to his prom so he could at least waltz without stepping on his girlfriend's feet. He was no dancer — he'd played football in high school and college.

Rocky Massaro went for a little less than

Tony, his winning bidder a nice-looking redhead at the next table over. Rocky got a stupid smile on his face, one he held on to until the music started playing and he escorted the lady onto the dance floor. If he was disappointed Natalie didn't make an offer on him, he didn't show it.

Tony stood and waited for whoever had won him to come forward.

A moment later, a throaty voice greeted him.

"Hello."

Tony's breathing slowing. The woman standing before him had an amazing presence, dressed in floor-length red satin and black heels. She was in her mid-thirties with long dark hair and a gorgeous mouth. She reminded him of Salma Hayek.

"Hey," he said, lifting his chin and turning on his best smile.

"I won you. You're mine."

He gave a light laugh, a slight shrug. "Well, okay."

The live band played an old tune, one that Tony didn't recognize.

"My name is Sophia. Have you heard of me?" Her eyes turned up slightly at the corners, their color a rich earthy brown.

"Should I have?"

"I own Sophia-Sophia. It's a ladies' clothing store on Bannock."

"I don't wear ladies' clothes."

She threw her head back and laughed, her throat an ivory column that captured his attention. The sound of her voice was low and sensual. She laid a perfumed hand on his shoulder, her fingernails painted red to match her dress. "Dance with me."

Maybe it was the way she took command with a rare self-assurance that had him following while she led the way to the dance floor. Perhaps there was a trace of ego involved — his. Or maybe it was because she had paid for the right.

Being won by a beautiful woman for the night was something he'd never experienced before.

He quickly discovered that he liked it.

Music drifted around Natalie, making her feel isolated and alone at the table while others danced. She was sorry that Sarah had been unable to come with her tonight. Her sister had had to go to a school event with her girls. Even the youthful Meagan would have been nice to sit and socialize with, but the clerk had had other plans for tonight.

So Natalie sat there, the table empty, wineglasses empty, and those who had been around her out on the dance floor.

She caught sight of Tony and a woman in red as they danced past.

Seeing him with the stunningly beautiful woman, Natalie wasn't prepared for the pang of something undefinable to assail her. She didn't want to consider it jealousy . . . envy, maybe.

She envied that woman.

Natalie's gaze connected with every place the couple touched. Their hands, their bodies, their legs as they moved flawlessly in unison.

Her breathing shortened, her muscles grew tense and in some place deep inside her she felt a void.

Stupid.

Why was she suddenly feeling so lost, so alone sitting by herself?

The dance ended and Tony's date — Natalie assumed she was the woman who'd won him — appeared quite content. When the bidding had ended, Natalie had tried to get a look at the woman who'd bought Tony for the evening, but the crowd had disbursed on the dance floor and the room had been pressed too tight with couples for her to get a look at anything.

Now she wished she hadn't seen Tony at all.

Natalie felt self-conscious sitting all by

herself. She'd just decided to leave, call the evening to an end, when Tony's voice came to her ears.

"The flowers you did for this evening look great."

Her chin shot up. "Oh . . . thank you."

Tony smelled incredibly masculine, wonderfully clean and musky. She'd noticed it before when they'd been talking earlier.

She thought he looked good beyond words in his suit. She never imagined he'd wear one so well. Of course he was Tony Cruz — anything he did seemed to be larger than life, and the simple suit and tie only enhanced his presence.

"Where's your date?" she asked, angry with herself for even voicing what she was wondering.

"The ladies' room." His eyes held hers. "Let's dance," he suggested, extending his hand.

A thread of panic wound around her, and she took a quick breath. "I wouldn't want your date —"

"Sophia's not my date. I came alone and I'll go home alone."

*Sophia.* Even the name was intriguing.

Her reluctance was met by a grasp of her hand and, the next thing she knew, she was being coaxed to her feet and led onto the dance floor.

Beside herself, she was in Tony's strong arms being turned around a parquet floor.

Over the strains of the music, he said, "You look amazing."

"Thank you," she murmured, not liking that he could so easily make her feel so nervous. This was ridiculous. The reaction she had toward him, as always, made her very aware she was female and he was male. There was no denying he was masculine beyond belief, so handsome he took coherent thoughts right out of her head, but that was no reason to get silly about it.

"I like your dress." His eyes were dark, a serious depth to the brown color as his gaze lowered and he made no attempt to hide his appreciation for her cleavage.

"Thank you," she repeated automatically. Then, before she could stop herself, she said, "You look wonderful."

"You think?"

"You know you do." She tried to put a teasing tone in her voice, anything to alleviate the butterflies swimming in her stomach.

"Yeah, maybe I look okay."

"More than that, and every woman in this room has probably told you as much."

"Sophia said I look like James Bond."

Amusement stretched a smile on Natalie's

mouth. Sophia was trying hard to stroke his ego — not that he needed it. "I wouldn't go that far."

"So, are you a Brosnan or Connery fan?"

"Connery, of course. He was hot in *Medicine Man*."

"You think?"

"I just said so, didn't I?" she bantered.

"Yeah, you did." His smile went straight to her heart.

She was very conscious of the feel of his muscles. Tony was solid, strong, and he carried himself with a commanding air of self-confidence. He was big and powerful, the rich outlines of his shoulders straining in the wool fabric of his suit. The white of his evening shirt was bright, the collar crisp. She liked his tie; it had a geometric pattern in hues of green and blue with a light dash of red.

She had to tilt her head back to get a full view of his face because he stood a good head taller than her.

The way he held himself, she couldn't help but notice every facet about him. His eyes, his nose, his face. The way his mouth curved, the faint scar at his temple where his eyebrow ended.

His black hair gleamed under the ballroom lights, cut short and neat. He had a rugged power that captivated her in ways that got to her. Why he did this she could only speculate . . . and she didn't like the answer.

He was her best fantasy come true.

There was something about him that drew her interest, sparked the sexual desire in her that could lead to poor judgment.

Eventually, when she was ready to be in a relationship, she wanted a good sex life and, in fact, thought more about it at her age than she had in her twenties or thirties. Maybe it was because she was settled in her early forties that she was willing to speak her mind now, willing to tell her partner exactly what she liked, what she wanted. Looking back at Greg, their sex life had been fine for the most part, but she hadn't always been the most uninhibited unless she'd had a few glasses of wine.

Strange that now she was discovering her sexuality, she had no one to explore it with.

Looking at Tony, she could imagine him naked, sprawled across her bed on the sheets . . . reposed and relaxed, waiting for her to join him and —

"I didn't expect to see you here tonight," Natalie said, willing illicit thoughts away.

"Why's that?"

"I didn't think you were a bachelor."

"I am as of last week."

"Everything went well?"

"It was all right." A distant expression caught on his facial features, his nostrils slightly flaring.

"I'm sorry."

"Don't be." His eyes fell on hers, locking her into a gaze that was both riveting and disarming. "I'm just fine."

The music ended and Natalie backed out of his hold.

She quelled the impulse to slip her arms around his waist, rest her cheek next to his chest, then tip her chin up and seek his mouth for a kiss. Instead she said in a somewhat shaky tone, "Thanks for the dance."

"Anytime."

His voice was smooth, his body language even smoother. He shifted his weight, his arms by his sides, his hands big and wide.

In a low voice, he added, "I wish it had been you who had bid on me and won. I could dance with you all night."

Before she could reply, Tony disappeared into the crowd.

His comment was unnerving, yet exciting. The implication set off warning bells inside her mind, things she should ignore but didn't. Not right away.

For a scant few seconds, she let herself

envision what it would be like to be held in his arms for the rest of the night.

With a blink of her eyes, she released those thoughts.

She was gun-shy about dating these days, very reticent about getting involved. Her track record wasn't very good, and falling for someone was low on her priority list — and barely even on the list at all. She had way too much going on.

Besides, he was too young for her; even though he did seem mature. Then again, he hadn't been divorced long enough to know what he wanted.

Steeling her resolve, she made a decision.

She had to blow the pilot light out before any kind of flame could be lit. Getting involved with him would only mean sure heartache.

# Nine:
## Blame It on Squirrels

This wasn't Fred Miller's neighborhood Target store and he felt discombobulated by aisles that weren't where he expected them to be.

"Where in the hell is the squirrel food?" he muttered to himself while pushing the red plastic cart. He rolled past laundry-detergent shelves, the smell of lemons and perfumes pressing in on him, making a sneeze tickle his nose. The cart's rear wheel rattled unless he pushed while applying pressure on the handle.

He was used to the Milwaukee location, the "old" Target. Against his better judgment, he'd come to the Eagle Road location after his dental visit on Chinden. He thought he'd check out the new store, assuming it would be a carbon copy of the one he always shopped at.

As soon as he stepped inside he realized the snack bar was in the wrong spot. And they didn't sell white-cherry slushies. This one had cola and wild berry. He disliked both. Whoever invented the cola slushy was a moron. It never tasted like cola.

The popcorn was the same and he bought a small bag along with a Dr Pepper. Roaming through the store, he took a sip through the straw, paused at the picture frames and picked one up. It was a double frame. He thought about the two photos he had of his daughters. Natalie and Sarah had given him five-by-seven pictures of themselves for Christmas and he'd yet to find a frame for them.

This one sort of appealed to him. It was black, about a half-inch all the way around with hinges in the middle. A little gilt sheen to it. Maybe he'd come back and get it after he found the damn squirrel food.

Pushing through the aisles, with different items stocked on either side of him, he realized how different his life was these days. He enjoyed it, but there was something missing.

He'd been thinking about that ever since he'd been at that veterans' home talking with Maynard. Maynard might have been an old fart, but he offered a perspective that Fred had never taken the time to think about in the last few years. Now he did.

He wasn't getting any younger and didn't want to die by himself.

His sweet wife had passed on twelve years ago after a battle with breast cancer, and he hadn't really taken great care of himself. Healthwise he was fine, but the house wasn't all that clean most often, and he didn't like to scrub his shower real good but once a month. He usually shot some of that contact-spray cleaner in there each week, but aside from that, he wasn't much into housework.

Speaking of which . . . he needed more of that cleaner.

He reached for his wallet in his back pocket and produced his shopping list. Then he ate some popcorn and stood in an aisle intersection of towels to the north, bowls to the east, electrical to the west and electronics to the south. It was as if he were in a foreign land. This was supposed to be something else entirely. He should have been standing in the music department looking for the latest Johnny Cash greatest hits.

"Well, hell." An oath was muttered once more, spoken to himself. A customer who happened to be walking past ignored him. "Where's the damn squirrel food?"

He caught a flash of red smock. A clerk.

Rolling ahead, he wobbled after her to get directions. Unlike most men, he wasn't about to waste all day looking for something when he wanted it right now.

"Ah, miss," he called after her retreating back. "Lady . . . ah, I'm lost."

She turned around and recognition hit him immediately — as if he could forget a face like hers.

Fred's eyes dropped to the clerk's name badge, just to make sure.

*Iris.*

He knew it! Irises for Iris. He'd delivered them to her himself.

"Can I help you?" she asked.

She obviously didn't remember him.

"I'm looking for the, ah . . ." He lost his damn train of thought when she gazed into his eyes. Not to mention, she wore red lipstick that drew his attention.

"Yes?"

"The, ah . . ." He couldn't form the sentence. Then, unexpectedly, he asked, "What department do you work in?"

"Housewares — kitchen appliances and gadgets."

"Oh." Fred drank a slow sip of Dr Pepper, the wheels in his head spinning like an old Ford pickup in overdrive. "I'm looking for a gadget."

Now, that was the furthest thing from the truth that Fred Miller had said today, aside from a slight fib to the dentist about using dental floss every night. Sometimes he skipped a night if he fell asleep before Leno came on.

"What kind of gadget?" she asked.

"Just a . . . ah . . . gadget. I'll know it when I see it." He set his soda pop cup down on the basket seat. "Maybe you can show me where they all are and I'll recognize it."

"I'd be happy to."

She was making him happy just by standing there.

Blame it on the squirrels, but Fred felt himself go a little nutty over a clerk named Iris.

# TEN:
## CATS AND FROGS

"Who's the smart-ass?" Walcroft growled, yanking the highlighted newspaper off his bunk.

Tony went on making his bed, pretending he didn't know what Walcroft was talking about.

The captain walked by, stopped in the doorway and couldn't hold back a laugh.

Walcroft wadded the newspaper and pitched it at Captain Palladino. "If you weren't the captain, I'd tell you where to shove that."

Unable to keep his humor in check, Tony busted up laughing. He and Rob had taken this morning's personal section of the newspaper and highlighted the men-seeking-men gay ads and left them on Walcroft's bed. It was juvenile, but damn funny watching his reaction.

"Shut up, Cruz." Walcroft got bent out of shape, but a smirk landed on his mouth as he snorted out a half laugh. "You guys are a bunch of pussies. You were looking at those ads for yourselves."

"Not me," the captain denied. "Tony."

"Bullshit," Tony countered, grinning. "If anyone's gay, it's Gable."

"What's the latest on that?" Walcroft asked. "Who's got the score?"

"I'm up one."

Tony and Gable had been playing tag ever since the omelet incident. The last prank Tony pulled off on Gable had been sneaking over to Station 3 and sabotaging the shower stall.

"I put a chicken bouillon cube in Gable's showerhead."

Walcroft grinned. "Now, *that's* fowl."

Captain Palladino shook his head with a grin. "Hey, let's get to daily duties. Grocery-store trip about three this afternoon? What do you guys feel like for supper? I'll cook."

"Chicken up the butt," Walcroft said. "Get a can of beer for it."

"Okay. I brought some new seasoning in. I'm not buying any rice or potatoes. I'm still on Atkins."

"Me, too," Walcroft said.

"Hell, I'm not." Tony was getting tired of no starch with his protein.

"Yeah, Rocky mentioned you guys drinking down some beers at that charity event. Major carbs." Wally finished with his bed and threw his duffel bag on top. "So did you get lucky that night?"

Tony kept closemouthed. He grinned and let Walcroft think what he wanted.

The truth was, he and Sophia had parted company after the dancing had finished. She gave him her number and they'd gone on the obligatory "date" she'd bought — a candlelight dinner at the Cottonwood Grill, but he wasn't interested in having sex with her as his dessert. He'd made up his mind to take things slow after his divorce. It was too easy to get caught up in a new relationship in order to forget the last one.

The morning progressed with firehouse chores, not giving Tony any time to think about his love life — or rather, lack of one.

A Shift at Station 13 had just finished lunch, and Captain Palladino was in his office doing paperwork while Tony and Walcroft spent time in the garage checking over the chassis of the engine.

The day was marginally warm for March, a high in the mid-forties. Tony and Walcroft were listening to the radio, the hood up on the engine as they did routine maintenance.

It had been a quiet morning. Only one call — a noninjury traffic accident in the commuter rush. Tony hoped they wouldn't be too busy tonight, although if it was quiet during the day, that usually meant they would be up all night. He wanted to get in a good workout, then watch *The Apprentice.*

Usually, evening television wasn't the high point of Tony's day, but he was keeping a low profile, staying in most every night. He wanted to form a new daily pattern with just himself, nobody else involved. But it was hard. He missed having company.

On more than one occasion, he'd thought about inviting Natalie over for dinner, but he cut off that idea and didn't go through with it. Seeing her dressed up at the charity event and dancing with her had revealed too much about how she affected him. He didn't want to admit to himself that he could fall out of love with his wife one month, and be attracted to another woman in the next. It felt too soon. But then again, his divorce had been a long time in the making.

A song came on the radio that Tony liked and he sang along.

"I think in a former life, you were a rock-and-roll singer 'cause you've always got to sing with the tunes, Cruz," Wally observed, squeezing a hose line.

"Because I sing good," Tony said matter-of-factly.

"And you sure aren't full of shit about anything, either."

Tony simply smiled.

Traffic moved past the fire station at a leisurely pace. They were situated near a residential area and a stop sign was just a block away.

A car sped through the intersection, causing both Walcroft and Tony to look up at the same time as skid marks shrieked from the vehicle's tires.

"Jesus Christ," Wally exclaimed, dropping his tools and running into the street.

Tony was on his heels.

At first, he wondered if the car had hit a child. Going round to the front of the red sedan and dropping to his knees, he didn't see a body.

"No kid," he shouted to Captain Palladino who'd come running out of the station to investigate.

The low moan of a wounded animal caught Tony's attention and he took a second look beneath the car.

A tabby cat laid on the blacktop beneath the driver's front tire.

"I didn't see the cat until it was too late!" the teenage driver cried, running to Tony's

side and peering beneath the car. "Is it
. . . ?"

The young girl began to sob.

Walcroft hunkered down and took the
injured cat out, cradling it in his arms. His
hand felt along the cat's spine and limp legs.
Then his gaze met Tony's. "She's busted
up. Won't make it."

"Ohmygod, I feel like crap," the teenage
girl cried into her hands. "I didn't see the
stop sign. Ohmygod."

Walcroft's hand stilled. "She's pregnant."

"I am not," the girl gasped, lifting her
head.

"The cat."

Captain Palladino took command as if the
cat were a patient. "Bring her into the
garage, Wally. Cruz, get out the medic kit."
The captain was running. "We'll do a
C-section on her and get the kittens out."

They delivered four kittens from the
mother cat who didn't make it. At no time
did they think about what they were doing;
it just seemed to be the right thing to do.

The teenage girl had called her parents
and they showed up at the station to find
out what had happened. Captain Palladino
spoke to them while Tony and Walcroft
made sure the kittens were kept warm as
they monitored their vitals.

By nightfall, the firefighters were trying to figure out how they'd get milk to the kittens. Tony made a call to Doug Frye, had him swing by the twenty-four-hour emergency animal hospital, pick up some supplies and bring them to Station 13.

It never occurred to the three of them to turn the kittens over to the animal shelter. Somewhere between James Walcroft carrying the mom cat into the garage and Captain Palladino making the lifesaving efforts for the unborn babies, the firehouse adopted those kittens.

"Dad smells like Brut," Sarah whispered as she and Natalie stood at the kitchen sink washing dinner dishes.

"I noticed that." Natalie's tone was hushed. "I didn't think they still made that cologne."

"Apparently so. Must be stocked next to the High Karate."

Natalie laughed. "What's up with him? He hasn't worn cologne since . . . Mom."

At that, the sisters' heads turned simultaneously in the direction of Fred Miller who was playing Frogger on the PlayStation in the living room. He swore at the controls, his posture rigid and his thumbs moving the knobs up and down as a frog hopped across the television screen.

"Goddammit," he muttered.

BreeAnn and Sydney giggled at their grandpa.

Natalie turned to Sarah. "He's got to have met someone. There's no other explanation."

"Agree."

Sarah's eyes narrowed. "I wonder who she is."

"Not a clue."

"Where would he meet a woman?"

"I don't know. Grocery store? Maybe Hat and Garden."

"I haven't seen him flirting with any of the customers."

"Dad would never do that," Natalie replied. "He'd play it cool."

"Should we ask him if he's seeing anyone?"

Natalie bit her lip. "I don't think we should ask him outright. You know how he gets defensive about things."

Steve Brockner walked through the kitchen, opened the refrigerator and said, "Want some pie, hon?"

"No. I'm still full from dinner."

Steve took out a half-eaten apple pie, set it on the countertop and began to cut a slice. To Natalie he asked, "Are you dating anyone?"

"Not since the erection guy," Sarah supplied.

"God, Sarah," Natalie said with a huff. "You told him that?"

"I tell Steve everything."

"Everything except how much you spend shopping," Steve quipped, shooting canned whip cream at his wife.

She laughed and ducked. Whipping the smear of white cream off the counter, she put her finger in her mouth. "Save that for later, babe."

Natalie felt a moment's discomfort. While she was happy for her sister's fabulous marriage, it left her with a lonely pang, wishing she had someone special in her life. Where that thought came from, she could only surmise.

The sisters went into the living room with cups of decaf to watch their father curse his way through the third level of the video game before giving the controls over to his granddaughters.

"I give up. Nobody can win that level," he said, rising to his feet and going into the kitchen for his second piece of pie.

"Grandpa, we can win it. We'll show you." Sydney proceeded to hop her way through the mazes and proved her point within a few minutes.

Grandpa Fred sat on the couch with his pie and frowned. "Well, I gave it my best try. You have to have the patience of a saint to win at that damn thing."

The girls moved up to the next level and Natalie removed her shoes and curled her feet beneath her. "So, Dad, what's new in your life?" she asked.

"Nothing."

His flat response didn't appease Sarah. "Seriously, Dad. Have you been doing anything fun lately?"

"Fun?" he said with a sour face. "I cleaned up dog shit in my front yard left by that worthless poodle who lives next door. They always let it out without a leash and it craps on my mugho pine."

"I'm sorry," Natalie offered, trying to keep a straight face. "So you haven't been doing anything different, going out any place special or —"

"Dad, we want to know why you're wearing Brut," Sarah cut in, literally cutting to the chase. "Do you have a girlfriend?"

The fork in Fred's hand stilled. "I have no such thing."

"Then why the cologne?" Natalie asked.

"Can't a man put on a quality aftershave

and not get interrogated about it?"

Natalie tried to smooth his ruffled feathers. "Of course, Dad. Nobody's picking on you."

"It feels like it."

"We're sorry," Sarah offered. "We're just curious is all. We wouldn't be upset if you were interested in someone."

"No, we wouldn't," Natalie put in. "We want you to be happy, to find someone."

"Someone you can add to your life," Sarah said with a smile. "Maybe take long romantic walks with."

"Romantic walks?" Fred's face blanched. "Don't you go getting any ideas. I don't want to talk about it."

He rose from the chair, put his unfinished pie on the counter, then stepped into the study to pester Steve while he was on the computer.

Natalie and Sarah traded glances. Natalie spoke first. "We hit a nerve."

"I think an artery."

"He's definitely got a crush on someone."

"No kidding."

BreeAnn and Sydney finished playing Frogger and punched the remote so that the television station came on.

The nightly news was airing, and as Natalie and Sarah drank their coffee, Sarah's chin lifted.

"Look! It's your fireman!" Sarah blurted. "He's on TV."

Natalie's attention was pulled to the television and the broadcaster's voice as she reported a story.

"The men at Station 13 have been up to extra duties this past week when they delivered four kittens from a cat who'd been run over in front of their firehouse. Dispatch rings down the station every two hours throughout the night so crews of firefighters can feed the kittens their milk. The feedings are something new for this bachelor who's never changed a diaper."

She put the microphone in front of Tony. "How does it feel to be a surrogate father?"

Tony folded strong arms over his chest, the blue of his IAFF shirt a contrast against his dark complexion. "It's no different than being a real dad. You do what you have to do."

Natalie sensed he was uncomfortable with the fame, maybe a little uncomfortable in front of the microphone.

"And what do you and your fellow fire-fighters plan on doing with the kittens?"

"We're going to adopt them out when they're old enough."

"Can the public request a kitten?"

"We're taking applications. We've already had a lot come in. Me and the guys on all the shifts are going to read through them, make sure the homes are suitable, stuff like that."

The reporter addressed the viewing audience. "You can find the fire station's address at our Web site as well as a form to fill out if you're interested in the adoption." To Tony, she said, "And all four will be available?"

"Three females and one male. The females are giving the guys a hard time already." Tony shifted his stance, looked down, then at the camera. He gave Boise a grin — the grin that Natalie had come to cherish, the one that would always give her a warm feeling inside.

"He takes a beautiful picture on television," Sarah commented wistfully. "He's not only handsome, Natalie . . . he seems to have a good heart."

Natalie merely nodded.

She couldn't form words around the lump in her throat.

Yes, indeed. He did seem to have a very good heart.

# ELEVEN:
## INDELIBLE SCARS

Natalie had been so busy all week, she hadn't gotten around to taking in her mail till Saturday. She made time on Sunday morning to stock up at the grocery store. Using facial tissues as emergency toilet paper had gotten old real fast and she could no longer put off a trip for supplies — namely food. That glass of cold milk with her lunch had never tasted so good.

She really had to stay more on top of her personal inventory. Since Hat and Garden's opening, it seemed as if she'd neglected her home life in favor of putting more energy into her business. While she loved the feeling of success, she didn't want it to come at the expense of keeping her home well run.

She'd spent this morning dusting and vacuuming and getting ready for Sunday-night dinner at her house tonight. Last week had been Sarah's turn and next week would be Dad's.

Something was up with her father, but he wasn't talking.

It somewhat infuriated Natalie that he could be so closemouthed. Did he think his daughters would disapprove that he was dating?

At that, Natalie wondered if the new lady was unsuitable. Perhaps she wasn't a good choice for her father and he knew it, but his infatuation caused him to cast a blind eye to his dating decision.

Natalie was going to call Sarah as soon as she came in from getting the mail to run the idea past her sister.

Natalie raised her face to the sky as she walked down the driveway to the mailbox. The days were finally warming up to the high forties and several afternoons this week they had hit the low fifties. Today had to be one of them. The sun felt heavenly and warm, a reminder that spring and summer were on their way. She couldn't wait to get into her garden and plant seeds. She'd spread Preen on her flowerbeds last fall and hoped she'd have better luck this year preventing weed germination. She didn't care for weeding. Last year she'd hired someone to clear the planters.

Opening her mailbox and gathering the mail, her attention was pulled to Tony's house as the garage door creaked and lifted.

She glanced in his direction and saw him inside the garage.

Holding her unopened mail, she made a decision, and crossed the street and walked up his driveway.

"Hi," she greeted, smiling.

"Hey." He wore a long-sleeved T-shirt and jeans. His hair was damp as if he'd just stepped out of the shower. He stood at his work bench with a small piece of wood clamped into a vise. "How're you?"

"Good. You?"

"Been okay." He tightened the vise, got a handsaw and started on the wood.

She tucked the mail in the crook of her arm as he worked the saw, a visible strain of muscle beneath his thin shirt. She swallowed. "I saw you on TV last week. I even read about you in the newspaper."

He sort of shrugged. "Yeah, it's gotten a lot of exposure."

"What you guys are doing is really nice."

"Yep." He finished cutting the small piece, took the wood out of the vise and examined it. "It's been interesting."

"How are the kittens getting along?"

"Fine. Growing up fast." Reaching for sandpaper, he began to rub the small wedge. "We've had hundreds of applications for them. You wouldn't think that, but people want a firehouse cat."

"Of course, because firefighters rescued them. It's honorable and noble and . . ." Her train of thought faded.

They were talking about cats, but she couldn't keep her eyes off him. The way his hands moved, the way he rubbed that slice of wood had her imagining what his hands would feel like all over her. She tried to push that thought to the back of her mind, but it just wouldn't leave.

"Uh, what are you making?"

"A wedge for my hat. I lost my other one."

"A wedge?"

"It chocks a door open after I go in when there's a fire," he explained.

He held up the small piece of wood, about three inches long.

"I always keep one in my helmet." He finished sanding the rough sides of wood. "A lot of guys do."

She noticed his firefighter helmet lay upside down on the bench, its rim marked with dings and scars. Inside there were crosspieces of black elastic bands and beneath one of the bands was a picture. He caught her looking and followed her gaze, somewhat hesitantly.

Seeing the object of her focus, he slid the

worn-out photograph from the elastic, and almost with embarrassment said, "I forgot to take this out."

It was a picture of his ex-wife and step-daughter, and she had the sudden feeling that there was more to the battered hat's scars than just the obvious. Tony had been scarred inside his heart, a place that he could hide, but it was obvious now that he'd been deeply hurt.

"I think it's sweet you kept a picture of the people you loved inside your helmet," she said, wishing for some utterly strange and unknown reason that a man would love her enough to carry her photograph into a burning building with him.

Tony didn't say anything. He took the photo and dropped it into one of the drawers of his tool chest. Then he put the wedge in his helmet.

"Can I see that?" she asked.

He handed the helmet to her and she examined the E–13 symbol over the front crown.

"How come the numbers come off?" she asked, referring to the way the E–13 badge was affixed with small fabric hooks.

"In case I leave one station for another. I don't have to replace my helmet — just put another patch on the front."

"Oh."

There was an eagle emblazoned on the dark helmet as well, and the helmet's overall weight was heavier than she'd anticipated. Just holding it, she was in awe of his profession. She wondered how many times he'd worn it, how many lives had been saved because of him.

"Thanks," she said, handing it back to Tony.

He opened the Ram and tossed the helmet onto the seat. Then to her, "Want to come inside, have a cup of coffee?"

She hadn't expected an invite, that hadn't been the reason she'd come over, and yet . . .

His cell phone rang and he collected it from the work bench.

"Sorry," he muttered to her, then into the receiver, "Hello?"

A look came over his face, a wash of "Been there, done this before" as he replied, "You'll have to call the fire station for that. We're taking the applications over there."

She watched him; his eyes grew hooded, disinterested, and yet he seemed vaguely flattered.

"I know that," he said. "Yeah. But I'm not the only one to give my opinion and you really need to fill out the form. No. I'm not available."

He shrugged apologetically at Natalie.

"No. I don't date women I don't know. Yes, I'm sure." He cut the call short, then half smiled. "How my cell-phone number has gotten out beats the hell out of me. But it's been ringing all the time."

It was no mystery to Natalie. Half the female population in Boise probably had sniffed out his number and wanted a date with him.

"Coffee?" he asked once more.

She smiled regretfully. "I've got to get back home and finish some things. But thanks anyway."

"Another time."

"Sure." But she knew she probably wouldn't.

As she walked down the driveway, she glanced through her mail to give herself purpose — something to do other than focus her every thought on Tony Cruz and wonder if he was watching her leave. Or if he felt anything at all for her . . . and why she even cared. Or wanted him to. . . .

Dead ends. Anything between them would be a dead end, or so she reminded herself. Neglecting to remove his ex-wife's picture from his helmet was testament to the fact he wasn't ready to move on, that he still mourned the loss of a family . . . that he probably wanted a family of his own and would begin one. But not with her.

Never with her. She was so done with that part of her life.

The return address in the corner of a letter caught her attention. St. Luke's B.C.D.C.— Breast Cancer Detection Center.

She slid her finger into the flap, withdrew the white letter inside and skimmed it, her steps slowing as she did.

Your mammogram has revealed areas of concern that need further investigation. Please contact our office to schedule an ultrasound.

That's all she saw, everything else blurred and the rest of the mail in her hand fell to the driveway as her footsteps ceased to carry her forward.

*Breast cancer . . . Oh, God, please don't let me have breast cancer.*

Natalie had an ultrasound on three spots the mammogram had picked up, and while they were smaller than pea size, they couldn't be aspirated and had to be removed for biopsies.

Several days later, she was admitted to St. Luke's Hospital for a needle localization and general surgery. The procedure was done on an outpatient basis and the preliminary results were positive.

She had fibroadenoma, small ones deep in the tissue. They were not cancerous, but given her family history, it had been safer to remove them.

She'd come home by noon that day — groggy, tired, sore and just wanting to sleep. The stress had worn her down and she'd crashed hard, her mind numb.

She woke sometime around four in the afternoon, the pain of her two small incisions starting to ache. Sitting up in bed, she looked down the opening of her top, pushed aside the lining of her bra and gazed at the white tape and gauze.

She'd have scars. Two of them.

The doctor said the incisions were each about an inch in width. The needle localization was something she never cared to experience ever again in her life. It had been hell on earth, the pain comparable to labor.

Emotions swirled in her head and she fought back tears of relief and upset, blaming it on the effects of the general anesthesia and drugs. She was beyond happy the procedure had turned up nothing, but the surgery left an imprint on her. Literally.

It was bad enough being in her forties with a body that wasn't what it used to be. Now she had to deal with changes that were out of her control. She had no idea what her breast would look like. But as she thought the worst, she quickly, and almost guiltily, shoved her worries aside knowing what her mother had gone through with the loss of an entire breast shortly before the loss of her life. What Natalie had to deal with was nothing in comparison.

Slowly getting out of bed and going downstairs, Natalie found her father sitting on the sofa watching *Oprah.*

"Hey, Dad . . ." she said, her voice sounding scratchy.

A worried expression painted her father's face. "I thought I told you to ring the bell if you needed anything."

Fred shot up from the sofa, came to her and put his arm around her waist to walk her to the oversize chair.

"I'm fine." She hadn't needed the small bell to chime for assistance. She wasn't in that much pain, but it was a dull throb. And she was fine to walk on her own.

He brought her to the chair and she sat. He quickly picked up the afghan and covered her legs and feet. "Do you want your slippers?"

Realizing she'd left them upstairs, she nodded.

Her dad was gone and back in less than a minute, slipping her feet into warm wool slippers.

Looking attentively at her, he asked, "How about some soup?"

"Later." She gazed at *Oprah,* not paying attention to the program. She felt a little foggy. "How's Sarah doing at the shop?"

"Good. I talked to her about an hour ago."

Her father had been with her since she'd gone to the hospital this morning. He'd absolutely insisted. He'd had a panicked look on his face that neither sister could deny — he feared he'd lose a daughter the way he'd lost a wife. He would be damned if he wasn't the one to be by her side throughout the whole procedure.

He'd stayed with her up to the time they took her into surgery, made sure she was all right in recovery while Sarah worked with Meagan in Hat and Garden. After school, Sarah's daughters were coming in to help, too. It was times like this Natalie was reminded how wonderful her family was.

"Dad, you don't have to stay anymore.

Go home and check on your squirrels and birds."

"I'm not leaving." Fred sat down on the couch, crossed his arms on his chest. "You look pretty good."

Her hand rose, smoothed her bed head and tried to tame a piece of hair. "I'm sure."

"I'm not talking out of the side of my mouth. You've got some color in your cheeks. You look really good. I'm just so glad that —" His voice broke, cracked. "Just so damn . . . glad you're all right."

Grateful emotions welled in her heart. "Me, too, Dad. I hope I don't have news like that again."

"You won't." Fred wiped his eye, blustered and sat straighter. He put on a cheerful smile. "I brought you something."

"What?"

He stood, went into the kitchen and then handed her a box. "It's to vacuum the crumbs off your table when you're done eating."

Quizzically, Natalie stared at the colorful picture on the outside of the box. It looked like a small, space-age DustBuster. She read aloud, " 'Great for crumbs, nuts and small messes that are too easily swept to the floor.' " Gazing up at her dad, she asked, "Do I have crumbs on my floor?"

"I've never seen any."

"Oh. Well, thanks, Dad . . . I'll . . . ah, thanks."

Fred took the box, his mouth souring. "I didn't really buy it for you, I bought it for myself and I know I'll never use it. If you don't want it, I can give it to Sarah."

"No, that's okay. I might use it. But, Dad, if you don't want it, why not take it back? Where'd you get it?"

"Target." Was that a tinge of red creeping across his cheeks, down the front of his neck? "I can't take it back. I mean, I don't want to."

"Why not?"

"I just don't."

"All right." Natalie sensed there was more to the story, but he wasn't supplying more information so she waited, hoping he'd add something.

"I went to the new Target."

"That's nice," she responded, thinking — *and what of it?*

"It's a good store. But they don't sell the flavor of slushy that I like."

Her father was a Target connoisseur. Everything and anything that could be bought at Target, he bought there. Christmas presents, birthday presents, everyday household items. Dad had his little ritual, she'd seen him do it before: popcorn, slushy, the latest circular and a list of items he needed. It was an event when he went.

"I think they change the flavors, Dad."

"Good. That's what I was thinking, too. That's why I'll go back to that new one. They had a nice housewares department. Do you need anything? Some drinking glasses or silverware?"

"No, Dad. I'm good."

"Are you sure?"

"I'm sure."

Natalie's mind wandered. There was something new simmering in her dad. A sort of spark, a joy, a fluster — she hadn't seen such a thing in him in a long, long time.

He'd had to contend with demons after Mom died, years spent trying to rebuild the emotions that had unraveled upon her death. He'd taken it hard, taken it the worst of them. It took five years for him to regain his sense of humor the way it had been. A year or so later to show an interest in all the things he used to do, even those he'd done without Mom.

Now he led an active life, kept busy and seemed to be in harmony with the world, his life, his surroundings and family.

But there was definitely a change in him.

Curious, she spoke aloud, "You sure seem

anxious to go back to the new store. Any particular reason?"

"No. None. Why?"

"Just wondering." She leaned her head back on the chair's cushion, an encouraging smile on her mouth, hoping he would spill his guts and just tell her he had a "new" friend. "Dad, do you think you'll ever be ready to date a woman?"

"Why do you ask that?" His response was spoken almost gruffly.

"It's not a bad thing. I was just thinking that it's been a long time to be alone. I want you to be happy."

"I am happy. Happy as a clam."

The latter was spoken almost as a reassurance to himself rather than a reply to Natalie's question.

"Even clams like other clams," she teased, trying to get him to smile. She shifted her position and grimaced.

"You should take one of your pain pills." Her dad was in the kitchen retrieving the pill bottle. "You'd better have some soup first."

"I will."

"What kind do you want?"

"Sarah bought some chicken noodle."

The click of the gas range came to life, a pan was put on the burner and soon the smell of canned chicken soup wafted from the kitchen. Her dad came back into the living room, sat across from her and held out the pills. "It says to take one. It's Vicodan."

"I've never had it before."

"You should eat the soup first." His silver eyebrows were bushy slashes above his eyes.

"I will. On one condition." She tucked her slippered feet beneath her, the pink shorts she'd slept in leaving her legs bare. Even in the wintertime she got too hot in bed with long pajama bottoms — those damn night sweats — but as soon as she got up, her legs were always cold even with the heater on.

Her shoulders were bare, the straps of her tank and bra offering her no warmth. The fabric, a soft white cotton, was wonderful to sleep in; she loved it. She owned three of the same shirt.

"What condition?" he asked.

"You go home now. You've been with me all day and it's been a long one. I'm going to be okay, so no more worries." She got up, shuffled into the kitchen and felt the minor pulse of a headache at the back of her skull. General anesthesia did that to her. It never failed. She ended up with a killer headache. "I can manage. See — I'm getting my own bowl."

"But you don't have to."

"I know that. But I can, Dad. Please." She turned, gave him a kiss on the cheek. "I love you. You were great to me. Now go. I'll be fine."

Indecision marked his eyes, his mouth pursed a moment. "Are you sure?"

"I'm positive. I wouldn't say it if I wasn't."

"All right then. I'll go home, but you call me if you need anything. I'll be back over before you hang up the phone."

"Deal."

"Okay. Deal."

She walked him to the door. A curtain of cold air rolled in as he let himself outside. It was cloudy and overcast with a damp veil in the sky, a breeze moving the twiggy bushes and bare trees. The cozy urge to snuggle under a blanket assailed her.

Natalie swallowed the pill with water, then sat at the kitchen table when she felt light-headed. As soon as the fuzziness in her head subsided, she'd get up and eat the soup.

The phone rang and she rose to answer, then went right back to the table while saying, "Hello?"

"Mom?"

"Cassie, hi."

Her daughter's voice was a comfort, and the distance between them suddenly didn't seem so many miles away. Trying to erase the pain in her head, Natalie forced a smile while listening to Cassie. "I talked to Grandpa after your surgery. He said everything went okay. How are you feeling?"

"Good." The answer automatic, somewhat stock. It was very close to the truth. Aside from a headache that was blooming like a firecracker on the Fourth of July, and the slight ache at her incisions, she was doing all right. "I'll be back to work next week."

"Mom, don't push it."

"I won't." Natalie rubbed her temple trying to quell the steady and slow throb, her stomach now suffering with a case of nausea. "I can't let Aunt Sarah have all the fun. And God knows what she'll do with the new line of teddy bears. She'll probably dress them up in something silly."

Cassie laughed, a joyful sound — but also twinged with something else that Natalie couldn't quite define. Perhaps it was a change in the pitch, as if she'd gone from a young adult's laugh to that of a woman's.

"How are things going for you?" Natalie took in a deep breath. "Are you and Austin still an item?"

A long pause greeted her by way of a response, and Natalie thought maybe the two had broken up.

"We're fine. I really like him lots."

"I had a feeling you did."

"I want you to like him, too."

"I don't know him, Cassie. Just make sure he treats you the way you deserve to be treated."

If she hadn't felt so awful, she would have kept Cassie on the phone requesting a rundown on all the details. As it was, she managed, "I hope you're doing well in your classes, Cassie. That's what's important."

"I know, Mom." She exhaled softly. "I wish you would have let me come down and stay with you."

"No. We discussed that. A trip midweek would have interfered with your classes."

"I don't care."

"Well, *I* care." Natalie fought the intensifying pain and light-headed effect from the pill. "Honey, I don't mean to cut this short, but I'm tired." She hadn't wanted to say she felt sick. "I want to lie down."

"Okay. Call me later. Promise?"

"I will. Love you."

"Love you, too."

Disconnecting the call, Natalie laid the phone down and buried her face in her arms on the tabletop, willing the sickness in her stomach to go away. The thought of soup had no appeal to her now.

She didn't know how long she'd been sitting in the uncomfortable position; she might have even dozed off. But the doorbell rang and gave her a start. Lifting her head, she gazed at the leaded-glass panel at the top of her front door.

A large silhouette of a man dressed in dark blue stood on the other side.

Rising on unsteady feet, Natalie went toward the door and could tell immediately who it was through the glass.

Tony Cruz.

Fighting off a renewed bout of nausea, she questioned opening the door. She felt like death warmed over, and was certain she looked like it. But she'd come this far, and if she could make out his blurred image, he could see that she was home and a hand's length away from the doorknob.

Sweeping the door inward, she willed the pitch in her stomach to go away. No luck.

"Uh, hi, Tony . . . it's not a good time. I don't —"

That's all she managed to get out when she turned around and ran for the downstairs bathroom to be sick.

She never heard him come in behind her. He hadn't been on her mind as she was throwing up that damn pill — or what was left of it. When she looked up from the sink moments later while running cold water over her face, he was there in the doorway.

"I came over to see how your surgery went. Are you all right?" His brown eyes were assessing and filled with a questioning warmth.

She talked to his reflection. "I think I am now . . . sort of." Daring a glance at her face, she grimaced. Dark circles smudged beneath her eyes, and her face had a paleness to it. Her black pupils appeared dilated and her lips were dry.

"No cancer," she murmured, easing her way to standing.

Before she knew it, he was behind her, his solid chest pressed into her back to support her. "I'm glad to hear that. So what's wrong?"

"I took a Vicodan on an empty stomach."

"That'll make you sick."

"Will it?" She gave him a half smile, unable to glance at their paired reflection in the mirror.

He was so handsome, so strong and big. She knew she was frail right now, weak and feeling hideously wretched. She wanted to lie down, curl up on her side and be tucked under blankets. Intuitively, he must have sensed this because the next thing she knew, he swept her into his arms and was walking her through the house.

"Where's your bedroom? Upstairs?"

She nodded into the crook of his neck, thinking his skin smelled like fireplace smoke from outside, like wintertime; sun and snow mixed in one. His body was strong and hard, warm and comforting. She hooked her arm over his broad shoulder, rested her cheek against the heaviness of his Boise Fire Dept. sweatshirt as he climbed the stairs. Not for a second did she think he'd drop her. She felt safe and protected, and reveled in the feeling for as long as it would last.

Once at the landing, he paused.

"Left," she said, directing him to the master.

Inside the bedroom, he laid her down on the unmade bed. Thoughts of curling up on her side were forgotten when she remembered the pain of the incisions and knew she had to lie on her back.

She tried to plump up the pillows behind her head, but he moved her hand out of the way and did it for her. When the pillows fit snugly at her back and neck, she settled into them. He took her slippers off, sliding them from her bare feet, gave a lingering gaze to her reddish-pink toenail polish. Then he brought the covers up to her chin, tucked them in at her sides and sat on the edge of the bed.

His weight dipped the mattress in a way that hadn't been felt since Greg moved out of the house and out of this bedroom. Come to think of it, Tony was the first man who'd ever sat on her bed. She and Michael had never spent the night at each other's homes; they went out of town when they wanted to be together.

Lying down with her eyes on Tony, she thought it remarkably strange that he was here in her small space of the world.

"Thank you," she said in a soft tone.

"You need to eat something."

"I have soup on the stove."

"I'll get you a bowl."

"You don't have to," she said weakly.

"I know that."

He was gone, leaving her alone long enough to close her eyes, to remember the day she'd read the letter from St. Luke's. She'd told Tony what the results were, had been numb with shock, and the words had just come out. It had felt natural confiding in him. For reasons that were still undefined to her, she'd kept him updated about the ultrasound and then her surgery scheduled for this morning.

When he returned with a cup of soup and some salt crackers, she tried to quell the affection for him stirring in her heart.

He cared.

He cared enough to come over and check on her. Cared about her welfare to bring up the soup . . .

Why did he have to be so nice? So wonderful? Why this man? Why not someone else who didn't offer complications?

Tony held the cup in front of her. "Can you hold on to it?"

"Yes."

"Where's a chair?" His face was chiseled, a day's growth of beard dusting his jaw and cheeks. The dark five-o'clock shadow made him look rugged, even daring and definitely more real-life man. She always saw him as bigger than most men, larger in body and proportion, and right here, right now, he was even larger in real life.

"Cassie's room, straight and to the right."

He was back with a chair before the first spoonful of soup had cooled enough for her to eat it. Propping the chair's back in front of him, he sat backward on it and faced her while she ate.

"How did everything go?" he asked, his eyes framed by dark lashes and eyebrows that were black slants, arched just slight enough to question.

She licked her lips, gazed at him and felt emotions building in her heart. It was curious how he'd melted into her life like an icicle slowly dripping and blending into the ground — her ground, her territory.

They had been building a friendship of sorts, a mutual admiration and a respect that she had never built upon as a foundation for a male-female association before. She liked that she could trust him in ways she found very comforting. Again, she wondered if it was because of what he did for his job — or was it more that he was a man who seemed open and honest and kind, someone who didn't play up attributes or traits he didn't have for the sake of looking good to others.

Tony Cruz, on many levels, mystified her. But he also intrigued her. She thought he was incredible. Too great for words.

Perhaps she did have a bit of a crush on him.

Frowning at that thought, she acknowledged she knew that she did. And it bothered her somewhat. There was no point in an infatuation; she was years older, he was newly divorced and he needed to adjust and make concessions to being on his own, finding out who he was without a woman in his life.

"Everything went fine. They removed the lumps." She took another sip of the soup, which did seem to help the uneasiness in her stomach. However, not enough of the pain pill remained in her to take the edge off the ache where her incisions were.

For some reason, she expected his gaze to drop to her breasts. Tony didn't look. His eyes remained fixed on hers. "You're going to be okay?"

She understood what he meant by "okay." Not okay in the sense of medically okay, but emotionally okay. That he could sense she needed to speak it aloud brought a rise of gooseflesh on her arms. She hadn't even realized that she had to make such a declaration.

"Yes. I am okay. Thanks . . . Tony."

The sound of his name on her lips caused her to smile briefly. She forgot about the horrid state of her appearance and took a large measure of peace and strength in his presence.

She finished her soup and he took the cup from her. Laying her head back on the pillow, she closed her eyes, then caught herself talking. "I fainted today. The first time I have ever fainted in my life."

When he didn't say anything, she went on, taking his cue of silence as one to continue.

"They put me in the mammogram machine and stuck a needle in my boob. Then they took a picture. It hurt so bad." She closed her eyes more tightly, tensing in remembrance. "He took a picture and made me wait in the damn thing with my boob smashed and then he came back. He didn't get the needle in the spot, so he had to take it out and try again. Took him three tries. It was the second needle that got to me. I think my body went into shock or something. He left the room and all I remember was saliva building in my mouth, my ears ringing, and I tried to get out of that X-ray machine but I couldn't. I woke up on a hospital bed with my feet elevated and a wet cloth on my forehead. I was hoping it was over. It wasn't. I had to go back in the X-ray machine and he had to get that second needle in. I have never in my life encountered such physical pain . . ."

The words trailed, she felt her body sigh. She swallowed. A hand came over her forehead, her hair was smoothed away from her face. She thought she was dreaming for a moment, then opened her eyes to view

Tony's face. He smiled at her, softly and slightly.

"I can't go through something like that again," was all she managed to say. She knew deep in her heart that if it came down to it, she would have to do the same thing. But it was hard to think about. She prayed it would be done now. Over. She didn't want such a scare again. But she knew there were no guarantees about the future.

Nothing was certain in life. No matter how badly she wanted things to be neat and orderly, to eventually find and meet the right man, she had no real control over that particular fate.

"You will if you have to," Tony said, his warm hand smoothing the hair from her forehead, tucking a piece of it behind her ear. His deep voice was solicitous, his words empathetic. She felt warmth breathe into her heart, her very core. He could make a shudder heat her body and cool her skin at the same time. She'd never encountered someone like him before.

She fought off a wave of emotions so deep and so profound, they gave her a shiver.

"Tony . . ." She opened her eyes. "I thought about dying when they took me into the operating room. I've never had a thought like that before. Do you think about dying when you're at work?"

"I never really think about the danger or dying." His expression was dark, emotion-filled.

Maybe it was the lingering effects of the Vicodan making her talk of truths and worries. Maybe it was wanting to know the little details about him and watch the play of light come into his eyes. She wasn't sure why, didn't really care. But she had to ask, "What's your biggest fear?"

He didn't readily answer, perhaps struggling for the right response to give her — either an unbridled truth or a reply that painted him in a heroic light. At length, he said, "I have a fear that something will go bad in a fire. That another firefighter will need my help and I won't be able to carry him out of the building."

She stared thoughtfully, considering something about him. He must be at the gym a lot, lifting weights and developing muscle strength. "Is that why you're so big? I don't mean tall-big, but big like muscular-big?"

He nodded. "I've been in buildings on fire, pitch-black with smoke and it feels like you're the only person on the planet. Only six guys have died in the hundred years the department has been around. I feel better knowing the Brothers will give me a really good funeral. So, no, I don't think about dying because I know it would be okay."

"It wouldn't be okay," she said quietly. "People would miss you."

*I would miss you terribly.*

Where that thought came from, she didn't question. It had to be the miserable way she was feeling — somewhat vulnerable and drifting in and out of a half-conscious state.

"Why do you do it?" She let out her breath in a slow release from her lungs, then waited. "Why are you a firefighter?"

His eyes were an intense shade of brown, his mouth full and curved very slightly at the corners. She could smell him on his clothes, that distinct masculine scent. "Because it's who I am."

Reluctantly, she fought against reaching out and touching his cheek with her palm. She felt things for him she had no business feeling.

She had to get him out of her head.

"How's your lady friend? The woman in red from the Valentine's auction — Sophia." She hoped he'd say he was in lust with her or something, that he was seeing her on a regular basis, taking him out of circulation. Off-limits.

Creases of humor formed at the corners of his eyes. "I wouldn't know. I haven't stayed in touch with her."

"Why not? She was stunning."

"She's also not what I'm looking for."

It was on the tip of her tongue to ask him just what he was looking for, but she refrained. She didn't want to know — well, yes, she did. But she didn't want to hear the answer.

"Hmm." Her response was more of a hum than anything else.

Tony's laughter penetrated the room. "You think too much."

Marginally affronted, she remarked, "Think about what?"

"About everything." His large hand rested on her thigh, its weight measured even through the thickness of her blankets. He gave her a pat, more of a pal-type pat than anything else, and dammit if she was disappointed it wasn't more of a caress. "Just relax. Take a nap."

"Hmm," she uttered once more.

"Make your mind go blank."

"It's never blank. Too much to think about. My store, my daughter, my family . . . my house and my —"

"Close your eyes, Natalie. Stop thinking."

She did as he suggested, but it seemed like a long while before she allowed herself the liberty of relaxing, of drifting off to a semi-conscious sleep.

The last thing she recalled was the woodsy smell of him taking over her senses, the feel of his hand on her leg and the sound of his breathing as he sat in her bedroom.

Later, when the phone rang and it was Sarah saying she was on her way over after closing the store, the bedroom was dark and the chair was empty.

Tony had gone.

# TWELVE:
## CHECK UNDER THE HOOD

Tony couldn't take Parker out to lunch on Sunday because he was on shift, so he made arrangements to take her on Saturday. Kim dropped her off at his house just before noon. Brian drove them, parking his pickup at the curb while Kim led Parker to the front door.

From the doorway Tony glanced in Brian's direction, no longer gripped by the intense anger he'd once felt. There was still animosity, a deep resentment and dislike, but at least Tony kept that tamped down most of the time. It only resurfaced when he had to deal with Kim, which had been less and less frequent as Parker adjusted to her new living arrangements.

"Toe-Knee," Parker said, hugging him.

"Hey, Parker." He laid a hand on her head and gazed at Kim. "I'll have her back at four."

"Where are you going?"

Before Tony could answer, Parker spoke up. "Can we go to Chuck E. Cheese's?"

Tony thought it over a second, shrugged. "Sure. Sounds good."

Kim left and Tony went inside to grab his coat. Parker ran into the garage to climb into the truck and was waiting for him when he punched the door opener.

Stepping toward the truck, he paused, thought for a second, then opened the Ram's door. "Parker, would you mind if I asked a friend to come with us today?"

"Who?"

"A lady."

She scrunched her small face, hair sticking out from beneath a knit cap. "Your girlfriend?"

"No. Just a friend who lives across the street."

"The snow lady?"

Tony smiled. "That's the one. I helped her shovel snow once."

"Okay, Tony. She can come. Does she like pizza?"

"Who doesn't?" He turned the radio on and presented Parker with a stack of CDs. "Pick which one you want to listen to and I'll be right back."

Tony walked across the street, wondering if Natalie would be home. It had been three days since he'd sat with her until she'd fallen asleep. He had seen her once since, walking out to the mailbox in the late afternoon. She had her slippers on, but she was dressed in jeans and a sweater. She had to be feeling better, must be going a little nuts in the house, so he was going to take her out of it.

He rang the bell and the door was answered a few seconds later.

"Hey," he said, smiling as she smoothed her bangs off her forehead.

She wore a pair of navy-colored sweats that fit nicely against her hips and thighs and a plain white T-shirt. The knits flattered her figure, hugging her body, curving and accenting in all the right places. Her hair was down, its blond color looking golden and warm. She'd put on some makeup, not much. Mascara, maybe some blush. No lipstick.

"Tony, hi."

"How are you feeling?"

"Better, thanks." She stood there, almost a little at a loss; he could tell by her body language, her posture. "Uh, I didn't get a chance to tell you thanks for staying with me."

"No thanks necessary."

"Well, I go back to work on Monday. I am

so ready." She gave a half laugh. "I'm going stir-crazy in here. I shouldn't be driving because of my stitches, but I'm half tempted to go for it and head up to the grocery store just to look at the produce or something — anything but staring at these four walls."

"I thought that's how you'd feel. Get your coat."

She questioned him with a tilt of her head. "Coat?"

"You're coming with me and Parker. We're headed out for pizza."

"But I —"

"I'm thinking your coat is in that closet by the stairs." He moved past her, let himself inside. Her house was warm, the air smelling like spices from something that had been baking, and another fragrance — it was the flowers on the kitchen table. A huge bouquet of them.

He picked out a camel-colored hooded coat, one with fur on the trim, held it out for her to put on. "Parker's waiting, so let's go."

"But I'm wearing sweats and I —"

"And you look great," he said, sticking one of her arms in the sleeves, then the other. "Get your purse and keys, lock the front door. We're going to Chuck E. Cheese's."

"Chuck E. Cheese's? I haven't been there

since Cassie turned ten."

He grinned. "Then you're long overdue."

Without further protest she grabbed her belongings, closed up the house and walked with Tony across the street.

Once there, he said, "Parker, this is Natalie."

The little girl replied with a beauty-queen wave. "Hi."

"Hi, Parker." Natalie climbed up into the high truck, sitting in the passenger seat while Parker slid into the middle. "How are you?"

"Hungry."

"Me, too, actually." Natalie's eyebrows rose. "Now that I think about it, pizza sounds great."

"I like plain cheese," Parker stated.

"Well, of course. That's what my daughter likes, too."

"How old is she?"

Tony watched Natalie's expression alter from relaxed to a controlled smile. "Eighteen."

"She's old." Parker opened a CD case. "My mom's twenty-seven. How old are you?"

Tony could have waylaid that personal question, told Parker it wasn't something you asked an adult, but he wanted Natalie to respond — even though he knew the answer. It would do her good to say it in front of him, and say it often so she knew that it wasn't an issue for him.

Plastering a smile on her mouth, she replied, "Forty-three."

"You don't look it," Tony said, turning over the ignition, taking the CD from Parker and slipping it into the player.

"Thank you," she murmured as the music came on, LeAnn Rimes singing her heart out.

For most of the drive, Natalie gazed intermittently out the window while Parker talked a mile a minute. Occasionally, Natalie would smile and add a comment, express her opinion.

Tony slid his gaze across the seat toward Natalie, took in her profile and pensively thought about what it was that made him comfortable with her, made him want to get to know her better.

Driving along Fairview Avenue, Tony was well aware of emotions that were normal after a divorce — feelings of setback, unworthiness, even loneliness. He had tried to put the lonely times from his mind, keeping himself busy on the job or around the house, hanging out with Rocky. He'd repainted his bedroom, bought new sheets, a duvet cover and pillows. The room was masculine now in rich tones of olive, brown and black. He liked it, liked what it stood for. Independence.

He sensed Natalie valued her independence as well, but on many levels they were both fighting long nights in beds without someone beside them to make the days seem fuller, the quiet hours bearable.

It wasn't as if he couldn't live by himself. He had no problem with that. He had just been thinking that he had been alone even when he was sleeping beside Kim. And there was nothing more lonely than being alone with someone. In retrospect, his empty feelings had been building for the past year, and had been a long time coming.

Maybe he'd worked through the divorce issues faster than most because he'd had a head start putting things behind him while he was still in the middle of being married. Who was to say? He didn't want to get too circumspect about it. Shit happened in life. His life was moving in a new direction now.

He slid another glance at Natalie. Her lips were set together, her nose tilted, and her jaw was set in a resolute manner. She was proud. He always sensed she was a strong woman. That was confirmed the day she told him they'd found a problem on her mammogram. She hadn't fallen apart, cried or gotten hysterical.

He had spent the last couple of weeks with her on his mind, catching himself in situations at the firehouse, doing something and pausing, Natalie's words or her face or her expression coming into play in his head. He was in the station kitchen the other day, the guys having put on a pot of chili, and he recalled putting soup in a cup for Natalie and taking it upstairs to her.

That she popped into his thoughts without warning said something to him. He was attracted to her maturity, her openness to discuss most any subject and her intelligence. Comparing her to women his own age, she was emotionally more stable than most he knew. Plus, she was sexy as all hell.

He liked her. There was no doubting that at all. Maybe he liked her too much for his own good.

He knew about the rebound woman a man was supposed to hook up with after a divorce, then figure out she was all wrong for him, move on and get real for something else more serious. He hadn't dated much since the divorce, if at all. The Valentine's auction was the closest he'd come to spending time with a woman for any length of time, but he'd realized after a few hours that Sophia only wanted him for sex and nothing else.

Not that there was anything wrong with sex. He liked it, missed it. But he was looking for more than that. Couldn't exactly explain why. Maybe because he could have sex so easily, he knew how empty it could be. He was tired of being empty, he wanted more. Wanted to feel full and have some kind of promise in his future.

He could have had plenty of dates with women whom he met through his job. Paramedics and nurses, even some female cops he crossed paths with on calls.

He thought about Alisa, the nurse from Swallow Hill who would date him in a heartbeat. She wasn't for him, and besides, he didn't want to get involved with anyone affecting his job. When he was off duty, he wanted to be off duty and not talk shop or compare notes.

That left the bars and he wasn't into the Boise bar scene, although he and Rocky and gone out to a few, but no one had peaked his interest. A hoseman on C Shift suggested Internet dating, but Tony wasn't thrilled about that — seemed like too much of a shopping market for the opposite sex. He'd rather meet someone when he was least expecting it. Find her where he wouldn't think of looking and let whatever happened, happen between them.

Natalie's voice intruded on his reflections. "I didn't think you'd like country music. You seem rock and roll to me."

"I love country music. Just not the twangy stuff. Travis Tritt, Montgomery Gentry, Big and Rich — they're some of the best."

"I like Montgomery Gentry, too. He's a good singer."

Tony laughed, slanted a smile at Natalie. "Montgomery Gentry is two people."

"It is? I thought it was one guy."

"Eddie Montgomery and Troy Gentry. They sing about life to the marrow — to the bones." Tony thumped his hands on the steering wheel in a mock salute. Then he patted Parker's knee. "Get out the CD that sings the bad word."

Parker's eyes lit up and she scrambled to find the case. She got it and stuck it into the CD player. She knew which track it was and the duo of Montgomery Gentry came through the speakers, Parker singing along and getting giggly when it came to the refrain of "Hell yeah!" She put a lot of spunk into it and he didn't mind she was swearing because it wasn't really swearing, it was singing.

Natalie got into it and the three of them sang some badass lyrics on the way to get some pizza.

Once at Chuck E. Cheese's, Natalie and Tony sat at a table while Parker happily ate up all the quarters Tony gave her. He sipped on a cola, watching Natalie look around the restaurant with a lightness in her eyes.

"I remember these days. They were fun times," she remarked, her gaze traveling to the arcade area and the hippo slam. "I never beat that darn thing."

Sitting back in his chair, Tony folded his arms across his chest. "I love Parker, get a kick out of her having fun but, one day, I'm bringing my son or daughter here and I'm going to make the same good memories."

Natalie met his eyes, grew thoughtful. "You want children."

"Absolutely."

A far-off expression caught on her face, and she grew quiet a long moment. "You're going to be a great dad."

"If I have a son, I want to play baseball with him."

"What if you have a daughter?"

"I think I'd be okay with that because I work around so many guys, I do a lot of guy things with firefighters. Kind of like a mentor thing for the new recruits. So, yeah,

I'd be more than okay with a daughter."

"Kids are wonderful, no question." Absently, she toyed with her straw wrapper, rolling the thin paper between her fingers. "I wouldn't trade a minute with my Cassie, even though we had some disagreements in high school that tested our patience with one another. She's the light of my life and I miss her terribly."

"I can understand that. I miss having Parker around. I don't see her as much as I used to, and there's going to come a day when I probably won't see her much at all. But for now, I like to take her out for lunch. She likes it, too."

"Is she adjusting okay?"

"I think so. I hope so."

"It's never easy on a child for its parents to live apart. Cassie was sixteen when Greg and I got our divorce. It was difficult for her, it still is. I sometimes wish that he and I . . ." The thought trailed and she didn't finish it. "It's not that I want to be married to him again. I don't. I just wish that it wasn't so hard for my daughter at times. I can tell she's gone through some changes since going to college. She just doesn't seem as, I don't know — innocent anymore."

"Parker's six and she's grown up a lot in the past months."

"I can see how that would happen."

Tony grew quiet a moment, looking at Natalie and wondering. He saw a very beautiful woman; someone with naturally nice features and a great smile. She held herself well. He asked, "Are you dating anyone?"

With very little hesitation, she replied, "No."

"Why not?" It wasn't his business, but he wanted to know. She had the option of not telling him.

She inhaled, thought a moment. "I live a full life. I'm finally at a place where I'm happy with it. When Cassie moved out, I never really had that panicky feeling of an empty nest. Of course I miss her, but I have such a vast horizon at my disposal." The sparkle in her eyes gave her a youthful appearance. "Eventually, when things calm down with Hat and Garden I want to travel. Ever since I saw the movie, *Under the Tuscan Sun,* I've wanted to go to Tuscany, Italy. To see the fields of wildflowers, smell the salt of the ocean and explore the villas. The whole idea of going just speaks to me."

"It sounds really great," he said, sincerely meaning his words. "But you aren't that old, Natalie. You can do everything you want and have a second chance at life with someone special, too."

"I agree. But I'm just not determined to have a date on a Friday or Saturday night the way I was right after my divorce. One day —" she smiled, a soft upturn of her mouth "— I will date again. I'd like to feel important to someone, to not live alone. But for now . . . I'm okay."

He realized she'd confessed a lot and he appreciated her candor. "I understand."

"Do you — really?"

"Yeah. It feels good to feel like you're important to someone."

"Yes . . ." She spoke with a soft exhale, a gentle caress of a sigh, one that he read volumes into.

She was lonely. She might not admit it, but she was. He knew the feeling, could define it in ways she probably hadn't thought about.

Easing into his chair, he asked another personal question, hoping she would answer. "How many men have you dated since your divorce?"

"Seriously or just had a first and last date with?" She laughed, trying to make light of the topic.

"Seriously," he supplied in an equally serious tone.

Her mouth sort of fell open a little, a parting of her lips as if she was indecisive about answering. At length, she responded, "One."

"How long?"

"Too long."

He waited.

"Four months."

"That's not long."

"It was long enough to become emotionally attached. It was a bad breakup."

"Why did you break up?"

"Not my choice. His. He said we didn't have chemistry."

Tony's eyebrows lifted. "It took him four months to figure that out?"

"Apparently."

She thoughtfully took a sip of her soda, then a crease marked her forehead and an audible sigh escaped her. "You men view dating in a whole different way than women."

"How's that?"

"Well, it's like . . ." She collected her words, licked her lips, then in a breezy tone, professed, "Here's a good analogy. Women walk into a car dealership, size up all the cars, then pick the red one because it looks pretty. Men walk into a car dealership and spend hours checking out all the cars, under the hood, the gauges and the tires before they settle on one particular car."

"And there's a problem with that?" he questioned, a smile tipping the corners of his mouth.

She swirled her straw through the ice in her cup, then elaborated. "The same woman, when choosing a man, will want to check his tires, under his hood, get all the stats on him — then decide if she'll go out with him. And yet, the same guy who spent all those hours on the car before buying it — he'll look at a line of women and pick the redhead without a single question. He goes by her appearance only because she's pretty."

Tony laughed. "So what's the point?"

"The point is, men are fickle. They'll invest more on a car than they will on a woman."

"Not all men."

On a half laugh, she sort of snorted. "The men I know."

Shaking his head, Tony concluded, "Then you haven't been with the right man."

She gave him a glance, a lift of her eyebrow. "Maybe not."

Their eyes connected, neither saying anything. Both maybe thinking two different things . . . or maybe not.

Tony didn't know how long the moment would have lingered if not for Parker butting up to the table.

"Tony, when's the pizza going to be here?" She sidled next to his knee, pushed her weight into him and stole a sip of his cola.

"Right now," he said, breaking away from Natalie's gaze as the server came to the table with a large cheese pizza.

They ate, talking about nothing significant until he mentioned the Idaho Steelheads and Natalie said she'd never been to a game.

Tony lowered his slice of pizza, wiping his hand on a paper napkin. "You're kidding me — you've never been to a Steelies' game?"

"No."

"Why not?"

"Not on my priority list." She pointed at him, and almost in an accusatory tone, asked, "Have you ever been to the Morrison Center and watched a musical?"

"No."

"Why not?" She teased him right back.

"Not on my priority list," he responded.

She laughed. He enjoyed the feminine sound, thought she looked years younger when she relaxed and wasn't so on guard.

Pizza was finished, the bill paid and the three of them drove Parker to her house. Tony brought her to the door, said good-bye, then it was just him and Natalie heading back to their part of town.

They didn't say much — they didn't need to. He felt at ease, was comfortable just listening to the music and not having to make filler conversation.

He pulled into his garage, got out of the truck, and she made it clear she was going to walk back home without him, because she started walking while talking. "Thanks for taking me out to pizza. It was fun —"

"I'll go with you," he said, shoving his hands into his pockets to ward off the chill. It might have been in the low forties at best, the sky clear and crisp.

"It really was fun." She stepped up to her porch, dug into her purse for her house key.

"I'm glad you had a nice time. So did I. We should do it again." He waited to see her reaction.

She gave him just the one he anticipated — a moment of indecision as if she wanted to but didn't want to let herself want to. It was all he needed to see.

He leaned his shoulder against the wood trim around her front door, folding his arms over his chest. "There's a hockey game tomorrow night. The Steelies are playing Vegas and they're going to tear up the ice. I'll pick you up at five, we'll grab something to eat downtown and I'll show you what you've been missing."

"Well, I . . ." She fumbled for something to say. "Don't you have some firemen buddies you'd rather go with?"

He grinned. "I don't date men."

"But this wouldn't be a date," she quickly rebounded. "I don't think we should date because I —"

"I told you, you think too much." He leaned in, gave her a kiss on the corner of her mouth, tasting just a hint of her. His was a brief touch, nothing sexually overt, but if she didn't get his message that he wanted to see her — and not just as a neighbor — he was going to have to spell it out in big letters.

Stepping down from the porch, he called over his shoulder, "You can check under my hood anytime, Natalie. I've got nothing to hide."

# Thirteen: Performance Anxiety

Iris stocked the color-cast, two-quart oval roasters. She loved the new color. She had the same roaster in red and blue in a four-and-a-half quart. She'd have to put this one aside, feeling the need for the green, too. Not that she could cook with two at a time, but the roaster was so pretty she just couldn't resist.

Each month, probably forty percent of her pay check went right back into Target's coffers via the cash register as there were just too many temptations for her to resist. This store was her world, her little niche that she loved to explore and she loved to see what new goodies came in each week.

She liked wearing her red smock, the bright red carts, was smitten by the Target mascot — Bullseye, the white English bull terrier with the red circle painted around its left eye. Whenever she got a gift card, she always picked the one with the dog.

The roasters were showing nicely, a colorful splash against the plain ivory-colored shelf. Her impending evaluation was put out of her mind as she performed the job she enjoyed so much.

Who would have thought she'd end up in retail? She'd started out her career as a court clerk back in the seventies, lasting for fifteen years before making a job change. Her husband at the time said she was crazy to start over so late in life. No wonder she'd divorced her son's father.

The man had never believed in her, not for one day, so God only knows why she fell in love with him. He was Mr. Negative. Doom and Gloom. Xavier now lived in Portland and she never spoke to him, never had to run into him in Boise — thank goodness. She knew from her son that he talked with his dad on occasion, but they weren't close. That made her sad sometimes. A boy should be the apple of his father's eye, but it wasn't to be and there was nothing Iris could do.

She finished aligning the roasters, making sure to save one for herself, then rolled her stock cart to the small appliances-and-gadgets area and took inventory of basic equipment — ladles, pancake turners, hand can openers, measuring spoons, etcetera.

Biannual personnel reviews always put her out of sorts. She didn't know why. She did a good job, always got a great performance review. Raises were given each year and she was due. She'd worked for the company coming up on three years and had rarely missed a workday. She had done her "goal setting," and felt that she had set realistic results.

Gazing at her distorted reflection in the large chrome soupspoon hanging off the pegboard wall, she brushed aside her reddish-brown bangs. She'd been thinking about growing them out. Maybe bangs made her look older. She wasn't all that old — at least she didn't feel old. She looked younger than her fifty-four, which was nice at times. Not so nice at others.

Men her age didn't ask her out. It was usually younger men, and she just didn't have a lot in common with them. They wanted "trophy" ladies to bring to the country club, to dine in the golf-course lounge, to spend a weekend in Sun Valley at a spa for "rejuvenation." Iris didn't need any weekend rejuvenating aka "a one-night stand."

Men in their mid-fifties were moving on in life at a rapid rate, one in which they feared mortality, although they had not voiced that to her — but she was smart enough to figure it out. It was because their children were having children. They were *grandpas.* And grandpas meant rocking chairs and Viagra. It was quite silly.

Actually, she was the oddball in not having grandchildren by now. Most everyone her age had at least a handful of grandchildren they got to spoil. Iris had none.

Her son wasn't married, had no one special to spend his time with. He had so much to offer and she wished nothing but the best for him, and hoped he would find someone to love and to be with for the rest of his life.

Iris took a deep breath, fought off the inevitable uncontrolled pang of wanting good things for her son, then took stock of the knives. Paring and grapefruit. Single blade versus serrated.

She was going about her job, lost in thought, when she glanced up to a cart rolling toward her.

It was *him.*

That man she'd sold the crumb duster to. He'd returned several times since to ask her opinion on other kitchen items. She'd talked up a parsley mill and he'd bought that, much to her surprise, as most men wouldn't have known what to do with it. Last time he showed great interest in the hard-boiled egg cutter and put it in his red cart.

She smiled, rather liked it when he showed up, this being his fourth trip to her aisle while she was on shift, and it confirmed something.

He wasn't just shopping for items . . . he was looking for her.

That thought sent a shock wave of awareness through her, right down to the toes of her Keds. Never in her history of employment at Target had a customer come looking for something that wasn't readily on the shelf. It could be nothing, maybe he was thinking she was nice and informative.

For some strange reason, Iris wanted him to keep coming back. It had been a very long time since she'd had more than a passing interest in a man. Why she'd pick this one was apparent enough.

He was good-looking, with a very nice head of hair. His jowls were a little on the full side, but they lent his face a great deal of character. The warmth in his gray eyes compelled her to stare into them when he spoke, while his straight teeth had caught her attention on more than one occasion.

"Hello," he said, coming to a stop.

"Hello." She felt a curious leap to her heartbeat. He smelled nice today. She was thinking maybe it was Brut. She had a good memory of that particular cologne from high school. Usually it was only old-school men who wore the scent — and she was an old-school woman who recognized and appreciated it.

"I'm just pushing through," he said, taking a sip from a slushy in his cart. "Thought I'd stop by and see what's new in housewares."

"Let's see," she returned, trying to figure out what she'd shown him before and what she hadn't.

She loved the obscure, the little knick-knacky things that could really add to a kitchen and make it more functional. Her gaze scanned the wall of gadgets and she pressed her lips together, trying not to be aware of his gaze on her back, feeling it there and trying to quell a delightful shiver.

"I just love this butter-and-cheese dispenser." She turned around, an item in her hand. "You can decorate your food with five shapes using butter or soft cheeses. Isn't it cute?"

She held it out to him, his gaze skimming over the box. "It's nice."

"It's very chic for dinner parties. Your guests will think you spent hours in the kitchen." She was going to set the box back on the shelf, but he took it from her.

"I'd like to buy it."

"Lovely." She smiled at his sheepish grin. Then she dared ask, "Do you have very many dinner parties?"

"No, but I was thinking I'd start."

For some strange reason, Iris wondered if the "I" was single or if the "I" meant he would have the parties and help a "we," meaning his wife or a girlfriend. A little too late to be mulling that over.

But if he were married, why would he keep coming back?

She had seen him four times now. The once or twice evoked little curious emotions about him. The third time she'd grown more intrigued, had even felt a moment when she thought she knew him from somewhere aside from Target, as if their paths had crossed before but she couldn't place it.

Today she gave him her full attention, and with more than a passing interest.

Iris inquired, rather on the sly side, but she had to know, "Does your wife like to host parties?"

"I'm a widower," he replied quite quickly.

Inwardly, she smiled over his availability. Outwardly, she offered the necessary condolences. "I'm sorry."

"She's been gone a long time, not that that diminishes the happy memories, but life marches on to the beat of a new drummer."

"Yes, it does."

"And you . . . Iris? Are you, um . . . married?"

His question was so cute, so hopeful, but he probably had the same thought as she — a little late for wondering about such things. She liked how he spoke her name. He made it sound like the flower.

"I'm divorced."

"I'm sorry to hear that."

"Why would you be? He was a grumpy bear."

His eyebrow rose, then a smile caught on his mouth. "But at one time you must have loved him."

"I believe for a few years I did. He gave me a fine son and a pain in my rear end."

He laughed. "Well, I have two daughters, so I know about pains in the rear end. You wouldn't believe how messy teenage girls can be. I almost killed myself on electric hair curlers lying on the hallway floor."

Iris grinned. "My son never wore curlers, but I twisted my ankle on his athletic gear on more than one occasion."

They both smiled, a lull in the conversation drifting around them as they reconnected with fond old memories.

Iris drew her spine straighter, then thought better of it. She was five feet eleven inches tall and this man was clearly inches shorter. He might not feel secure being around a woman taller than him.

On a soft exhale, she slouched.

"I don't mind that you're tall," he said, causing her to let out a half gasp.

"Oh . . . well, yes — I am tall."

"It doesn't make me feel less like a man's man or anything. Not that I'm not a man's man. I open doors for ladies and help them with their coats and things like that."

"That's very admirable. Very nice."

"My wife liked it."

"My husband didn't do that for me."

"Then he was a louse," he commented sourly, then reined in his personal opinion and muttered, "I shouldn't have said that."

"Quite all right. I've called him worse than a louse."

He sipped his slushy once more, a flush of color rising up his neck. He formed words, then spoke them in a soft tone as if he'd been thinking how he would speak them one day. "My name's Fred Miller."

"Hello, Fred."

"Hello, Iris."

Putting a foot on the cart's lower rail, he leaned his forearms on the handle. "I'm . . . ah . . . This isn't my usual Target. I shop at the one on Milwaukee."

"Oh."

"Yeah, it's a good store in Boise. They have the slushies that I like. I got a mango one today. It's not as good as the white cherry, but it'll do. You could say I'm a Target regular — like church on Sunday. You'll find me here with the new circular on Sunday mornings."

"Today's Friday."

"I came early."

That pleased her for unexpected reasons. She had never engaged in an extended or recurring conversation with a customer until now.

She merely smiled, was happy that he'd visited her aisle. The items in his cart were telltale evidence that he'd come straight to housewares, as everything he had in his basket was the found at the front of the store — some hand lotion, a Johnny Cash CD, number-ten envelopes and a disposable razor pack. What a man bought said a lot about him.

Fred Miller seemed pretty grounded, stable.

"Are you retired?" she asked, curious about it.

"Retired postal employee who never went postal." He chuckled. "I put in my time, now I've got plenty of it to spend on the things I like."

"And that is?"

"I like to feed my backyard squirrels and birds, and I help out at my daughter's store. I make the deliveries. I get to meet a lot of people that way . . ." His voice trailed, he stared hard at her. "I remember everyone who I make a delivery to and I wonder if they remember me."

Then he said nothing further, but she had the strange feeling she should have added something or made a comment.

"I'm sure you're good at it," was all she managed, thinking that in a familiar way, she should know what he was talking about, but why couldn't she remember?

Damn menopause anyway; it messed with her memory sometimes.

"Is there anything else I can help you with?" she asked, not really wanting him to leave, but she did have that review, and her performance would be under scrutiny — much as it was now. Her performance as a woman, that is.

She felt as if she was saying the wrong

things, perhaps acting as if she wasn't interested in him when she was, and yet, she wasn't the kind of woman to throw herself at a man. It was usually the other way around and they did the throwing at her.

Fred was different. He appeared very cool under pressure, or maybe he wasn't interested in her in the way she felt she could be interested in him.

That thought made her frown. Perhaps she had misread him.

"Yes, there is some thing else," he replied.

And it was then that she knew he was interested because he got this vague blush across his cheeks that touched the tips of his ears.

She waited for him to elaborate.

"I was thinking . . . since you aren't married and neither am I and I was thinking that maybe when you get off work you might want to meet me in the snack bar and we can talk more . . . maybe. If you aren't busy after work. I was just thinking maybe . . . but it's up to you. You can say no."

"Yes." She didn't take a second to contemplate it — she responded in an impulsive manner.

"Yes?"

"Yes, I would like that, Fred." She slid her

fingertip down the price-scanner gun, her thoughts running together. "But I don't get off until six and then I have a performance evaluation."

Fred did something completely unexpected when she said that. He burst into laughter and she was momentarily taken aback.

"I feel like I've had some performance anxiety just asking you to meet me in the café. I don't do this sort of thing, you know."

"Neither do I." She laughed with him. "You're the first customer to ask me to meet him after work."

"As pretty as you are, I find that hard to believe."

Now it was her turn to blush. "I can call you when my evaluation is over so you don't have to wait. I'd need your cell-phone number."

"I don't have a cell phone."

"You don't? I like mine. It's very handy."

"I don't call many people. Just my girls, the dentist and the doctor. I called the rug-cleaning outfit last week to have my carpets cleaned, but I didn't need a cell phone to call them." He rubbed his jaw. "I don't mind waiting. I'll come back at six o'clock, find a good table, and when you're able, you can join me."

"All right — since you don't mind."

"Not at all. I'm planning on buying the latest *Popular Science,* so I'll give it a look over while you're being given the look over by your boss." He took a sip of his slushy and added, "I hope you do okay."

"I don't worry too much about it. I've worked here for three years. If I can't pass a performance assessment by now, then I'd better start looking for another job."

"What would you do?"

Iris pondered that a moment. "Honestly . . . I don't know. But I'd think of something. I'm not one to rest on my laurels. I have to save for my retirement."

For some reason, what she said made him smile. He spoke with a quiet tone, one reserved with admiration. "I'm looking forward to this evening, Iris."

His smile was infectious, a spark of something burning to life in the core of her heart. "Me, too, Fred."

# Fourteen:
## Guns and Hoses

"Aunt Natalie, I think you should wear this top instead of the one you have on."

Natalie gazed at the slinky, black silk blouse on a hanger that BreeAnn held for her inspection.

Sydney agreed. "Yeah, it's sexier."

Her eleven-and thirteen-year-old nieces had come over with Sarah. They'd said it was to bring back the lawn chairs Sarah had borrowed. If it hadn't been six months ago and the weather too cold to sit on the patio, Natalie might have bought into it. But since she recalled telling Sarah she could have the chairs, the excuse was thin, not to mention, concocted.

The three of them had come over to offer their clothing and makeup suggestions to get her ready for the hockey game.

In hindsight, Natalie never should have told Sarah that she'd gone to Chuck E. Cheese's with Tony, much less that he'd invited her, as *friends,* to a Steelies game.

But with a careless comment on the phone this morning during her conversation with her sister, she'd blabbed. Maybe it had been the rush of excitement that Natalie had been trying to keep at bay — whatever it was it had gotten the best of her.

She didn't know why she was so anxious about tonight. Probably because her sister and nieces had gone into overdrive making sure she looked perfect.

The special attention was unnerving.

BreeAnn and Sydney were like miniatures of Sarah; they liked to dress the same, wear makeup and their hair was always styled. Natalie thought it a bit much, but then Cassie had preferred to play sports than take an hour to flatten her hair. BreeAnn was the queen of hair design.

Grudgingly, Natalie allowed BreeAnn to fix her hair and it had turned out really good. Great, in fact. BreeAnn had gotten the layers to curl just right so that they fell in soft curves around her cheeks and lay against her neck.

Sydney was the makeup expert. She wore hers a little too dark for Natalie's tastes, but Sarah had no problem with it. Natalie had to admit, Sydney did a nice job applying eyeshadow for her. When she did it herself, she usually applied two colors, a light and a dark and hoped for the right contrast. Sydney had used five different colors of browns and applied them in layers, but not heavy. The look was natural, yet it was apparent that she had on eye makeup. Her green eyes seemed to pop, her lashes even longer. Lash primer — that's what Sydney said was the magic trick.

Natalie rose from the chair she'd been sitting on in the bathroom while the girls worked on her, Sarah sitting on the toilet with the lid down.

"I think that top is too much for a hockey game," Natalie protested.

Sarah joined her in the bedroom. "I don't. I think it looks great. Hey, the tag is still on it."

"I've haven't worn it yet."

"Why not?"

"No place to wear it."

"Put it with jeans," BreeAnn suggested.

Natalie frowned. "Jeans?"

"Sure," Sydney chimed in. "You can wear anything with jeans."

Sarah took the blouse, held it up over the top Natalie was wearing, which was a plain white cable-knit sweater. Nothing fancy, but it was very pretty and practical to wear inside a cold ice arena. The silk . . . she'd be freezing in that.

"I think you should wear the blouse." Sarah held it out to Natalie and she was forced to take it as her sister invaded her closet. "And I think you should wear these shoes with the jeans."

She held up a pair of four-inch heels Natalie reserved for a business suit. "Those? They won't look right with jeans."

"Sure they will." Sarah propelled her to the bed, sat her down and within several moments, the three of them had swapped out a perfectly good sweater and Doc Martens for a black silk blouse and heels.

They urged her to stand up and give them a turnaround. She felt self-conscious — it was too much. "I can't wear this."

"But you like him, Aunt Natalie," Bree-Ann said, her face beaming. "You have that look in your eyes that Sydney gets when she likes a boy."

Raising a hand to her cheek, Natalie replied, "I do? I mean, I do not."

"Yeah, you do." Sydney brought the blush brush over and dusted a final trace across the bridge of Natalie's nose.

BreeAnn fussed and fixed her hair one last time, then the girls went downstairs to microwave some popcorn.

Sarah stared at Natalie so long that she

finally said, "What?"

"I think you should just have fun."

"I intend to, but you're making a huge deal out of this. It's nothing."

"It could be something. The man was just too gorgeous for words when he was on TV. He's intelligent and, from everything you've told me, he's adjusted to being single in a relatively short amount of time. The fact that he asked you out says he's ready to move on."

"I keep telling you, we're going as friends. This is nothing. He's not ready to get involved. I saw a picture of his ex-wife and stepdaughter in his fireman's helmet. He took it out in front of me, made an excuse why he'd left it in there."

"Not necessarily a bad thing," Sarah justified. "That shows he's not vindictive. He's sweet and compassionate. He didn't have to take the photo out in front of you, but he did. That says a lot. Who knows, you could be 'the one' for him. After all, he gave you those fabulous flowers."

"As a thank-you for *friendship*. I am absolutely not 'the one' for him." Natalie walked through the bedroom. She got her watch, put it on; then selected a pair of hoop earrings. "He wants kids, he told me. I have a daughter in college and the next baby I hold will be my grandchild."

"He didn't ask you out tonight to make a baby with him."

"I couldn't do it even if I wanted to — I'm sure of it each month when my period is late or early or whatever it decides to do." Natalie smoothed her hands down the blouse, still not convinced it was the right choice. "So why invest in something that won't go anywhere?"

"How can having fun be a bad investment for the night?"

Not responding, Natalie sat on the bed, composed herself and took a deep breath. "I shouldn't be going anywhere with him. It's like leading him on or something. I think maybe he's hoping there could be something more. But if I'm wrong, it would be extremely presumptuous of me to blurt out I can't have kids. I can't win for losing. I never should have said I'd go."

Sarah sat beside her, took her hand. "I think you're nervous because you like him more than you're willing to admit. You said you had a great time at Chuck E. Cheese's. Why not have more great times?"

Quiet a moment, Natalie said softly, "I can't afford to get attached to him. I think I could . . . very easily. It scares me."

"Don't be scared."

Natalie met her sister's eyes. "After my surgery, my outlook on life changed. I've thought about it — I don't want to have doubts about things, I want to plunge in and hope for the best in everything. To live each day to the fullest."

"That's what Mom wanted for us," Sarah said quietly.

"I know. And I forgot about what that meant until I woke up on that hospital bed and had a reality check." Natalie looked at her hands and the pink polish she'd painted on her nails. "I don't know what's ahead for me. I want to stay hopeful that I'll find the right man eventually, but I know it's not Tony Cruz. He's at a totally different place than I am, wanting different things in life than I do. If I were ten years younger and had never had Cassie, I'd be on him so fast he wouldn't know what hit him."

Sarah's soft laugh filled the bedroom. "And he'd love every minute."

Natalie lifted her chin. "So would I."

"Then don't let anything stop you. Have fun with him."

"I will, I do . . . Yes. Fine. You win. I'll be happy tonight and he'll never know that I'm giving him up for a good cause — his own future with the woman of his dreams." She straightened and gave Sarah a silly grin. "Now get out of my house."

Sarah put on a face of mock indignance. "How's that for gratitude? We come over here and get you beautiful and you kick us out before we can greet him at the door."

"My point exactly." Natalie stood and headed downstairs to let her sister and the girls out. "I don't want you guys here when he comes over. You'll all drool on him or say something that will embarrass me."

"We would never."

"Maybe not on purpose."

Sarah rounded up her daughters and they departed with well-wishes. As soon as they were gone, Natalie went back upstairs, took the heels off and put on her Doc Martens, and swapped the blouse for the sweater.

She felt more herself, although her nerves were still stretched thin.

A quick check of the clock. Tony would be here in less than fifteen minutes.

She had thought about his kiss on more than one occasion, not even bringing it up to Sarah who would have had a field day with it and put far more into the kiss than she should have.

Natalie wasn't sure why Tony had done it other than he was a charmer and perhaps that was just how he was . . . or maybe not.

Who was to say?

All she knew was she hadn't been prepared to have such hot feelings for sex hit her so soon. But the second Tony's mouth brushed the corner of hers in a kiss good-night, she was a goner.

He was so masculine, so incredibly solid and strong; it had taken all her willpower not to lift her arms around his shoulders and hold him close, enjoying and savoring the way he felt.

It had been so long since she'd wanted to be wrapped up in someone's arms, to have them be inside her and fill her mind, body and soul.

The rapid, almost reckless way she'd reacted to Tony's chaste kiss both thrilled and frightened her.

Natalie hated to acknowledge the signs. He had ignited in her a driving need to kiss him again, and to kiss him fully on the mouth . . . with more than a quick touch. She fantasized about slipping her tongue around his, tasting him, putting her arms around his broad shoulders and holding him close. Bringing him home, taking him upstairs and undressing . . .

Blinking, her mouth went dry. Her pulse was tripped up, missing a beat. She felt flushed, anxious. The very thought of him sent a warming shiver through her body.

She was in trouble. Deep trouble.

The Bank of America Centre came alive with cheers from the crowd as the Steelheads skated out on the ice. The fans had been given boxes of macaroni and cheese when they came into the arena and everyone went a little nuts shaking the boxes and making noise to spur on their home team.

The orange chairs were filled to capacity, the fans wild and very different from those who were regulars at the BSU football games. Followers of the Steelies were a different breed. They were loud, rowdy and always liked a good hip check that ended in a fight on the ice.

Tony slanted his gaze at Natalie who stood next to him shaking her macaroni box and keeping her eyes on the rink as the players' names were announced over the PA system. Over the deafening noise of cheers and the clabber of air tubes that fans smacked together, it was almost impossible to hear any of the names being spoken.

Natalie's eyes were intent on the arena, taking everything in — and there was a lot to take in. She was oblivious to him staring at her, which was good. He wanted to take his time, to observe and study. To smile at her and watch her expressions.

She seemed to be interested so far. Hockey wasn't for everyone. A bit of a blood sport at times. Teeth got knocked out, knees cut, fingers got broken, foreheads sliced by the blade of a skate. He knew firsthand about that one. That's how he'd gotten the scar on his temple.

He was a skater.

Funny thing, big as he was, he glided on the ice as if he were meant to be there. He played on the firemen's hockey team, loved the game, the challenge and adrenaline rush that was different than he experienced on the job.

Natalie glanced his way, smiled and he smiled in return. Or maybe he was already smiling.

A sparkle lit her eyes, a hint of curiosity and wonder before returning her attention to the ice.

She looked great in a white sweater that was very feminine. Her jeans rode a bit below her waist, something he thought was sexy and when she moved, just a hint of skin showed between the bottom of the sweater and the waist of her jeans. He liked that. Her coat was draped against the back of her chair in case she got cold in the arena.

She'd done her hair differently, put on her

makeup a little differently, too. Just when he thought he knew her — rather, could predict her — she did something out of the ordinary.

He liked that, too.

She surprised him in ways that made him happy.

Her cheeks were flushed pink, the neckline of her sweater was low enough to show a slight valley of cleavage but not too much that he could see any outline of her bra. She had a great body, a flat stomach and nice breasts. He wondered if her surgery had affected her, not in a particular physical way, but in an emotional way. He knew of people's lives that had been changed by scars and accidents. Minds were reset to live differently, to think beyond appearances. He could only speculate if she thought she was less of a woman, if in any way she felt less desirable. She didn't look less desirable to him. In fact, she'd never been more beautiful.

"It's crazy in here," she laughed, her lips shiny with gloss and the overhead lights picking up varying strands of blond in her hair. "Is it always like this?"

"Absolutely."

"Wow." She returned her attention to the rink, then the announcer called for the start of the game.

The puck was dropped and sticks started slamming as the period got under way. Tony explained several things to Natalie when she asked. He had to lean toward her, talk into her ear. Whenever he did he smelled her perfume and was tempted to bring his lips to the shell of her ear and give her a kiss.

If she had any clue how much she affected him, she didn't show it. There had been a time or two when her question wasn't really a playing question, and he sensed maybe she asked just to get him to come closer.

All he knew was he was enjoying himself more than he had in a long time.

In between periods, they walked around the arena, nudging through the crowd. He wanted to buy her some pucks to throw on the ice.

She lagged behind him due to the tight congestion of people, and he instinctively reached out his arm, took her hand in his.

She was warm and soft, her fingers curling around him. He felt like the luckiest man in the place. Men looked at her, something she had to be used to, but perhaps she wasn't paying attention.

He steered them toward the puck booth, then stopped when he saw Walcroft wearing his blue volunteer EMT shirt.

"Hey, Wally." Tony didn't let go of Natalie's hand and she came up beside him. She shifted her weight as if she'd slip out of his fingers if he loosened his hold and free him from any obligations to keep tabs on her, but that wasn't happening. He wanted to keep her close.

"Cruz." Wally shook his hand, then moved his gaze to Natalie. "Hi."

Tony made the introductions. "I work with this guy. He's one of our hosemen."

"Nice to meet you."

He could tell Wally was impressed, not that it made a difference to Tony. He already knew he had something special. And he planned to get to know her much better and really figure her out.

"We work the games for nothing," Tony explained. "In return, we get ice time."

"Ice time?" she questioned.

Wally filled her in. "We're on the fire department hockey team."

She slanted her gaze up at him, her lips parted. "You are?"

"Yep. This coming Friday we play the police department in the third annual Guns and Hoses charity event."

"Boise's bravest whip the asses of Boise's so-called finest," Wally joked.

Tony knew Wally's words were optimistic

— the fire department had lost the last two years, but this time it would be different. "We're going to smoke them this year. Rocky's out for blood."

"Well, hell," Walcroft said, "if Massaro is going for broken bones, the cops better look out."

Tony gave Natalie's hand a squeeze. "Come on, let's buy you some pucks."

At the booth he paid for ten of the yellow rubber pucks and handed five over to Natalie. He kept five for himself.

"What do I do with them?" she asked.

"In a minute, we're going to toss them."

"Oh . . . okay."

He kept hold of her hand and they resumed their seats. When the announcer made a call, everyone who'd bought pucks threw them on the ice. The one who came closest to the center circle won some money.

Natalie concentrated and made a toss; it was anyone's guess where the puck landed. She got close to the center-mark circle, as far as he could tell. He pitched the pucks he'd bought for himself. It was good fun. Neither of them had the number of their puck called out as a winner.

The toilet race started, his interest not really into the icecapades, but rather the woman beside him.

"You look nice tonight," he said, his voice loud enough so she could hear him but not so loud everyone else in the row could, as well.

She turned to him, gave him a playful bat of her eyelashes. "You already said that when you picked me up."

"I meant it then, and I mean it now."

She smiled. She had a great smile, one that got to him in the core of his heart. While sometimes he was sure he wanted to get crazy-deep involved with her, other times he held himself back.

The night moved quickly, the game was over and a sea of macaroni boxes ended up on the ice in celebration. Afterward, he asked Natalie if she wanted to go to Bardenay for a drink. She said yes and, rather than move his truck from the parking structure, they walked Capitol Boulevard and crossed the street to the Basque District.

Everyone else apparently had the same idea and the pub was packed with people. He found a table in the back by the distillery.

Holding out her chair for her, he then sat down himself.

There was a bar menu. "Are you hungry?"

"I'm still full from dinner. It was so good."

He'd taken her to Opa's on Ninth Street. The Mediterranean decor and food was something she hadn't experienced before. He was glad he'd chosen it.

"What do you want to drink?" He glanced at the mixed cocktails, opted for something straightforward.

"Wine would be good. Chardonnay."

The server came and he ordered a Corona and her wine. When they were alone again, he settled into his chair, brought his foot to his knee and sat back. He watched her, said nothing until she got self-conscious.

"W-what?" she stammered.

"Just looking."

"Why?"

"Because I like looking."

"Well . . . it sort of makes me nervous."

"Why?"

"Because it just does."

He kept staring, smiling. "You're cute when you blush."

She put a hand to her cheek. "I'm not blushing. It's the lighting from the television. There must have been a Pepto commercial. All that pink hit me or something."

He laughed. "Don't think so."

She laughed, too. "It could have been possible."

"Don't think so," he repeated. He laid his

hands on the arms of the chair, felt relaxed. Content. "Where'd you go to high school?"

"Borah. And you?"

"Boise. Class of '87."

"I was Class of '78."

His eyebrows rose. "She's getting better. She admitted to graduating nine years before me."

"Funny how that nine years just stays between us, huh?" She tried to make a quip. "I might as well keep reminding myself."

"I don't think of it as a reminder, so you're wasting your breath."

The drinks came and Natalie took a sip of wine, her fingers sliding down the stem and a thoughtful expression lighting on her face. "Do you have any brothers and sisters in town?"

"Nope. Only child. I know you have a sister. Any others?"

"Just my sister who you met at Hat and Garden. She's younger. Although sometimes I think I'm younger."

He nodded. "This is good."

"Not really. She's a lot more out there with her thinking than I am, so I feel inexperienced at times."

"How so?"

"I married the first man who asked me, didn't date a lot before him. Now that I'm single, it's like I'm going through that awkward stage all over again."

Tony cracked an easy smile. "I don't look at it like that. I'm smarter now, I know what I want. I have a better perspective about what's going to make me happy for having gone through what I did."

"I don't doubt that. But I've been on some dates that I wish I'd never gone on. I tried that speed-dating service. A disaster."

He drank some beer, rested the bottle on the dark wood table. "That kind of dating isn't for me. I think the best things come when you aren't looking for them."

She lowered her gaze, then lifted her chin. He couldn't read what was in her eyes, wished he could, but her words were more telling. "So you're not looking for anyone?"

It was the first time she'd admitted to being interested him, even if she didn't come out and state it — even if she didn't realize what she *didn't* say was just as revealing.

He grinned, gave her one of his best ones. "If I don't look, she'll fall right into my lap."

Music drifted around them, each looking into the other's eyes. The atmosphere was lively, the lighting soft. Noises from the kitchen were a muffled sound in the distance. People walked past their table to use the restrooms in the back. None of it seemed to matter. It was as if they sat by themselves, alone. Just the two of them.

Something changed in that moment, he felt it course through his body. Knew she was considering giving herself over to things she fought. He couldn't tell for sure, just had a hunch by the way she looked at him, the way she smiled slightly.

They left and drove home, each in thought. At her door, he took her keys and unlocked it for her.

Moths batted against the porch light she'd left on, illuminating the small space.

She stood with an awkward posture and a tight hold on her purse, maybe wondering what she should do. He wasn't going to do anything because she expected him to do something.

The last time he'd had her here, he'd kissed her. That didn't mean he didn't want to now. He did.

Her hair was soft, the blond buttery and golden. Her lips were pink and her cheeks blushed from the cold. From the close way he stood next to her, he could easily take her into his arms, kiss her firmly on the mouth and make her melt.

But that's what she assumed.

He wasn't all that predictable. Besides, he'd rather kiss her when she wasn't tensed up waiting for it.

"Good night, Natalie. Thanks for coming with me."

"Oh, well . . . thanks for asking."

He put his hand above her, rested his palm on the doorframe and leaned closer. He could feel her breath against his jaw, watch the part in her lips. She swallowed.

"Next Friday, come watch me skate. The Guns and Hoses event starts at four just before the Steelheads play. I'll come by and get you about two."

Confusion marred her forehead, a sense of what to do came to play over her features. "I usually work on Fridays."

"Can you make arrangements for someone to cover you for late afternoon?"

"I . . . Tony, I think we're better off if we just stay friends and —"

"Friends watch other friends skate. There's no commitment to doing anything else but that, Natalie."

She struggled, then said, "Yes, I suppose you're right. It's just that —"

"Then I'll see you at two." He pulled himself taller, backed away and stepped down from the porch. "Have a good week."

As he walked toward his house, he pushed his hands into his pockets to ward off the cool spring night, yet his internal temperature was blazing. It was all he could do not to turn around, pull her fully against his chest and cover her mouth with his.

# FIFTEEN:
## CHEMISTRY TEST

Boise Fire Station No. 13 was located near downtown, a redbrick building built in 1951 and remodeled in 1994.

Natalie viewed the firehouse through Tony's eyes as he took her in through the main entry.

"See that Dalmatian?" He motioned to a three-foot-tall, black-and-white-spotted ceramic dog sitting by the front door. "The cost of that's in the city budget. All the stations have them."

"Oh, really?"

"Yep."

They proceeded past a type of library, and then the hallway cut left and right, as well as straight ahead. Tony went straight and she followed.

The Guns and Hoses hockey game had just ended, and they'd left the Bank of America Centre right after and come to the firehouse. The fire department had won, and several of the guys who worked at Station 13 and played on the team had wanted to stop by, see the guys on shift, and celebrate their victory. Rocky, Tony's friend, had come along, too, with a brunette who'd watched him at the game tonight.

Natalie had watched the game with the wives and girlfriends. It felt strange, as if she were an outsider to a small community established with longtime friendships. It wasn't as if the women treated her poorly. To the contrary, they were friendly and nice, asked her questions, told her Tony was a good guy.

She met Wally's wife. She was petite, dark-haired and wore bangs. Natalie liked her right away. They sat beside one another and talked when the noise level permitted.

Watching Tony speed across the ice wearing a jersey evoked a feeling of pride in Natalie. She was proud of him, and of the way he gave his time for a good cause. And very glad she had been there to cheer his team on.

She'd kept her gaze fastened to Tony as he wielded his hockey stick, shot the puck into the net to score a goal. She couldn't believe he could be so agile, so fast and accurate. He amazed her.

Watching him, warmth had seeped across

her skin, making her tingle. Her heart swelled and she'd suddenly felt tears burn behind her eyelids. She rapidly blinked them away. She hadn't been sad or upset, just hit by overwhelming feelings.

She told herself she had only gone to have fun. That that's what she needed to do. Not think things through and get so serious. Just enjoy, let herself be in Tony's company and not worry about anything else.

But last week on her porch, she had wanted more. So much more.

When he didn't kiss her, she was disappointed. She shouldn't have been. No strings attached, no "dating." That's what she'd told herself she wanted. Why then had confusion assailed her when he left her without a quick brush of his lips against hers?

She followed him down the hallway toward a row of rooms on both sides.

"This one's mine when I'm on shift." He came to the end of the hall and showed her a room with a twin bed, a television and floor heater. The bed was unmade; no sheets or pillow. A man's unzipped duffel was strewn on the floor, a pair of tennis shoes tossed in the corner.

"Doug Frye is working tonight. He uses the room when I'm not in it. He hasn't made the bed yet. Probably will sleep on the mattress and throw a blanket over himself." Tony chuckled.

"You don't get bedding?"

"Sure. It's in the linen closet. The sheets are taken off after every shift and each guy has to make his own bed. Frye's probably in the TV room watching *Blind Date.*"

Tony took off his jacket and threw it on the bed. "You can set your purse and coat in here. Nobody will bother it."

She put her purse down, slipped out of her wool coat and red scarf. Tonight she'd worn comfortable jeans and a simple cashmere sweater in a pale shade of green; she didn't have fanfare from Sarah and the girls when it came to getting ready. Natalie had drawn part of her hair back in a clip, selected silver hoop earrings and applied light makeup.

"It's kind of cold in here," she commented.

Before she could react, Tony ran his strong hands down her arms in an effort to warm her up. It didn't take but a few seconds. Sometimes all he had to do was look at her and her skin grew heated.

With his hands on her shoulders, then slipping down her arms, he explained, "Some guys like it cooler, so you have to have extra heat. I don't remember where I got that heater. It's mine. I just leave it here."

"Oh," was all she could manage, distracted by his closeness. His hair was damp at the ends from a shower he'd taken after the game. She could smell the fragrance of shampoo and soap on him.

He stopped warming her up, but didn't step back. Her chin rose and she met his gaze. She couldn't think, couldn't move. She just stood there and waited, hoped that maybe now he'd kiss her.

But he didn't.

And she had to remind herself once more that it was fine that he did not. More than fine . . . okay. She drew in a breath of much-needed air.

"So what else is there to show me?" she asked, collecting herself.

"Come on."

He went down the hallway once more. They passed a closet and he opened the doors. "Stuffed animals."

"Hmm. What for?"

"When there's an accident involving kids, we give a stuffed animal out at the scene. It helps calm them down, gives them something to hold on to."

"Good idea."

"Here's the sheets." He pointed to neatly folded white linens.

Tony moved on, walked past a small desk. "This is the library."

There was a shelf, cupboards, a desk with an old computer, some fire manuals and training books.

"We keep copies of *International Fire Fighter* here."

She listened to him, watched as he walked around the room. She tried to keep her mind focused on what he was saying and not let rampant thoughts about how great he looked get away from her.

He wore a long-sleeved navy T-shirt with Boise Fire Dept. in white lettering across his broad back, faded jeans and black, gym-type tennis shoes. His hair was cut short and combed away from his forehead. When he pointed to a painting on the wall, she focused on his hand. An abrasion ran across several knuckles.

"This guy lives in Meridian. He paints pictures for the fire stations."

"It's really great."

"Yeah, he works out at Gold's Gym. I see him in there every once in a while." Moving ahead of her, he said, "The weight room is down this way."

Seeing Tony in his element, observing the

emotion in his expression as he talked about the things around him, what mattered to him, allowed her to have a better understanding of who he was, what he valued and what his code of ethics was. He had people who cared about him; his character was obviously placed in high regard.

She realized they were more similar than different. Both of them put all their effort into the jobs they worked. Pride in what they did was important, and they clearly got a feeling of satisfaction out of doing what they did. While she didn't save lives or put out fires, there was a similarity in their strengths and in the way they viewed things. Perhaps even how they wanted their lives to be.

Where he was physically strong, she could be emotionally strong at the times when she had to be — her latest encounter with her surgery had really tested her. Where she had the memories of raising a child, he wanted to create the same for himself. She saw self-assurance in everything he did, yet all the while he sought a relationship he had never had before. She knew that about him from how he'd talked about his ex-wife that day she'd brought him wine. He hadn't come out and said it, but she'd read between the lines.

He wanted to make himself a better person so that he could be ready to find real love. She understood this, too. He wanted more than what he'd had in his marriage.

It amazed her how she began to see this clearly when she wasn't fighting against the two of them being any more than friends. There were more commonalities between them than dissimilarities. Except for one big issue. A baby.

For now, she just took in everything he showed her and she let her imagination picture him in the weight room working up a sweat. Or just walking the hall wearing his fireman uniform.

They came upon the captain's room. "I work with Captain Palladino when I'm on A Shift. Just like the firefighters, he swaps out his room with the other captains who come on and off duty. The captains have their own bathrooms."

"What do you do if you're in the shower and a call comes?" The question slipped out before she could stop it.

He grinned, that irresistible grin she had come to recognize wasn't always accidental, but well timed to make her blush. "If we come back from a bloody call or mostly a fire, we shower." It suddenly felt as if he stood too close to her; heat fanned across her collarbone, up her neck. "I can take as many cold showers as I want. We also shower after our workouts. So I could be wet and naked two or three times a day."

"Oh." Her response didn't sound all that coherent to her. She would have taken a step back, but she realized the wall was blocking her on one side and Tony was right in front of her.

In a lowered voice, he went on, "I have gotten caught by a call. You just rinse off fast and get dressed wet and run out."

"Oh," she repeated, swallowing.

The corners of his mouth curved higher. "Come on." He laid his arm over her shoulder and steered her in the direction he wanted to go. "I'll show you the engine."

The garage was a large and tall expanse of space that housed an old red Hummer used for brush fires in the foothills, a workbench area with tools, and of course, the fire truck — rather, the engine.

It was a monstrous thing. She'd never looked inside one before and Tony took her to the driver's door that was ajar.

"You're going to run down the battery," she commented, thinking an open vehicle door would do that.

"Nope. Shoreline." He pointed to a thick

cable plugged into the cab of the engine. "Get in."

She reached for the chrome handles and lifted herself onto the seat. A smile found its way on her mouth, her pulse kicking into a faster beat.

"I've been driving lately," he said, pulling himself up next to her and standing on the diamond-plate platform.

Sitting in the big engine gave her an awesome feeling. No wonder he liked it so much. So did she.

A small hula girl was propped on the dash. She reached out with her fingertip and swung its grass skirt. "Yours?"

"I don't know who put that there. It's been on this engine for as long as I can remember."

"What are all the buttons for on that panel?"

"Lights." Leaning over her to switch them on, his muscular upper arm connected slightly with the side of her breast. She sat still, hardly daring to breathe. "Warning lights — master, light bar, wigwag — makes the headlights wobble — intersection lights and rear beacon."

She tried not to let the smell of him affect her senses, but he smelled so good. He was too close. Pushing herself back into the seat to give them a wedge of space between, she tried to stop her heart from hammering against her ribs.

"Uh, when you're not driving, do you sit in the passenger seat?" she asked.

"Nope. That's for the captain. I sit in back."

He got down, held out his hand to help her down from the high seat. She noticed how smooth his fingers were around hers. How warm, strong. It was all she could do not to slip her arms around him.

He looked into her face with brown eyes, his smiling catching her unaware. "What are you thinking?"

"Um, just thinking how exciting it must be to go on a call."

"Yeah, every time that buzzer goes off, it's an adrenaline rush."

"I can only imagine."

Tony showed her the rest of the engine, the corners of the garage and the duty list. She found everything fascinating.

She found him fascinating.

They returned inside and he took her into the kitchen were a group of firemen sat around a Formica table. Some were on duty and some were not. They'd played on the hockey team.

The room was large and bright with a

patio that led into the dark night. She could see the edge of a gas barbecue through the glass. The sinks were spacious and a dishwasher was located along the wall next to a refrigerator.

It looked like a normal kitchen with a full-size stove, but there were many more cupboards. Some had locks on them. She noticed an ant trap on the floor, but thankfully didn't see any ants. A large plastic container of a weight-lifting supplement drink was on top of the fridge.

Off duty, Wally Walcroft sat next to his wife and Natalie was introduced to the men on shift.

"That's hoseman Burt Schmitt, driver Doug Frye, Captain Henrico George — but we call him Captain Rico."

"Hi," the captain said, a can of diet cola before him. He was a dark-complected man, probably in his mid-fifties, with a thick head of black-and-silver hair.

"What did you ladies make for dinner?" Rocky asked with an easy grin, his hand looped through his date's hand. The woman was attractive, and she'd fit right into the lively group, joking with Rocky.

Natalie didn't immediately get the "ladies" reference, but soon gathered it was a quip against the firefighters being domestic.

Doug replied, "Captain Rico made stuffed Cornish game hens."

"Did you get out the fine china for it?" Rocky teased.

"You got that right, Rocky." Captain Rico leaned back in his chair. "You're just pissed because the ladies at your station only know how to punch a button on the microwave."

"Can I get you something to drink?" Tony asked her.

"Ice water would be fine."

It felt a little strange to have him wait on her when what he did here for his duties was so much more important. She felt as if she should get it herself. Perhaps he read her mind because as he handed her the glass, he gave a laugh, "Don't worry about it. I clean the toilets and mop the floor."

She smiled. "Okay. Thanks."

Good-natured comments and jokes were exchanged about tonight's hockey game and victory. Natalie listened, added here and there, enjoyed the camaraderie and thought this was a real family. The heart of the fire station was in this kitchen, the lingering smells of spices from this evening's dinner in the air.

The movie *Backdraft* was brought up and dissed.

Doug Frye said, "It's pretty much Hollywood. There are no fires in the walls and no way they'd have sex on the engine."

Rocky nudged the woman he was with. "I told you."

She opened her mouth. "I never said I wanted to do that."

Laughter went around the table and she took it well. Natalie gave her a well-intended smile.

Wally added, "Now, *Ladder 49* — that was a good one."

All the men nodded in agreement. Tony said, "Captain Palladino, who never cracks, shed a tear in that flick."

"I think we all did." Doug Frye's expression grew contemplative.

Natalie hadn't seen the movie, but made a mental note to rent it.

Captain Rico reminisced about a prank involving frozen silverware in the dishwasher, when a succession of three buzzers came over the speakers. A slight hitch in the captain's voice was the only acknowledgment of the call, but she felt the tension in the room, the anticipation to see if it would be for them.

"Engine 13, code blue —"

Natalie didn't follow the rest. Chairs were scraped back and three pairs of legs propelled three men into fast action.

Tony took her hand, had her follow them down the hallway and into the garage. She stayed on the sidelines and watched as the firefighters bypassed their big boots and turnouts and jumped directly into the engine. The tall garage door rose while the motor rumbled to life. Lights flashed, casting a red-and-yellow splash against the white walls. As the engine rolled out, the siren came on and the crew left.

In their wake, the garage door slowly wound down and the area was quiet.

Natalie hadn't realized she put a hand over her heart as she watched it all being played out before her.

"I thought I had an idea . . . but I really didn't," she whispered with a sigh of awe.

"I know," was all Tony said.

They went back into the station and he took her in to the main sitting room, a large space with five worn La-Z-Boy chairs lined up in a row. The television beamed a picture into the darkened room, giving enough light that she could see Wally and his wife seated in one of the chairs together, she on his lap.

Rocky said he and his date were taking off, and he and Tony clapped each other on the back, congratulating themselves on the win.

Tony put his hand on the back on one of

the chairs, an old metal TV-tray table beside it. "Can we stay for a while and then head out? I want to hang around and see how the call went."

"Yes. I understand, of course." Then she asked, "Which way is the restroom?"

"Down that hall by the kitchen, on the left."

After using the bathroom, she stared at her reflection in the mirror and asked herself how she'd gotten here. It seemed as if a friendship had been building with Tony for months. She'd never had this happen before. She'd always started out with the possibility of being romantically involved and letting things go from there. This was the first time she'd had a male friend who had touched her heart in ways she hadn't been prepared for.

This was Tony's world, his place, and it had a profound effect on her. She liked being here, liked sharing this with him. She felt accepted in this firehouse, even though not so long ago there had been a Mrs. Cruz who came and visited. But nobody seemed to mind she was with Tony. It could have been that they knew he'd been unhappy and now he was . . . happy.

She'd seen it in his eyes, felt it coming from his heart. He'd smiled at her in the kitchen, thoughts surfacing in his eyes that maybe he was content for the first time in a long while. Those same feelings were stirring in her. She couldn't believe how easy it would be to fall if she let herself. Dared to let go . . .

Leaving the bathroom, she started back down the darkened hallway, then remembered she'd left her water glass in the kitchen. She turned around, looked up and saw Tony coming toward her from the illuminated kitchen.

"I need to get my glass —"

The rest of what she was going to say was cut short because just as she was passing him, he took her hand and pulled her back so she could advance no farther. She let out a soft gasp. His splayed fingers gripped her hip as he brought her to him, then his mouth covered hers in a kiss she wasn't remotely expecting.

His lips were soft and warm, inviting, and evoking in her a jumble of feelings and sensations she'd thought were long dormant, and maybe even nonexistent.

Heat washed over her, through her, inside the marrow of her bones. It came from the pressure of his fingers slightly digging into the soft flesh covering her hip and under the fabric of her jeans. He held her close, yet didn't have both arms around her. She kept herself more captive than he did, frozen still and reeling in the overwhelming physical need that one simple kiss in a hallway could fan into life in her.

Sexual awareness preoccupied her every thought until she had no thoughts left at all.

Her lips were moist from his, from the way he slanted his mouth and took her with a kiss. What she felt was like warm silk against her tender mouth and then a soft nip of his teeth. She sucked in her breath, her arm raising on its own accord to cup the back of his neck and hold him close.

Her bottom lip was more sensitive than the upper and he nipped at it once more, just briefly enough to make her want him to do it again, yet at the same time causing her pulse to beat so erratically at the base of her throat she almost grew incoherent.

He explored the seam of her wet lips with the tip of his tongue but didn't enter her mouth. He stroked the plumpness, the corners, the bow on her upper lip until her mouth parted with a moan.

As soon as she did that, the spontaneity of the moment was over as quickly as it began.

His hard, chiseled face was above her, his eyes dark and intense and presently unreadable. And just as unexpectedly as he'd taken her into his arms, he released her and she felt a rush of cold air swirl around her and almost bring her to her knees.

"Your water's on the table where you left it," he said, leaving her to go back into the television room.

To steady herself, Natalie braced a hand on the wall, her breathing coming in short, choppy intakes of air. She looked over her shoulder to see if he would be coming back . . . wishing he was. Hoping he wasn't.

She had to get her head on straight.

What had he just done to her?

It was more than a kiss. So much more . . .

# Sixteen:
# The Balloon
# Bunch

Natalie Goodwin was losing her mind.

She'd never been one to walk around with her head in the clouds; it wasn't her nature. She was sensible and practical most of the time, although she could get distracted like anyone else.

Right now, Tony Cruz distracted her even without being in the same room.

She hadn't seen him in several days. He'd worked on Saturday and Tuesday, and she'd been busy at the shop. Yesterday he'd called to invite her to the Macaroni Grill for dinner tonight. She'd turned him down, said she had a big wedding to do. At the time she needed an excuse not to see him, to really back away from what she was feeling for him.

Her excuse had been real, however. Just how real it would turn out came as a surprise this morning when her biggest shipment of flowers had been delayed. She'd be working extremely late tonight — probably until one in the morning just to get everything done.

Meagan was helping when she wasn't on the floor with customers, but Natalie stayed in the shed making basket arrangements out of classic deep red roses, twigs, green hydrangeas and bells of Ireland.

Music played from the CD player, and a floor heater kept the space warm, but not too warm to damage the flowers. She felt cool, but not too cold. She let her thoughts go numb while arranging, trying — but without much success — not to fixate on one man's face, the resonant sound of his voice, the touch of his mouth against hers.

At certain times of the day when her mind ran with these images of Tony holding her, kissing her, speaking softly to her, there didn't seem to be enough oxygen in the room.

For a second, Natalie wanted to pick up the phone, to call him back, to tell him she'd have dinner with him another time, but she never made that call.

Smart. Wise. Sensible.

A knock sounded on the shed door and she looked up to see her dad come inside.

"Hey, Dad," she said, cutting the stem of a rose. She wore her apron and its front was stained blush red and a verdant green from flower petals and stems.

"I got all the deliveries done," he said, milling around the doorway.

"Thanks. I appreciate your staying late and doing that for me."

Carl, her BSU student who worked part-time as the delivery driver, hadn't been able to come in this afternoon; he'd had to take a test.

Her dad didn't readily leave. Rather, he closed the door and came inside. She kept working, but looked over her shoulder at him.

She waited for him to say something. He didn't.

"Is everything's okay?"

Fred proceeded to her long workbench strewn with vases, reels of ribbons, scissors, knives, floral foam and myriad other things she needed.

"Why wouldn't it be?" he said almost in an accusatory tone.

"I don't know. You're standing around and not saying anything."

"What do you call what I'm doing right now? I'm talking, aren't I?"

She let it go. Sometimes there was just no appeasing him.

He walked around the shed, looked at a

few things, took in the floral refrigerator, then the helium canisters and balloons. Then he came to stand by her once more. She glanced at him.

He looked good. In fact, he looked great. Well rested, happy in the countenance — especially around the eyes. They were warm and bright; a light twinkle in the gray spheres. He'd gotten a haircut recently, the spot above his ears clipped to neat perfection.

He held back, watched over her shoulder. "What are you working on?"

"A wedding for tomorrow. My bells of Ireland didn't come in until four this afternoon. They should have been here at eight this morning."

"That's too bad."

"Oh, I've had worse happen. This isn't anything I can't handle."

"I'm sure you can."

Natalie stuck a gnarled twig in the basket, glanced at it for symmetry, and put another in at a different angle. She worked on the arrangement a little more, then paused to gaze at her dad once again, feeling unnerved by his hovering.

"What?" she asked, turning toward him.

"I need something," he blurted.

"What-something?"

"Something . . . like flowers."

"What do you mean — like flowers?"

"I mean . . . I don't want flowers. I only get flowers for your mother's grave."

She nodded, understanding. "You'd like a gift for someone, but you don't want flowers."

"Right."

"Well, what's the occasion?"

"No occasion."

"Oh." She had a feeling he was buying something for that woman he was seeing but wouldn't admit to seeing. She opted to test the waters a bit and gauge his reaction. "Then you want something for 'I Love You'?"

"Way too soon! I mean, not that I couldn't ever love anyone again, but no. No love stuff."

"How about a 'Thinking of You' theme?"

"That works. What do you have?"

"No flowers?"

"No flowers."

"A teddy bear?"

"No."

"Balloons?"

"Um . . . yeah. Okay. I like the idea of balloons."

She pointed out the selection of balloons she had. "What colors? I have everything."

"I don't know."

"I think pastels would be nice. Pinks, maybe a little purple."

"Okay."

She began gathering the colors. "Can I ask who these are for, Dad?"

"No." He gazed at his shoes, then at her, then stuffed his hand into his coat pockets.

"Why not? I can tell you're involved with someone you like. I don't mind. Honestly. I'm glad for you, Dad. So who is she?" Her eyebrows lifted, a smile touching her lips as she blew up a small bunch of balloons and tied ribbon on them.

Almost sheepishly, he confessed, "You wouldn't know her."

"No, I doubt I would, but I'm curious."

"Well, it's someone I'm getting to know, and I like her. Nothing you need to be worried about. I won't marry her or anything."

"Dad, I don't care if you get married again. I think you should if that's the direction your heart takes you."

With that, he pondered the balloon bunch, then said, "Put one of those in there, too."

She followed his gaze. "A red heart balloon?"

He flustered, a stain of red working up his neck. "You're right, that would be too much. Never mind."

"No, no . . ." She blew up the balloon. "I didn't say it would be too much. In fact, I think that's a very cute idea."

She added the red heart to the pastel bunch and handed them to her father. "I think it's perfect."

"You do?"

Kissing his cheek, she said, "I do."

"All right. Thanks, Natalie. I'll pay you for them."

"Don't you dare."

"I'll put the money in the cash register."

There was no point in arguing.

After he left, she wondered who the woman was that had captured her father's attention. She must be very special indeed.

Tony questioned his mom's lack of appetite. "Mom, aren't you going to order anything more than a salad?"

"No, I'm not that hungry." She curled the edges of her napkin, then confessed. "I'm meeting someone for dinner at eight."

"Then why'd you say you'd have dinner with me?"

"You asked."

"You could have told me. I would have eaten by myself."

"Oh, no. I didn't want you to do that."

He'd wondered why she begged off him

picking her up, agreeing instead, to meet at the Macaroni Grill. The Italian restaurant was one of his favorites; he'd wanted to bring Natalie tonight, but she'd had to work.

He had a feeling it was more than that, but he didn't push the issue. He'd talk to her about it, though. He took away something from his failed marriage and he realized that communication was key.

He wasn't one of those gamma-phi-beta males — or whatever the hell they were called — a guy who reflected on shit in the shower or anything else overly profound for any length of time. Things happened, he dealt with them. He wasn't a person to dwell. His job cinched that trait for him. He saw things, he processed them, and he moved on. If he didn't, he'd go nuts.

But there was something about Natalie that kept her right at the edges of his mind. He thought about her. A lot. He thought about that kiss he'd given her, the way she'd kissed him back. He knew she'd be a passionate woman. Knew it by the way she wore that black cocktail dress at the Valentine's Day auction. She might come across as refined, a little closed off sometimes but, underneath, there was a woman who possessed a strong inner will and confident sexuality. She may not recognize that about herself, but he did.

"So who was this woman you wanted to have dinner with?" his mom asked him, drawing Tony out of his thoughts.

"My neighbor. She lives across the street."

"That makes things interesting. You don't have to go far to see her."

Tony shrugged. "I would have driven across town to see her if that's the way it worked out."

His mom grew thoughtful, quiet. He could tell something was on her mind and she was working on how to phrase it tactfully.

He helped her along and offered, "Just say it, Mom."

Her brown eyes filled with worry when she spoke. "You've only been divorced for a short time. Don't rush, Tony. I know you weren't happily married with Kim for a while, but you don't want to do anything too soon."

While her words were well intended, he felt slightly put off by her caution, as if he weren't capable of a good decision. "I'm not rushing."

"Good."

"I enjoy her company, though. She's smart, funny, and I like her."

"I can see that." She absently aligned her

silverware. "You deserve to be happy."

He got an intuitive thought. "So do you. Who're you having dinner with?"

"Did all the kittens go to good homes?" she asked, disregarding his question for one of her own.

"Yeah, we made sure of that." With a frown, he asked, "So who's the guy?"

She exhaled. "A very nice retired man."

"That's it?"

"That's all there is for now."

"Okay." He decided to let it go. For whatever reasons, his mom was keeping this one under wraps. She'd dated in the past but nothing had gone anywhere. Maybe this time she'd found someone special and wasn't ready to talk about it until she was sure he'd be in her life for a while.

"Just don't go too fast," he cautioned, giving her a grin and a dose of her own advice.

She frowned. "What goes for me is different for you because I'm older and have more experience."

He didn't agree with that rationale but let her continue.

"If you seriously involve yourself with someone too soon after Kim, you might get hurt. I don't want to see you get hurt."

"If I do, I do. Life has no guarantees."

"I know that." A wistful look came over

her face and lit into her eyes as if she was thinking she wanted a guarantee.

He thought about the possibilities of getting hurt if he got too close to Natalie. A part of him said not to get attached to her in any kind of way, to get out there, enjoy his freedom being single again. But going to nightclubs or bars and doing bachelor stuff had never been something he was into. Meeting new women on the weekend or having sex just for the night wasn't what he was all about.

The last year of his marriage he had lived a lie. He was sick of it. So a larger part of him wanted to explore something with Natalie. A woman who intrigued him, fascinated, made him want to get to know her better.

Maybe he wouldn't like everything he saw, maybe it wouldn't work out. But he was willing to invest the time to find out.

There was a note on Natalie's garage door when she got home at one in the morning.

She had just punched the opener to lift the door when she noticed a paper on the panel. She hit the button again to make the door come back down. Getting out of her car, she pulled the note off, went back into her car and hit the interior light.

If you aren't too tired, come over whenever you get home. I'll be up. Tony

Natalie gazed at the handwriting once
more, noticed it slanted in a bold way, then
she pulled into the garage.

Entering her house, she had every intention of ignoring the note, of not going over
there. But each time she walked through
the kitchen, she stared at the words Tony
had written.

Conviction began to melt.

She was bone tired, had worked a
seventeen-hour day, but the sight of Tony's
note lifted her spirits in ways that confused
her. She should have been perfectly fine
coming home to her quiet house. No phones
ringing, no teenage girls, no one to talk to.
Just the way she liked it.

The very fact that Tony wanted to see
her, had gone out of his way to invite her
over . . .

Maybe it was time to set the record
straight.

The next thing Natalie knew, she was
knocking on his front door.

Soft lights cast shadows on the inside.
Shivering against the cold, she should have
thrown on a coat.

The door opened and Tony, in dark T-shirt

and jeans, stepped aside to let her in.

"I got your note," she said, feeling a sudden surge of breathlessness.

She grew vaguely aware she'd forgotten to take off her apron and she noticed her hands were stained with petal and stem pigments.

Usually she was indifferent to how she smelled after work — she was used to the floral perfumes that came in contact with her skin; right now she noticed she smelled pungently like flowers.

"Sit down." Tony steered her to the sofa strewn with throw pillows and an afghan — a sofa that hadn't been here the last time. It was leather, a rich dark brown color. Very soft and very inviting.

It felt wonderful to rest her feet, to take the weight of the day off her legs. She never sat when she arranged, she moved around too much. She leaned her head back and removed her shoes. She wore jeans and a pullover knit top that was pink and had a V-neck. Reaching behind her, she pulled on the ties of her apron, tossed it to the floor beside her shoes.

"I smell," she said, staring at the green stains on her hands.

"You smell good."

"I don't always smell the sweetness, I

smell the sap from twigs or the bitterness of greens. What do I smell like to you?"

He knelt in front of her on the floor, situated himself between her legs and put each foot on one of his knees. "Roses."

"I worked with them all night for that wedding tomorrow. I need to be at the church by seven to get everything set up." She exhaled, tried to make her muscles go slack, but it was a battle against a fatigue that held her in its clutches. "I'm so tired."

"Lean your head back."

"No, I can't. I need to tell you something." She resisted brooking an argument, and trying not to think about the fact Tony was right here, touching her legs and within reach of her mouth if she wrapped her arms around him.

"Tell me what?"

She suddenly grew quiet, unable to form the words. This wasn't going to be as easy as she thought.

"What, Natalie?" he coaxed. "You can tell me anything."

She gazed at him and gathered her thoughts enough to speak them. "I like you, Tony. You're smart, good-looking, funny — I enjoy being with you."

"I enjoy being with you, too."

"But we need to have the parameters defined."

"Why did I know you were going to say that?"

"Because I have to be truthful with you." Natalie sat straighter. "I only had one child because that's all I can have. I'm not thrilled to tell you I'm going into perimenopause because of my age, but it's a truth I can't avoid and you have to hear it. My cycle has always been uneven. So even if I wanted to have a baby with you, if it ever came to that, you won't get from me the very thing you want so badly. And I am not blaming you at all for wanting a child. In fact, I'm encouraging you to find someone you can have that bond with."

Tony said nothing for a long while. "That's it?"

Baffled, she questioned, "Isn't that enough?"

"Maybe if you're a scientist and you have an equation for the world's biggest problem. This isn't a problem, Natalie. I just want to spend some time with you. Isn't that okay with you for now?"

"But what about the future? I can't be who you want."

He sort of laughed, but she didn't think anything was very funny. "You know, you women are so intellectual. You analyze this and that to death until you take all the fun out of something. Guys are visual. If we like what we see, we screw all the emotional stuff and just go for it. You told me that." He brushed his fingers across her cheek, his expression softening. "Natalie, right now I like what I see. That should be enough."

Goose bumps rose on her arms. She didn't have a ready answer.

"Sit back," he urged. "Relax. Close your eyes. It's been a long day. Stop thinking about everything."

"But what I told you —"

"I appreciate your honesty," was all he said.

And that was that. No more conversation about it. He nudged her back onto the sofa and she lay there, tense.

"Close your eyes," he said once more. "You are so stressed out."

"I'm not that stressed out."

"You are so lying to me."

Maybe just a little fib.

She gave herself permission to close her eyes. To try and slow down her breathing.

With her eyes closed, she grew more aware of her sense of smell. He filled the room with his scent; he smelled good, intoxicating. Like warmth and wool from the sofa's afghan.

"Did I wake you?" she asked, thinking he must have been lying here sleeping, waiting for her.

"I don't sleep in a deep sleep."

"Still, I woke you." She lowered her chin, opened her eyes. Gazing into his face, she said, "You're tired." But he didn't look tired. He looked great, wonderful. So handsome with his dark features, his rich brown eyes that held her captive. She was tempted to touch his hair, to comb its short length through her fingertips. She refrained, trying to maintain control and composure.

"I'm not that tired. But you are." His arm reached out, and he put a hand on her shoulder, nudged her back into the sofa's soft depths. "Close your eyes."

She didn't want to fight him on this. It felt too good to let the energy of the day drain from her. He took her foot in his hand, massaged the sole of her foot, her heel, the arch.

"Mmm." The grateful sound rose from the back of her throat before she could stop it. What he was doing felt so wonderful. Her body tingled, gooseflesh rose on her skin. "That feels good."

"It's supposed to."

"Mmm."

Natalie let her mind go blank. . . .

Tony watched as Natalie's expression finally relaxed. She finally let go and the slight fists that had been by her side were now open palms, the fingers softly curled and unmoving.

As he massaged her feet, he discovered she didn't relinquish stress easily. A control thing.

She'd tried to take control of his feelings, tell him what he needed and wanted. Maybe part of her thinking was right about them. But he'd challenge it until she could prove otherwise.

There was always a way out, a clear path to a resolution. He'd learned that in the fire academy. No matter how intense a fire was, no matter how difficult it might be to see through the smoke, there had to be an option to get out. He may not see the solution right away, but it was there.

Natalie's lips parted, her breathing grew slower. She wasn't sleeping, she was just in a state of pure relaxation. It made him smile.

She made him smile.

He rubbed her other foot, focusing on her ankle, kneading her calf, running his hand under her jeans leg. He slid her socks off. They were a thick blue. She didn't protest their removal, just increased a breath to pull in a deep drink of oxygen.

Her bare feet were cute. She painted her toes. Ruby pink. He liked the shape of her feet, the softness of her skin. She was soft. Really soft.

And she smelled amazing.

He smelled no bitterness, simply sugar. Sweet sugar from flowers.

He watched the rise and fall of her breasts, the way her pulse beat at the base of her throat. Her skin was awash in the muted light of his lamps that burned low in the living room.

He'd bought furniture. Not much. A sofa and chair, a kitchen table. He had to keep things simple for now. The divorce lawyer and court fees set him back financially, not so bad he was hurting, but his salary couldn't afford to refurnish an entire house in one month.

Having Natalie here felt right, felt nice.

He was more mentally tired than physically. He had to be at work tomorrow by seven. But after years on the job, he never slept deep and hard anymore. Sometimes he did if he was completely burned out, but that was rare.

Tony eased himself onto the sofa, sat beside Natalie and put his arm around her.

She opened her eyes, exhaled a slow breath and gazed at him through the heaviness of her lashes.

She smiled. "Hello."

The greeting was simple, but uttered in a sexy-sleepy voice, one that had his arm curl around her and bring her flush against his chest. In the hollow of her collarbone, where the skin was soft, he rubbed his thumb on the exposed area at the crook of her neck.

She was overtly feminine in ways he was masculine rough. Her skin was smooth, like the texture of a rose petal; his jaw and cheeks were rough from a day's growth of beard.

He cupped her cheek, caressed her ear and jaw, gazed into her eyes and angled his forehead to touch hers.

Pulling in a breath, he did think and wonder about her. About them. Where this would go.

But the thoughts were quickly diminished when he brought his mouth over hers and gave her a slow and arousing kiss that trapped his heartbeat, causing his breath to come out in a muted hiss. Heat expanded in his lungs. He angled his head to take her parted lips fully, completely. His tongue slipped inside her mouth, danced with hers.

Natalie's body arched to his. His fingers

tightened around the curve of her shoulder, pulling her closer as he eased back on the sofa's cushions, taking her with him so that she lay on top of him.

Her arms lifted and fit snugly around his neck as she kept him close. As their tongues touched, discovered, he tasted her warmth, the moist heat in her mouth. Her lips were so soft; they fit perfectly next to his. Exploring, arousing, tempting.

His hands slid down her back, slowly tracing the curves of her waist and hips. He cupped her behind, keeping her next to him. A hard heaviness pooled in his groin.

He wanted far more than to taste her mouth. He imagined what she would be like naked, envisioned the shape of her breasts and curve of her bare waist. The swell of her hips, the patch of hair between her legs.

Raw with need, it took every ounce of control not to undress her.

He could do just this. Kissing. Savor it. Her lips pressed against his. Her tongue sliding over his.

His fingers tingled, he felt her trembling. So it wasn't just him. She was affected, too. This was different, he knew it.

His mouth grazed her soft skin at the corners of her lips. He nipped and sucked her lower lip, teasing. She moaned. He didn't loosen his hold on her, kept her pelvis to his. Hard. Firm. Unrelenting.

He lost himself in his wants, her needs. Kissing. Just kissing.

The enjoyment of it was pure and new. He lost track of time.

When he released her mouth, she gasped for breath and he let her go. She rolled onto her side, tucked her head in the crook of his shoulder and laid her arm over his chest.

"You kiss . . . good," was all she managed, her breathing choppy.

His every muscle felt taut, tense — but with a pleasure-pain that he held in check.

"You kiss good," he said, a smile on his mouth. He pushed her hair from her forehead, held her tight and tried to slow his breathing down.

"I've never been kissed like that before," she admitted in a wondrous tone.

That broadened his smile. "I'm glad."

"Me, too. Sort of. Makes me want it some more."

He chuckled. "Okay."

She looked at him. "But not right this second. I have to catch my breath . . . I have to . . ." She brought a hand to his cheek, touched him. "You are so damn good-looking."

"So are you."

"Oh . . . God, no. It's you." She licked her lips, sucked on the lower one as if to taste him there. "You're good-looking and young and . . . what am I doing here?"

"You're relaxing."

"If this is relaxing, I don't ever want to stop."

He smoothed her hair, brought her closer. "Close your eyes. Feel your heartbeat. Remember how it feels to relax."

"Mmm."

Stroking her hair, the shell of her ear, he kept her next to him until the last thing he consciously remembered was the sweet fragrance of roses curling in his lungs, taking him to places he had never been before. Giving him good thoughts to close his eyes to.

Peace and contentment washed over him.

And at last, he slept. Soundly. Deeply.

With Natalie Goodwin in his arms.

# SEVENTEEN: FOR HERE OR TO GO?

"Austin, stop it . . . I'm trying to study." Cassie's plea for him to stop nibbling on her ear didn't have much of a threat to it. She liked it when he kissed her like that, but she really was trying to memorize her notes for an art history test.

They were in her dorm room lying side by side on the narrow bed, shoes off and their legs entwined. She wore crew socks and so did Austin; he kept rubbing the top of her foot with his toes.

"But you taste so good," he said, his breath warm against her skin.

"Mmm." Her moan was covered by his mouth over hers and he was on top of her before she could protest.

Their make-out sessions had been getting progressively more carried away. She didn't know how much longer she could hold out. She thought she loved him, maybe not "in love," but she did love him.

She'd only known him a short time, but she'd fallen hard.

She recalled that day at orientation when she'd first seen him. He wasn't her usual type. Tall, thin, quiet in ways she was outgoing. He had spiky hair, a crooked nose and slightly crooked teeth. The clothing style he chose wasn't what she'd ever pick out. Baggy pants, big sweatshirts. But he had a great body underneath. He'd been on the high-school gymnastics team. That "pretty boy" sport didn't seem to fit him, but he'd done well and had taken home a state-championship medal in two events.

He didn't hang with the popular crowd at school, didn't care about that. Which was what drew her to him. She'd never been one of the "It Girls" in high school; thought they were stuck up, and most of them were on birth control and not virgins.

She loved the color of his eyes. They were gray, like the silver lead of a pencil — expressive as if he could create scenes with a glance, a look. She couldn't define it — but when he looked at her, she melted. Just melted.

And when he kissed her . . .

She kissed him right back.

His tongue entered her mouth, his hand fell on her breast and he squeezed. Then he did that thing with his palm, lower, between her legs. He was the first boy she'd ever *really* made out with. She'd never had a steady boyfriend before and she liked it.

Austin in her life was almost crazy-reckless when she let herself go.

And she knew where this was going if she didn't stop him.

But sometimes it was hard to stop.

Her cell phone rang and its chirp immediately sobered her. She sat upright, grabbed the phone and punched the answer button.

"Hello?" she said, breathless.

"Cassie?"

"Mom. Hi."

"Were you running?"

"Um, no."

Austin kept his hand on her hip, slid his fingers down her arm and he did those little motions with his thumb around her navel. She jerked back, frowned at him.

"I was calling to see how you're doing." Her mom's voice was clear and warm, genuinely interested. It would have been easy to fib about not having time to talk if her mom didn't sound so nice.

"Good. Been busy." Cassie got off the bed so Austin couldn't touch her anymore. "There's a trip to the museum next week and I signed up to go. It should be fun."

"I'm glad to hear that. And your grades? You're studying hard?"

"Yes. That's what I was doing when you called." She slid her gaze to Austin, who snapped his textbook closed, got up and waved goodbye while walking toward the door.

She waved him back, urged him to stay. "Um, Mom . . . I really need to get back to the books. I don't mean to cut you short but, you know . . ."

"All right, honey. Send me an e-mail when you get a chance."

"I will. Okay, Mom. I gotta go. Love you."

"I love you, too, Cassie."

Cassie finished the call, went to Austin. "Don't leave!"

"You were on the phone."

"I got off." She put her arms around him, kissed him. "But I really do have to study," she murmured against his soft lips, liking how they felt on her mouth.

"You can study me."

He kissed her back and the next thing she knew, they were on her bed again.

She wished she had more willpower, but the way he made her feel, it was like fighting nature.

In those few minutes, he had her bra hiked

up and he was unzipping her jeans.

Cassie gained enough composure to put her hand on his. "Austin, no. I'm not ready. I told you . . . no."

He jerked way without argument, sat up and ran his hands through his hair. "Cassie, sometimes you really make me nuts. You know you want to."

Panic filled her, along with a thread of fear. She'd pushed him away again. Maybe one too many times now — he'd find another girl to be with. There were plenty of them on campus and he was so cute.

Sitting up, Cassie put her arms around him. "Austin, I'm sorry. I don't mean to make you nuts. I feel the same things for you, but I'm just not ready to take things further. It's a big step for me. I'm a virgin, you know that. I'm not like the other girls you've been with. . . ."

He took her face in his hands. "I know. That's what I love about you, Cass. You're so sweet. You're just too cute."

She smiled, pleased. Happy. Very happy.

"I'm hungry," she announced, in the mood for a sub. "Let's take a break and go to Chicago Carryout."

"I don't have any money."

"I do. My treat."

She rearranged her clothing, got her coat

and hat, and the two of them left the dorm building.

Chicago Carryout was at Harrison Street and Wabash Avenue, and the café was always packed with students.

"Did you ask your mom about Easter?" Cassie asked while reading the signboard menu as they waited their turn in the sandwich line.

"I forgot."

Disappointment hit her. "I thought you were going to ask her when you talked to her yesterday."

"I told you, I forgot. I'll ask her. I'm sure she's cool with you coming home for Easter with me."

"I need to know so I can tell my parents. My mom's already bought me a ticket for Boise. I can change it, but I think I should let her know soon."

Austin moved up in the line. "Can you change it to Minneapolis?"

"I think so, if the airline flies there. That's why you have to ask your mom as soon as you can. I can't keep letting my mom think I'm coming home if I'm not."

A part of Cassie regretted ditching a family get-together, but how often did she have the opportunity to go to her boyfriend's house for Easter? Never. She'd always been with her parents. She was eighteen. It was her turn to choose where she wanted to go. She just really needed to let her mother know as soon as possible.

Cassie was a planner, like her mom. And Austin's inability to remind himself to ask his mom bothered her. She wished he could be more on top of things.

"What do you want?" Austin asked, glancing toward her, then at the pretty cashier. "Hey," he said to the girl, giving her a grin.

Cassie held off the stab of jealousy that pricked her. He was always doing this. He was a hopeless flirt, and in front of her, too.

"Hi," the clerk replied, her lip gloss shiny and sexy. "I know you. We have the same poetry workshop class."

"Oh, yeah. I've seen you. What's your name?"

But the clerk didn't have to reply. Austin stared at her name badge that just happened to be right over her breast.

"Candi," he said with a smile. "You'll have to say hi to me."

"Okay." She giggled and Cassie wanted to smack her. She encircled her hand around Austin's upper arm, keeping him close.

They placed their orders, Cassie suddenly not so hungry for a turkey sandwich anymore.

"Do you want this for here or to go?" the clerk asked, looking only at Austin and not her.

"For here," Austin replied.

"To go," Cassie said, gazing into Austin's eyes. "I want to go back to my dorm room and we can be alone."

He shrugged and she paid for their lunch.

While they waited for the sandwiches to be made, Cassie grew quiet and thoughtful. There were times when she wasn't sure about Austin, if he was really the right person for her. Other times, she was very lonely at school and she was so glad to have him in her life.

Her mood grew sullen.

Outside, the weather was bleak like a water-faded, old newspaper. It was windy, too. That wind always had so much bite to it, it could take a person's ears off if they didn't cover them. While Idaho winters weren't that great, Chicago winters were the worst. The streets were always littered with sheets of paper and debris that spilled from office doorways and then were sucked onto the streets. Chaos.

*Chaos.* A good word. She'd write that in her journal tonight.

Her first year in college felt like chaos at times.

"Austin," she said, snuggling next to him and feeling those butterfly feelings stir in her stomach. "Do you love me?"

"Of course. I tell you, don't I?"

"Yes . . . but I mean it — do you *really* love me?"

"I do. I mean it, Cassie. I love you."

Relief poured through her body, her hands and legs and toes. She needed to hear that, needed the reassurance that he was only interested in her.

"I love you, too," she said, but questioned just how deeply. How real. She had nothing to compare it to.

Austin Mably was her first big crush.

# EIGHTEEN:
## SEX BED

Tony had never been to the Boise Art Museum. Just hadn't been on his list of places he felt like visiting. It wasn't what he expected. A little more urban, maybe.

The floors were colored and lacquered concrete, a small gift shop was to the right of the main entry. Exhibition rooms veered left and right, all full of art.

The exhibit was flowers in still life by various artists.

"This one is great," Natalie said, walking several feet ahead of him. She kept her tone lowered at a respectful volume. He felt as if he were in a library or the Catholic church during mass.

"I like the pastel color palette," she commented while studying the large painting. "And I like the arrangement. It's not symmetrical. I have to try and not do that so much."

"Why?"

"Because abstract can be better."

He was truly clueless. "Why?"

"Just because it tricks the eye. You don't want everything to be just right, so perfect."

He shrugged, moved along and viewed the other paintings. The side room wasn't lit real well, the walls making him feel closed in. He said he'd come to this, to see a piece of her "world," but an art museum wasn't his thing. While it didn't turn his crank, he respected Natalie enough not to tell her that this place went unappreciated on a guy like him. Give him a beer and a crowd; he preferred loud sporting events or anything outdoors.

"That one's nice," he said, just to say something positive.

A sunflower painting was illuminated by a light beaming above it. There were some nice strokes of paint on the canvas, the yellow and gold colors bright. Other than that, it was just a vase of sunflowers.

"I like it, too." She gave it her attention.

He gave her his attention.

She wore jeans and a thick sweater, and a coat that was unbuttoned. He liked her when she was carefree. That was one good thing to say about the art museum. Natalie Goodwin felt comfortable here. She walked with a casualness, an ease he didn't normally see in her. The art exhibit brought out her smile, sometimes laughter or thoughtful words.

She was enjoying herself.

He appreciated that.

They'd agreed not to decide anything about their relationship and just continue as friends who did things together. It was an easy compromise for him to do — if one called it a compromise. He'd already made up his mind he was only going to date women who had the potential to be his best friend. Kim had never been that for him. He'd never been able to really go to her with things that were deep issues for him. He vowed never to have that isolated feeling again.

They wandered the rest of the halls, walking into a large room with a sculpture of metal. He couldn't see the attraction to it, but she stood and studied it for a long while.

He studied her.

She'd pulled her hair back in a claw, pieces falling along her cheeks and neck. Diamond stud earrings sparkled from her earlobes. When she'd turn her head, they'd catch the light. Her eyes seemed greener, her lips were pinker, fuller.

He recalled sleeping next to her on his sofa. They'd woken up in the early hours of morning when the newspaper hit the front door around 4:00 a.m. He knew right away who he was with, where he was. His sleep had been surprisingly deep and sound. He woke with a clarity about his senses and was glad to have this woman in his arms. She smelled great, too, was so soft and warm.

He'd felt himself need her, want her. His body stirred slowly, like a drug that came to the surface of his senses. There were things about her that made him desire more than a casual friendship. Her independence and strength, the way she smiled and looked at him.

When he was being a realist, he was aware that she wanted different things at her age and was at a different place. But boundaries were like firebreaks. Sometimes a spark leaped over them and started a fire. Issues that seemed to be hurdles could look differently suddenly. Sometimes seeing too much wasn't the best way to deal with something. Sometimes going by feel, relying on a sense of touch, was better. It was how he was trained. Love didn't come with instructions.

When they'd finished looking at the exhibit, she buttoned her coat. "Do you want to get something to eat?"

"I was hungry an hour ago," he said before he could stop himself.

"You didn't like the show?"

He held the door open for her. "It wasn't that I didn't like it, it's just not something that I would do on my own."

She smiled at him. "And I wouldn't have gone to a hockey game on my own."

"So we're even."

"But I liked the hockey game. You didn't enjoy this."

"I didn't say I didn't like it." They walked through the barren rose garden to the parking lot. "I just didn't find the same appeal in it as you did. I thought some of the paintings were really good."

"They were."

"So there you go."

He unlocked the Ram and opened the door. She got up inside, and he still liked how she did that. She put a hand on the grip and pulled her body up to climb in. He got a nice view of her behind.

Closing the door, he went around to the driver's side. Once behind the wheel, he asked, "Where do you want to eat?"

"Anywhere. I'm starved."

"Cobby's?"

"Perfect."

He took the side streets from downtown to Chinden and they didn't have to drive far to the landmark sandwich shop. Once inside they ordered, then got a table. He ate, thinking it felt really comfortable to sit here with her.

She asked, "What will you do at work tomorrow?"

"What do you mean?"

"I mean — like, if there's no call to go on. Do you watch daytime TV?"

"I only do that when I'm at home doing laundry," he laughed. "I was a former *Days of Our Lives* watcher. Don't tell anyone."

A smile curved the corners of her mouth. "Okay."

He swallowed a bite of sandwich, wiped his hands on a paper napkin and said, "I get there a little early, talk to the guy I'm relieving. I ask how the day before went. I'll wash the engine, make more coffee if the pot's empty. I don't drink a lot of coffee, though."

"Why not?"

"Just don't need it."

"Do you have a hard time getting up?"

"Snooze button, babe."

She laughed, then her expression grew more serious. "You woke up just fine the other morning."

"Because I wasn't alone."

She gazed down at the sandwich paper, then at him, a hesitant smile touching her mouth. He would have liked to know what she was thinking in that head of hers. Probably too much. She worked too hard to analyze things. She didn't do herself any favors.

"I liked having you sleep next to me."

She said nothing, and he sensed there was more on her mind than she let on. He'd had that feeling for the last thirty minutes, even though she'd tried hard not to show her preoccupation.

"I liked it," he reiterated. "I like having you around. I like kissing you even more."

He leaned in and gave her a kiss on the mouth. Her lips were soft and sexy; they moved beneath his as he traced hers with the tip of his tongue, a light and easy stroke. He felt her shiver when he pulled back.

She licked her lips, said nothing.

"Natalie, you should just give up the idea that this is bad. We can have good times."

"Is that what you want?" she asked, a frown on her brows.

"Your meaning?"

"Good times . . . fun. Nothing else. Just a . . . you know. Just fun."

Folding his arms over his chest, he carefully chose his next words. "No. This will sound conceited and I don't mean it to but, on any given day, I run into women who would sleep with me. I don't go there. That's not who I am. I don't need to put a notch on my bedpost just to prove to myself I'm a man. I'm just me. Just Tony."

She quietly looked at him and he could see she was trying to figure out how to say something.

"Just say it," he prodded. "You've had something on your mind all morning. I know you enough now to be able to tell."

She came out with it. "Are we going to have an affair?"

"An affair?"

"Sex. No strings attached."

He pulled in a breath. "Is that what you want to call it?"

"I don't think there's anything else we can call it."

"How about a relationship? I thought we agreed to be friends."

"That won't work and you know it."

"Why not?"

A nervous reaction, she tapped the table with her fingertip. "All you have to do is look at me and I forget about being your friend. I want to be your lover. We're both mature adults with level heads. If we go into this with our eyes wide open, I think an affair would be better."

"You make it sound very cut-and-dried."

"Wouldn't it be?"

"I don't think so." Tony balled the leftover paper from his sandwich and finished his beer. "So you're saying you just want to have sex?"

She contemplated a response, her green eyes filled with something he couldn't quite define. Then it hit him — lust. She'd revealed her lust for him. It excited him.

Pulling in a breath, she said, "I want to be your friend, but I also want more than that so long as we're both clear that we don't get involved in other ways. Namely, doing something stupid like falling in love or anything that revolves around feelings that could get hurt."

"So you think you can be my friend, only sleep with me, and not fall in love with me?"

Once more, she licked her lips. "Yes. I do."

Everything in the Victoria's Secret store was pink. Pink walls, pink displays, pink panties, pink bras, pink hangers, pink sexy teddies and pink pajamas. It must have been Pink Day in Vicky's.

"I can't believe I said what I said to him." Natalie wanted to blot out the world, forget her discussion with Tony at Cobby's.

"Well, frankly," Sarah replied, "I can't believe it, either. You've come a long way."

Natalie frowned. "So you're encouraging me to just sleep with him?"

"I didn't say that." Sarah looked at a bra with sparkles sewn on the cups. "But I do think that if you are intimate with him, you'll let go of all these hang-ups you have about him being younger. You'll probably swear off men in their forties."

"If things don't work out in a cut-and-dried sex situation, I'm swearing off men. Period." Natalie bit her lip. "Sarah, do you think I'm ready for just *sex?*" That last word squeaked out between her lips. Even she had a hard time saying she was going into this for sexual pleasure and that was all. How dumb did she think she was?

Actually, she didn't think herself dumb at all. She considered herself very reasonable and adult, which was why approaching this thing on an affair-only basis sounded so sensible. She liked him, he liked her. There was no reason they couldn't like each other naked. In bed.

"I don't think any woman is just ready for sex. We all think we are," Sarah said, holding up the bra to herself, then checking the price tag. "We want to get paid like men, we want to be accepted like men and we think we want to have causal sex like men.

But it's crap. We want love and romance. Not just sex. So, in my opinion you're setting yourself up to either A — fall in love with him, or B — get hurt. Or maybe you'll fool us all and choose C — which is multiple orgasms and still stay friends with him. Although I think the likelihood of that is remote. And I'd hate for 'B' to happen after the damage that Michael did. So I'd suggest 'A' — falling in love with the fireman."

"That's absurd."

"Is it?" Sarah put the bra back. "Then why do you get hearts in your eyes when you talk about him?"

"I do not."

"I think you should buy something that will just completely blow him away. He won't know what hit him. Remember, you're representing the over-forty crowd and you've got the body to pull it off." Sarah moved along to the teddies.

"I didn't come in here to buy sexy. I came in here to buy something I think is tastefully sensual."

This time Sarah frowned. "If you want to seduce him with tastefully sensual, I have a pair of bunny slippers and a short nightie."

If the suggestion hadn't provided such a visual, Natalie would have kept her thoughts to herself. Instead she couldn't help laughing. Then she gave her sister a hug. "You're my best friend, Sarah."

Sarah hugged her back. "Of course I am. Which is why I won't steer you wrong. Come on, let's see what this place has."

Sarah and Natalie lifted up thongs and compared the cuts.

"I couldn't wear something like this *before* I had kids," Sarah said on a sigh while looking at the two-inch triangle of sheer fabric and thin elastic strings. "You'd have to be a Barbie in order to fit into it."

Natalie examined the pair she held. "This one's for Skipper."

"What size is that?"

"Medium."

"Are you sure it's not extra small?"

"Positive."

Sarah's eyebrows rose. "I guess we're at the wrong pantie display. Even I'm intimidated."

"That says a lot!" Natalie put the underwear down and they made their way to the back of the store.

She couldn't believe she was in here, looking for something sexy to buy. An involuntary shudder washed through her when she thought back to yesterday. And worse yet, couldn't believe that she'd actually said what she'd said to Tony about having an . . . affair.

Had she been crazy to say that?

She'd been conscious of him the entire day at the museum. Where he stood, how close he was to her. How he smelled, what he said, how he said it. The way his eyes focused on a painting, then on her as if she were the only thing in the room that mattered.

He took her breath away, made her heart beat faster. It was crazy.

Whenever she was around him, she lost her common sense, and in its place, every sense she possessed was heightened. She knew when he was behind her, even if it was a foot away. She could feel him. There had been many times she'd wanted to turn around, take him in her arms and just hold him, have him hold her. Stroke her hair from her forehead the way he had the morning she'd woken up with him.

She couldn't believe she'd spent the night on his sofa. She'd been so tired she'd just drifted off. Every muscle in her body had relaxed from the foot rub he'd given her, then when he'd put his mouth on hers . . .

Bliss.

That's the only way she could describe it.

She'd never been kissed the way Tony

Cruz kissed her.

Natalie struggled to maintain a level head, a reasonable perspective. But she couldn't. Whenever he was near her, whenever she even thought about him, reason fled.

It was stupid to suggest just sex. What had she been thinking?

She'd been thinking about sex.

What was wrong with a woman her age having sex just because she wanted to? It wasn't as if she'd be irresponsible.

Her eyes were wide open, unlike before with Michael when she so desperately wanted a relationship after her divorce. She could disconnect from anything emotional with Tony — because she wouldn't allow herself to be emotional.

No strings attached.

When she'd said that, she'd seen a shadow of something come over his face. What had it been . . . ? Disappointment perhaps? No . . . a struggle between two issues. That was it. His *want* to have sex and something else that ran deeper. His want of . . . her.

She knew it. He'd all but said it. And that want wasn't just for intimacy. It was a want of the emotional. Well, she couldn't do it. She knew too well that he deserved someone younger, someone who wanted the things he wanted. He might think that by looking the other way things would be all right. But they wouldn't.

She was still who she was . . . he was still who he was.

At least she'd put the baby issue out on the table and he couldn't say she hadn't been up front about it.

Even for all her honesty, she saw that look in his eyes. He desired her. She knew that.

It made her feel good to know that at her age she was desirable to a man nine years younger. Which is why she didn't want to disappoint him. So she was determined to buy something sensual, something that would make his mouth drop open.

She couldn't remember the last time she'd made a purchase in this store.

"What about this?" Sarah held up a bra and pantie set.

A black feathered-and-jeweled skimpy set was dangled in front of her.

"Not what I had in mind. I need more coverage."

Sarah homed in on a pair of fuzzy mules. "Oh, my God, look at these. Steve would just die. I wonder if they have my size? I'm going to ask."

Sarah wandered off to get help and Natalie was left to her own devices. Which was fine with her. She wanted to pick something that suited her own tastes, but it had to look good on her body. She needed breast support . . . which was a different issue entirely.

She wasn't real comfortable yet with the way her breast looked, and wondered if she'd ever be comfortable with it. She had two slashes for scars, not that big, but still — they marred the ivory skin of her breast and it did bother her a little to think about Tony seeing them. Which is why she wanted to buy something that had a built-in bra, something that looked so great he wouldn't want to take it off on top. At least that was her hope.

Natalie picked a few things, took them to the dressing room with her, and once inside the cubicle, she started the daunting task of trying on.

Two women in the next dressing room were talking, and while Natalie's subconscious had been focused on how she looked in her first selection, she grew aware of what the women were saying.

"This one looks better."

"No, it doesn't. It's cotton."

"But it's expensive cotton. I like to sleep in a cotton T-shirt and cotton shorts."

"That's fine. I like sleeping in cotton, too, when I'm sleeping in my bed. But when I want to spend the night with Chris, I wear silk for a sex bed."

*Sex bed.*

Natalie paused. That's exactly what she was buying something for. A sex bed. . . .

Gazing at her reflection, her hands rose to cup her burning cheeks as she studied her face and the expression that greeted her. Who was she? She was forty-three and trying on skimpy teddies for a thirty-four-year-old fireman's sex bed.

She swallowed, smiled. Then thought — yeah, that's what she was doing and it felt really good. It was exciting . . . promising. Wicked.

"But if I buy this for a sex bed, it's a lot of pressure," one of the women continued.

"Pressure for what?"

"An orgasm."

"Oh. Well, you can always fake one if you have to."

"Wouldn't he be able to tell?"

The woman heaved a sigh. "Fake orgasms, fake phone numbers. You give it to the guy because that's what he wants to hear."

Natalie began dressing in a black lace teddy and thought about Tony and how he was built, his strength and confidence. The way his lips felt on hers and the way he touched her.

With a certainty she would have bet

money on, Natalie wouldn't be faking anything.

# NINETEEN:
# REALITY CHECK

"Her name is Iris," Fred Miller announced over dessert.

The weekly Sunday dinner at his home quickly quieted down as he waited for the onslaught of questions. And he knew there would be a hell of a lot of them.

Sarah was the first to ask, "Where did you meet her?"

"Target, sort of."

"I knew it," Natalie replied, bright-eyed, as if she'd just won the lottery. "You got all bent out of shape about Target with me that day you gave me the crumb duster."

"I did no such thing."

Steve, his son-in-law, rose from his chair, reached across BreeAnn and shook his hand. "Good for you, Fred."

Fred took Steve's hand, thinking it a bit stupid. So what was the big deal? He had a woman he was dating and he liked her. No reason to take out a headline in the damn newspaper.

It had been increasingly more difficult to keep his feelings under wraps with his two daughters so suspicious of his every cough or sneeze.

He and Iris had been enjoying time together on her days off. They'd gone to the zoo yesterday. He'd forgotten how much he liked the Boise zoo. Afterward, they'd walked through the park holding hands like two lovebirds. It felt good to be out with her, look over and see her in the passenger seat of his Elantra with the sunroof open, wind in her hair.

"Did she like the balloons?" Natalie asked, ignoring the bowl of vanilla ice cream in front of her.

"She did. Very much."

Natalie smiled.

Sydney chimed in, "What balloons?"

Sarah supplied the explanation — Natalie must have blabbed. Why wasn't he surprised? "Grandpa got some pretty, round balloons and a red heart one and he gave them to Iris."

"Why do you like Iris, Grandpa?" Bree-Ann scooped her ice-cream bowl clean.

"Because I just do." He felt his cheeks grow hot, red. He didn't like the scrutiny. Scraping his chair away from the table, he went to put away the dishes.

While it wasn't as hard as he thought to confess his love interest, he felt a sense of guilt just the same. Guilt for bringing a new woman's name into the family-dinner conversation. God forgive him.

But Fred was alive. And he wanted to live it with someone who put a skip in his step.

Iris was the bright spot of his day.

"We're glad you met her, Dad," Sarah said, coming to stand next to him and rinse her plate. "I'm not surprised she shops at Target."

"She works there."

Natalie joined them. "Really?"

"Housewares."

"That explains the new kitchen gadgets."

Fred sheepishly shrugged. "I can't resist."

"Her or the gadgets?" Sarah teased.

Putting hands on her hips, Natalie said, "Well, I think we should meet her. I want you to invite her for Easter dinner at my house."

Fred felt an instant's panic. He'd just barely gotten over admitting he had a thing for Iris. Now they wanted him to bring her into their fold? His daughters might question her to death and scare her off.

He begged off. "I'm sure she has other plans."

"She might not." Natalie held firm. "Ask her."

"Maybe."

"Dad, please." Sarah snuggled up next to him. "We want to meet her."

"But Easter is for family." He rejected the idea, didn't want things to get mucked up too soon.

"Oh, good grief," Natalie said. "I invited Greg and his girlfriend, so it's already going to be a merry bunch."

"You invited Greg?" Sarah's gaze widened.

"He's picking Cassie up at the airport on Easter Day and driving her to my house. It would have been awkward if I hadn't invited Greg and his girlfriend in for a drink and hors d'oeuvres . . . I don't know. I figured I'm an adult and I should act like one."

The fact that Natalie had invited Greg was pretty big.

Fred mulled over the possible scenarios if Iris came, and the best he could say was, "I'll let you know. Maybe I'll ask her. We'll see."

His daughters smiled, two broad smiles that worried him. They'd be after poor Iris like fingers in icing on a cake.

He didn't know if he was ready to do that to his Iris.

■ ■ ■ ■

Natalie stared at the phone when she got home from her dad's. She took a long hard look at it and decided it wasn't going to get any easier the longer she waited.

She picked it up, dialed a number and waited.

The line was answered on its second ring. "Hello?"

"Hi, Tony. It's Natalie."

"Hey. What's up?"

She bit her lower lip, gathered her thoughts. "I was wondering if you were free on Tuesday to come over for dinner."

"Sure."

Just like that. Sure. "Well, great."

"What can I bring?"

"Wine would be nice."

"Merlot?"

"Whatever you want would be fine."

She tucked her hair behind her ear, paused, and tried to think of something else to say. She couldn't. She grew anxious, uncertain.

This seemed so staged . . . so set up.

"Thanks for inviting me, Natalie," he said, pulling her from her thoughts.

"I wanted to." Before she could change

her mind, she said, "Why don't you come over about seven."

"Sounds good. See you then."

He hung up and she disconnected the call.

Natalie sighed, straightened her shoulders and set the phone down. It was a done deal now.

She'd just sealed her fate. The ball was in motion.

Heading for the stairs, the phone rang and she had a moment of dread.

*He's calling back to say he can't make it after all.*

Natalie glanced at the caller ID, saw it was Cassie and let out a sigh of relief.

"Hi, Cassie."

"Hi, Mom."

The distance between them seemed so far. Sunday nights weren't the same without Cassie with them, and this Easter it would be nice to have her back.

"How're things going?" Natalie asked, walking through the house and turning off lights to head upstairs for the night.

"Good."

There was a pregnant pause.

Cassie didn't have to say anything. By the faintest sound of her daughter's breathing, Natalie could read into the length of silence. It wasn't good news.

"What happened?" she blurted, fearful.

"Nothing, Mom. Geez."

"Well, something's on your mind. I can read you like a book."

Cassie waited a few seconds, then she said, "I'm not coming home for Easter. I'm going to Minneapolis with Austin."

The news didn't readily register.

"You're what?"

"I'm taking spring break at Austin's house with his mom. I already changed my ticket, so you can't say no. Northwest flies into Minneapolis and the fee to reroute me wasn't that bad."

"Cassandra, I paid for that ticket," Natalie reasoned, trying to keep her voice calm. "You had no right to change it and have my credit card billed with the higher fee. Not to mention, you should have run this past me first."

"If I had, you would have told me I couldn't go."

"You are so right. We had plans for Easter. You knew you were expected here."

"I know, but Austin —"

"Austin came for Christmas and I was nice about it. I'm not going to be nice about this. I'm upset with you."

Natalie felt her ire rising. Cassie might be on her own, but she still had certain family obligations, especially when that airline ticket was already bought and paid for.

"Mom, I don't want to get into it with you and I'm sorry if I hurt yours and daddy's feelings."

"Greg knows about this, too?" That dinner invite was going to be yanked right out from under him if he had any clue about the change in plans.

"No, I was hoping you could tell him for me."

"Absolutely not. You'll have to call him."

"Okay. I will." Defiant, she continued, "Mom, this is important to me and I wish you could understand. Austin asked me to go to his house and that's a big deal for him. He wants me to see where he lives."

Once more, silence stretched between them, Natalie thinking how extremely unhappy she was.

And how she wished her daughter had never met Austin Mably.

"Mom?"

"I'm still here."

"Mom, please don't be angry. I'll come home soon. We'll look on the calendar and we'll set a date for a long weekend. Okay?"

Natalie dragged in a breath. "I'm disappointed."

"Oh," Cassie groaned. "Kids always hate

it when their parents say that. Please don't."

"Well, it's true. I'm disappointed you didn't check with me first."

"I'm sorry."

Natalie couldn't say much of anything else. The reality was, an eighteen-year-old who thought she was in love thought she knew all the answers. But the real truth was Cassie didn't have enough experience to know that they weren't all the right ones.

In a case like this, Natalie had a feeling her daughter was just going to have to learn the hard way. And maybe the increase in airline fare was a small price to pay for the lesson.

# Twenty:
## Sheet Music

Tony couldn't remember the last time he'd had a dinner cooked for him. Kim had never been big on domestic skills but that had never really been a problem for him. He knew how to cook, plus he ate a lot of his meals at the fire station.

Going out to dinner was a nice break from cooking. He had his favorite places and liked being waited on. But a home-cooked meal by a beautiful woman was far more preferable.

Tonight Natalie had set the table with place mats and red napkins. She'd put flowers in the center and had lit candles, as well. He sat sipping a glass of wine, watching her at the stove. She was doing something with pasta. If she was nervous, she didn't show it. She moved with efficiency, much as she probably did at work.

He was glad she'd invited him over for dinner. And he knew full well she would be offering herself for dessert.

While he wasn't planning on turning her down, on a core level, he wanted to be in love with someone, and that sort of surprised him. He would have figured after the divorce he'd be turned off love and not wanting to fall into it again.

But, in rethinking his marriage, he realized that he'd been trapped in the emotional aspect of Parker needing a dad, and unconditional love for Kim had been part of the equation.

His gaze followed Natalie as she moved a pan from the stove to the sink and drained the water. The house smelled like garlic and onions, some kind of sauce — tomatoes in it maybe. She threw some spinach in another pan and put a lid on it. She had pine nuts on the counter. He was hungry.

He liked everything he saw, and the smells had his stomach growling.

"Can I pour you more wine?" she asked, taking a sip of hers. She'd been drinking at the counter, pausing every now and then to pick up her wineglass.

"I'm good."

"Dinner should be done in a minute."

"No rush."

And he meant it. He had all the time in the world tonight. He knew she had to work tomorrow, but he didn't. Having forty-eight hours off was one of the perks about his job that he enjoyed. He could take two days off at a time and do things he wouldn't normally get accomplished if he was a nine-to-fiver.

"Do you usually work six days a week?" he asked.

"It depends on the time of year. Around holidays, yes. I'm crazy this week with Easter so I've gotta be at the store by eight. Sometimes earlier."

She stood at the sink, her hip resting against the counter. She wore a pair of black slacks and a black-and-pink top. It clung to her skin, the sleeves long, the neckline a deep vee that cut to the middle of her cleavage. She looked great. Her hair was down, in a long and layered cut. He liked it. A lot of women in their thirties cut their hair. Even though Natalie was in her forties he liked that she chose to wear it longer.

"Everything's ready." Her voice drifted into his thoughts. "I'll serve you, if that's okay."

It was more than okay.

She picked up the plates, put food on them and returned the plates to the table.

"I'm impressed," he said, looking at what she'd served him. It was angel-hair pasta with shrimp, tomatoes, pine nuts and spinach with a rose-colored sauce. "It smells really great."

"Thanks. I hope you like it."

Now, as she sat down close to him, he could see that nerves were setting in. He reached out, touched her hand. "Relax."

She took a sip of wine, gazed at him over the rim, smiled while she drank, then set her glass down. "Of course. Yes. I will try."

She tried to make light of her sudden bout of anxiety, but she wasn't very good at it. Why he could still make her nervous after they'd been together in so many different situations, he wasn't sure. He just knew he wanted her to be herself, to enjoy the evening.

They ate and talked about her daughter not coming home for Easter.

"I have a feeling this boy is bad news for her," Natalie said, taking a thoughtful sip of wine, "but sometimes there's no talking to a teenager."

Genuinely interested, he asked, "Was she a good kid in high school?"

"An 'A' student. Honors classes. Very bright. She's at Columbia College Chicago on a scholarship. She's studying graphic arts. She likes drawing, advertising, that kind of thing."

"That's great."

"This boyfriend of hers . . . I just can't picture her with him. I don't know him well enough to make a final judgment. Just call it mother's intuition. Wait until you have kids of your own. You'll know what I'm talking about."

The comment was made casually, but it lingered in the room and Natalie looked down at her plate.

Without changing the inflection in his tone, Tony said, "I'm sure I will."

To that, Natalie gazed at him. "Cassie seems happy with Austin, but the last couple of times I've had her on the phone she's anxious to get rid of me. She's distracted, like he's in the room with her and she can't talk freely or something."

"He wouldn't be abusing her or anything?"

Natalie took a bite of shrimp, then lowered her fork. "I don't think so." Then with conviction. "No. He might be flaky, but I can't see him as the type, and Cassie would tell me if she was in trouble."

"Kids do things you don't expect. I went on a call where a teen girl delivered a baby in the bathroom — her parents never even knew she was pregnant."

Natalie's face blanched. Tony reached over

and touched her hand. "I'm not saying that's your daughter."

Somewhat reassured, Natalie resumed her breathing. "I don't think she'd ever do something like that, but I do know that college has brought a lot of new pressure to her. And I just hate to see her do something stupid. On one hand, I need to let her go and test her wings. Find out about life. I'm so ready to be done and free of the worries. On the other hand, I know I'll always worry about her even when she's married and a mother herself. It's just a parenting thing."

He let her talk, smiled while she spoke. She suddenly let up, looked at him. "I'm sorry. I put my foot in my mouth again. I didn't mean to sound like you have no experience with parenting. I know how involved you are with Parker."

"I didn't take it the wrong way." Then, to alleviate her concern, he nodded in appreciation over the taste of the food. "This is really good."

"Thanks."

"Don't take this the wrong way, but I didn't see you as a cook."

She frowned, then smiled. "I do have to eat, you know."

"I know. But I didn't think you'd cook something so elaborate. I sort of figured since you had to be creative at work, you wouldn't be as creative in other areas."

"But maybe since I am creative at work, I'm creative in a lot of other ways."

The implication of what she said caught his attention. He didn't think she meant it in the way he was interpreting it, and when he gazed at her, she looked at him, then away. She understood what she'd said, maybe didn't even regret it.

He took it that she liked to be creative in bed.

That worked for him. He would try anything and he wanted to try a lot with her.

Sleeping together wasn't something he wanted to plan or think out. He just wanted to make sure she knew what she was doing, what she was offering.

Dinner was eaten leisurely and the bottle of wine finished. She got up to clear the table and he rose to help her.

"You don't have to do that."

"I want to."

"Well . . . okay."

"I take it your ex-husband didn't help."

"No. Not all the time."

"What did he do for a living?"

"Micron. He developed software."

"Are you on good terms with him?" Tony brought the plates to the sink and Natalie rinsed them before loading the dishwasher.

"Better. Actually, we were never on bad terms. We just didn't like each other." She dropped forks into the silverware tray, then looked at him. "I've invited him and his girlfriend to Easter dinner. It should be interesting. If I show up on your doorstep, have a shot of tequila waiting for me. I might need it."

Tony laughed. "How come you invited him?"

"Initially — harmony for my daughter's sake. I have no quibble with Greg. If he's happy, then I'm happy for him." Letting out an exhale, Natalie sighed. "Besides, he was planning on picking Cassie up at the airport. It would be awkward now if I uninvited him and his girlfriend just because our daughter canceled. And when I told him Cassie wasn't coming, he did his usual two-minute tirade, then he asked me what time he should be here for dinner. I was trapped. What are your Easter plans?" she asked, wiping the counter.

"I'm working a half shift for someone. They have family coming in that morning and they're eating at noon, so I'll stay at the station until he comes in."

"Why doesn't he take the whole day off?"

"Needs the money, I guess."

"That's what's wrong with this country — firemen, policemen and teachers don't make enough money," she stated, swinging the dishwasher door up and into place. Then she glanced at him. "I mean, I'm not saying that you don't earn a decent wage . . . I . . . uh, oops. That didn't sound right."

Tony went toward her, pulled her into his arms and looked into her eyes. "I know what you meant and I didn't take it as anything negative." He dropped his mouth to hers, gave her a soft kiss. "You worry too much about saying the right things."

"Not all of the time," she replied, her breath teasing his lips. Their foreheads touched and he savored the feel of her shirt fabric. He didn't know what it was, but it was soft; it felt really sexy.

"You look nice," he uttered next to her mouth.

"Thanks. So do you. You always do."

"I could argue that but I won't."

"Seriously, I'll bet you look just as great with soot on your face and your hair damp with sweat."

He simply smiled, brought his mouth back over hers and kissed her long and leisurely. She tasted like wine, sweet and sugary. Her arms rose around his neck, pulling him close. He let himself go, surrendered to the kiss and let her take it over.

She opened her lips and took him in the direction she wanted to go as she nibbled on his lower lip. Her tongue swept over the seam of his mouth and his lips parted. She entered him, their tongues meeting and tasting. His body tightened, he reacted and grew hard. He wanted her, but once he had her, there would be no going back. For him, this was something different. It wouldn't be casual and she had to know that.

He lifted his head, gazed into her eyes. Her face was flushed with a sexual heat that colored her cheeks. She breathed in short little gasps, a strand of hair brushing her eyebrow. He touched her, swept the hair back and then traced the outline of her ear.

She seemed to hold her breath, tense and waiting.

Expectation filled her, a flicker of indecision in her green eyes. She was deciding — was it worth going ahead and being a little reckless, maybe even dangerous? Did she really want this?

He read her like yesterday's news.

He was having the same thoughts, the same pattern of looking ahead and wondering how this would change things between them. Anticipation. Apprehension.

"I don't know how to do this," she murmured. "I don't know how to just be a gender-appropriate friend. I thought I wanted you just as my friend, but . . ."

"We're more than friends."

"Not yet. We aren't lovers yet."

"Is that what you want?"

"Yes, I told you."

"But you're having doubts?"

"No. That's the problem. I'm not really doubting anything, but I am questioning my sanity."

"Why's that?"

"Because I've never had sex without being in love — or thinking I was in love."

"I understand." He traced the side of her neck, grazed his fingertip over the pulse point at her throat.

She sucked in a breath. "I thought I was so in love in my one and only relationship since my divorce — you know that feeling when you crave someone?"

"No . . . I don't." Tony swallowed, tried to explain. "I loved my wife, but I didn't have those feelings for her. I thought I did, but I didn't."

"How sad."

"Yeah, it was."

She reached out, touched his cheek. He'd shaved before he'd come over, his jawline and face smooth. Blinking several times, her eyes filled with a deep and curious longing. "Do you think you can ever crave love? Feel it strongly in your heart, mind and soul?" As soon as she asked, her hand withdrew and she shook her head, fingers touching her lips as if to remove the words. "I shouldn't have asked that. It's irrelevant."

"Why's it irrelevant?"

"Because we aren't going to fall in love, me with you nor you with me . . . so it doesn't matter. I don't know why I even asked."

"Yes, you do."

He waited for her to give him her reason; he knew she had one.

Natalie's lips pressed together, their fullness and pink color catching his attention and distracting. He would have kissed her if she hadn't been forming words of explanation.

"Some men think they want to be in love, but they don't. Not really. It's the chase, the pursuit that interests them. When they win a woman over by doing everything right, when it comes time to make a commitment, love leaves the picture."

"I hear bitterness."

"I'm sorry. I don't mean to be, it's just that I'm a lot more cautious these days."

"Caution is good. Just know your limits."

That caused Natalie to roll her eyes, step out of his arms and brace her hands on each side of the sink. She lowered her head, stood in silent thoughtfulness, then came back to him.

Before he could react, she had both hands on the back of his head and was kissing him soundly on the mouth.

He could feel her body trembling as she spoke. "I'm done thinking. Come upstairs with me."

Natalie wasn't sure if Tony would follow her — she just began walking and hoped he would. With each riser she climbed coming closer to her bedroom, her heart jerked into a more frantic pace.

What was she doing?

Ha! She knew damn well what she was doing. She'd known since being in the dressing room of Victoria's Secret trying on underwear and lingerie.

Once on the landing, she walked into her bedroom. She'd placed candles on the bedside tables, put flowers on the bureau and on the side of the bathtub. The room was perfumed with waxy fragrances. Fresh sheets were on the bed, the pillows plumped. The lighting was low — she'd left the dimmer on a low setting. In every way, she had planned the last detail of her . . . seduction.

*Seduction.*

What a name to call this. She shouldn't have put so much thought into it . . . Should have just — just what? Just not done anything and gone on as if Tony didn't matter, as if she didn't need him or this.

She felt him stand behind her, his hands holding on to her shoulders and bringing her back to his chest. He rested his chin on the top of her head.

"It looks nice in here. Different."

Then she remembered he'd seen it when she'd had her surgery. The chaos and clutter of the room, the rumpled bed, her in it after she'd gotten sick. She vividly remembered the cup of soup he'd brought her and set on the night table, relived how he'd sat backward on a chair and talked to her. Such a different time, a different mood. This now felt different, strange, as if she were disconnected from that past experience. As if it hadn't been her. As if she were a different woman now.

She couldn't quite pinpoint it, but suddenly she questioned if she'd done the right thing. The timing . . . the planning.

She was a planner; felt better knowing what was to come. But did a woman really plan out a sex bed? Could it really work?

Maybe Tony was thinking she was nuts.

She turned in his arms, needing to rest her cheek on his chest. He cupped the back of her head, held her close and just kept her near him. She heard the beats of his heart, the strength within his body pulsating through his chest. He was indeed strong, battle-hard from his job.

Tony Cruz was like no other man she'd ever met.

If only she could be the kind of woman he needed and wanted.

If only . . .

For some stupid reason, she got a tear in her eye, blinked it away and held on to a curse beneath her breath. Funny how she felt things for him she'd never felt for a man before. Funny how their differences put a wedge between them that she could see no way to build a bridge across. And yet it was those very differences that attracted her to him.

"Do you want to go back downstairs?" she asked.

"No."

She hadn't expected that answer. "What do you want to do?" She held her breath.

"Lie down."

"Lie down?"

"Yes. I want to lie down on the bed with you, hold you in my arms, and I want to feel all the damn stress inside you leave. I'm not getting up until you let it go."

"I'm not that stressed," she lied.

"The hell you aren't." He moved away from her. "Sit down."

He nudged her toward the foot of the bed and made her sit. He took off her shoes, then he sat and took his off, as well.

Tony lay back, brought her with him as he scooted up onto the pillows and fit her into the crook of his arm. She lay there, tense and anticipating something more. But nothing else happened.

He settled in, rested on his back with her tucked next to his side. She gazed at the ceiling fan above the bed, thought about the summer months when it rotated slowly and kept her cool. The room was warm right now, the heater tripping on in the house. Outside it was quiet, a hazy darkness having settled. Her blinds were closed.

Natalie put her hand on Tony's chest, amazed that he could control the beats of his heart to slow, normal and steady. His ability to relax with ease was something she envied. She closed her eyes, willing herself to do likewise. She felt the pressures slipping away from her.

No sex bed . . .

It was okay. It was all right. She was happy like this. Just lying next to him as she had on his sofa. There was an infinite peace that came with lying beside someone — the right someone. She defined it as a comforting strength, a contentment that wasn't there when she was alone.

Again, she wondered if it was because Tony was a fireman and he represented heroic qualities, or was it Tony himself? She had a feeling it was both, but more so the man.

Tony was more than just any man. He was someone she could fall for if she let herself. If she didn't think about the future, if she put the past behind her and she only thought about right now, this second, this fragment in time — she could let her heart open up and take him inside.

So she let the thought drift, let her muscles slacken. She swallowed, feeling herself relax. He stroked her hair, her shoulder; he touched her in a soothing way that rose gooseflesh across her skin, at her nape, on the soft surface of her lips.

She found that dormant place within her that trusted, that didn't need explanations or validations or reasons.

She smiled, thought it felt great to know

herself once more. To feel a sense of belonging. She hadn't realized how much she had wanted this, but she hadn't known how to get it.

Tony must have known. He took her there with a touch, without a lot of words. Just being here with him, holding him close, not falling into the sex bed with her — that had been what she needed.

Her smile deepened, her heart lightened and her body released the last fragments of tension.

She slept.

It could have been minutes or hours, but Natalie woke to the steady cadence of a heartbeat beneath her palm. As she roused to consciousness, she realized her hand was on Tony's chest. He lay on his back, her body fitting snugly next to his strength.

The length of her left leg rested between his, the angle of her pelvis pushed against his hip. She stirred slightly, felt the pressure between her legs and grew aroused in a drowsy way that had long been dormant in her.

Darkness bathed the room, lit only by the LCD reading from the bedside clock and streetlight filtering in through the blind slats. Tony slept, a deep and sated sleep —

or so she thought. He moved, very slightly. It was almost like a twinge, maybe a dream that flitted through his mind with lightning speed. Whatever it was, she brought her hand to his face to give him comfort.

He didn't readily wake.

She felt his jawline and the bristle of beard. He was rugged and so very masculine. He was all male, sculpted by hard contours and smooth planes of flesh. Even through the heavy fabric of his shirt, she could tell his arms were ripped with muscles.

She wondered what he'd look like without clothes.

That thought hovered within her, giving her pause . . . had her closing her eyes and imagining. It would be far better to see. To feel. To touch and discover.

In that span of time just after midnight Natalie made a decision. She didn't come to it lightly nor quickly.

Slipping out of bed, she rose to her feet. Tony stirred slightly, a soft rise and fall of his chest. She went into the bathroom and got a book of matches. Going from candle to candle, she lit them until the bedroom flickered with low light from flames.

She was glad he didn't wake as she undressed down to her new bra and panties.

Her pulse beat, her skin cooled from the room temperature even though the heat was on.

Leaning over Tony's legs at the end of the bed, she began to slowly crawl toward him until she straddled his legs and gazed into his face.

His hands came around her waist before he even opened his eyes.

Once open, he stared at her with a sleepy expression on his face and a smile curving the corner of his mouth.

"Hey," he said, his voice low and whiskey-smooth.

"Hey," she whispered, lowering herself on top of him so she spanned the length of his body.

His arms slid down her back, keeping her close. She loved the feel of him, the hard muscle that pushed into her breasts. There was no time to feel self-conscious in the underwear she'd chosen.

She'd bought pink lace, next-to-nothing panties with a matching bra. They were satin with ivory trim. The panties were French-cut with lace panels. She felt sexy-feminine in them.

Tony's hands moved down her spine, cupped her behind.

"I can't see what you're wearing. Stand up."

The notion of modeling what she'd bought for him sort of gave her a brief panic. While she wasn't overweight, she didn't have a flawless body. After all, she'd had a baby eighteen years ago. What used to be firm and perky was now softer and more pear-shaped.

"Stand up," he said once more, his tone scratchy — not from sleep but from a desire that heated his skin. She could feel it. He was hot to her touch.

She backed away, took a step from the bed and stood there. It took all her willpower not to cover herself with her hands. Having a younger man examine her was new and unnerving.

Tony's body was perfect. She didn't have to see beneath his clothing to know he wasn't carrying an ounce of extra weight. She'd felt the ridges of his abs when she'd lain on top of him, the swell of his pectorals.

His eyes traveled her body, from her breasts to waist, her pubic area, hips and legs. "You look great."

The words of affirmation made her smile, relax a notch. "Thanks."

"Really sexy."

"I wouldn't go that far, but I appreciate

the comment."

"Natalie," he half snorted. "I never bullshit anyone. Especially not you. Come here."

She went back to him, stretched out on top of his hard body and he kissed her.

He bunched her hair in his hand, keeping her head close, his mouth locked over hers. He had the nicest lips. So soft, smooth and warm. He knew how to master a kiss, to apply just the right amount of pressure. Not too wet, not too dry.

Explosive currents raced through her, a drugging sensuousness that gave her courage to let herself go. Be herself.

The kiss sent fire through her blood. Its mood changed from sweetly soft to devouring, urgent, exploring.

She felt his body flex, perhaps an involuntary response.

Her head rose; she gazed into his eyes. He had a mask of control on his face.

Spoken with resonant tightness, he said, "I want you, but I want more than you just for the night. You know that."

"Yes. But I can't promise anything but right here and right now."

"I understand. That still doesn't change the way I feel."

"I know."

She didn't want to argue the point with

him, nor try and reason. She just wanted. Wanted him.

Maybe it was stupid to dust details under the rug, but she'd never felt this desired or felt this excited to be with someone.

Sharp need rose through her. She trembled for him to touch her, to fit himself inside her heat. She imagined locking her legs around his waist, taking every inch of him and having him fill her up and move steadily within her.

He was gorgeous. Just looking at him could suck the breath right out of her.

Getting off the bed, she stood, knowing what she was about to do.

Her heart slammed hard into her ribs as she unhooked her bra and discarded it. The skimpy pink panties were slid down her thighs, passed over her knees and calves and pooled on the floor at her ankles. As she stepped out of the satin puddle, her chin lifted higher.

Breath caught in her throat, almost solidifying and causing her to become dizzy.

An endless heartbeat stretched between them.

She stood naked, not daring to lower her gaze to herself without the cover of clothing. She already knew what he saw.

The skin on her body was an ivory tone,

her breasts a creamy white, the nipples rosy pink. She didn't want to think about the two scars. They unsettled her, made her feel less attractive. She would have preferred to leave the bra on. That's why she'd bought such a pretty one.

Her pulse raced in her throat. She wouldn't speak.

Tony got off the bed, came to stand by her.

"Undress me."

She almost stammered that she couldn't. In that brief second when time ticked off, she realized she'd never undressed a man before. Wasn't that strange . . . she honestly never had.

The challenge of doing so gave her confidence.

She reached out for the tiny buttons of his shirt and started at the top. First one, then the second until the bottom. The fabric was soft, a brushed cotton. The rich blue color looked good against his skin. As the material parted under her touch, she spanned her hands across the T-shirt covering his chest. She thought it was black. Too dim in the room to tell. It had a V-neck.

Slowly peeling the shirt away from his body, she bunched the T-shirt in her hands and began to lift. Tony's arms rose to accommodate her and with a tug, the T-shirt was off. She tossed it to the floor.

Gazing at him shirtless was divine ecstasy. His body was even better than she had envisioned.

Every plane and valley, every surface of skin was toned and ripped. Muscle defined him, the hard slabs rippling slightly as he breathed.

"I'll bet you could carry a refrigerator out of a burning building," she caught herself saying. The comment was sublime, dumb, but uttered just the same.

"Never had to," he replied, his voice deep in the dark recesses of the room. "Don't think I ever will."

The muted softness of his laughter curled around her.

She licked her lips, extended her hands to the button fly of his jeans. She flicked the metal button open, then dragged the zipper down.

Her knees went weak as he leaned in and gave her a kiss on the side of the neck. Shivers cascaded through her body, a shudder held her in its grip.

She couldn't quite manage to get his jeans off his hips. He helped, then stepped out of the faded denim. He wore cotton briefs, the kind that went down his thighs. That thin knit fabric cupped and hugged, leaving nothing to her imagination.

He was thick and large.

She never doubted he wouldn't be. But seeing for herself, emotions whorled and skidded.

She'd never been with anyone like him before.

"I don't think I can take off the rest," she said, half the words lodged in her throat.

Tony removed the briefs, tossed them aside.

They were naked before one another. The heat of his exposed body reached out to her skin, seared her flesh beyond measure.

He reached out, traced his fingertip over her parted lips, slowly down the side of her neck and to her collarbone. Then lower across the swell of her right breast . . . then lower. To the two scars.

An involuntary reaction caused her to tightly grip his wrist, trying to stop him.

She had no more effect on stopping him than she would a freight train.

He met her directly in the eye and tenderly urged, "Don't."

"It looks ugly."

"Don't," he repeated. "Nothing on you looks ugly. You're beautiful."

The hot sting of tears threatened. Not out

of sadness or embarrassment, but out of a deep-seated emotional state.

She released him, stood tense and expectant.

His thumb and forefinger touched her nipple, gently pinched and aroused. She grabbed his marble-smooth shoulders to steady herself, to give her strength.

He spent a long time touching, exploring the fullness of her breasts, creating gooseflesh across her skin, causing her nipples to ache, to tighten into hard peaks. He ran his hands down her stomach and hips. Then to the juncture of her legs.

His fingers covered her, one slipped inside. Her legs almost buckled.

He must have known she couldn't support herself. He took her to the bed, laid her down and lay beside her.

"Touch me," he whispered.

For all her courage under fire at work, at life, in dealing with Greg and the variety of other hurdles she'd overcome, touching Tony in the way he was asking took every fragment of her resolve. It wasn't as if she didn't want to. She did in the worst way.

She just had a moment when she wondered if she could please him as much as he pleased her. It was a stupid and inopportune thought, but she had it just the same.

She slid her hands down his chest, lower to his navel. He had a modest amount of hair on his body, not much. She liked the smooth feel of him, the way he smelled. Musky. Masculine. She liked the sound of his voice in the room, the way his breathing echoed against the walls.

She traced a circle around his navel, then swallowed. Lower. She moved lower to the nest of hair at his groin.

He thrust out, firm and rigid. She touched him. So smooth, warm. Pulsating with heat. A bead of moisture was on the tip and she rubbed it into his flesh, slowly and with a massaging motion.

He groaned, touched her breast with his hand, then pushed her into the bed and covered her nipple with his mouth. He pulled and tugged, a light suction and just enough rough pressure to drive her crazy.

Need consumed her, the moist folds of her flesh aching for him.

She encircled him, slowly pumping and moving. His hips arched, he moved slowly with her.

His hand found where she pulsed, touched, and his fingers went to the spot that stimulated her to the edge of sexual release. She hung on, not wanting to let go. Not yet. He stroked and rubbed, sucking on her nipple at the same time.

Time ceased to be measured. It dragged and ebbed, each of them touching and exploring one another. He felt like a part of her and there was no room to breathe, to think.

Natalie tingled everywhere. The jolt of his thigh against her pelvis ignited him, evoking a tremor.

His mouth broke free of her nipple and he kissed her, a half groan that smothered her lips. Everything inside her pulsed tightly, a consuming tenseness that begged to be unwound.

Her legs spread and she wanted him now, this second.

She'd never felt so slick, so ready.

"I have something in the nightstand." The words came out in a choppy breath. "I can't reach . . . you'll have to get it."

She didn't need to say what it was. Tony reached over her, opened the drawer and came out with the condom. Thankfully he didn't ask her to put it on him; he did so himself, quickly.

She just wanted him back beside her, in her, next to her, on top of her.

He was there and she gripped his buttocks as he lay over her, her legs opening wide and feeling him at her entrance. She arched her hips, moved higher, wanting so badly . . .

And then she felt the tip of him, hot and aroused.

He moved forward a little, not all the way inside. Torture.

His arms were braced on either side of her, his facial expression in deep control and concentration. She wanted to tell him to stop it, to just be inside her. Yet at the same time, it was the slowness of it all that drove her to near frenzy.

"More," was all she could utter.

He gave her slightly more. Then a little more.

Her legs rose and she hugged his hips, urging and pushing herself to contain him completely. Until he obliged. With one long thrust, he was inside, and the gasp that left her throat couldn't be contained.

She struggled to regulate her breathing but failed miserably. On the brink of losing all control, she focused only on the face above hers. His eyes, their color. Briefly, they caught hers, then they closed.

His lips parted. A sheen of moisture covered his forehead.

He moved with a slow and rhythmic pressure that drove her forward, to the edge. She burned and throbbed, felt incredibly filled. The rotation of her hips grew faster, harder. She met him in the middle of each thrust, her hands moving down the length of his back.

There was no place between them that didn't touch, abrade, cause a pleasurable friction. She undulated, her flesh tightened around him.

The movement became less exploratory, more steady and stronger. She was on the edge, that place where she would be able to let herself go. She didn't want to hold back any longer.

Natalie reached for it and let go.

Her entire body convulsed around him as her nails sank into his shoulders, keeping him close, her legs locked around him.

Several more thrusts, and he sought his own pleasure, pulsing within her body and releasing. She closed her eyes to the overwhelming intensity of them being together.

He collapsed on top of her. A jagged breath left his lips in a low rasp as he buried his face in the crook of her neck.

A moment later, he lifted his head and kissed her fully on the mouth. He didn't move; she wasn't ready for him to leave her and he knew. He still felt hot within her; a sensation she wanted to savor.

Trembling, she lifted a hand to his face.

She spoke nothing. Didn't need to.

Everything she felt, but was unable to say, was reflected in Tony's eyes.

In the flickering light, listening to the thrum of his heart beating against hers, Natalie dared to embrace a truth she had tried to keep at bay.

She feared what had started out as sex would turn to a profound and intimate connection leaving her wanting more.

A lot more.

# Twenty-One:
## Premonitions

Natalie was late for work, missing an early-morning meeting with a vendor and forgetting her cell phone at home.

She never thought she'd oversleep with Tony next to her in bed. She hadn't slept all night with a man in so long, she figured she wouldn't doze off, much less drop off into a coma. So she hadn't set her alarm. Big mistake.

When she finally opened her eyes, the clock had read 7:45 a.m. Panic set in, then an instant awareness of the body beside her, an arm draped over her middle and a strong chest butted against her back.

She'd thrown off the covers and dashed for the shower. When she got out, the smell of coffee drifted through the house and the bed was empty.

She met Tony in the kitchen. He stood in his jeans, the top button undone. He'd slid his arms into his shirt but left the front open. His feet were bare.

"I have to leave right now," she'd said. "I'm sorry."

"It's okay."

She looped her purse through her arm, collected her briefcase containing invoices she'd been meaning to look over. "Can you lock the front door on your way out?"

"Yeah."

"Thanks." Adrenaline pulsed through her, she turned to leave then stopped. Facing Tony, she gave him a smile. She knew what she was about to say would be a huge mistake, a step in the wrong direction and a sure disaster . . . but she spoke it anyway. "Can I see you tonight?"

He flashed her a grin. "Count on it."

Careless pleasure had washed through her over his response. Then she'd dashed out of the house.

Her day proceeded at a frantic pace, the pressures of running a floral shop during a holiday really weighing her down. She barely had a moment to reflect on last night and how she felt about it.

Rather than spend a spare thought on the subject, she ran through the day getting things done. She rescheduled the meeting, placed orders, connected with her glass supplier, had to balance those invoices and pay bills. By closing time, she was exhausted.

Before pulling into her driveway at dusk, she glanced at Tony's house. The interior lights were on.

Last night had been incredible, amazing. She'd never felt so alive, so fulfilled. Just as she feared — or at the very least had tried to deny, there had been an emotional connection between a man and a woman. She supposed there simply was no sexual intimacy for her that wouldn't involve her heart.

Thinking about it, she realized she didn't want to be a one-night stand. She wanted more than that with him.

Conflict ran through her, sharp and painful. The picture was clear, but she preferred looking at the cloudy version. If she didn't view the whole truth, she could still see him, still fit herself in his arms . . . sleep next to him.

Natalie entered her home and switched on the lights.

In the kitchen, a bottle of wine sat on the island countertop. It was one of her bottles. Tony must have taken it out of the wine rack. A note was taped to the bottle's front.

*Bring this over when you get home.*

Climbing the stairs, Natalie went into her bedroom and noticed the bed. It was made. The sheets had been rumpled this morning.

Now the duvet was pulled up, the pillows plumped. Everything nice and neat as if two people hadn't slept together in it last night.

She took a shower and rinsed off makeup and the day's stress. She toweled dry, smoothed a light coat of moisturizer on her skin, then picked out a pair of jeans and a comfy sweater to wear.

Back downstairs, she snagged the bottle of wine, locked the front door behind her and walked across the street.

Lantern lights softly glowed from everyone's front yard, brightening her path. She knocked on Tony's door, feeling an instant's pleasure when he opened it and she saw him.

His height dominated the space, his dark hair appearing a little spiky and shorter since this morning.

"Did you get a haircut?"

His masculine chin rose, that familiar gesture he made with a killer white smile. "Yeah."

"I noticed. I notice everything about you."

He wore dark jeans, a long-sleeved, black knit shirt that stretched over his chest and arms. He dressed in an effective manner; maybe he didn't see that the fit of a shirt emphasized all the muscles beneath it, but she did.

How did simply looking at him stir heat in her? Make her want to pull that shirt off over his head and . . .

She walked in, wrapped her arms around his neck and kissed him, the bottle of wine dangling loosely in her grasp.

He kissed her back, a greeting that made her forget the busy pace of her day. Her arms tightened around him and she felt as if she were home.

The slow and hot punch of the kiss caused air to clog in her lungs, making breathing an effort. He tasted like cinnamon. The house smelled like something had been baking. A sugary sweetness that still lingered on Tony's lips.

"What have you been eating?" she asked against his mouth.

"Those cinnamon rolls out of the can."

She smiled against his lips. "Really?"

"I know how to cook."

"Is cracking open a can actually cooking?" She softly laughed, the vibration of her mouth against his sending a dart of heat through her.

He didn't reply, merely kissed her thoroughly until she felt unsteady on her feet. Passion roused in her so profoundly it almost troubled her that she could be affected this way by him.

When she looked into his eyes she was hoping she'd find a shadow of fear or hesitation to mirror her own. But it wasn't there. He was still confident as ever, the brown eyes gazing at her hooded and comfortable, if not sexual, along with that easy grin.

"What?" he asked, his forehead touching hers as he looked at her so very closely.

"You scare me," she uttered in a half whisper. Then repeated it just to make sure he heard her. "You scare me."

His heart drummed fast; she could feel it next to hers. He took her chin in his fingers, lifted it so that she was looking directly at him when he said, "You scare me, too."

"I do?"

"Hell, yeah."

She wasn't expecting him to say that. "I thought you knew what you were doing."

"Not even close. I like you, Natalie. I can see myself with you, but I know it's taking a chance to give you my heart. You're set one way and I'm set the other. I keep thinking there's got to be middle ground."

"I don't think there is."

"I'd like to keep trying to figure it out."

"But what if we do something stupid?"

"Like what?"

"Like . . ." She didn't want to say it aloud. "Like get too attached. One of us will get hurt. I don't want to hurt you, Tony."

"I think we're both in this too deep already. It's too late. If one of us walks away, the other's getting hurt."

She wondered if she could walk away. She tried to tell herself she wasn't even remotely attached. But after last night . . . after walking over here when she came home tonight — if that wasn't getting attached, she didn't know what was.

Even so, ever the one to reason, she tried to talk herself out of it.

"Well, if we quit now, the hurt won't be so bad."

Tony let her go, and she didn't realize until afterward that she'd been holding on to him. She staggered a little, caught herself.

"If you want to leave, then you can leave."

His words jolted her, surprised her.

"Do you want me to?"

"You know I don't."

Natalie stared at him, saw he was giving her a dare. He didn't want her to leave any more than she did, but it was her decision. She was the one who was conflicted. She looked for the easy out, the noncommittal goodbye and go on her merry way . . . back home to an empty house and an empty feeling inside.

It wasn't a good way to live. Risking

heartache suddenly seemed like a good plan. Maybe. If she could just let herself not over think things. When they were together, she saw colors in every shade, like the flowers in her cooler. But she still knew that a future for them was just too gray.

Tony turned, went down a hallway. She knew where he was going without having ever been there before.

His bedroom.

She stood in the entryway, poised with a bottle of unopened wine she could take back home across the street, or drink here after . . .

. . . after she went down that hallway and followed a man who could make her forget all logic.

Flickering doubts vanished. She accepted his unspoken invitation so easily, caught herself moving.

Once in the bedroom, she set the wine on the bureau.

His room was richly painted, dark and masculine. The bedcovers were in tones of burgundy and gold, the furnishing black lacquer. It was a very detailed room, too. He'd decorated with black-framed photos of still life on the wall. Ivory vases were filled with greenery, a very little hint of bright color. Wall sconces were gold, the shades an ivory tone to match the vases.

Tony stood at the foot of the large bed. The frame was a heavy wood, its king-size dimensions dominating the room. The bed almost needed a step to get up into.

Without words, she went to him and kissed his mouth. That's all he needed to have. He locked her in his hold, lifted her off her feet and took her to the bed with him. She skimmed her hands up his warm neck, held his mouth close to hers. She could feel ripples of muscle on his back; the play of powerful sinew and masculinity was something she found intriguing.

Hands explored, mouths tasted, tongues met. Everything heated at one time in a sensory pool that tingled in every pore of her body.

Need swallowed her and she grew impatient.

Clothing was discarded. He sheathed himself with protection and her body yielded to his. Gooseflesh rose as she felt him sink into her slick internal heat. The friction and tempo that followed drove her to the edge, pleasure streaking mindlessly through her head.

She didn't let emotions get in the way this time. She simply accepted the physical pleasure. The purest of joys and fulfillment.

Her body tremored as she cried her release. She wrapped herself around him, feeling him let go then uttering a low groan from the back of his throat.

In the ensuing seconds while their breathing caught and mingled as mouths touched softly and intimately, she knew what was different about making love with him this time.

This time, she gave him her trust.

The call came in and Tony knew it was going to be bad. Sometimes he could sense it, like a premonition.

That buzzer didn't go off because someone was having a great day. It always meant crisis, whether it was an obese woman who couldn't cook her own dinner and was calling for help, to an electrical spark coming off a dryer connection. The fire department responded to public problems.

Captain Palladino was in the engine before anyone else — which was saying a lot. He'd been dead to the world, sleeping in a recliner while a rerun of *Seinfeld* played on the tube. As soon as the PA announced the call to Station 13, adrenaline went in to full throttle and propelled everyone into action.

Tony drove, every muscle in him tense and stretched to the breaking point. Hoseman Walcroft sat in the back. After the mobile data terminal was engaged as "en route," and an address was located on a map, a lot of easygoing exchange transpired through the headsets as if they had to keep things light for as long as they could.

Laying on the horn through the lit intersections, Tony gassed the big engine through a red light. The hula girl on the dashboard danced with a smile on her face, her fringy grass skirt swaying when the wheels of the big truck hit bumps in the road.

The powerful truck moved at a decent speed, turning the corner and pulling into a residential neighborhood.

Tony steered the engine down the street to the address the captain directed him to. A dark cul-de-sac came into view under the headlights. Somewhere in the end was the address, but it was too dark to make out with limited light from the streetlights. Tony had to put on the brakes and stop.

"First on scene," Captain Palladino said and they all knew what that meant.

A female dispatch voice came over the radio. "Engine 13, stand by. Staged for code four from P.D."

Frustration knotted in Tony's shoulders,

his hands gripping the big steering wheel, the engine idling beneath him. The three of them waited, a helpless feeling creating a deathly silence in the cab. When the police had to go in first, it was for the firefighters' safety because the subjects involved could be armed and dangerous.

After what seemed endless minutes, finally the flash of police-vehicle lights came into view. They pulled up to the semidark home.

Tony's foot itched to hit the accelerator, but they still had to wait until the police declared the scene safe to enter.

"Code four. Engine 13, proceed."

Sweat had popped out on Tony's forehead and he engaged the engine in a jolt forward.

They were in the house less than a minute later.

A dynamic charge of raised voices from a grandmother and mother, police interrogation, a teenage girl's hysterical crying echoed off the living-room walls while the firemen and arriving paramedics team tried to calm the sixteen-year-old down by taking her to one of the tiny bedrooms.

She was distraught, her long black-and-pink hair hanging in her face. Her pale complexion looked like milk. Her hands were wrapped in towels, blood seeping through. One of the female paramedics was able to get her vitals, calm her down, while a line was started on her.

The mirror over the girl's bedroom bureau was broken, shattered. Much like the girl herself. Her eyes were haunted, a shade of blue that Tony wouldn't soon forget. She gazed at him once, briefly, and her look made him feel as if a hand had closed around his throat.

She didn't want help.

She had given up.

If they came out a next time, the scene would be different.

An hour later, Captain Palladino called dispatch to say Engine 13 was back in quarters.

Tony went to his room, taking a minute to compartmentalize the varying emotions that ran through him so he could deal with the reality.

He sat on the bed, picked up his cell and dialed a number without a glance at the clock. On the third ring Natalie picked up.

It was 12:05 a.m.

"Hullo?"

"God, I'm sorry. I didn't realize it was so late."

"Tony? Is everything all right?"

He laid back on his bed, stared up at the

white grid ceiling. "We just got back from a call."

He could hear as she shifted the phone from one ear to the other. She must have been lying in bed asleep. A place where he wanted to be right now. Next to her. "What happened?"

"A sixteen-year-old girl tried to kill herself. She cut her wrists with a piece of mirror."

"Oh, that's terrible, Tony."

"I hate to see something like this. You'd think after so many years, I'd be immune to it, but every now and then sometimes a call happens and it affects me in a way I'm not really ready for."

"I can only imagine."

Tony pressed fingers to the bridge of his nose. "It made me think about your daughter. From what you tell me, she seems like a good kid, even if she isn't coming home for Easter."

Natalie's voice softened with fondness. "She is a good daughter. I get frustrated with her every now and then, but that's bound to happen."

"I know it's none of my business, but I hope you tell her you love her a lot."

"Of course, yes. I do. Tony, is there anything I can help you with?"

"No. I just don't like to see someone so young think they'd be better off dead. Sometimes the call is just for help, but in this case, I saw a look in her eyes. She really tried to do it."

"That's so sad. Can't she get help?"

"They'll take her to Intermountain Psyche and put a watch on her. She needs some therapy, but it's not always mandated. There's red tape. You can only hope for the best."

"And you know that you did your best when you went out there to help her, Tony."

"Yeah." The tightness in his chest began to subside, his lungs didn't feel so closed off. It felt very natural to have called Natalie. He had never called Kim at night. With a particularly bad scene, he always called Rocky if he needed to air his thoughts.

Natalie grew quiet a long moment, then she said, "Do you still have to work a half shift on Easter?"

"Yep."

He could hear her breathing, a soft exhale. "Would you like to come over to my house for dinner when you're done?" Before he could give her an answer, she hastily went on, "Tony, my family will ask questions about us. It could get uncomfortable."

"I can handle it."

"I don't know if I can," she laughed without humor.

"Natalie, you can handle anything."

She reflected on his words a moment, then tenderly said, "Thanks, Tony. That means a lot to me."

# Twenty-Two:
## Leaving Normal

The aromas wafting through Natalie's house were savory, making her hungry. The rich scents of ham, brown sugar–baked beans and onion-cheese scalloped potatoes drifted through the house. In the fridge was a bowl of cabbage-pea salad, homemade applesauce and fresh fruit. She had a cookie sheet of butter rolls that she would put into the oven in a few minutes.

Each room in the house had a freshly cut floral arrangement — even the downstairs bathroom. The sweet smells of flowers mingled with the Easter meal cooking in the kitchen creating a warm, homey atmosphere.

Natalie had taken great pains to make this day as perfect as possible.

Sarah and her family had been the first to arrive; Steve had parked himself on the sofa watching sports, while Sarah and Natalie stood in the kitchen with wineglasses in hand. BreeAnn and Sydney were upstairs in Natalie's room with MTV on the television.

"I can't wait to meet Dad's girlfriend," Sarah said enthusiastically after popping a green olive into her mouth. She selected another and ate it. "I wonder what she'll be like? I picture him with a very elegant lady, someone who wears her hair short and styled in a beehive bubble."

"Nobody calls hair a beehive bubble anymore," Natalie responded, a twinge of butterflies hitting her as she thought about the soon-to-arrive guests. But she vowed to herself not to show her sister she was a little bit unhinged. "I think Mrs. Price was the last teacher I had in elementary school who did her hair in a helmetlike sprayed bouffant. I don't think Dad would date a woman who had an old-fashioned hairdo."

Sarah's eyebrows rose thoughtfully. "Probably not. Remember when Mom sold your hair to the lady next door so she could make a fall out of it?"

"I totally remember that. It's a little creepy now to think about it."

"You always grew such pretty, long hair, then you chopped it off each summer so you didn't have to mess with it after a day at the lake."

"I know. I can't believe I did that."

Natalie adjusted the plates of hors d'oeuvres, even though the trays and bowls of gourmet goodies were already nicely aligned and presented.

She had nothing more to do. Right now she was very organized, but she needed to keep busy or else she'd spill the news to her sister that she'd invited Tony over, too.

She'd thought about telling Sarah beforehand, then opted against it. Better to have Sarah's attention focused on Iris than on Tony. Sarah would know soon enough when Tony showed up. There was no point in making a big deal about it prematurely.

Tony should be here within the next thirty minutes.

Everyone's arrival time pretty much centered around three o'clock. Everyone, that is, except for Cassie. Natalie frowned, trying not to dwell on that disappointment.

The doorbell rang and Sarah was halfway to it before Natalie could take a step.

"I'll get it," Sarah said, swinging the door open. "Dad! Hi. And you have to be Iris. Come in."

Glad her dad had extended the invitation to Iris, Natalie ran her hands down her apron, checked the oven clock to make sure she wouldn't be late putting the rolls in, then went to greet her dad and his friend.

Iris was very pretty. Her glossy hair was swept into a soft style. She was dressed in a nice pair of slacks and a light sweater that complemented her skin tone. She was tall, statuesque, with a wonderful smile on her lovely face. Her smile was charming, engaging and it reminded Natalie of someone else's.

That thought came from nowhere and Natalie quickly discounted it.

Ridiculous.

Fred wore a sports coat and slacks, his hand on the small of Iris's back as he ushered her inside the wide foyer and then into the kitchen area. He was visibly nervous, made evident by the way he kept a smile plastered on his mouth, those dentures of his looking a little too predominant.

Natalie warmed up to Iris immediately, liking the lavender smell of her perfume; very fragrant and sweet.

"This is my youngest, Sarah," her dad said, making the introduction. "And this is my oldest, Natalie."

"Hello," Iris said, but her demeanor was distracted as she glanced at Fred. Then she broke into a smile, disbelief alight in her brown eyes. "I'm sorry, but my mind is still elsewhere. I just told Fred about an amazing coincidence when we pulled into the neighborhood and parked in front of your house."

Sarah, her usual vivacious self, asked, "What coincidence?"

With her pulse spinning, Natalie didn't have to wait for Iris to say it; she had a strong hunch she knew already. That smile had tipped her off.

"My son, Tony, lives across the street." Iris smiled a Tony-smile, still looking incredulous. "He told me he was seeing one of his neighbors. Knowing my son, she's young and pretty and blond. So, Natalie, do tell me where she lives and maybe I'll pop over there to get a good look at her."

Her words were spoken harmlessly. Of course, she'd conclude her son was dating a young and beautiful woman.

If Tony hadn't been coming over any minute, maybe Natalie would have played along. But she wasn't in the mood, and failed to see the ironic humor in any of this. In fact, her heart sank.

And while Natalie was nice and blond — albeit courtesy of the beauty parlor — she was not younger, nor very perky or anything else that described a thirty-something woman who probably had fake boobs.

The tension of the moment wove itself between Sarah and Natalie, and Sarah, bless her, spoke up. "Well, now, Iris, that is a coincidence, and you will be so glad to know my sister is the neighbor. She's pretty and I think she fits your description perfectly."

Fred Miller stared between Iris and Natalie, his jaw slackening. "Is that true, Natalie?"

Suddenly needing to check on the ham, Natalie ignored the question and opened the oven door. A wave of heat slapped her face, burning and leaving an imprint of . . . what? Embarrassment?

Why in the world would she be embarrassed by seeing Tony Cruz?

Because it defied convention, went against stereotype.

Hot firefighters dated hot women. It was a given.

She, on the other hand, was a former PTA president, a mother of a college-age daughter and a divorcée who had had two years to find Mr. Right and had, instead, found Mr. May who'd set her heartbeat racing out of control.

Natalie closed the oven door, turned and faced the group. "Well, it is a coincidence, isn't it? Tony and I are friends."

Iris's eyes softened. "Oh, I didn't mean to sound as if I . . . Oh, I'm so sorry. I don't disapprove of *you.* It's just that, I was assuming that he would have . . . Oh, my."

Oh, my was right.

At that moment, the doorbell rang again. Silhouetted behind the etched glass was Greg and his girlfriend.

*Wonderful.*

Natalie didn't think he'd actually show up even though he'd called the other day to confirm the time. He had this annoying habit of saying one thing and doing something else entirely.

Leave it to her ex-husband to follow through on this particular day, of all days.

With a slight sigh of annoyance Natalie opened the front door. "Hi, Greg," she said almost bluntly. She had to remind herself to breathe correctly. She'd never met his girlfriend and, after everything that had happened in the last few minutes, she had no inclination to do so right now. But she put on a civil face and chiseled a smile onto her mouth.

"Hi, welcome," she said, greeting the girlfriend.

Greg came in, bringing a rather plain-looking woman with him. She was petite, wore glasses, had red hair and freckles. She looked about forty with laugh lines at the corners of her eyes.

"Hi, everyone," Greg said, shaking Steve's hand.

Steve Brockner had been taking everything in stride so far, watching as the scene had played out around him. Now that his former brother-in-law had arrived, Steve stood in the middle of the group. "Hey, Greg."

Greg Goodwin's palms were sweating because he wiped them down the sides of his jeans. Natalie watched, the gesture familiar and slightly annoying. "This is Renee O'Neil," he introduced.

Natalie, still feeling shell-shocked over Iris being Tony's mother, was helpless to do anything but give Renee a quick, "Hi."

Sydney and BreeAnn came bounding down the stairs just as Natalie was wondering if anyone would notice if she left right now and didn't come back.

"Miss O'Neil?" Sydney said. "What are you doing here?"

"You know her?" Greg's puzzled tone hovered in the air.

BreeAnn supplied, "Oh, this is so weird. She's our new history teacher at the middle school."

Miss O'Neil looked like a history teacher now that Natalie took a closer look.

"Hi, girls," she said, her voice sounding

very bookish. "Isn't this fun? What a coincidence."

Natalie couldn't take another coincidence.

She excused herself and grabbed the tray of rolls, shoved them in the oven and set the timer. The sooner everyone ate, the sooner they could all leave.

"We were just talking about coincidences," Iris said. "My son lives across the street and he's dating Natalie."

Greg shot Natalie a look — as if it were okay for him to have a postdivorce girlfriend, but not okay for her to have a boyfriend.

And Tony wasn't even her boyfriend!

"Can I pour anyone a glass of wine?" Natalie asked, and a chorus of adult yesses filled the kitchen.

As glasses were filled and the adults relaxed, the conversation began. They briefly covered the territory of Tony being newly divorced, Greg and Renee's last trip to McCall, Miss O'Neil's class project due after spring break, the sunroof on Fred Miller's Elantra acting up, Iris announcing a big Easter sale at Target, Steve mentioning that Micron stock had taken another header in the market and Sarah talking about getting food poisoning once from an undercooked ham.

Not bad for fifteen minutes and two bottles of wine.

Just as everyone was getting comfortable with one another the doorbell ran again.

Natalie's head shot up as Sarah said, "Gee, who could that be? You want me to get the door, Natalie?"

"No, no, I'll get it, thanks."

With a mixture of dread, excitement, confusion and just plain terror, Natalie opened the door, knowing it was Tony.

The expression on her face caused Tony to ask, "Nat, are you okay? You look kinda stressed."

"Oh, I'm stressed all right. You better prepare yourself. When I told you this might be awkward I had no idea."

As they walked into the kitchen even the calm, cool and collected Tony Cruz paused for a moment as he met the quizzical gazes of eight pairs of eyes. As he looked from one to the other, his eyes suddenly did a double take.

"Mom?"

"Hi, honey, imagine seeing you here," Iris squeaked. "Tony I'd like you to meet Fred Miller, Natalie's dad. Fred and I are dating."

The confused expression on Tony's face turned to incredulity. "Natalie?"

At that moment Natalie's composure was at the breaking point, so she asked Sarah to make the introductions while she murmured something about needing to check the oven.

The rolls were browning, but not quite ready. Natalie turned toward them all, put her hands on her hips and announced to the crowd, "Dinner should be ready in just a few more minutes. Now, if you'll excuse me for a moment I need to . . . need to do something."

The temperature in the room had grown suddenly stifling. She needed air.

Natalie walked through the living room, past the downstairs bath, and went into the cold garage. She took in deep gulps of air that smelled like automobile oil, and tried to regain a semblance of composure. She walked back and forth over the concrete, hands on her hips as she pulled herself together.

Her dad and Tony's mom? How did that happen?

She was still trying to digest the news when Tony appeared in the garage and leaned against the fender of her car.

Folding his arms over his chest, he asked, "What are you doing?"

She all but barked, "Trying to figure out this mess."

"So let me get this straight — that silver-haired guy in there is your dad, and he and my mom are dating?"

"You win the prize," she said, instantly regretting her sarcasm. But honestly, this was just too strange for words. "So what are we going to do about this? Your mom and my dad are a couple!"

Calmly, Tony responded, "There's nothing to do."

"It's not normal for my dad to date your mom after you and I have, you know — been together. My God, it's almost like incest or something."

Tony's eyebrows shot into a frown. "It is not."

"It's still weird." Natalie felt the cool bite of the air in the garage, and rubbed her hands up her arms.

"It's not weird. It's no big deal."

"It is a big deal. She expected me to be younger than you and have fake boobs."

"My mom said that?" he asked, his voice rising an octave.

"No . . . no. She didn't have to. I filled in the blanks."

"Jesus, Natalie, you're coming unglued for no good reason." Tony's ability to take everything in stride rattled her. "Was that your ex-husband in there with the redhead?"

"Yes. She's a schoolteacher."

"I never envisioned your ex would look like that."

Natalie's chin rose. "How did you picture him?"

"I'm not sure. Not like him. He's sort of short and he looks so much older than you."

Not sure if that was a compliment or not, Natalie let it go.

Maybe she needed to let Tony go, and this was a rude awakening.

"I have to check on my rolls," she uttered, moving past him. But his hand caught her and he pulled her to his chest, engulfed her in his arms.

"I don't know what's going on, but nothing's changed between us, so whatever you're thinking, get it out of your head."

She closed her eyes, breathed in the scent of him on his shirt, took comfort in his embrace and his body, so solid and confident.

"I don't know what to think," she said in a small voice. "This is so out of my comfort zone. I can't handle it."

Tilting her chin up so she could meet his eyes, she saw the dark look he gave her. "The Natalie I know would never say she couldn't handle something. So cut it out."

She swallowed, knowing he was right.

Damning herself for even having the thought, and so thankful he didn't let her get away with it.

Reaching up on tiptoe, she gave him a kiss full on the mouth. "I'm so glad you came."

"Me, too."

With that, Natalie reentered the house, the buzzer on the oven going off, but before she could take the rolls out, the doorbell rang.

"Again?" Sarah said, glancing toward the door, then at Natalie. "Who else did you invite and not tell me about?"

Natalie shrugged, her shoulders slumping. "Nobody else. Who in the world could it be now?"

Natalie went to answer the door and stood back as Cassie and her carry-on luggage filled the threshold.

"Cassie?" Natalie gasped.

The steady notes of the oven timer kept sounding and the smell of burning dinner rolls filtered through the house in a waft of acrid smoke. But Natalie didn'tnotice.

"Mom." Just that tiny utterance of her name, and Natalie knew that something had happened.

Cassie flung her arms around her mother, holding tightly just as the smoke detector triggered and ear-piercing beeps resonated through the house.

With brief instructions to Sarah and Tony to start dinner without them, Natalie ushered Cassie upstairs. While the guests pitched in getting the windows and doors open to air the house out, and laying out the Easter dinner, Cassie began to cry and cry in her mother's bedroom.

Just then the smoke detector finally stopped screeching.

Natalie couldn't get much of anything out of Cassie except for the news that Austin had done something upsetting.

On hearing that, Natalie tensed to the breaking point. Cassie's explanation could very well be every parents' worst nightmare.

Natalie felt as if she were being sucked into a current of floodwaters. Suffocating. Drowning. The weight was a sinking feeling the likes of which she had never before felt in her life.

"Cassie, you need to calm down and tell me what happened."

In between gulps, Cassie said, "Her name is Candi and I hate her."

Taken aback, Natalie held Cassie's hands as they sat on her bed and faced one another. "Who's Candi?"

"She's the girl Austin cheated on me with.

I hate him, too." Cassie's mascara was dark smudges beneath her eyes, her lashes spiked with tears. "She works at Chicago Carryout and he was flirting with her right in front of me, and then I went to his dorm room last night — and he was with her. In bed. I caught them *doing it.*"

The way Cassie said "doing it" with a negative ring and connotation gave Natalie a thread of hope that her daughter had *not* "done it" with Austin.

Compassion filled her response. "I'm so sorry you had to go through that." Natalie moved to hug her daughter, but Cassie straightened, angry. The tears subsided and she sniffed.

In a vengeful tone, Cassie blurted, "I hate Austin Mably. I wish I'd never met him."

"You're upset with good reason."

"I'm not upset. I'm so mad, I want to kill him." With that, Cassie broke down and cried again. She'd been hurt, her voice bitter. "How could he do that to me, Mom? We were supposed to be going to his house for spring break and then he does something like this to me. Why?"

Natalie wished she had a viable answer. She hated to be real honest about it: Austin Mably was a jerk. She'd sensed it when she'd met him and she'd had a feeling something like this was going to happen. But how deep the damage was, was yet to be determined.

Downstairs, the guests were forgotten, as well as Greg's look of concern as Natalie had ushered their daughter upstairs.

"Cassie . . . did anything happen between you and Austin other than what you found out? I mean —" Natalie selected her words carefully "— did you and him . . ."

"God, Mom. Just ask me." Cassie's eyes swam with tears. "I'm still a virgin. I held out. That's why he went to someone else. If I'd've let him, we'd still be together."

Relief came out in a whoosh of words. "No, Cassie. He would not have stayed with you. I suspect he's the player type. He would have liked you for the short term, but he would have moved on."

"I'll never know, will I?" Cassie got up, went to the bathroom and yanked a line of toilet paper off the dispenser to blow her nose. She gazed at her reflection. "I feel like crap and I look like crap, and it cost you big bucks to change the airline ticket again. You can yell at me if you want. I think I deserve it."

"Oh, Cassie, no . . ." Natalie patted the bed beside her so Cassie would come back. "I'm not mad."

Cassie sat down, wiped the underside of her nose, the corners of her eyes. "You should be. If I was my mom, I'd be royally pissed at me."

Natalie reached out and hugged her daughter, loving the soft feel of her, breathing in the smell of her hair. "At a time like this, I am so incredibly proud of you."

Muttering in Natalie's ear, she asked, "What for?"

"For being true to yourself. For coming home when you needed a friend, and for considering me your friend *and* your mom."

"I always thought you were my best friend, Mom. I've never stopped thinking it. I'm sorry if I forgot to tell you lately."

A tear slipped down Natalie's cheek. She held Cassie's face in her hands. "I'm so glad you came home. And I am so glad I showed you that *Playgirl*. See — it paid off."

Cassie's laughter was the first sign she was on the way to recovery, however marginal. Of course, there was the trauma of discovering the boy she'd had a thing for had been unfaithful. At any age, that would be hurtful. "Mom, looking at a nude-guy magazine did not make me hold on to my virginity." Gazing into Natalie's eyes, Cassie went on, "*You* made me hold on to it. Sex was never an off-topic subject in our house. And the way you were always talking to me about how special it was to wait until your wedding night — I listened. And that's what I want to do."

Swallowing the lump that had formed in her throat, Natalie sighed. "I'm so glad you think that way. These days it's uncommon for girls to wait. You'll think it's worth it when the time comes."

"I know. But that's not to say I don't like to make out."

"Um, yes . . ." Natalie gave a nervous laugh. "Well, maybe I don't need to know about the details."

Cassie blew her nose once more, tore apart the tissue in her hands. Then with a puzzled frown that wrinkled her forehead, she asked, "Who are all those people downstairs?"

Venting a half laugh, Natalie informed, "That would be Grandpa's girlfriend, Iris. Your dad's girlfriend, Renee — I think you already met her at Christmas at your dad's house — and my friend, Tony."

"I know who Tony is. He's hot."

"Yes, I believe you've mentioned that already."

"Are you dating him? Because if you are, I'd think it would be cool."

At this point, assailed by confusion, Natalie wasn't sure what she was doing with Tony.

Iris's house was decorated with a homey touch. Her hardwood floors gleamed a golden color while a red, green and gold Persian rug lay beneath the coffee table.

Fred wished this evening's visit with Iris could have been under more normal circumstances instead of drinking coffee and talking about what had just transpired at his daughter's house.

Easter dinner had begun on very shaky ground but, oddly, had ended on a happy note. Cassie's surprise visit was the glue that had put things to rights.

When she came downstairs with Natalie, Cassie gave her dad a hug and declared that everything was great now that she was home. A sigh of relief had been breathed by Fred — and everyone else.

The revelations of the day were forgotten — or at the very least, not discussed any further. New acquaintances were formed, maybe even some friendships. In the midst of it all, Natalie had a full crowd at her dinner table. And there was nothing more wonderful than family gathered for a holiday meal.

Iris joined Fred on the sofa. The cushions were comfortable, the back a row of down-filled pillows. He thought it was nice. The throw pillows in green and black were a good complement.

"You have a nice home, Iris."

"Thank you, Fred. I got most everything at Target." Iris set her hot cup on the coffee table to cool. "You'd be amazed at the versatility that store has."

"I believe you. I'm a regular shopper."

They sat next to one another, quietly thinking a moment.

Fred almost didn't know how to handle himself. He was still a little nervous around Iris at times, but he was grateful she'd invited him in to sit and visit after he brought her home.

"So . . . our kids are dating," he stated. "Interesting, isn't it?"

Iris, her eyes a rich brown like coffee, didn't readily comment. When she did, it was with thoughtful words. "I'm not surprised. You've spoken nothing but wonderful things about your daughter and you know how fabulous I think my son is."

"Who's to say what will happen between them," Fred said, realizing that he and Iris had only just begun to skim the surface when it came to learning details about one another. "And I hope I'm not talking out of turn, but I thought ahead to the fact if they ever got married or something, how that would relate us."

"I had that thought, too. We'd be in-laws." Iris picked up her cup, held it close to her mouth, but paused before drinking.

Fred pondered the idea and came up with a different explanation, but this time, he didn't speak it.

They both drank their coffee, the room growing quiet as they both lost themselves in reflection.

"Iris . . . it was me who delivered those irises to you that day . . ."

She looked into his face. "I know. I finally figured that out the day you brought me the balloons."

"Why didn't you say something?"

"I thought you might want to tell me yourself, when you were ready."

"And I thought whoever sent those irises to you might have been your boyfriend or someone special."

"They were from my aunt Edna who lives in Wyoming."

"I'm glad you have an Aunt Edna."

Iris beamed at him.

After a while, Fred put his arm around Iris's shoulder and slid her closer to him.

She felt wonderfully soft, feminine, with so many features and qualities he enjoyed.

Leaning back slightly, he gazed into her face. She smiled, her mouth so sweet, her lips so red. His heartbeat tripped and skipped, his breath felt tight in his chest.

"Iris," he whispered, tingles rising across his skin. His pulse caught, held still. "I want to kiss you, but I haven't kissed a woman in so long."

"It's still done the same way, Fred."

Smiling, Fred lowered his mouth over hers, his lips gently brushing across the fullness of hers. She tasted like coffee and cream, a little hint of sugar. So sweet, so nice. Very pleasurable.

His first kiss in forever and it reminded him of what he'd been missing. He'd loved his wife and would have given her the moon, sun and the stars. It had been a good marriage, a loving one. But it was over. That part of his life was gone. He'd been living in the present, but not fully experiencing life. Tomorrow was his future and, if he let himself, he could have daily sunshine again.

He was ready to send the clouds away.

He was ready to find love. With Iris, if she would have him.

Iris's arms tightened about him, as did his around her.

And all the world seemed to be right for the first time in a long, long while.

# TWENTY-THREE:
## BREATHING ROOM

Tony saw Natalie digging in her front planters, a flat of pansies by her side as she worked the soil. A lot of her shrubs were leafing out, and her yard was coming back to life after being dormant throughout the cold winter months.

He crossed the street, walking with purposeful strides toward her house. Since Easter Sunday, Natalie had spent her time with her daughter, but he'd heard from his mom that Natalie had put Cassie on a plane back to Chicago yesterday morning.

"Hey," he said, causing her to turn in the direction of his voice.

She was on her knees, wore a sweatshirt and jeans with tennis shoes. "Hi, Tony." Her smile was pleasant.

"How've you been?"

"Good. How about you?"

"Fine. Did you have a good visit with Cassie?" He stood over her, shoving his hands into his pockets.

"Yes. It turned out really great that she came home. We had some good times, stayed up late and watched old movies. I was sorry to see her go, but she had to get back to school."

"And everything's okay with her?"

"Now it is. That boyfriend she had cheated on her. It was horrible and she had to work through the hurt of it. I hope he doesn't try and get back together with her. I don't think she'd allow it. She was pretty set in her resolve when she left."

"I'm sorry she got hurt."

"It's okay. Sometimes, in order to grow and evolve, you have to get hurt in the process."

"She seems strong. Just like her mother."

"Thanks, Tony. I appreciate that."

He nodded, giving Natalie time to say something further. When she didn't, he said, "I had a good time at your house on Easter. Having both sides of our families there was interesting. I wondered how it would go, but it was great. Sometimes your family drives you crazy, but it's a good crazy."

"I know exactly what you mean."

He sat on her porch, its concrete warm from the afternoon sun. The day was cloudless, the air warmer than it had been in a long time. He put his face up to the sun, enjoying its heat on his skin. Then he straightened.

Natalie's shoulder-length blond hair was twisted into a hair claw, wispy pieces framing her face. She continued to work the ground, using a spade to overturn the earth, then she planted a purple pansy.

She dusted her hands off, sat back on her heels. "I wanted to come over many times, but with Cassie here . . . I just couldn't."

"I understand. Can you come over tonight?"

"I . . ." She rose to her feet, came to him and gave him a kiss. "Yes, I was hoping you'd ask me."

Later that night, as they lay naked in bed together, Tony wondered when the time would come that things would change between them, that they'd take a new direction. Now wasn't the time to talk about it.

He rolled onto his side, caressed Natalie's cheek and kissed her. Her arms rose, cupped his neck and brought his mouth closer to hers. He loved the feel of her naked, the touch of her body pressed next to his.

For now, this was enough.

But a week later, after Tony and Natalie had taken turns spending the night at each other's houses, after long hours of making love and getting to know every intimate inch of each other, he felt he needed an answer. A definitive place to go in the relationship.

They were in her big bathtub, Natalie settled between his legs and the bubbles of the bath surrounding them. Candlelight flickered off the walls, the fragrance of roses in the air. Her back was pressed next to his chest and he kissed the side of her neck.

"Natalie, I think it's time we got serious." His statement caught her attention. "I really want to spend more time with you."

Her response wasn't immediate. "We spend a lot of time together."

"But it's filler time — and I don't mean that in a negative way. I want quality time. Assurances that this is for real."

She turned toward him a little; he studied her profile.

"Tony, I care about you, too, but I'm just not ready for that kind of commitment right now. I'm actually scared about taking that step with anyone, so it's not just you."

"Then why does it feel like it's me?"

"Because you're the one I have to say it to. Keeping our relationship the way it is works for me. And if you want more . . . I can't. I really care about you, but my marriage ended, my daughter is in college and my business is keeping me running. I know you don't mean to, but I feel like you've been pressuring me to make more out of us than there is, than there ever will be. I'm just not ready." She looked directly into his eyes, a sadness coming into her gaze. "I'm sorry . . . I wish I could give you a better answer. Maybe we need to spend a bit of time apart. I have to think about all this."

Tony's eyebrows pulled into a frown. He rubbed his jaw, but didn't say what he wanted to say. There was no point, not right now. "Okay."

If she wanted time, he had just as much of it as she did.

"I went to the doctor and had my hormones tested."

Natalie and Sarah were cleaning out the floral shed, and Natalie blurted out her next words. "She said they're normal. She suggested I go on the Pill, but I told her no. I'm going through this cold turkey and I *know* I'm perimenopausal."

"How can that be if the hormone test was okay?"

"Then why am I having these damn hot flashes and night sweats?"

"I don't know. Changes in your body that can't be explained." Sarah swept the floor, then paused and in an accusatory tone asked, "Why did you *really* get your hormones tested? I think it's because you're thinking about Tony and a baby, aren't you?"

"Absolutely not." The response was spoken a bit too quickly and too defensively. She sighed, frowned. "Maybe a little. Yes. I had that thought in the back of my mind, but it was more to prove to myself that I can't get pregnant, so why even give it a second thought?"

Sarah set the boom aside. "Why aren't you seeing him anymore?"

"We're taking a break."

"Oh, I hate that phrase. It's the kiss of death whenever someone in a relationship says that."

"Maybe you're right. I want to end it. Being with Tony made me get involved, lose my head a little. I'm halfway out, have been struggling with this for weeks. I can't go back now. I'm going to call him tonight and tell him."

"But you don't have to."

Natalie lowered herself onto the chair. "I have to." Then with more conviction, as if to convince herself, "I have to because it's for the best."

Later that night, Natalie called Tony.

"Hi, Tony, it's Natalie." Why did her voice sound so distant?

"You're calling things off," he said, not waiting for her to say anything further.

"Yes . . . it's for the best. I'm just not ready."

"Would you ever be ready, Natalie? Do you ever think the timing is right for anything?"

His defensive tone made her sit up straighter. She was hurting him and she felt awful about it. "I don't know. Right now, I just don't know what I'm doing."

"Then take more time."

"But I —"

"Take more time to think about it."

Then the line disconnected.

Tony and Rocky Massaro drove up to McCall for an overnight fishing trip. They'd spent hours out on a rowboat, baiting hooks and casting lines, talking about what women wanted, if they even knew or would ever have a clue.

At the end of a long day, they sat in the hotel bar over beer and fried onion rings with ranch dip.

"I don't know, dude," Rocky said. "I think I've had the most success with women when I've treated them like shit. Some of them want you to treat them badly." He knocked back the last of his beer. "I feel your pain, but you're asking me my opinion and all it's worth is what it's worth, which is nada."

Tony sat back on the bar stool knowing he'd never treat Natalie like shit. So if that's what she wanted, forget it.

"Let's check out that nightclub over by the shore," Rocky suggested, throwing a bill on the counter to pay their bar tab.

Tony stood, thinking some loud music and another beer would be a good time killer. "Okay."

The next morning, they decided to go to the Pancake House for a late breakfast. They hadn't gone to bed until three and were dragging when they sat in the booth and ordered two cups of black coffee.

There must have been some kind of women's retreat in the resort town because the restaurant was filled with them.

When the waitress came back to top off their coffee, Tony asked, "What are all the women doing in here?"

"Holistic convention."

"A what?" Rocky asked, his eyebrow quirking. His hair was ruffled since he'd neglected to comb it after he'd gotten out of bed.

"They're spiritualists. They channel rocks

and stuff." The waitress moved on, and Rocky made a face.

"What's that mean? Rock channeling?"

"They talk to rocks and are into water-falls." Tony drank his coffee. "I think it's like energy healing."

"Hey, I smoked weed in high school when I wanted to talk to a rock and it worked."

Tony chuckled.

The women's voices rose octaves too high for the slight hangover Tony was nursing. Each time a woman walked by their table, she smiled at him; some giggled and others were more blatant with their gazes. One even dropped her purse just so she could bend over and get it, allowing him a good view of her behind.

Rocky said, "I don't know why you're asking me what women want because you seem to have it in spades. You don't even have to do anything and they want you."

Tony didn't recognize what it was about him that made him so appealing. Yeah, he was okay to look at, but these women didn't know him. He might have had a rock for a brain — but then, they liked rocks.

As their breakfast order came, Tony said, "Maybe women do find me attractive, but I'm not some boy toy."

"Oh, Jesus, Cruz, we all want to be boy

toys. You're full of it." Rocky shot ketchup on his eggs. "Talk like that, you sound like you're in love with her."

Tony didn't say anything. He couldn't.

Maybe he had fallen in love with Natalie. God knew it felt as if he were headed in that direction sometimes. Other times, he'd prevented himself from letting go because he hadn't been ready.

What started out as just having an enjoyable time, having fun with each other, had turned serious for him. He wanted her in his life, but he wanted her on his terms. No barriers. Whatever happened, happened.

And yet, he wasn't willing to give up his dream of being a father. He wondered if she'd consent to fertility treatments. Would that be an option she'd be willing to explore even though she'd made it clear she was done with parenting?

He'd been getting to a place where he had to make a decision about Natalie — if he wanted to continue to give her time to think about what she wanted, or if he should just give up. Maybe he should start seeing other women. The trouble was, no other women interested him.

He was comfortable with Natalie, felt good around her. The sex was really good, too. Great, in fact. He missed having her in his bed, sleeping next to her.

He didn't like being alone.

Maybe he had been putting too much pressure on the women in his life. Maybe that's why Kim left him, and that's why Natalie needed breathing room.

Tony pushed a grocery cart through Albertson's and headed into the produce section. Because he was with the fire department, he'd gotten into the bad habit of shopping daily or every other day, rather than once a week to stock up. The firemen always pooled their money to buy what they needed for dinner that night, then they'd drive the truck to the store in the late afternoon, pick up steaks or ground beef, sometimes chicken in the summer for a barbecue. The station usually had condiments, but that didn't mean they were edible. The refrigerator wasn't cleaned out all that frequently, and sometimes it was better to buy a new jar of mayo than trust the one that had been in there with the lid not screwed on tight.

Selecting some navel oranges, he dropped the plastic bag into his cart. Tony was pushing forward when a familiar voice greeted him.

"Well, hi there! I thought that was you." Alisa, the floor nurse from Swallow Hill, came up to him.

"Hey, Alisa."

"I haven't seen you in a few. C Shift has been getting the majority of calls." She laughed. "Sometimes I wish that one of the patients would get a case of something on your shift."

She stood closer; he could smell perfume on her. Store-bought. Not the same soft and floral scent that clung to Natalie.

Tony almost wished he could be attracted to Alisa.

"You never can predict what'll happen," Tony said, pushing forward to continue shopping. "Sometimes we're called out to the same place two or more times a night. Other times, we never get there all week."

"Oh, I know. I just like seeing you."

He was well aware of that. She couldn't be more obvious. He hated to come right out and tell her he wasn't interested; he did, after all, have to work with her to a degree and it was strained enough as it was with all this polite bull he tried to keep up. He kept hoping she'd get the hint.

Alisa followed him to the lettuce as he selected a head and tossed it in a bag. "What have you been up to?"

"Nothing much."

"Aren't you anxious for warmer weather?"

She gave him no opportunity to reply, and answered the question herself. "I am. I'm looking forward to summer. Do you ever go up to the lake?"

"Sometimes."

"Me, too. I like to go to Lucky Peak. I go with my girlfriends or I go with my cousin. She was dating a guy who had a boat, but they broke up over Christmas so there goes that. I was teasing her about getting a new boyfriend who has a boat."

His mind half heard what Alisa was going on about as he glanced up and saw Natalie pushing a cart toward him.

Their eyes met at the same time, a warmth filling his heart, and he gave her a lift of his chin and a smile. It was automatic; he was really glad to see her.

"Tony," Alisa was saying and he grew aware of her hand on his while it rested on the grocery handle. He gazed at her, then slid his hand away. The gesture had taken him off guard for a second. "I'd like to ask you out. I know you're not married anymore. I asked. I really want the chance to get to know you."

Just as Alisa said the latter, Natalie came within earshot. She paused, uncertain, then changed direction, obviously thinking he was interested in Alisa. How the hell she

471

got that impression, he had no clue.

Natalie bypassed the produce, rounded the corner and headed down the coffee aisle.

Gritting his teeth, Tony turned to Alisa. "You're a nice girl, don't get me wrong, but I'm not looking for anyone right now."

"But . . ."

"Alisa, let it go. We have to work around each other, it would just be too uncomfortable."

"But . . ."

"I gotta go."

Tony left the produce even though he wasn't done shopping there. He searched the coffee aisle, didn't see Natalie, carried on and found her at the baking mixes studying a box of brownies. He had to smile.

"Life's treating you that bad?"

She met his gaze. "This is for emergencies."

Everything inside Tony suddenly felt right, put back together. He hadn't realized just how much he'd missed hearing her voice, seeing the color in her eyes and a blush from the cool air dust her cheeks.

"How have things been going?" he asked.

"The plumbing is messed up at my shop again. I got a violation code on my sign and I might have to take it down for a smaller one, and one of my regular customers'

checks bounced. Other than that — fine."
She put the box back on the shelf, selected
another with double-chocolate chunks. She
tossed it into her cart.

"How are *you* doing?" She tried to look
nonchalant, unaffected. He was glad when
she showed vulnerability.

"I have my moments. Mostly at night. I'm
not sleeping too well."

"Me neither."

She folded her arms over her chest, smiled
a small smile, then remarked, "She was very
interested in you."

For a moment, he didn't know what Natalie was talking about, then he remembered. He shook his head, as if shaking the
nurse out of his mind. "She works at one of
the assisted-care homes we get called out
to. She's had a thing for me. I don't think
about her like that."

"She looks persistent."

"She's wasting her time." Tony grew
marginally perturbed, he didn't know exactly why. Maybe because Natalie was assuming he'd moved on so quickly — would
*want* to move on to someone else. "Natalie,
nothing has changed for me. I backed off
because it's what you wanted. But now
you're looking at me as if you regret it."

"I don't," she said quickly, almost too quickly.

"You've thought about me."

She grew quiet, then said, "Of course you cross my mind. It's hard not to when you live just across the street."

"You know you can come over anytime you want."

"I . . . no. I've been fine. I don't need to come over."

"You used to come over for no reason at all."

"But that was then . . . before."

"Before what?"

She drew in a breath. "Before things got complicated."

"If they did, it's because you complicated them."

Natalie licked her lips as his gaze fell on her mouth. He wondered what she would do if he leaned in and kissed her, pulled her into his arms and slid his tongue into her mouth. He had half a mind to do it, and to do it in the grocery store where everyone could see. But if he did, she might think he was only doing it in case Alisa came by. Which he hoped she wouldn't. The fact that she hadn't followed him was a good indication she'd finally accepted he wasn't going to go out with her.

"Tony, I need to finish my shopping," she said as she began to move away.

He blocked her cart with his, a subtle movement that kept her still a few seconds longer. "You know where I live."

"Yes," she whispered.

If she was going to give them a chance, she would have to come to him. They had reached a point in their relationship where she had to ask herself what she really wanted. As much as he would have liked to, he couldn't answer that for her.

Not even a fireman good at rescuing people could rescue Natalie out of the fears she kept in her heart. Only she could do that.

"Natalie?" he asked.

"I don't want to lose your friendship," she said in a half whisper, her body betraying her; she trembled.

"You don't have to."

"But I don't know if I can give you anything more permanent."

"I'm not pushing."

"I know . . . it's just that you're young and handsome and you should be meeting women, dating them. That nurse — you should go out with her."

Strong reproval resonated in his voice. "I don't want to."

"Then look up Sophia from the auction, go out with the guys to a bar and meet someone you might like better than me. Younger and —"

"Natalie, shut up."

Tony took her chin in his fingers and brought his mouth over hers in a soft kiss that she had no problem yielding to. It surprised Natalie that she allowed him to kiss her in a grocery store. But he felt so good. She had missed him so much.

His lips teased hers, his fingertips tight over her chin as he held her still. She welcomed him; the sensual slip of his tongue into her mouth to discover and remember. She took the peace and pleasure he offered, her hand resting on his hard thigh and her pulse beating erratically.

He stirred within her a lazy and languid feeling of desirability, of being wanted and cherished. She loved it, embraced it. Felt comforted by his presence in ways she could barely comprehend. He meant the world to her.

In spite of everything she told herself she would not do, Natalie had fallen in love with Tony.

That thought made her go still.

"Don't think, Natalie." Tony's words sluiced over her parted lips in a moist heat.

"I can't help it." She struggled, fought against the familiar tug to let him go.

She wondered if the answer would ever come easily. The things in life that were worth having were sometimes hard-fought. Maybe this was one of those times when she just had to ignore the voice of reason in her head. Because the harder she tried to let go of the truth, the more it persisted.

She loved Tony Cruz.

# TWENTY-FOUR:
## DIRT BIKES AND
## SUNDAYS

Cigar smoke drifted in pungent gray curls. The firefighters of Engine 13 sat out in back of the firehouse puffing on cheap stogies. They'd had a box of Fuentes last time, a real "walking the dog" cigar, but for some reason or another — maybe it was because they were local boys — they liked the kind of smokes that didn't take a huge chunk out of a man's wallet.

"Good smoking," Captain Palladino commented, taking a puff.

Tony got a full-bodied taste of tobacco as he smoked. It was almost a licorice flavor that filled his mouth. "Who bought these?"

"C Shift," Walcroft said, his voice tight as he exhaled. "You owe the contribution box a couple of bucks."

Nodding, Tony made a mental note to himself to drop some singles in the cigar fund.

The fire station operated on a city budget,

but whatever personal items the firemen wanted, they had to pay for themselves. The morning delivery of the *Idaho Statesman,* cable television and the box of candy bars in the TV room were funded by the men.

The three of them sat in a half circle on kitchen chairs, Tony tilting on the back legs of his.

The evening was warm for the first night of May. Remnants of the sunset streaked the western sky. The smell of a freshly mowed lawn from the fire station's small piece of yard filled the air with a grassy scent that mixed with the cigars.

Hoseman Walcroft straddled his chair backward, his legs on either side of the seat. He'd traded out shifts on a regular basis with another one of the firefighters so now he was permanently on Tony's shift.

A crooked smile relaxed Wally's face measurably. "Nothing beats a long, hot summer and a motocross race. The good Lord probably mixed my system with a little too much testosterone, but that's what dirt bikes and Sundays are for."

"Are you riding at OMC this Sunday?" Captain Rob Palladino rolled his cigar, knocked the cherry off in the chrome ashtray the guys used. It was the top to one of those hotel stands, but without the bottom cylinder. They kept the bowl on the black-top, each of them leaning forward on occasion to drop their ashes in it. At least that was the intention. They didn't always make their target.

"I have the need for speed." Walcroft got a thoughtful look on his face. "Who said that?"

"Steve McQueen," the captain supplied.

"Naw. I've seen *On Any Sunday* a bunch of times, and it's not in that movie."

Growing contemplative a moment, Captain Palladino said, "Then it had to be Keanu Reeves."

"What movie?"

*"Speed."*

A name lingered around the edges of Tony's mind, then it came to him. *"Top Gun."*

"Yeah, it was Tom Cruise." Walcroft folded his arms over his chest.

Tony shook his head. "It was Anthony Edwards."

"Who's that?"

"The guy on *ER.*"

"The bald one?"

"Yeah."

"No, shit. I thought it was Tom Cruise."

"Nope."

"Shows you what I know." Walcroft tapped his ash. "Are there any peanut M&M's left?" He was a little on the stocky side, solid and strong. Definitely the kind of guy who would watch your back in a bad situation.

Tony lowered his chair, reached forward and tapped his cigar over the ashtray. "You're going to eat candy with a cigar?"

"No. For later, smart-ass."

"There's a couple of bags left. I ate one."

"What's on television tonight? Anyone look up HBO?" Wally had a penchant for all the HBO channels. He could find anything to watch, even if it wasn't worthwhile.

"Nope." The captain studied his cigar. "This is a good cigar."

"Yeah, you can't beat the gas-station special," Walcroft laughed, a pair of dimples creasing his cheeks. "Hey, did you guys see Plummer at the Hazmat training? I swear to God, he's on 'roids. His arms are like fucking coconuts."

Captain Palladino's expression grew thoughtful. "I noticed that."

"Because you have gay tendencies," Walcroft teased.

Rob shot him a glare. "Shut up, Shorty."

"Hey, I'm five foot ten in my bare feet."

"I'm six feet five inches. I've got you by seven."

Tony chuckled as dispatch alerted Station 3 of a medic call. He had a moment when he'd been on alert, then his teeth clamped around the cigar as he relaxed once more since their engine wasn't being called into service.

The station phone rang and the captain got up to answer it in the garage by the service bay. His voice was muffled, then he scratched the back of his neck while nodding. When he hung up, he gazed at Wally.

"Flag call."

Walcroft's face soured. "It ain't dark yet."

"Close enough. Bring it down."

The station got calls from time to time from citizens who either lived in the neighborhood or would be driving by and see the flag still flying near dusk and tell them to take it down. Some people needed to get a life.

Tony set his cigar in the ashtray and went to help Walcroft lower the flag. He folded it, then passed the flag off to Wally.

Resuming his seat, Tony asked, "We washing the engine?"

"In a little while," the captain responded, his blue eyes glancing over the back of the red engine. "We could make a run in it like it is."

Walcroft came back. "My wife's been after

me to get our daughter a puppy. She says Molly's old enough to take care of a pet. I know what'll happen. I'll end up cleaning the dog crap or mowing over it."

Tony's mind drifted to Parker and the kitten he'd given her in what seemed like years ago. He'd only taken her out once in the past six weeks. Things at Parker's house were changing, keeping her busy with a wedding taking place this Saturday.

Kim was pregnant.

When Tony found out, he'd felt a slight stab in the gut. He couldn't fathom why. Kim and Brian were expecting in six months. A part of him was unhappy that she was having a baby with someone other than him. Which was ignorant on his part since he'd had the chance and he'd said no.

His feelings had more to do with himself. The lack of fulfillment he felt in his own life.

He'd forced himself to take out a woman Rocky had set him up with, but he knew before he'd even picked her up it wouldn't go anywhere. They'd played pool, had some beer — just a fun night. But Tony wasn't interested in her the way he was interested in another woman.

He saw Natalie in the neighborhood from time to time. They'd never spoken again since that day at Albertson's grocery store.

He'd begun to let her go. In small ways, he'd stopped thinking about her at certain times of the day.

"I think you ought to get the puppy," Tony said. "A child needs to be taught what it's like to take care of a pet. Just make sure she cleans up the crap."

"Easy for you to say, you don't have kids."

Tony let the comment go; he didn't show Walcroft how much it got under his skin being reminded of the fact he wasn't a parent. Wally didn't say it in a demeaning way. People with children often took their status for granted.

"Not yet," was all Tony commented. "But I will. One day."

"Better get married first," the captain said, brushing ashes off the dark blue cloth of his pants.

Not readily responding, Tony took a puff of his cigar. He opted to change the subject. He didn't feel like talking about kids and getting married. Not tonight.

"I know how I'm going to get Gable back." Tony's eyes narrowed in anticipation. The pranks between Gable and him had been really heating up lately. They'd been ping-ponging each other for months.

"What?" Walcroft took a sip of cola from

the can resting between his legs.

"Remember that woman who won me in the Valentine auction?"

"Never saw her, but Rocky did. Said she was a looker."

"She owns a dress store. She'll call me every now and then."

"Wants you to put out her fire?" Walcroft ribbed.

Tony made no remark; the fact was, Sophia would rather start a fire with him, but he'd told her he wasn't looking for an affair. "She offered to let me borrow one of her mannequins."

"What are you going to do with it?"

"Lippert and Anderson said they'd help me out. We're going to put the female dummy on the john and when Gable goes to use the bathroom, he's going to think he walked in on one of the female paramedics."

The captain and Walcroft burst into laughter.

"Good one," Wally said. "Too bad we can't see his face when he gets a look at that."

"I know." Tony mulled that one over. "I wonder if I can get them to mount a camera in the john."

Captain Palladino chimed in, "They're

talking about putting cameras in the stations."

"Hell no. We don't need the public seeing what we're doing." Wally chewed on the end of his cigar. "Remember that time Captain Rico staged a dead snake on the truck steps? Gave the driver a fucking heart attack when he was getting in for a call."

Tony's mouth curved in recollection. "Or the time we had a tennis-ball fight in the hallway."

"Hell, I remember that." The captain leaned forward. "Where did we get a bucket of them?"

"Frye, I think."

"Didn't Frye rig the toilet to spray water out when you flushed it?"

"Yeah, he got the back of my shirt wet —"

*Beep. Beep. Beep.*

The female dispatcher's voice came over the speakers. "Engine thirteen, Engine one, Truck two, Engine five, Battalion two, structure fire on 2012 Twelfth Street, map section N32 cross of Grand and River."

Cigars were tossed into the ashtray and the trio stepped into Danner boots and Kevlar pants. Turnouts were slipped on over their long-sleeved blue shirts.

"Tony, you're chauffeur." Captain Palladino stepped into the engine as the wide front door rolled up and open.

Tony took his seat, punched the engine's motor to life and the truck rolled out of the firehouse with the warning lights and wig-wags flashing in alarm.

Nightfall sharpened the effect of neon lights in parking lots and the marquees on roadside businesses. Headlights blurred past as Tony turned left onto the street the captain directed him to. An adrenaline rush surged through Tony as he punched the ac-celerator. Sweat gathered on the back of his neck, wind from the open window blowing through the cab.

Walcroft's voice carried through the head-sets. "This building's been boarded up for a year."

The captain's gaze was on the hydrant grid. "One block up, Tony."

Lights from other fire engines came into view at the end of the block; the ladder truck from Station 1 was pulled up in front of the building. Moments later, the engine from Station 5 appeared.

Smoke rose in gray ribbons from the upstairs windows. A plywood board had been removed; the remaining glass was broken and spidered with cracks.

Tony stopped the engine, and then the three of them went into action. First in was the engine from Station 1, their driver running the pump while the captain and hoseman went in to attack the blaze. It was organized chaos around them with the ladder company, as the rapid-intervention team, on standby.

Hydrants were tapped, lengths of hoses unrolled. Men in reflective turnouts worked around each other, helmets on heads and faces masked with the somberness of their duties.

Flames began to lick at the upstairs floors, a flicker of orange and red recessed deep within the building.

A bystander ran toward them, her voice raised with panic. "There's some homeless people in there. A family. I know there's two kids."

The battalion chief ordered Tony's engine to aid in the fire attack.

"Pull a line off Engine 1," he said with authority. "The three of you go in."

The battalion chief spoke to the woman, while the captain, Walcroft and Tony fit their oxygen masks on and prepared to enter the burning building.

The Engine 13 hose line ran down the street, hooked into a line from the Engine 1 pump and, once water was released, the hose rose to life as it filled with pressure.

There was no time to think about what they were doing. Two of the other firefighters were already in on the first floor. A thick gray haze made it difficult to see. Tony swept his gaze through the rooms, Wally forging on ahead toward the base of the stairs while holding the hand line, the captain motioning which direction they should go. Meeting the two of them at the stairs, Tony climbed the risers and they met the blaze on the second story.

"Fire department!" Captain Palladino called out. "Fire department! Hello?"

No answer.

Wally motioned to the left. Tony held back, studying the perimeter in their immediate area. Flames licked the wall ahead, closing off entry to a passage on the right. A third stairwell climbed to another floor of the Victorian-era building.

The seed of the fire got darker before it got lighter. It was extremely hot and Tony could hardly see objects in front of him as he surveyed the area to his right. A knocked-over chair, boxes, fast-food bags. He had to do everything by feel, relying on his sense of touch. He followed the hose string from Engine 1, then stopped and listened to the fire.

His breathing sounded surreal in his ears,

an echo inside his oxygen mask, it was slow and steady. He felt as if he were on another planet.

Both of them manned the hand line, Wally crouching low beneath the smoke and leading the way. Tony held on to the hose, keeping a closer distance to Walcroft than he did to Captain Palladino. Tony saw the reflective back of the captain's turnout. In his mind, Tony made calculations on how he'd drag Wally or the captain out if he had to. He was bigger than Walcroft, equally as big as Captain Palladino, and would be able to carry either of them down the stairs. Still, the thought of not being able to help his fellow firefighter out stabbed at the back of his head. He was on full alert, ready at an instant to make a move.

The roar of the fire blew up behind him, a crash and billow of sparks as the third-floor ceiling near the stairwell began to give way. The hose line jerked, breaking Tony's grip for a moment; long enough that Walcroft took a step ahead of him.

Tony looked up and saw a storm of cinders raining down, felt the sweat bead on his eyebrows and run into his eyes; he blinked, trying to focus better in the ashy haze as it suddenly grew impossible to see. And then he heard the telltale groan of strained timbers.

Not one second ticked off as time ceased to measure on the clock.

And in the following instant, everything around him went black.

The last thought on his mind was Natalie and regret over not telling her that he loved her.

# Twenty-Five:
# Learning Middle
# Ground

Fred had invited Iris to his home for dinner. He wasn't much of a chef, but he knew how to spice up an easy skillet meal and he'd made it taste better than the box intended hamburger to taste. Anytime he added fresh ingredients, their flavor doctored up a processed dinner.

He'd spent all morning cleaning his house. He did a deep cleaning, getting into every nook and cranny. For Iris, he wanted his home to look inviting. It mattered to him to impress her every time she came over.

During their leisurely dinner on the patio, they'd been entertained by the squirrels and birds. His yard was made up with mature trees and he'd taken time this spring to do some summer planting. Those bushes and a bed of flowers were starting to bloom.

They'd sat outside until dark, holding hands in the new lawn swing he'd bought and assembled. Those damn instructions had been a bear to follow, but worth the effort to snuggle next to his sweetie. Now he asked her inside for some dessert. He put some fresh fruit in a bowl, spooned strawberries on top. "Would you like some whipping cream, Iris?"

"Without is fine."

He handed her the bowl. She looked nice in a white summer dress that came to just above her knees. She was a fine-looking woman, one he was proud to be seen with. They'd done so many things together; walks on the greenbelt, the Discovery Center science museum, which he'd forgotten about until she suggested it, dinners downtown, a movie at the Egyptian Theatre. Getting to know Iris these past few months had been some of the best times he'd had in years.

"Would you like to sit in the living room?" he asked, always trying to remember his manners. He tried never to swear in front of her.

"That would be great."

He joined her on the sofa, each of them eating their dessert. He had a good hold on his bowl so he wouldn't screw anything up, but dammit if a strawberry didn't roll off his spoon, land on the carpet and leave a red splotch. He'd just had the carpet cleaned not that long ago. "Son of a bitch," he uttered, then quickly wanted to cut his tongue out for having cursed.

Iris burst into laughter. "I was wondering when you'd finally let one fly."

Aghast, he gazed at her. "What do you mean?"

"I've heard you cut yourself off several times, and it's not that I don't appreciate it, but Fred — nobody's perfect." Then she added, "Even though I think you're perfect for me."

"Iris," he said, smiling at her lovely face. She had such shiny hair, so pretty and soft. "You're a peach."

"Thank you, Fred." She had a very kissable mouth. And he had kissed it often.

Feelings of love stirred in his heart, very potent and profound. He'd often wondered how he would feel when they happened for him again. He wasn't afraid. In fact, he welcomed the rush of emotions.

They set their empty dessert bowls on the coffee table. He asked, "Would you like to watch a little television?"

That was their code for "Would you like to snuggle and smooch?"

"Definitely," Iris responded, scooting closer to him.

He settled her next to him, the clicker in one hand and his other arm around her.

The television came to life. A picture focused as he began to scroll through the channels, pausing every so often.

A newscaster announced, "City officials have confirmed that one firefighter has been killed in a blaze that ripped through an abandoned building near downtown Boise."

"Wait!" Hands on her cheeks, Iris was on the edge of the sofa so he wouldn't flip to another station.

The images on the screen were that of an old building engulfed in flames.

"Several Boise fire companies responded to a blaze that broke out about nine o'clock tonight. Firefighters still don't know the cause and an investigation is under way. It was thought that homeless people were living in the building at the time, but the building was vacant. Tragedy struck just the same, and the name of the fallen firefighter hasn't been released pending notification of his family."

"Tony . . ." Iris's face went chalk white. "Tony. I have to call Tony."

Fred was already getting the phone for her.

*The Fireman's Prayer*

"When I am called to duty God, wherever
    flames may rage,
Give me the strength to save some life
whatever be its age.
Help me embrace a little child before it's
    too late,
Or save an older person from the horrors
    of that fate.
Enable me to be alert and hear the weak-
    est shout, and
Quickly and efficiently put the fire out.
I want to fill my calling and give the best in
    me;
To guard my every neighbor and protect
    his property,
And if according to Your will I am to give
    my life,
Please bless with Your protecting hand,
    my children and my wife."

James "Wally" Walcroft, who died on May
1, is to be buried today. He saved lives for
more than nine years with the Boise Fire
Department.
    Walcroft's casket will be carried on the

same fire engine that took him to the fire in which he died. The truck will lead a procession expected to include as many as fifty pieces of fire equipment from across the state. It will stop briefly for a prayer at the Station 13 firehouse where Walcroft worked.

Walcroft, 37, leaves a wife and two young children behind. He got caught in what's called a flashover, which happens when the fire gets hot enough that everything inside bursts into flame. Officials say he'll receive full department honors.

The funeral will be held at 11:00 a.m.

Wind whispered through the ash and maple trees. The afternoon was so quiet that the leaves were soft music in the sunshine. Heat promised to settle into the day. Already it felt warm, suffocating.

Tony wore his Class A uniform with a blue dress shirt, black tie and black slacks, the suit coat's collar at his neck prickling his skin, making him hot. He removed the miliary-style hat, tucked it beneath his arm as he walked through the cemetery in a somewhat mindless manner. He had no direction, no destination.

Behind him, James Walcroft had been laid to rest and the mourners began to break apart. He'd given Mrs. Walcroft his condolences, then he had to get away, be by himself before they all left for the reception. He didn't even want to be around Rocky right now. His friend stayed behind at the grave site and talked with the other mourners.

This was the first time he'd ever dealt with losing a fellow firefighter, much less a friend. The only funerals he'd been to had been those of elderly family members. He'd been fortunate enough not to have to deal with this sadness until now. It was all the more powerful because Wally had been a friend he'd lived and worked with. Someone he cared about as only Brothers in the IAFF could relate to.

Tony's sunglasses toned down the glare of the day as he viewed the expanse of lawn and headstones ahead of him. It was a nice cemetery. Well kept with manicured greens. Peaceful. Serene. If he had to be buried somewhere, Tony wouldn't mind coming here.

But, hell . . . what a way to spend the rest of a young life.

It just wasn't goddamn fair.

Tony had relived that day in his mind a hundred times, wishing he'd done things differently. But he knew there was nothing he could have done that would have made a difference. Walcroft had been separated from him, timbers coming between them, and the fire too intense. There was no way anyone could have gotten to him when that third-floor stairwell gave way.

Even so, it was one of those nightmare things that returned each night. A recurring panorama of events, waking him up in a helpless bath of sweat, with a chill to his body.

It had only been four days since Walcroft had died, but in that time frame, Tony had aged a lifetime.

He wasn't the same man.

Who he was, what he wanted, how he viewed the world around him all took on new meaning. Life was short. He either got busy living it the way he wanted to, or he could stop everything and pretend he was in the slow lane with traffic going around him.

He didn't want to live like that anymore.

He wanted to drive ahead. He didn't want to pass up chances, seek what was in his heart. There were a great many things he had to do, things he was compelled to go after.

"Tony?" The soft voice carried to him as he stood beneath a shady tree. Towering above him was an enormous pine tree that must have been a hundred years old.

He slowly turned, saw Natalie and leaned against the tree trunk.

She'd come to the funeral, like so many others who'd met Wally and his family. Tony had glanced at her a time or two during the service, and had thought about her more than once during the last few days.

Her frantic voice on the end of the phone the night Wally died was a comfort he hadn't realized he'd needed until he heard her. The call came in to the emergency room when he was at St. Luke's being checked over for smoke inhalation. Natalie called right after his mom and later, when he returned to the station, the messaging system on his cell phone was full from people he was acquainted with. Even Kim had called.

He'd assured both his mom and Natalie that he was all right. His mom had come right down. Natalie had said she would but he told her no.

Now he almost wished he hadn't told her to stay away. He wished he would have let her come see him. But, at the time, he'd needed to have his space, needed to process what had happened without being influenced by a woman whom he cared very deeply about.

A woman he was in love with.

He recognized those feelings when the sparks and flames had come crashing down around him and he thought he might not make it out.

There was no doubting his love for her was real and strong. It had felt right for a long time, but he'd kept those feelings at bay over the recent weeks they'd been apart. He now knew that his love for her was within the very core of his heart; she was the reason it kept on beating.

But since the night of the fire, he hadn't fully allowed himself to explore what those feelings meant in the long run, or how she'd fit into his life. He'd put off what he hadn't been able to deal with.

"It seems like too nice a day to not be feeling the sunshine on your face," he said, his voice far-off and sounding strange to his ears. "Wally was talking about taking his boat out this weekend."

Natalie came to him, stood close enough that he could smell her skin and see the flecks of gold in her green eyes. "I'm so sorry, Tony. This must feel like losing a brother."

"Yep."

"Is there anything I can do?"

"No." Tony ran a hand over his jaw, felt the smooth closeness of this morning's shave.

She hesitantly reached out to him, touched the shoulder of his uniform. She didn't say anything, didn't need to. He could feel what was in her heart just by that simple touch. He could read what was on her mind by looking into her eyes.

"Something like this makes you reassess the priorities in your life," he said, taking in a breath of clean summer air. He didn't allow her to respond, his gaze drifting to the crowd of mourners who were disbanding. "I've got to go to the reception hall. Are you coming?"

Natalie's eyebrows furrowed. "I didn't know him that well and this is an important, private thing. I think I'm just going to go for a drive."

"Where?"

"To the top of Bogus Basin — that fire ridge you took me to that one day."

He remembered. They'd driven up there after Easter, watched the sunset over the valley before heading back down and going to her house to make love until the sun rose again the next day.

"I want to say a prayer for Wally and his family," Natalie continued. "Bogus is the closest place to God I know."

He nodded. Then he let her go. It got easier each time.

Bogus Basin was the local ski resort. The season had wound down, and the road to the top was no longer blanketed with snow at the lower elevations. It had been years since Natalie had skied.

She turned off on a rutted road and drove a few minutes up the hill. The terrain was mostly sagebrush that gave way to an area of pines and bushes. She angled her car in such a way that when she looked out over the dash, she saw a wedge of the Boise valley.

The air at this altitude was crisper, cleaner. Natalie rolled down the power window and dragged in a deep breath.

It smelled good. She'd forgotten how pure the air was.

Rebirth. New things.

The quiet whisper of the mountain settled over her, a peaceful and tranquil state that washed through Natalie. She knew, for the first time in weeks, a true calm.

Why, then, did silent tears belie her comfort?

Because she couldn't forget that the last time she was here, she'd been with Tony.

They'd sat close to each other in the front seat of his silver truck, holding hands and watching as the day ended.

She closed her eyes and prayed for Wally and his family.

Prayed for Tony.

She loved him. When she thought it might have been him who'd been killed, she'd been frantic. Hearing his voice on the phone had been a relief like nothing else she'd ever heard in her life.

She cared so much about him. She'd wanted to be there for him and he'd told her no. He didn't want her to comfort him, to be close to him that night.

She shouldn't have been upset about his rejection. She only had herself to blame. It had finally happened. She'd gotten her way.

Natalie Goodwin was facing the future alone. Just the way she thought she wanted it.

And now she knew she'd made a horrible mistake.

Actually, the night of the fire, she knew she'd made a mistake but she hadn't been able to tell Tony. Now wasn't the right time, either, but if she didn't tell him how she felt right away, she feared she'd never get the chance.

She dialed his number on her cell phone.

Nothing. No service.

Frustration worked through the cords of her neck. She wanted him to meet her up here when he was done at the reception. How could she let him know?

She tried dialing again. Nothing.

Sometimes in McCall, she couldn't get service. But she could text message. She typed out a short message:

*Drive up the mountain. I'll wait for you.*

She pushed Send. It went through.

Anxiousness overcame her. She leaned back into the seat and put a CD into the player.

An hour went by, then another, until she lost all track of time. Natalie feared he wouldn't come, perhaps didn't want to. Then she saw the Dodge Ram pulling off the road and heading for her on the fire-break.

She got out of her car and met him by the side of his truck.

"Tony." She breathed his name, loved the sound of it in her ears. "I'm glad you came."

His brown eyes were dark, questioning. "What's the matter?"

"Everything."

He climbed out of the truck and rested his backside against the wheel well and folded his arms over his chest. He looked so handsome in his uniform and she held back from kissing him, from throwing herself into his arms.

"There are a hundred different things going on in my life, but there's only one thing to me that's really important," she said, her voice soft. "When I thought it was —" her breath hitched "— you who'd died . . . I came apart. I didn't know what I'd do without you, Tony."

He said nothing and just let her talk.

"I can't give you up and I'm not going to. If you still want to be with me, I want to be with you. We can work through this together, but the most important thing for right now is that we are together."

Sunlight reflected in his eyes. She wished she could read his mind, know his thoughts.

"Tony?"

She worried he wasn't going to say anything, that he was no longer feeling the same things.

"I want to get married to you," he said, firm in his conviction. "And I want a family if that's the way it works out for us, but if it doesn't, then it'll be okay."

"Okay," she agreed, tears swimming in her eyes. His nearness made her senses spin yet she took great comfort having him so close. Elation overwhelmed her.

"Sometimes you make decisions you thought you'd never make for the love of that person." Tony was resolute in his words, strong in the way he expressed himself. "Because of the significance of the relationship, you do things you never thought you'd do."

She nodded.

Natalie gazed into Tony's face. She was so in love with him she felt it inside her soul. It was a physical ache, but with that ache also came a reservation. And it was dead center in the middle of her being.

Middle ground.

She'd learned it, knew how to embrace it now. But that didn't offset what she knew he wanted in his heart.

She had to tell him. "I don't think you should be denied those feelings of connecting with a child. You're wonderful. The best man I have ever met." She touched his cheek. "You're smart and kind, generous and loyal. You've shown me pieces of myself that I didn't know existed. I fell in love with you. I still am . . ."

His face was chiseled with emotion as he tilted her head up to look deeper into her eyes.

"So will you?" He waited for her to give him an answer.

She gave him her heart. "Yes. I want to marry you, Tony. And if something wonderful happens, then it happens. I'll be okay no matter how it goes, as long as I'm with you. And if by some miracle . . . well, I can't promise anything. I know you hate to hear it, but at my age, things might not be easy."

"Nothing worth having is easy." Finally, he gathered her into his embrace and she felt as if she were home. "Look at how long it took us to get here."

Natalie's arms rose and lifted to come around his neck. She took such comfort in the feel of him, the closeness. His smell, the hard planes of his muscular body and the strength of his physique.

The wind blew softly, the tree boughs rushed in a silky sound. Time ebbed slowly as they both stood there, facing one another, their heartbeats pounding in the same rhythm.

"I missed you," she said, her voice cracking.

"I missed you, too, babe."

His sensual mouth searched hers in a kiss that was both consuming with heat and tenderness.

"I love you." His voice fumbled through his chest; a feeling of total contentment spread through her.

"I love you more than I ever thought possible. You are the beat of my heart."

Tony's hands held her cheeks, his smile shining down on her. She loved the way his white teeth flashed a grin that she found so irresistible.

"When you give me that grin, it makes me go nuts." Natalie shook her head. "The first time I got a real good look at it was in Home Depot."

"Oh, yeah?"

"Yes. And I think you know that grin affects me. It gets me all hot and bothered."

In his firefighter voice, he asked, "Hey, lady, where do you want me to put out the fire?"

Pulling him closer, she whispered, "I don't. Let it burn." Her mouth covered his, and she murmured, "Let it burn. . . ."

# Twenty-Six:
# In the Pink

Hat and Garden was decorated with lots of pink in honor of Mother's Day. In the two and a half years since the flower shop had been open, it had become a neighborhood favorite. Natalie's clientele were loyal to a fault and today several customers gathered to shop for bears, angels, teacups and any other items that caught their attention.

She was behind the counter, ringing up an order when her dad and Iris came in. They'd gotten married shortly after she and Tony had, and they had all celebrated with one big reception, filled with family and friends.

"Hi, Iris," Natalie greeted, stepping out to give her a hug.

"Hello, Natalie!" Iris Goodwin was a beautiful bride, still carrying her honeymoon glow.

"Hey, Dad," Natalie said, giving Fred a

hug, as well. He engulfed her in a big bear squeeze.

"Well," Iris said, beaming, "I finally talked him into it. We're going to pick up our baby right after we leave here."

Her father's face soured. "I buckled under the pressure."

Natalie laughed. "So what are you going to name her?"

"Princess."

Fred grumbled, "I think Duke would have been better."

"Oh, Fred," Iris said, linking her arm through his. "You can't call a female poodle Duke."

"I know what I've called a poodle in the past." His eyebrows arched in thoughtful reflection. "And it wasn't Duke or Princess."

Sarah came out of the bathroom area, disgust on her face. "Okay, so it's happened again. The water pipe is leaking. When is it ever going to be fixed?"

Natalie simply smiled, unaffected.

Looking at Fred and Iris, Sarah said, "Hi, Dad. Hi, Iris." Then to Natalie, "Doesn't it bother you it's still broken?"

"Not really. I think I've gotten used to it. The leak sort of feels like it belongs here now."

Sarah threw up her hands. "Okay. They're

your pipes."

"Is Cassie still planning on coming home for the summer?" her dad asked, checking out a Saint Thérèse figurine, lifting her up and turning her over.

Cassie had gotten over Austin, and several months later, she'd met a boy named Ryan. He was her age, originally from Bozeman, Montana, and they'd become inseparable. Natalie had met him and his parents this last Christmas and she couldn't approve more. It wouldn't surprise her if Cassie and Ryan got married.

Natalie moved a greeting card that had been put back in the wrong slot. "She's going to work in the store again this summer, just like last year."

"That'll be good."

"Where's Tony?" Iris asked. "Isn't he supposed to stop by? I talked to him earlier and he said he was coming to the shop."

Natalie's heart warmed whenever she thought about her husband. "He should be here any time."

And at that moment, Tony Cruz had just parked his truck in the lot out back of Hat and Garden. He walked up the flower-shop steps, holding his precious daughter in his arms.

He'd dressed her in a red-and-white

polka-dot dress, white socks and black Mary Janes. He hadn't a clue what those shoes were a year ago, but now he thought girl stuff was cool to shop for. He loved taking care of her on his days off. She was his world, his everything. So was his wife.

"Are we going to see Mommy?" he asked, kissing his one-year-old on the cheek. Her skin was smooth like satin, her cheeks so plump and soft he could kiss them a dozen times.

She made a fist, put it under his chin and grinned.

"Are you giving Daddy a bruise in the chops?"

She giggled, two teeth on the bottom of her mouth showing in her wide grin.

He tickled her side, loving the sound of her laughter.

Tony pushed open the shop doors, to be surrounded by family, glad to see his mom and his father-in-law. "Hey, guys. Look at who I brought with me."

"Oh, McKenzie," his mom declared, coming over to her granddaughter and giving her a kiss. "Hello, baby girl. Grandma loves you."

Fred moved right in, crooned over her, as well. "Hi, Killer, it's Gramps."

McKenzie put her face in Tony's shirt for

a moment, then looked at the two grandparents and smiled.

"Hey, babe," he said to Natalie, bringing their daughter to her.

As soon as McKenzie saw her mother, her arms stretched out and Natalie took her. "Hey, boo-boo kiss." She nuzzled their baby, gave her downy-soft hair kisses. "Look at how pretty Daddy dressed you." Then to Tony, she said, "You got her all dressed up just to come over here?"

"Nope." A smiled worked its way over his mouth. "I got her dressed up to go pick up these."

Tony reached into his back pocket, producing an itinerary and airline tickets.

"What's this?" Natalie asked, her face bright with wonder. She was so beautiful to him. Motherhood had changed her, softened her features and put a glow on her skin. Her complexion was flawless and dusted lightly with a blush across her cheekbones. The dark plum of her shirt brought out the green in her eyes.

"We're going to Tuscany. McKenzie, too." Leaning forward, his lips touched hers in a tender kiss. "Happy Mother's Day, Natalie."

"Tony!" Iris gushed.

"That's my son-in-law," Fred said proudly.

Sarah put her hands on her hips and just

smiled, then laughed and said, "Well, Steve is really going to have a hard time topping this one."

Tears formed in Natalie's eyes and she blinked them back, her lips parting. "Well . . . oh, my. Tony. I don't know what to say."

"Say you love me." He grinned that grin that he knew shot straight to her heart.

With every emotion shining in her eyes, she said, "I love you."

And he felt every bit the luckiest man on the face of the earth.

# ABOUT THE AUTHOR

**Stef Ann Holm** is the bestselling author of twenty novels and one novella. While researching *Leaving Normal* she had to hang out with good looking Boise firefighters, eat and watch TV with them at the stations, ride on the engines, respond to calls, see some weird and gruesome things — all for the sake of making this novel realistic. It was a rough job, but she had to do it. You can send her your sympathies via her Web site at www.stefannholm.com or, if you prefer, snail mail at P.O. Box 1206, Meridian, ID, 83680-1206.